BRIANA CHEN & ELIZABETH ZHOU

GREDIAN

FIVE SEALS

Gredian
Five Seals Book 1
Published by Ink Bird Pres, LLC
Denver, CO

ISBN: 978-1-7332179-0-3
YOUNG ADULT / Fantasy / Epic

Cover design by Donna Cunningham

QUANTITY PURCHASES: Schools, companies, and other organizations may qualify for special terms when ordering quantities of this title. For information, email info@inkbirdpress.com.

This book is printed in the United States of America.

INK BIRD PRESS, LLC

To family, by blood and not

CHAPTER

ONE

IT'S GOING TO BE OKAY.

Teeth gritting. An uncontrolled scream scraping against a raw throat.

It's going to be okay.

Skin splitting and shredding like paper. Tears and sweat stream down, adding a drop of silent dew to the violent background.

It's going to be ...

"Cease." The new king stepped in front of a man whose silver hair was barely distinguishable under the thick layer of blood. The room was illuminated only enough for one to see stones of ebony, brown, and moss stacked upon each other, climbing up, up until they began to curve toward each other, joining in an arch a few feet above the king's head. There was a grate at the peak, a circular opening no bigger than a fist, the source of the glow. Pure white light peeked through it, casting a heavenly aura onto the figure kneeling on the floor.

A floor that was splattered with gore. A vile work of abstract art.

"I think he's tasted enough of his own blood already," Adaric Amptonshire said, his voice a low tremor. He cast a cruel glance toward the guards holding the man down, and the silent order was understood—"If you want to live, don't let him go."

A woman stood just outside the rusted dungeon door, her back pressed against the wall, lungs searing against the overwhelming smell of sweat and metal. She was taking a risk just coming down here, even though she wouldn't go in. She glanced into the cell. Two dying torches, flickering beacons in the dark, hung gleaming on the stone arch; there was one on each side. Their ebbing flames lapped ravenously for air.

She shrunk back as the figure in the grate's spotlight shifted, stained with blood that contrasted sharply with the green-hued atmosphere. Bruises littered his skin, his jawline, his knees (which had been slammed into the soiled floor over and over again just because he refused to kneel). A bruise bloomed around his left eye, sealing it closed. She caught a glimpse of the shredded skin on his back and resisted the urge to vomit.

He was barely even twenty.

"You'll taste your own soon, Adaric," Chais Nevermoon ground out through blood-stained teeth, "once this empire burns under your rule. Once I hunt you down for everything you've done." And he smiled—despite everything, despite his condition, he smiled. The woman could see his blue eyes glaze over, maybe from the pain or maybe from the mention of his world's future. She wanted to run—wanted to run so badly, to tear her eyes from this sick show of ripping the dignity from a Gredian soldier.

But she didn't. She reminded herself that this was just for information.

The king laughed, a twisted caw. The slow trickle of water made its way along the ground, curving and snaking sporadically, glowing an unnatural green from the room next door. Iron bars barricaded a small window to her right. Iridescent. That was the only word to describe it; a lonely torch was mounted to the wall, and when her head shifted, the flame's colors flickered in shades—emerald green one moment, then as scarlet as the wounds on Chais's back. Violet. Gold. Blue, a blue so vivid it could be compared to the waters of the Qlihr, tinted with a hint of ice from the Northernlands.

The woman drew her gaze away from the allure of the light and tried to focus. She couldn't see the king's features, not with the shadow drawing a cover over the bridge of his nose and the bones of his cheeks, but she didn't need to. She could remember Adaric's face well enough—his thicker brows, angular jaw, and thin lips were qualities that would have looked handsome in any other combination, but the king's appearance resembled more of the masses. Average. Someone they could relate to.

There was a light splash as Adaric walked closer to the kneeling figure. "As much as I'd like that, I'm afraid you'll be dead before you even see the light of day." He twisted his thin lips into the semblance of a smile.

Silence. Thick, choking silence that could freeze a man's blood. There was only the dripping of something. Its sound seemed both distant and close at the same time. The woman could make out a glimmer of a fight inside Chais's eyes, like a shard of ice amidst a sea of cold water.

"What did you do with Havard?" Chais snarled, curling his lips back to expose his canines. He was another person altogether. Beneath all the gore and grime, she supposed he was handsome, more so than the court's heartthrobs, even. She felt that lasting twinge of jealousy that she'd harbored for him after so many years ... But that didn't stop the pang of fear that closed around her heart like the jaws of a demon.

"You thought this was out of the blue, dragging you down here the second you got back from the frontlines?" That snake-like laugh again. It made her bones tingle. "It's not that simple, Chais Nevermoon," Adaric spat, the name a poisonous curse on his tongue. His eyes, the shade of Exagogh's sun, widened just slightly. Despair glittered vibrantly, but when she looked again, it was gone—replaced with the shattered glass of triumph.

"Because Gredian's king, Havard Avington," he smiled, "is dead."

She caught that moment—the moment when the ice in Chais's eyes sunk like a ship at sea, the moment when all the breath in his body left him, when his knees could no longer hold his weight. His eyes dropped to stare dully at the ground, and it was at that moment she knew that Chais Nevermoon could be broken.

Adaric seized that moment of weakness. His gaze flickered down, briefly, to scan the blood on the ground as an artist would stare at a completed painting. Pleased.

"Throw him in a cell," he shouted for more guards, who entered through another door, their grips all lingering near their weapons. "And make sure he stays there. We wouldn't want this

...” he gestured at the blood on the floor, “to go to waste now, would we?”

Lynara Merran backed away from the door and, with the steps of a feline, she ran.

ΤΗΕ ΤΗRΟΠΕ RΟΟΠ was darker than when he'd last seen it.

Its ceilings were still as high, however, and they hadn't changed the glass chandelier that loomed above the throne, ablaze, the first thing visitors would ever see if they had the privilege to visit the castle. It had a simple design, really, an oval of glass shards, then beams that extended upward to meet the main shaft, creating a line of stability that allowed it to stoop to such a height. Polished stone supported the pillars at either side of the throne, and sable marble stretched over the floors. A long red carpet led directly to the king's throne, wide enough for three people to stand side by side at once.

Since the grand magistrate had mysteriously disappeared without a trace a few days before the trial, Gredian's capital turned to its next wisest members—the king's advisory board. Naturally, as the board's premier, Adaric would be the one to ascend, as the king had passed away without any living relatives or appointees.

Quick, efficient, and biased. Lacking any real formalities. That was the nature of Gredian trials, whether the people wanted to believe it or not.

Adaric fixed the man with an impartial gaze. One that Chais held, yet no one could spot the embers that sparked between them.

"Colonel Chais Nevermoon," Adaric's voice was calm, devoid of emotion, a far cry from the voice he'd used in the dungeons so far beneath the surface; it was the perfect tone to convince the court of his unbiased view on events. "Did you murder King Havard Avington after you returned from battle, roughly two days ago?"

The court was silent. Even the noble families who had gathered in the balconies that loomed above didn't utter a whisper. Many of the royals leaned over the ebony wood railings, intricately carved with legends that went back centuries. Grotesque features of demons stared out from the carvings, red eyes alight with the desire for slaughter.

Chais didn't break Adaric's stare as he said, with a strength that few men could muster, "No, I did not."

There was a sudden influx of heated conversation in the wings. Adaric pressed his lips into a thin line, impatience showing in his brow. The empty throne was close enough to picture the previous ruler who had resided upon it; Chais could almost reach forward and feel the soft velvet of the steps that led to the base, had his cuffs permitted. The torches were stationed on each pillar of the elongated chamber, providing just enough light to make it dark. Two banners as long as the throne "room" draped over projections in the stone wall. Their velvet was embroidered with a silver border, along with a key and arrow in black. Its tassels, also silver, hung from bolts on the ceiling, reaching the same height as the chandelier.

The balconies finally died down. Somehow, though, there was a sinister vibe that hadn't been present when Havard was here.

"Then, where were you when he was killed?" There was a tug at Adaric's lip too small for anyone to see, anyone except the man kneeling at his feet—again. The question took him by surprise.

That bastard. Chais couldn't—wouldn't—dare tell of the time spent in the dungeons. In this empire, that marked anyone as a criminal, even the ruler. It had happened before when a queen that everyone and everything loved was thrown in a cell, and Gredian turned its back on her. Regardless of what good she'd done, how she pulled her beloved empire out of depression—no one even shed a tear when the noose was fitted around her neck and the blood drained from her face. In these dungeons, execution was a mercy.

And Adaric Amptonshire knew. He knew that even Chais Nevermoon wouldn't dare lie, not while he had all the weapons in his arsenal—not while the entire court, save for a few people who'd unconventionally vanished, was watching. He knew that while he was busy breaking Chais in an attempt to instill fear, someone had been on their way to murder Havard Avington. And he had done absolutely nothing to stop it.

Adaric took the silence as an answer. "Are there any witnesses on Colonel Nevermoon's behalf?"

No one stepped forward. Chais scanned the crowd—Where were his soldiers? The men he had fought beside, against the Fey? Who had sworn their lives to him in the midst of this bloody war?

They couldn't have been absent ... unless ...

"Are there any witnesses on His Majesty, King Avington's, behalf?"

Adaric. Unless Adaric had done it, had pulled strings just like when Havard was killed. His men wouldn't have missed the trial if their lives depended on it.

A man stepped forward—one of the guards who had kept Chais locked in place while the whip broke his skin into tatters.

His eyes held a green that could only be from Lastor, a city-turned-ruins by the Fey.

"I saw him go up the stairs, to King Avington's chambers, after I finished my rotation," he spoke as if he'd rehearsed it. Shaky but practiced. He had an accent, however, and Chais couldn't tell where it was from.

"Did you see him murder the king?" Adaric stood perfectly still, holding the mask he put onto his face to convince the audience of his credibility. A red-haired woman shifted somewhere near him—Chais recognized her. Merran. Was she going to do anything about ... this?

The guard began trembling, slowly at first, but then becoming increasingly exaggerated. The man's white-knuckled fists were clenched so hard the blood had drained out of them. When the man released his grip on his own skin, his nails had left crescents in the palm of his hands. If this was an act, it looked too real, felt too real.

"Did you see him murder the king?" Adaric repeated.

With a molten glare, the guard stared at Chais. "Yes," he said at last, barely in control. "I saw him slice the king's throat." A roar of outrage erupted from the balcony and, with it, the witness snapped. He lunged for the colonel on the ground, grabbing him by the collar. Chais kept his face placid, meeting the man's furious eyes with his own.

Calm. Stay calm.

"You killed the king," the guard snarled, taking comfort in the fact that Chais's wrists were bound in metal cuffs. "You killed the man who supported me, the man who supported my daughter!" Spit landed on Chais's cheek. There was a long, deadly pause, and still, no one made a move to drag him off.

"I'll be glad when I see your body hanging from that noose," the guard said finally, his tone laced thick with malice before he backed away. Chais stared at the empty spot where the guard's eyes had once been. He knew that he had been thrown, bleeding, into shark-infested waters.

"I can confirm that." A woman dressed in simple maid attire stood. "I was in the king's chambers at the time."

Adaric's golden irises were aflame as he said in controlled measures, "What were you doing?"

"Making tea," the woman answered. There was a hardness in her eyes that was difficult to create. One foot was poised in front of the other, as if she was about to run.

"And what happened, then?" Adaric pressed.

Another pause again, a long one that kept the royals on the edge of their seats, fingernails digging into the cushioning. "He came through the door, slit the majesty's throat, then ..."

"Then what?"

"Then he knocked me out. But not before I got a good look at him." The balconies were soundless; viewers kept taciturn, looking onward in anticipation. There was truth somewhere in their stories, or they wouldn't have been so genuine about it; none of them had studied acting for the theater that was now being played out. There was truth somewhere, but it didn't make any sense.

Adaric gestured for the maid to take a seat, then turned to the nobles—men, women, people who were convinced that the man on the ground with blood running down his back and with a face full of cuts and bruises ...

"Are there any other witnesses for King Havard Avington?" Silence—everyone already had their mind made up.

"We now call for a vote. Those in favor of Colonel Chais Nevermoon being guilty of murdering King Havard Avington?" There was a wicked glare in Adaric's eyes. Fists crossed forearms—the arrow and the key: Gredian's insignia. As each member of the court, in turn, crossed fists over forearms, Chais felt his heart sink deeper and deeper and deeper until he couldn't feel his soul anymore, as if it were six hundred feet under.

Adaric Amptonshire gestured to the soldiers keeping the colonel grounded. Chais felt the lacerations on his body tear open as they dragged him up. The blood—his own blood—fell onto the carpet, blending in with red.

"Those in favor of Colonel Chais Nevermoon's innocence?"

Chais could almost hear the liquid hit the floor. Nothing moved. No sign of Gredian, no outburst, no one standing up for the man who had dedicated his lifeblood to this empire, for the man who shed his very soul for it.

Dripping. One second passed. Two. Three.

Slowly, Adaric turned to the colonel so that his feral smile went unseen by the people in the balcony. The expression in his eyes turned dark as his hair, and he said, "Chais Nevermoon. By the Gredian Empire, you have been charged guilty of murdering King Havard Avington. You are to be executed publicly by the end of the month, and should you escape it, you will be condemned to slavery for the rest of your life. Chais Nevermoon," Adaric lifted his chin as he inhaled, shoulders moving up toward the infinite ceiling, "You are hereby stripped of your title as a lieutenant colonel."

As those words were uttered, something broke in Chais. It was what kept him from fighting back when the guards pulled him toward the dungeons. It kept him from screaming the fact that no, it wasn't him, it wasn't him who murdered the man whom he saw as his own father … It kept the harsh realization from surfacing—that Havard was dead, that Chais would soon be, too, that the Gredian Empire was destined for destruction. It was a block of pure ice that settled in his stomach, spreading to his fingertips and veins, invading his body with cold waters that drowned reality.

And he might have only imagined it, but as he descended to the dungeons that reeked of sewage and bodily fluids, he heard a voice in his head. Hang in there, it seemed to say, for this won't last forever.

He still felt that block of ice as his body hit the grungy stone floor. The cell door squealed shut behind him. With the little energy he had left, Chais dragged himself up into a sitting position, that arctic breath within him dulling the pain of his wounds. He could barely make out, under the flickering torches hanging from the dripping ceilings, Adaric's silhouette.

"I have to say," Adaric had lost the image of a trustworthy judge and instead morphed back into a sick, manipulating man, "our guards did quite a number on your back." Chais was on his feet in a heartbeat, his skin splitting. He clenched his teeth against the pain.

"Don't you dare talk about me as if you have been through what I have." Chais spoke with lethal quiet, pinning the man to the ground with his eyes alone. "Don't act like you have nothing to do with this."

Adaric's smile faded from his face. "I didn't know how badly I wanted this until you opened your mouth," the king said, meeting his gaze.

"When you walk up there to inform them of Gredian's new ruler, you won't feel a thing," Chais said. "You won't feel a thing in that hole where your heart is supposed to be, knowing that you just murdered an innocent—another body to add to your long list of soldiers sent to the frontlines, isn't that right?"

"Aren't you guilty too?" Adaric roared. The magic in their hall prevented his voice from reaching the ears of curious listeners. "Aren't you also guilty of not feeling? Of killing? Chais," Adaric addressed him by his first name, and his voice trembled slightly, "you are no less a criminal than I."

"I don't allow myself to feel," Chais said thinly, "because we are at war, and too many lives are at stake." His resolve cracked but did not crumble. "I kill," his throat caught, "for Gredian's sake. But your reasons—for sending soldiers to suicide for nothing, for getting *rid* of a colonel just so you can claim your throne …" Chais paused, and all of a sudden the air in the dungeons seemed to grow colder. "… are not for the empire or for our future—only for you and your own selfish life."

Adaric opened his mouth in a retort, but it fell dead in the tension. The king was the first to break eye contact, pulling his gaze away to rest on the dirtied metal door at the end of the hall. A few moments passed in silence before he said, "Your execution will be in two weeks. I will send people down to help with your healing." The smile returned. "After all, your special day is coming up. We want you looking good for it."

With that, Adaric left. Chais listened for the slamming of the metal door before he backed away slowly, his breath returning to him.

It's going to be okay.

His knees gave out, and he painfully connected with the bloodied floor. Shaking, he buried his head into his hands.

The voice returned, still soft, as if spoken from far, far away.

ONE

Hang in there, for this won't last forever.

This won't last forever.

Chais couldn't help but wonder what, exactly, that meant.

CHAPTER
two

A FIGURE CLAD in muted colors stood at the edge of the courtyard. His eyes were half closed, but his intense gaze was locked on the young girl playing with the pixies. A warm and rather calming spring breeze stirred the dandelions and sent small fluffs of soft wispy clouds swirling through the air. The hazel-eyed child giggled as the breeze ruffled her golden locks and the small fairies pulled at her curls and slender, pointed ears. Streams of sunlight danced off of their translucent wings. A kaleidoscope of pinks, blues, and yellows spun across the little princess's pale skin, her snow white gown the perfect backdrop for the reflected lights.

A taunting and annoying voice pierced the concentration of the dark figure watching the child. *Well, this doesn't look creepy at all.* With a great amount of willpower, he ignored the commentary. Instead, he waved his hand gently, a single ring glinting on his left pinky.

The girl turned when she felt the air cool around her. A wide smile spread across her face when she spied the man, and then suddenly, a large blast of air sent her tumbling with a gleeful shriek. She rolled over, paying no heed to the strands of grass the fairies were already picking out of her hair and waved cheerfully at her green-eyed watcher. The man shifted away from the wall, and the wind sent his long, ebony hair snapping around his face. He took a single step forward when the voice rang in his head again, worry thickly coating each word.

Elwood, Aldridge is in trouble.

"He's always in trouble," Elwood muttered quietly as he withdrew and leaned back against the wall, giving the girl a half-smile. The blond pouted before being distracted by the small, winged mischief makers once again. She nearly tripped over her long dress in the process of chasing the small creatures around. He retied his long ponytail and watched the scene before him with detached amusement.

He's in a bind he can't get out of, the voice warned, tone urgent.

"How can you tell?" the Fey asked, his annoyance growing as his tolerance for the unwanted interruption dropped faster than a soldier thrown off a cliff.

He's practically sending his power in waves. It's kind of hard to miss. The voice almost snorted. It sounded rather amused that his comrade was desperate for aid.

"How is it normally?" the Fey murmured. He tried his best not to slam his head into the wall.

A low hum. Aldridge hates asking for help. The voice was starting to sound annoyed and maybe a little concerned about his apathy. Good. He really didn't want to deal with demon keys right now, but instead of giving himself a concussion and possible brain damage, Elwood leaned further into the wall, appearing uncaring about the dire situation that could be taking place with Aldridge. The sunlight caught the dew drops, allowing the grass to shimmer with unearthly beauty and light, and the gentle breeze caused the bits of water to shiver on the thin blades. Yet, the water clung on, he noticed, never falling off, at least not until the unruly princess barreled through them, leaving nothing but crushed blades in her wake.

"Huh. Then he must be in a lot of trouble." His tone was unchanged, unconcerned. He was simply trying to enjoy the beautiful dawn and warm wind. The sky was painted with the brightest of colors and lined with gold. This world was alive with the whisper of grass and the creaking percussion of trees. The princess's playmates sang a harmony of taunts and giggles, accompanying the girl's twinkling laughter and chime-like melody. He hated to think about important things when everything was so peaceful.

"What do you want from me?"

Elwood. The voice sounded impatient. Perhaps he was pushing his patience too far, though the thought certainly amused him.

"What?" Elwood snorted, finally willing to listen. He decided that he had avoided it for long enough.

Elwood. You know what you need to do. The voice was commanding, like a general would speak to a subordinate. Elwood hated it when the voice talked like that. After all, they shared a body—his body, for that matter. So shouldn't *he* be the one in charge, not the annoying voice in his head?

"Can't one of the others do it? My place is by Princess Syellian and my king. It's my duty," Elwood argued. He had just recently gotten back from the frontlines; he wanted to stay by his best friend and family a little longer before leaving again.

It's also your duty as a host to help protect the other hosts. One is ... undetectable by my power; not gone, but not there either. The other two are in fragile hosts, far too weak to handle this kind of activity. You. Must. Go. The voice boomed with authority, loud and echoing within his mind. Elwood really wished the voice would speak quieter, especially considering they were sharing the same head. Whenever Relevard used that voice, in particular, it always left him with a headache—one of the many problems of two souls sharing a body.

"Holy hydras, Relevard. Tone it down, would you? You're giving me a headache. Besides, I can't just leave. What about the princess?" Elwood asked, knowing the answer, yet still hoping for a different one.

She knows your duty. Elwood knew he wouldn't win this argument. Why couldn't he just get a break for once?

"Elly?" A small voice interrupted his seemingly one-sided conversation. He turned to the girl, who looked no older than ten—looks were deceiving when you didn't quite age. Elwood knew the young princess was at least fifteen decades old. He, himself, looked no older than sixteen. The princess smiled lightly. Her hands were clasped behind her elegant white dress that was embroidered with pale pink and red roses with small smears of grass stains and mud bleeding into the edges. She tugged lightly on her hair and elegantly skipped over.

"Yes, Syellian?" Elwood knelt down, bangs hanging back into his eyes. Once the princess knew, there was no more arguing.

"Is something wrong?" the princess asked. Wide brown eyes, flecked with green and amber, as if a small forest thrived in her gaze, blinked at him. Her curls perched like butterflies on her shoulders, two small braids pulling her hair out of her eyes. He hated his job sometimes, but it was not a job he could simply hand to someone else, not unless he decided to have kids. Which, to be honest, wasn't going to happen anytime soon. He had a war to fight, a royal family to protect, and now, another long-dead warrior to save. His life was too complicated for him to settle down now.

Looking up, he sighed. "I apologize, but I need to speak to Callum."

"Awww ... but you just got back," Syellian mumbled. She sounded like the ten-year-old body she occupied. "I just learned how to grow forests too ..." She looked up, eyes pleading, her small hand tugging once again on her hair.

"Maybe some other day, all right?" Elwood tried for a smile before he leaned down and placed a gentle kiss on the girl's forehead, then ruffled her hair.

He boosted himself over the low, crumbling wall surrounding the small garden and headed for the archway framed by honeysuckles. A stone wall immediately shifted to close off the entrance. Now, if only he could find the throne room ...

Striding with an air of purpose, Elwood walked through the twisting maze toward the center glade. Anyone who didn't grow up in the ever-changing Atrelian court would have gotten lost in the labyrinth of ten-foot, vine-choked hedges. This is my home, he thought proudly. The sun streamed through canopies of copper wire blooming with flowers. Small will-o-wisps bobbled in the darker corners, resting for the day before terrorizing the masses once the moon rose.

Fey and mythical creatures alike nodded in respect as the knight to the youngest princess and friend to the recently crowned king walked through the court. There were fewer people than usual—the normally loud and crowded palace felt empty, as a majority of its inhabitants were on the frontlines defending the kingdom. The late king (after over 800 years of sitting at a throne, bashing political heads together) led the charge, leaving his young and rather inexperienced son to run the kingdom and deal with the terrifying monster known as "politics." While the new king, Callum, was more than four centuries older than Elwood, he was still young and new to the concept of ruling.

Another demon seal had finally shown up after all this time. Relevard had only given him the minimal amount of information—five hosts, five souls, each a key that made it impossible for the demons to enter their world on their own. It forced the monsters to rely on mortal summoners. If Aldridge was truly in danger, their continent—or even their world—could be at risk. It would be the Demon War all over again, with seemingly immortal demons running free to create havoc. They didn't need that again, not with the current war so close to ending.

He had heard that the human king who started this whole mess had passed away from age since he had left the bloodbath. Good riddance. If the new king, Havard, was anything like that man, the war would never end. Rumors, however, had come back saying that the new monarch had been pulling back his forces—sending ambassadors, trying his hardest to stop the five-decade-long war, one that Elwood had been in since he was one hundred and fifty years old.

It would be strange, not having to fight anymore.

He shook the morbid thoughts from his mind and continued

toward his destination. Weaving through the tall hedges that acted as a natural defense, he entered the throne room through an archway of roses. Two tall trees stood proudly in the center of the clearing. The evening light filtered through the leaves and cast soft shadows on the thrones carved straight from the great oak tree. Designs of vines and leaves crawled up the backrests, reaching for the Atrelian emblem etched at the top before stretching out into sturdy branches and thick leaves. The grand oak wood almost glowed in the filtered light, and the vines appeared to writhe, growing and grabbing, while small flowers released a soft, alluring scent. Colorless roses bloomed and shielded the sharp, twisting needles from view. Despite the cover, the thorns still glistened predatorily for blood.

Quickly looking away, Elwood tried to clear his mind of the bloodthirsty plant life. Everything in Atrelia was covered in beauty and blades. One of the thrones was empty; in the other sat a Fey who radiated ancient power. He had donned a spring green robe lined with gold; he appeared no older than mid-twenty, yet the wisdom and age that shone in his sea-green eyes said otherwise. A tall and elegant wreath of silver branches crowned his head. His straw gold hair glimmered as fireflies perched on his headdress like glowing flower petals. Unassuming but deadly poisonous plants slithered their way across his arm as he idly picked at the small purple blooms dotting it.

Kneeling before the king of Fey, Elwood waited patiently for the monarch to address him.

"Elwood! Nice of you to come see me! How's my little beauty? Not causing you any trouble I hope?" The king was cheerful, a wide grin on his face as his eyes twinkled playfully. The plant life that had shielded him only moments ago withered, yellowed and dried. Small daisies popped into existence all over his throne. It gave him a wild look as the small white flowers took over the king's crown.

"Syellian is delightful, as always. I only wish the same could be said about her old man." Elwood rose and threw a rueful smile back to his king and closest friend.

"And here I thought we were friends," Callum pouted. He tilted his head to the side, looking like a curious child. A few flowers dislodged themselves and fell to the ground. "What are you here for? Surely not just to insult me!"

"Can't I just come to greet my king and friend?" Elwood answered, pushing his bangs out of his eyes and flashing his brightest grin. He could have blinded a man.

The ruler of Atrelia blinked. "And here I thought we couldn't lie." Straightening in his throne, his carefree expression morphed into a serious one.

"State your purpose, Zefire."

"Sir, Relevard has warned me that another of his kind is in dire need of my assistance." Elwood stared straight forward, eyes hard.

"Where is the host?"

"He is currently in the mortal kingdom of Gredian."

"Mortal kingdom?" The immortal ruler of Atrelia wondered why a key to the demon seal would be in a mere mortal. Elwood nodded but didn't say anything.

"I suppose you need to go investigate," Callum sighed as his normal personality began to leak through the cracks in his mask.

"Yeah," Elwood muttered, "Obviously not by choice." The thought of entering the mortal kingdom both excited and scared him—he had lost too much to the mortal army and still had so much he could lose. He couldn't say he hated mortals; they were just fighting for their loved ones like he was. But he held no love for them either. The thought of being able to wreak havoc upon their land was something he looked forward to. But infiltrating so deeply behind enemy lines also awakened the fear that he might not come back.

"Well, be careful. You'll be deep in enemy territory," the king whispered, as if reading his mind. Worry colored the powerful Fey's words. "But don't forget to have fun!" he added, trying to lighten the mood. He was rewarded with a chuckle.

"I can promise that I will enjoy every second of havoc I'm planning on causing," Elwood assured. He bowed once more before turning to leave. The winding paths outside the arc straightened in a direction he knew—at least he wouldn't be spending the next hour trying to find the exit.

"All joking aside," the king's voice forced him to stop in his tracks, "Do come back in one piece."

Elwood threw his war buddy a lopsided grin. "Of course, my king. I promise I'll return alive. After all, you'd be horribly lonely without me." His eyes met the king's. "And Callum," the king barely even flinched at the use of his given name, "you and I both know we can't break a promise now, can we?"

Callum smiled. "No. No, we cannot."

And, without a formal dismissal, Elwood saluted and walked through the ring of roses, feeling a wave of power wash over him as the hedges shifted once more. He would need to grab supplies for the journey, and that included his bow. At the thought of his weapon, he stumbled to a halt. Where had he put the thing?

CHAPTER
THREE

ON THE DAY OF HIS DEATH, the voice came.

The first time after the trial, it was something fabricated from Chais's brain, something pulled from the sea of turbulent thoughts riddling his mind. This time—this time, it was different.

Chais leaned against the slimy stone wall. The dungeons were too dark to see what coated them, but he couldn't care less. The colonel—ex-colonel, he reminded himself—pushed off. His steps were far too loud in this near-abandoned hallway. A blade shone in his right hand, its steel edges catching the dim light from the flickering torch. At least from that light, he could see very well what coated the walls, and he didn't want to look again.

Another blade emerged in his left hand, its leather handle rough and compacted from years of use. Chais made his way toward the opposite wall. Indistinguishable liquid squelched beneath his boots. He leveraged the only relatively clean thing he could reach in the dungeon—the slab of stained stone pressed against the wall, serving as a place to rest and to sharpen his knives, which were hidden in his uniform. The guards had recovered several, but he still had a good amount left.

Now facing the bars that barricaded his exit like sliding iron teeth, Chais Nevermoon palmed his daggers. The first attack—try to bring the opponent's guard down. Sparks flashed through the dungeon as he cut across the iron. Second—move in with a hit to any open area. He slashed at the bars, sweat dripping down his back over wounds that were in the middle of scarring. Third—if they're still standing, change that. Chais reared back with a coiled kick, striking the metal. The impact against an immovable object sent him skidding back, no thanks to the slippery stone floor. The ex-colonel sank to a knee and studied his opponent.

Two weeks. Two entire weeks, during his waking hours, he'd trained against the bars. Yet, even though he had struck the same place over and over again, the gleaming iron showed no sign of it. The shallowest chip that he would normally make against metal didn't appear. Magic it was, then.

Chais walked up to the bars. Craning his neck, he could barely see the end of the hall. It was too dark. Somehow, the one torch, its sickly yellow glow flickering as if it couldn't make up its mind, made the environment all the more creepy.

But what would he do if he escaped? He was a criminal in Gredian's eyes, and Adaric had said it himself: by code of the empire, should he manage to escape death, he would be a slave for the rest of his life. The nearest place was Atrelia, home of the Fey, but that was the race that humans had fought for thousands of years now—that he had fought for his entire life. And it was near impossible to catch a ride to the other continents when they were knee-deep in their own matters.

Chais wiped the sweat off his brow with his sleeve, which was now crusted with red-brown blood. He looked up—looked up at the waterlogged ceiling that he'd analyzed so many times already, but the ancient stone didn't yield a clue. He listened. Dripping in a corner, a liquid that smelled of Gredian's slums hit a puddle between the cracks in the floor. The three-second intervals between drips were enough to make a dent in a new prisoner's sanity.

A healer is coming.

The ex-colonel was immediately on his feet. A voice? Pungent yet familiar odors reached his nose as he moved to each corner of the cell, checking for something, someone—anything to confirm the fact that he wasn't hearing a voice in his own head.

Nothing. There was absolutely no one—

Sit down! Whoever it was—whatever it was—growled into his ear, tingling at the end of his brain. *They will be suspicious!*

"Who are you?" Chais kept his voice steady. The reassuring touch of leather pressed against his palm, and he traced a bloodied finger down the hilt. Clouds of frigid air coalesced in the damp, musty cell.

Silence. His gaze flickered back and forth, senses on high alert.

Aldridge. My name is Aldridge. The liquid in the corner fell. *Now, will you sit down?*

He heard a soft splash as it connected with the puddle. Chais drifted to the corner of the stone slab. He barely felt his fingers as they searched for the bed's rough outline. Aldridge? Where had he heard that name before …

There was a sudden deafening clang of steel, and Chais felt his heart jolt. The healer. Aldridge had said a healer was coming.

A woman entered the cell. Behind her, Chais could spot four guards, their sashes bearing the key and emblem, move into place. He eyed their weapons, wondering if he could knock them out fast enough before they could trigger the alarm—or before they could get to the doors at the end of the hall and seal Chais in until Adaric sent someone to haul him out.

Seal him in. Seal …

Aldridge … the Fey warrior from the Demon War. A key to the seal that kept the monsters trapped in their own universe. No wonder the name sounded so familiar; every human and Fey had heard of that story—the legend of a clash between worlds where the warring human and Feykind faced a threat from a third entity, a realm of demons that promised havoc and destruction no matter what race you were. It was almost surreal, how two enemies united under a common peril, utilizing magic and five sacrificial vessels to seal the demons away forever.

Then that would mean …

Another loud reverberation as the healer left, surprisingly quick. She left behind a steel basin—an average bathtub but not as large or heavy and certainly not in such good condition. One of the guards approached the bars of the cell, and Chais rose to meet her.

"You will be escorted outside in an hour," the woman said. The shadow of the dungeon and her hood obscured her features. "Get dressed. His Majesty insisted on you wearing your training gear." Her voice was deep and rich, with a slight accent from another continent, maybe Xilan. A pause as the guard passed him a neatly stacked pile of clothes: his clothes. She tilted her chin up, waited for Chais to take the gear, then left. Her footsteps echoed off of the walls, and the flickering torch cast her receding shadow in an ominous light.

"You're a key?" Chais hissed as soon as she was out of earshot. He set the stack onto a dry area of the bed—a tunic, pants, and a belt, all as dark as midnight.

... Yes. And you're a host. Before you ask, Aldridge cut in as Chais opened his mouth to speak, *the reason you only hear me now is because my previous host died.*

Chais discarded his tunic, the back of it already shredded and stained a darkened maroon. "This just made my escape a whole lot more important," he muttered and faced the bars again. Reaching an arm through a gap, he searched the slick walls on either side. Like always, his hand came back soaked in nothing but green-tinted slime.

Stop. There's no use in trying to escape. Aldridge's voice was stern and weathered, the voice of a seasoned warrior. It made Chais wonder what the Fey looked like in Aldridge's time—over two centuries ago.

"I just found out that I'm one of the reasons this world still exists, and you expect me to sit obediently and wait to be put into a noose?" He wiped his hands on the scrapped cloth and filled the basin, ignoring its grimy exterior.

The first part, yes. The second, well ... yes. That too.

Chais felt a tick in his brow as he moved to pull the tub out from underneath the dirt-covered faucet. While it was a relief to wash the layers of blood and filth off of his skin, he realized Adaric's intention was to make his last days in the castle worthwhile before his dignity was stripped from him—again, and this time in public.

"I'm going to get out of here. Alive," Chais inhaled as he lowered himself into the cold water that caused his bones to tremble. The dulled pain of his scarred wounds numbed underwater, and it took everything in him not to make a sound. Instead, he scrubbed at his skin. Flakes of dirt and dried blood fell off and into the basin.

You will. But not without a little help. It sounded like the Fey warrior inside his head was smiling.

Chais paused. "From who?"

I sent a signal to another one of my kind. The host is on his way.

The ex-colonel savored his hour before he climbed out of the tub, sparing a glance at the water that was now clouded a red-brown. He grabbed the small towel, which was surprisingly clean, and thought over the Fey's words.

"There's another host? In Gredian?"

No. The host is from Atrelia. Long, dark hair. Green eyes.

"A Fey?" Chais struggled to keep his volume in check. His fingers were numb, and the tips gave off a blue tint. He trembled as he got dressed, his own breath appearing in front of him. Chais tucked his hands under his arms and tried to fit a foot inside the boot. "A damn ... a damn Fey is coming to save me? In case you've forgotten, Aldridge, our species aren't on very good terms."

You mean the humans and the Fey aren't.

"My species and the Fey—" Chais cut himself off. He stood and dumped the contents of the basin in the drain, then resorted to pacing the cell. He ran a hand through his hair. "Are you implying that I'm not ...?" Chais almost whispered.

THREE

Somewhere down the hall, footsteps sounded.

Guards. The cell door opened and, almost immediately, iron shackles clamped his wrists together. A part of him reared at the non-healer contact, and his hand instantly reached for a knife. But he couldn't, no matter what that night—those nights—on the whipping block had done to him. He couldn't give himself away.

So, Chais let himself be hauled up the steps, through a darkened passageway, and into the courtyard. The morning sun was blinding. It cast his vision into a stupor, where anywhere he looked became a heavenly white. But it was so warm on his skin, on his frozen fingers and lips, that he thought he was already dead.

The guards didn't spare him a moment as they dragged him ... somewhere. He tried to memorize his steps on the packed dirt, tried to blink the light away, and the shadow came in the form of spots. The fact that he was outside and under the sun drove his blood to his head, and the world slowly came into focus. A small structure—where all victims went before their execution. That was where they were taking him.

If it weren't for Aldridge's reminders that someone was coming to save him, Chais doubted that he would've been this calm. He allowed a guard to leash him by the cuffs, which were thankfully in front of his body. That made killing much easier than if he was shackled in the back. But Former Lieutenant Colonel Chais Nevermoon was going to die today, so why bother? At least, that's what everyone else believed.

Footsteps. Chais knew who it was before he spoke.

"Ah, Nevermoon," Adaric strode in, accompanied side and flank by Gredian guards. The vivid red and silver were almost too much for his eyes to handle after being in the dark for so long. Chais managed a grim smile.

"Amptonshire," he said coldly, meeting the king's eyes.

"That's *Your Majesty* to you." Adaric's gaze turned sour.

Chais snorted. "Over my cold, dead body."

"That won't be long, then," Adaric took a few steps toward him. There was no furniture in the building, just velvet draped over the simple wooden structure (to hide from the spectators who was dying today). The king halted mere inches from Chais's face.

"Do you hear that?" Adaric whispered. Through the curtains, the voice of the announcer was just barely muffled as the man stepped onto the raised wooden platform in the center of the courtyard—the platform where a noose dangled from the top. Chais heard his name escape the announcer's lips, then the deafening roar of the crowd.

"That's the sound of hatred." The king backed up slowly. "And it's all directed toward you."

Before Chais could reply, a guard beside him lifted the curtain. The sheer amount of people gathered at the execution was enough to give him a headache. Colors swarmed, royal blues and blinding whites, peasant brown and forest green. He scanned the thick audience for a head of ebony hair, but there were just too many people.

He's here.

It was all the confirmation he needed. Chais could see a glint in Adaric's eye, as if he were imagining all the things he'd be freed of after this day. Now all that was left was his execution.

Or, as he hoped, his rescue.

CHAPTER

FOUR

ELWOOD WAS IMPRESSED. Through the vegetation he was hiding in he could see a town housing what could be no more than thirty people. This tiny village, with its wooden shacks and cobbled paths, was situated with its back pressed against the war zone. Dried leather and meat hung from wood buildings with leaking roofs, and the smoking pits behind the homes still wafted the scent of last night's meal. People dressed in earth tones milled around, chatting about meaningless things; it felt far too peaceful for a place so close to the blood-soaked fields. Granted, it was in a completely forsaken part of the Gredian border, so neither army really cared for the land, but still, most towns this close were either evacuated, made into army camps, or burned to the ground by Fey forces. He felt very lucky to have stumbled onto this residence; it would save him the trouble of sneaking past absurd numbers of border guards. The last five days could not have been described as fun, and the fact that his map had been eaten by some rabid sand monster on day two before he left the Unknown certainly didn't help. Fortunately, the map had served its purpose in leading him around the Unknown, where the battle between the two races took place. Unfortunately, he had no idea where on the Gredian border he was, and he had to get to the capital in two days, then disrupt a public execution. He groaned at the thought of just how much work it would be.

Stop complaining.

"Shut up," Elwood muttered, wishing he could glare at the spirit he shared his body with ... it was quite queer when he really thought about it. Actually, a lot about his current situation sounded odd when reflected upon. "You're not the one who needs to sneak his way into the enemy's capital."

Technically, I am you and you are me, so strictly speaking, I also need to sneak into the enemy's capital. Relevard sounded smug as his annoying voice buzzed in Elwood's mind. Why was it so hard to play nice with a dead general's soul living in your body?

"Technically, you're also dead," he grumbled under his breath and ran a hand through his tangle of hair before tugging out the tie holding it back. Dirty streaks fell across his shoulders and back, tickling his neck where it bunched up at his hood. Elwood reached up and arranged the locks around his ears. He covered them as best he could before pulling on his hood. The forest green fabric framed his vision and shadowed his too bright eyes and too sharp features. It should be an adequate enough disguise for the time being. Deciding to test his luck, he walked into the village and approached the nearest civilian. The human was a middle-aged woman with watery blue eyes. A thin and worn shawl was draped over her head, and there was a small basket of dirty clothes in her hands. Considering the early time of day, Elwood guessed the mortal was on her way to do her daily chores.

"Excuse me, miss." He stepped into her path and placed his sweetest smile onto his face. He knew that mortals found Fey charming, and he was more than willing to use that to his advantage. Maybe she would be too smitten by his charms to wonder where he had come from and why he was here. "I wish to ask you something, if it is not too much trouble?"

"Oh." The woman blinked in surprise, a faint blush coloring her pale skin. Smile marks branched from her eyes as she grinned, "Of course, young lad! How may I help you?"

"You see, miss," he rubbed the back of his hood in false nervousness. The soft cloth rustled, and he had to adjust it before it fell off. "I wish to get to the capital; I have dire business that I need to conduct there. But I do not have any means of travel that can get me there in time!" He carefully twisted his words so nothing he spoke was a lie, but nothing he said gave away his identity either. A Fey's immortal life span is reliant on the fact that they didn't lie; each lie made them more mortal, and each broken promise was returned with retribution from the gods themselves.

"What business are you attending to that puts you in such a hurry?" the lady asked. Her eyes narrowed slightly at the vague answer, seeming to realize something about his presence was unnatural.

Shoot. He had to distract her. It would be really annoying if he had to level the entire town with a tornado just because some stupid lady asked too many questions. Using every bit of acting he had learned over the years, he released a nervous chuckle and kicked up the dirt at his feet. His leather boot dug a small trench before forcing the dry, barren particles into the sky. The small dust motes spun in the morning air and clogged his nose. Bad idea. Elwood forced away a sneeze and assumed the role of a desperate young lover. Paying attention to every word he spoke, he tried to explain. "There is a person that I need to get to before it is too late."

Realization dawned upon the mortal. "A special someone?"

Elwood nodded eagerly—a key to the demon seal was a special person after all. Just ... not how the human was interpreting it.

"Please, miss," he pleaded, calling forth every ounce of frustration he had gathered over the past days and using them to twist his words with desperation, "I must get to them before I lose them forever."

"Well ..." Elwood saw her eyes warm—mortals and their softheartedness. He laughed internally; how foolish and naive. "My husband is taking the horse and wagon into the city to trade for some coin. I'm sure he wouldn't mind bringing you along. Once in the city, there should be transportation to bring you where you need to go." Elwood smiled and thanked the woman profusely. If he played his cards right, this would be easier than he thought.

ELWOOD SLIPPED OUT of the wagon where he had hitched a ride without the driver noticing, glad to be out of the mountain of wool. The man must have been some kind of rancher, as he was on his way to the capital to trade his quality sheep wool. The Fey gagged and pulled fluffs of fleece that clung to his coat in vengeful burrs; the smell was choking him. The street he had landed on, stone polished from years of travel, led to the wall. He couldn't help but shudder as he stared at the tall, foreboding walls. Crossbow turrets lined the lip. Heavy bolts already rested on drawn strings. One order and the dozens of men standing guard would open fire with polished muskets and forged iron bullets. Iron. The stink of it stung his nose and stirred his stomach. The putrid metal was fatal to Fey—just touching it burnt their skin, sapping at their strength.

Having picked up rumors of the man who killed the king, Elwood had no doubt that the man being gossiped about was the same one he had to save. It was a bit of a shame since the king was supposed to have been a rather good ruler, someone hoping to end the war and the horrors that came with it. The general uproar about his death proved that those assumptions were at least close to correct. A part of him didn't want to save the criminal who perhaps killed the only man in the next hundred years with the ability to end the war; however, the life of a demon key was more important than the death of a murderer. Considering that the man, Chais, was accused of killing the king, Elwood could easily guess that the execution would be a large public event ... making it that much easier to get close, and that much harder to get away.

"Relevard," Elwood whispered. He left the middle of the road and headed for the cluster of shops that surrounded the capital wall, which were inhabited by those not quite rich enough to live in the capital but who still wanted to be close to the action. A well-maintained inn was bustling with people, no doubt coming to watch the execution. He weaved through the crowds of people, noting some were dressed in nothing more than glorified rags and others in false, woven gold. Elwood entered a small tavern, guided by the smell of booze, careful that his hood was up and his waist-long hair covered his ears. "I should be able to get to the execution stand by simply following the crowd, right?"

Yes—from what I gathered, the execution will take place in the main square, surrounded by civilians and protected by at least fifty well-armed guards. The new king should be there as well, surrounded by his personal guards.

"Would I be able to get away with a grab and run?" Elwood asked as he sat in a corner booth and ordered a beer. The important part was to blend in. Maybe he should get a snack also; his soon and inevitable use of his power was absolutely going to sap his energy. How was the pie here? It had been a while since he had had anything but dried bear jerky ... Relevard jerked him out of his food fantasies with a lecture.

It would be impossible to get away without encountering the mortals. Battle is inevitable. Besides, you would have to flee across the entire country with the army on your tail, whether or not you encounter resistance while stopping the execution.

"Well then, I suppose I just need to do what I promised the king." A small, sadistic grin spread across his face, his unnaturally sharp canines glistening, "I'll wreak some havoc." Maybe this was actually going to be fun.

I have no doubt you will. Relevard sounded almost gleeful at the thought of tearing through the capital with a wanted man.

Elwood rose from his seat and downed the mug—sticking a tongue out at the sour taste it left in his mouth—and left, tossing a few coins onto the table. Only he knew of the irony of the coins, as those were the very same coins he had swiped from the waitress when she served his beer. He strolled out of the tavern; pity he didn't have time for pie.

He readjusted his hood and approached the looming gates. They were open—after all, what was the point of a public execution if no one could see it? Many mortals, more than usual, were entering the large gates. Crowds of people flocked toward the center square, eager to find justice served for the death of their beloved monarch. The rich stood out with their sparkling robes and enough jewelry to drag them to the bottom of the ocean, their hair styled and oiled and their servants trailing them like lost puppies. The poor looked for entertainment; they were mostly barefoot and wearing rags, giving a wide berth to the well-dressed upper class and smelling of cheap booze and mildew. He stuck with the merchants in bright colors and false jewels that were just passing by. He could tell they needed to see a man killed to make the day more interesting.

Being so close to so much iron made him want to throw up. The smell of death radiated from the metal. Elwood shuddered and walked through the gates as fast as he could, only to groan as he realized that the guards were checking for Fey. Did someone see him? He had heard rumors of Fey in the kingdom ... it was foolish of him to just dismiss them. Men and women alike were stopped and forced to show identification, and most were let go after seeing that their ears were human. Elwood was going to be in a load of trouble if they saw his ears.

He carefully approached one of the guards and casually flicked up his right hand. A sudden breeze came through, knocking the soldier's helmet off his head. The iron headwear rang a loud, hollow clang against the polished stone and rolled clanking away down the slight slope. While the human was distracted, Elwood smoothly walked past him. No one gave him a second glance, as most were bracing themselves against the sudden wind or watching the soldier comically chasing down his runaway helmet. The faery knight smirked lightly and entered the capital. One hour until the execution. If he hurried, he could get a good spot.

Elwood stood before the execution stand and got as close as he could without being noticeable. A mortal announcer pulled out a scroll and took his place in front of the noose. He was cautious not to stand on the trap door that would fall out once the noose was fitted around the accused's neck. The stage was hollow underneath so that everyone could witness the moment that the noose took the weight of the victim. The rough yet simply cut wood beams held up the stand and stretched above the announcer's head, standing with all its grim glory. The rope swinging in a phantom breeze seemed to mock the viewers, loose and ready to be wrapped around the neck of a seal key. The shadow thrown across the stage made it appear as if the announcer was being hanged by a shadow noose. He began to list the crime of the man who would soon be hanged. Elwood tuned him out, far more interested in watching the crowd's reaction and planning his attack.

At some point, a curtain parted, and a soldier forced a man onto the stage. He was only a little shorter than Elwood and appeared to be in his late teens or early twenties. His hair, a metallic silver, stuck to his forehead, still wet from a hasty bath— no doubt to make him presentable to those gathered to watch him die. He had eyes that were a startling electric blue, burning with the will to fight and live. His body was that of a warrior's, coiled muscles tense as his sharp eyes scanned the crowd, searching for Elwood. Something about the accused man's gaze and features were eerily familiar; maybe they had met on the battle-field before. But he knew one thing immediately: this man was not the murderer that the public made him out to be. The underlying sorrow was not directed at his approaching death, but at the loss of a loved one—at the loss of a leader, the loss of a peace bringer. Elwood wanted to hear his story.

That's him.

"I can tell," he mumbled, making sure not to draw attention to himself. His faery steel bow was on his back. Considering most people carried weapons, no one really gave it much mind. Some, however, noticed that he didn't have any arrows and simply labeled him odd. Things were going to get really interesting really soon. There were twenty guards around the king, two holding the accused—he would have to terminate them—ten around the immediate perimeter, five in the crowd … no, make it six. Twenty circling around the crowd, over fifty around the wall, guarding the gate. Patrols in pairs of two at five-minute intervals, all armed with an iron broadsword and iron bolt crossbows, dressed in iron chest pieces adorned with a blood-red sash. The King's Guard carried muskets, which he would have to avoid at all costs. He had seen what those did to Fey. He narrowed his eyes so they were glowing slits. Blood. Chais was recently wounded, badly, although the injuries had healed a bit. That would certainly complicate things. Elwood took a steady breath and planned his course of action.

Fingers inching toward his bow, he started to focus his power. The noose was fitted around Chais's neck. The flare of anger in his eyes was obvious. His gaze locked onto the false king, and if looks could kill, Adaric would be six feet under. Speaking of Adaric, the man looked far too pleased. He wasn't a newly burdened king sentencing a man to death but a manipulator watching his plans solidify before his eyes.

The trap door unceremoniously fell away with a deafening crack, and Chais was suspended; he started to pale as his air was cut off. A wide smile stretched across Adaric's face, like a viper gleefully examining its dying prey. He watched his victim, absorbing each and every second of the man's agony and relishing in it.

NOW! Relevard growled. Faster than any human eye could see, Elwood whipped out his bow and sent a spinning funnel of wind at the rope. Before he even confirmed its connection with the target, a sweep of his left hand sent a blast of wind toward the king, catapulting him through the air and into the crowd with a rather high-pitched scream. The King's Guard rushed into the crowd. They cut down anyone who slowed their path to the king, staining their blades red. Screams rose through the air at the sudden attack. Meanwhile, with the rope cut, Chais had fallen to the ground, a little dizzy but otherwise unharmed. His neck was going to have a nasty bruise by the next day, but at least he was still breathing.

Elwood leaped with inhuman grace and downed the two guards before his feet even landed on the platform. Kneeling by the warrior, he smiled and pushed his hood back to reveal his dark hair and pointed ears. His green eyes shone with mischief.

"Hello," Elwood greeted. He removed the noose from the poor man's neck and examined his shackles. They looked way too tight. "I'm Elwood Zefire. My demanding brain voice told me to come help you, the bossy son of a bitch."

Chais stared at him, as if unsure whether or not he was serious. "We can save the introduction for later. The guards are starting to rally."

"Sure," Elwood grumbled. Great, another order-giving bastard. He leaned in to cut through the lock with a concentrated blast of wind before his instincts screamed at him to stop. "Or not." He blinked and wrinkled his nose at the iron. "Your shackles are iron; I can't touch them. Just stay close to me. We're going to have to plow through them." Chais cursed under his breath, but Elwood's sharp hearing caught the words, and he let out a low chuckle. "Is that any way to speak to your rescuer?"

"You're not my rescuer yet," Chais pointed out with annoying logic. Great, he was a smart ass too. They were going to get along fine.

"Then I suppose I will have to do just that," Elwood answered before releasing a torrent of wind, knocking back the approaching guards. The civilians had scattered, though the blood of the unlucky ones was already seeping into the ground. Time to slaughter some mortals. With a deafening battle cry, he left a path of carnage behind him.

CHAPTER
FIVE

CHAIS ADMIRED FOR A SPLIT SECOND how the warrior fought—powerful, swift, with a feline grace that sparked with his every move. A moment passed where nothing sounded except the screech of metal against metal, screams that reached octaves higher than he could comprehend, and the relentless pounding of his heart—his heart—crashing, drumming, the music of a thousand soldiers marched in the midst of a rain-trodden battlefield with nothing but the white-hot fires to guide them.

And then the leather soles of his boots met dirt, and a flicker of electricity raced along the bone of his shin before he dug his toe into the earth and launched himself forward. He was sharply aware of the cold metal pressing against the skin of his wrists, the strong iron odor that rose from it, and the bodies that were piling around him. A hiss of wind from ahead. An explosion of blood and gore and bone.

Chais ducked his head as he wove through the crowd, seeing swarms of brown and black leathers and poorly woven fabrics the color of dungeon walls. The mass of his shoulder collided with another. Breathlessly, he ignored the yells of startled civilians.

The King's Guard indiscriminately cut innocent people down, while the other guards watched who they were aiming at. Although Elwood wouldn't be able to distinguish between the two, Chais chose a side with fewer royal guards and more common townspeople. He hoped the fleeing Fey would catch on.

There was a dull pain that was now pulsing through the muscles of his back as the wounds restitched themselves with a new, strange magic. Aldridge's voice was a steady rhythm in his brain, throwing warning after warning.

On your right—

Chais swung around and raised his cuffs. The sword of a soldier slammed into the metal, and a vibration echoed through the bones in his forearm. Almost immediately, Chais clamped the blade between the manacles and twisted. He delivered a swift kick to the guard's wrists. The weapon came free. Chais flung it to his left and caught it on the grip with both hands. Another strike to the stunned man's stomach left him temporarily incapacitated.

Ahead—

Chais flipped the newly claimed sword so that it hung at an angle and sprinted after the Fey, his steps blending into the chaotic surroundings. There was a gap ahead of them where civilians were few, and there was nothing but a wide courtyard, a wall, and a stone bridge that signaled their freedom. Beyond that bridge was the city of Silvermount, where hiding was as easy as hitching a ride on the back of a passing cart. And then ... and then where would he go?

The stab of reality faded into the background, to be replaced by the stern voice of a demon key.

They're closing the gates! Aldridge's voice was laced thick with panic, but he still somehow managed to maintain his composure. The iron barrier rumbled and clanked loudly as it sunk slowly toward the ground, manned by soldiers. Too far. It was too far away.

"There's no other way out," Chais hissed, eyes darting back and forth across the crowds as he zigzagged. An arrow hurtled past the skin of his cheek—the guards were starting to shoot now that there were fewer civilians strewn about. A sickening lurch sounded as the gate hit the ground and trapped the crowd inside the capital. A string of scared spectators began to pound at the rusted bars. The men who stood next to it and violent outbreaks temporarily threw Silvermount into a panicked frenzy.

"Unless ..."

Chais steeled himself. Over the heads of the people, he could catch a green cloak and an inky ponytail. A cart on the path beside him, someone's form of transportation, exploded into a million splinters of wood. Alarmed, Chais threw a glance behind him. Guns. Shiny barrels, iron bullets, and smoke. The screams heightened tenfold.

Elwood. Iron was poisonous to Fey.

Driven with a new type of desperation, Chais sprinted after the wind maker. The muscles on his calves screamed from lack of use, and his lungs burned with the extra energy. Think, think, think.

"Elwood!" Chais yelled, "Can you fly?"

The Fey's pale face was smeared with the crimson blood of guards. He grabbed a soldier by the face, not breaking eye contact with Chais.

"Of course!" Elwood said, pupils lit up by the fire of battle. His fingers twitched, and the man in his grip screamed in agony as high-speed winds shredded his face. Chais took an instinctive step back, but it didn't prevent the man's eyeball juice from spilling over his tunic. Chais's face twisted in disgust.

The Fey had the nerve to look innocent. "What?"

Chais tightened his grip on the sword and pivoted to catch an approaching guard by surprise. He aimed a blow to the man's forearms, toppling the gun that he had rushed to load. A pouch of iron bullets spilled across the cobblestone path and into the cracks, but the soldier had only a few seconds to comprehend this before Chais knocked him out.

"Let's go," Chais said. He searched for a spot on the wall. It was close enough to run up to in seconds, smooth enough to deter thieves, and high enough to make him pale at the idea of flying over it.

"Wait!" Elwood knocked over a merchant's cart as he approached, and apples spilled across the road. The Fey moved swiftly, an embodiment of the element he controlled. There was a spear gripped tightly in his hand.

"Hold still," Elwood said, and then he sliced down.

The chain holding Chais's cuffs together snapped into two. Without restraints, the newly acquired range of motion stunned Chais long enough for Elwood to run up and grab his arm.

"And now, hold on tight!" he whispered. The giddy, delirious edge to his tone snapped Chais out of his reverie.

"Now? Wait!" Chais shouted in vain as he was forced to stumble after the Fey, arrows, and bullets narrowly missing flesh, "We're still too f—"

They rocketed off of the ground at a neck-breaking speed; a single burst took them halfway up the thirty-foot wall. Chais cursed loudly this time, and impulse enabled him to launch his sword at the shrinking group of guards who were separated from the throng of civilians. Immediately, the burden that Elwood had to carry lightened, and a second burst sent them soaring over the top of the wall. The soles of Chais's boots barely brushed the stone surface. He cast a glance behind him.

Citizens and soldiers alike stared at the odd duo, mouths agape and the nerves in their bodies refusing to react to orders. These people had never been on the battlefield, where walls of fire much higher than this one incinerated bodies in the blink of an eye, where tsunamis tore mortals apart and scattered the remains, where creatures morphed into wolves and bears, their jaws glistening with fresh blood. Some of these people were royals. Some of them watched children forced onto the battlefield when they could barely hold a sword.

He knew how it felt. And a part of him loathed the nobles with jewelry perched over their collarbones as they took pleasure in seeing his childhood—all of their childhoods—stripped away.

Elwood laughed suddenly, a sound too strange and unfamiliar to Chais's ears. They were still flying, steadily gaining height, and the safety of the wall's surface was already out under their feet. Just a little ways to go before they were over. The Fey gestured toward a seemingly discarded sword on the ground. Chais followed his gaze.

"You're a horrible shot," Elwood sniggered as a burst of wind propelled them forward. Chais growled in response.

"Shoot them down!" a familiar voice shrilled from down below. He looked back to see Adaric, royal robes rumpled and his expression contorted into absolute lividity. His eyes burned with anger, and his face was flushed a bright red.

As if revived by an unseen force, the soldiers discarded their momentary shock and lifted their weapons. Arrows and bullets battered, like pouring rain, at the figures above the wall.

Cursing, Elwood sent a burst of wind to his side, redirecting his trajectory, trying to avoid the sharp projectiles. Chais's grip tightened on the Fey's forearm. Wind, expanding outward like a pillow, supported his body as he flew. He twisted around and felt the cushion spread to his back as he acted as a lookout for the Fey warrior. Now that they were at an angle above Silvermount, he could see the soldiers as they cocked their guns and drew back their bowstrings.

A low bang echoed before a bullet tore through Elwood's coat, barely missing his skin. Minuscule scraps of green fabric flew off, carried by the wind. The bridge, a thin line with two lanes, was crowded with escaping citizens and wooden carts, many of which came dangerously close to falling into the waters below. In the distant skies, dark and hazy shapes vaguely resembling hawks circled over the treetops, demons on their patrols.

Elwood dove and spun, sending controlled blasts of wind to different parts of his body. Chais felt a sharp prick of pain on his arm as a bullet barely grazed his skin. The agony only flared briefly before Aldridge brought it under control and the wound began knitting itself together.

Almost there ... Aldridge whispered, a calm voice in an otherwise chaotic world. Chais looked back at Silvermount, his former home, his heartbeats pulsing in his eardrums. With Aldridge's shared eyesight, he could make out every detail of every person in the square. In his peripheral vision, he caught a group of archers draw their bowstrings.

"Six o'clock!" Chais shouted. The Fey made a sudden loop through the air. He barely avoided the projectiles. Wind whistled as the arrows flew by and into the water. Just a few feet to go; then they could land and blend in with the townspeople until they were out of the empire. There was no destination right now. Their first priority was to survive.

Chais could sense the shift in Elwood's flight pattern. Abandoning caution for speed, the Fey directed his power into a mighty boost at his feet and propelled them past the turret near the outer wall.

There. Aimed directly at them.

As soon as the gleaming barrel entered his line of sight, Chais opened his mouth.

"Veer left!"

On his last word, the low echo of a musket sounded. Elwood slammed wind into his right side, sent them shooting left, and prayed they would be able to dodge it.

There was a burst of fire and a spray of crimson. Chais cursed as the Fey jerked, agony and nausea clouding Elwood's senses, the bone in his upper arm shattered from the bullet. Chais felt himself beginning to slip and gripped tighter onto the warrior. They were falling now, toward the open water, leaving a red ribbon trail. Elwood's forest green eyes faded in and out of consciousness.

"Stay with me—" Chais breathed as he pressurized the Fey's wound. The wind holding him up was weak, but it was enough. Damn. Damn. Damn—

Elwood's eyes snapped back into focus, and he inhaled sharply. All of a sudden, the Fey tightened his grip around Chais before redirecting his remaining power to his feet. A burst of energy sent them soaring over the bridge, over the rooftops of Silvermount, as far away from the capital as Elwood could go. The roars of rage from Adaric died along with the wind.

And then there was nothing, nothing but air and the sensation of falling and a silence so deep he could hear the blood rushing through his veins, his heart beating to the music of soldiers. Chais struggled to gain control over the limp Fey in his arms, surprisingly light as they hurtled through the sky and into the unfamiliar woods below.

The branches came, leaves populating their surfaces after the harsh winter. They stretched toward each other over the clearing, sharp and thin. As the two figures careened toward the ground, the branches left bloody marks on Chais's skin and were tearing at his clothes. He curled around Elwood to shield the warrior. Pain rushed through his body as new and old wounds opened. In a flurry of leaves and blood, Chais fell, back first, grasping the body of the unconscious Fey.

And they crashed into the ground.

Something broke. Chais stifled the initial scream, distracted wholly by the blinding agony. He flinched as his bones cracked unnaturally. Gently, gritting his teeth through the pain, he nudged Elwood to the side. The Fey was mostly untouched, save for the grotesque wound in his bicep. Chais grimaced and squeezed his eyes shut. His chest moved rapidly as he searched for air.

"Aldridge?" His voice was merely a whisper, yet it sounded deafening.

Working on it. Focus on your breathing right now.

"Thank you," Chais murmured. There was a pause.

"And just so you know, I really mean that. Genuinely."

I know. Now, I hate to use this phrase, but shut up before you make things worse.

Chais chuckled but decided to stop when his torso flared with pain. He glanced up, not willing to move his neck in order to assess their surroundings.

They had landed in a clearing. Tall trees, full enough to provide good shelter, stretched toward the sky, bent as if he were looking through a lens of some sort. Small breaks in leaves cast icy spotlights onto the ground. A leaf dislodged from their crash drifted toward him, trailed by numerous others. And a stream—he only realized now how thirsty he was—bubbled somewhere near them. Small, yellowed blades of grass shot up from between the roots of the trees.

The pain in his ribs and spine dampened to a dull throb. Chais sat up slowly, shuddering at the noises that his joints were making, and crawled over to the fallen Fey. There was still blood leaking through Elwood's coat. It formed a dark red stain on his bicep area, but much less than if Chais hadn't pressurized it briefly. Chais pulled himself into a sitting position and tugged the Fey's arm out from the sleeve. It was harder to see the blood through Elwood's black tunic, but Chais braced himself anyway and carefully peeled back the fabric.

"Gods," "That does *not* look good," he muttered before he stood to face the stream. An errant hand ran through his hair. If he was going to deal with Elwood's wound, he'd have to clean up.

... No, it does not.

Chais kneeled. He glanced briefly at his battered reflection before he plunged his hands into the creek. Dirt spread, moved downstream by the sedate current. The water was cold and clear. It pumped with an electricity that didn't seem quite right, even after everything that had happened. Chais waited for the grime to disappear and was about to cup his hands for a drink when a sudden burst of energy radiated through his fingers and exploded outward in a constellation of white light.

He jolted, instantly retracting his hands. He looked back at the stream, but there was nothing unordinary about it. The multicolored stones still gleamed beneath the current of water, silvery shapes of fish darted in between the white foam, and a bird landed silently somewhere nearby.

Chais realized that there was a knife in his grip, the only weapon that wasn't confiscated from his training outfit, hidden in a spot that the guard probably didn't bother to check. He turned the blade over and momentarily examined its surface before sheathing it. Hallucinations? Side effects of being a seal? A demon seal. He was a demon—

Are you okay?

Aldridge's voice came as a shock. Right. Elwood. There was a dying Fey in these woods.

"Yes," Chais said slowly. He took a quick drink of water and stood, casting a quizzical glance at the stream. "I'm fine."

He pushed the thoughts to the back of his mind as he wandered back to an unconscious Elwood. If Aldridge hadn't felt the pulse of energy, chances were, it wasn't real. Chais shook his head slightly, as if the action could make everything better.

He rolled Elwood's sleeve up to gain access to the wound. The edges were blackened and cracked, dark blood oozing out slowly, not clogging up the wound as it should. Tints of yellow surrounded the wound, hardened and rough. The skin further away from the wound was pale and slick with sweat, and the veins around Elwood's bicep were darkened to an unnatural ebony. Chais swallowed.

A healing lesson would be perfect right about now.

He noticed bits of iron, shards that could barely glint due to the blood covering their edges. He could remove the larger ones, but at this rate ...

Chais took a deep breath. The sun, even though it only cast itself onto the ground in spotlights, felt like a foreign entity through his new Fey-given lenses. Sounds of wildlife formed a consistent backdrop, relentless despite the bloody heap of Fey in the middle of it all. He tilted his head to the side. The wind was barely alive, but it was fluttering as if its last breath were approaching.

Careful to avoid the shattered bone and major artery, Chais secured a larger shard of iron and guided it out, forcing his hand to stop shaking. He could feel Aldridge following along in tense anticipation.

You might want to bring him closer to the stream so that you can clean out his wounds better, Aldridge suggested after the first piece was removed.

Chais sighed and wiped the sweat off of his brow with the back of his hand. He half-dragged the Fey to a grassy clump next to the water, finding a spot that provided more shelter from the heat. He resumed his work methodically, almost not noticing what his hands were doing. The water ran red for a second as Chais started to clean the wound. Somehow, the sounds of the river flowing and brushing gently against the rocks on the bank calmed him, despite what had happened at a stream not so far away from here, despite being a seal ...

Chais carefully pulled out the last iron shard he could dislodge without causing more harm. He realized that a medic was necessary for further treatment. But ... to move Elwood now, when he was unconscious, could result in his warrior instincts surfacing and causing him to lash out. It was better to wait for Elwood to wake up.

"Aldridge," Chais murmured. He decided to pass the time by gaining information.

Yes?

"Why—how did I become a demon seal?" Chais shook his head. The words coming out of his mouth were ludicrous, alien. He was just a soldier from Gredian, not some otherworldly entity that would determine the future of mankind. He was just a soldier whose mother died with his birthplace. His father ran away to the army so many years ago, detached so suddenly from his life that Chais had assumed he had died in battle. But if Chais was a seal, and seals were usually transferred through blood ...

"He was still alive." There was a long pause.

He was. Aldridge's voice blended in with the gentle breeze and the current of slow-moving water.

Smoke.

Screams.

Fire.

Chais took a deep breath. "Do you know if he died ..." he bit his lip, thankful for the independent nature of the forest, "happy?"

Yes. On the battlefield, near the place he used to call home.

Chais swallowed and looked up. Spotted white light shone

down from the sky, such a vivid blue. The place he used to call home—Alryne—was gone. And no wonder Chais had never seen his father; they were battling in completely different places.

Smoke.

Screams.

Fire.

He wiped at his eyes with the back of his hand. It came away dry.

"Explain to me how demon seals work," Chais breathed, overcome with a faceless emotion. "How they're passed, the magic involved—"

He had too many questions and too small of a world to hold them all.

We are not made to be burdens, Aldridge began. *We are made to be strong—born from tragedy and passed on through death.*

The shadows in the clearing stretched and birds cut off their song, as if something, someone ancient, was speaking words that could make or destroy the universe.

Demon seals grant enormous power that takes a while to develop and master, from element affinity to increased physical capabilities. The hosts also own the ability to hold the rift together; as a result, they're highly valued. However, if one person were to harness the power of these five seals, they could reopen the fissure, if they possessed enough summoning potential.

Aldridge took a silent breath. Images flooded into Chais's brain, memories that weren't his, faces that he didn't recognize. But there was Aldridge, standing with four others—Fey and human—in front of a tear in the sky. Demons poured out of the rupture, a pitch-black ocean teeming with legs, claws, and bright red eyes.

We were just five warriors who wanted to save the world, Aldridge said. His words were forlorn, but his voice was not.

Using a long-forgotten sealing scroll, we sacrificed our lives to stitch back the veil between humanity and demonkind.

The flashbacks disappeared. There was only the soothing flow of the river water and the gentle breeze that had picked up moments before. Chais closed his eyes and tried to go back, tried to find some sort of clue …

We were born to protect. So don't take it so hard, Chais. A warm flow spread to his fingertips as the seal said his name for the first time.

Elwood's awake. You'd best tend to him before the pain gets to his head.

Chais glanced over and, sure enough, the Fey was stirring. Chais searched quickly through Elwood's supplies, which he had brought from Atrelia, and found a half-empty leather canteen. He had barely refilled it when the Fey warrior groaned loudly and cracked open an eye.

Chais kneeled by his side, to which Elwood responded by shifting and groaning again. The pain from the wound probably wasn't registering yet.

Chais helped the Fey to a sitting position and placed the rim of the canteen on Elwood's lower lip. Elwood took a small sip of water, his next words muffled. Chais glanced at the bullet wound and noticed that the previously black veins had begun to return to their original color, but if he didn't remove the smaller shards, Elwood dying from poison was highly likely.

As if on cue, the Fey flinched suddenly, his eyes wide and rimmed with red. The water from the canteen dripped uselessly onto his black tunic before Chais tilted it back, helpless as to what to do. Elwood grabbed onto Chais's arm for support.

The Fey's breathing became measured again in only a few moments; Chais assumed it was the voice inside his head that was calming him down. Upon closer examination, Chais realized that there were dark circles under Elwood's eyes and his skin was sickly pale. Combined with the blood and dirt from the previous fight, the Fey wasn't faring very well.

Elwood whispered something, but his words were lost in the wind.

"What?" Chais asked, now crouching in front of the Fey who had sought a trunk to sit against. Despite Aldridge's pep talk, which had settled some concerns about being a seal, there was still the situation at hand. The more he thought about going to Atrelia, the land of the species he had spent his entire life fighting against, the more it got to his head. Had he been fighting for an enemy and against an ally? Had he been raised upon lies? Doubt flooded his brain as his questions seemed to carry no meaning.

"Can you ..." Elwood's voice was hoarse, and even though it was obvious how much effort he was putting into speaking, his words only came out as a whisper. He swallowed and tried again.

"Can you kindly remove the damn iron bullet from my arm," Elwood growled, "before it kills me?"

"You think I don't want to?" Chais snarled back, "I don't know how!"

Elwood tilted his head back against the tree trunk, and a massive sigh escaped from his lips. Here they were, in the middle of an unknown forest, an unknown distance from the capital, a lieutenant colonel who had just escaped death and was now being hunted by the empire he used to call home and a Fey warrior who had a voice inside his head and had just been shot by a bullet made of poisonous metal.

"Great," Elwood moaned. His emerald eyes closed. "I'm going to die."

CHAPTER
SIX

CHAIS TOOK PERSONAL OFFENSE at Elwood's lack of faith and hauled him to his feet, ignoring the loud protests and completely justified whimpers of pain. Relevard unhelpfully ran diagnostics and pointed out just how low the chances of their survival were while complaining about how keeping him from going into shock was giving him a headache. Elwood moaned in pain as the stupid colonel dragged him over what felt like every boulder. He leaned more of his weight onto the man and immediately felt his companion stiffen before pressing onward. Perhaps Chais had an issue with physical contact.

Elwood couldn't help but notice that the back of Chais's shirt looked significantly more bloody and his breathing was not what he would deem normal. Did Chais cushion their fall? That would explain the reopened wounds and broken ribs. Considering he was regaining breath more and more easily each step, his key must have been working overtime to mend the damage.

Still, how foolish for him to wound himself further when he knew that Elwood would be incapacitated after that bullet. Stupid human. No, he wasn't human ... at least not completely. A Feykin, how interesting. Those were rare, and this one hadn't even inherited a Fey's power, it seemed. Where were they going?

Black spots danced across Elwood's vision, the result of fatigue and pain. Sunbeams streamed through a light canopy of leaves and reflected off the bubbling brook they were following. It gave his pounding skull even more to complain about. But none of the scenery gave any clue as to where they were heading.

"Where are you taking me?" His words came out in a near whisper, so he cleared his throat and tried again. "Where are we going?" Chais came to a sudden stop, as if he just realized he had been dragging a dying Fey for a good twenty minutes with no explanation.

"We're going to find you a doctor ..." Chais muttered. His hand clenched and unclenched where it was wrapped around Elwood's waist to keep him semi-upright. "There is a village nearby, it should be a couple of miles through those trees. I know it. I've been there during a hunting trip ... I think ..."

"Oh, that makes sense," Elwood slurred, his mind foggy. He felt a wave of irritation that ripped through the fog.

Are you insane? What's stopping them from turning on you at the moment they realize you're not human? Relevard growled. Exhaustion tinted the edges of his speech.

"W-wait!" Elwood yelped as Chais began to pull him forward again. He dug his heels into the wet riverbed mud. "They will just turn us in!"

"If we don't do something, you're going to die and so will I!" Chais hissed. He scanned the trees as if a cure for iron poisoning was just going to appear. Finding nothing, the Feykin growled and eyed a nearby tree like he was hoping it would catch fire. Maybe he was just pissed off that he was too stressed to realize what a horrible move he had almost made.

"Just ..." Elwood winced. His body was numbing—most likely from blood loss, which was not a good sign. Positive thoughts ... at least it didn't hurt anymore? They needed a solution quickly, before he died; Elwood had a fleeting curiosity about what could happen to him if he broke a promise by dying. Normally, a broken promise created the worst kind of karma, as if the world was punishing a Fey for breaking a promise and therefore lying. But if he were dead ... No, hold on. Not the time or place for this kind of discussion. Think, Elwood urged himself. 'Use that mind that got you promoted to general!'

And then he had a horrible idea.

No! Relevard immediately said.

"It may be the only way. Better than dying, right?" Elwood noted morbidly. A dry chuckle escaped from his throat. It was going to hurt like hell. He looked back at his arm, hoping it wasn't as bad as it initially seemed; he really didn't want to do this. The wound did not appear better; if anything, it had worsened. The black veins had come back. They pulsed against his pale skin, looking like night snakes ready to burst out of his body. The area directly around the wound was no longer a hardened yellow but an inflamed red, puckered in the middle of dried, diseased skin.

Elwood grimaced.

You would bleed out. Relevard was grasping at straws. He knew that Elwood was right. Elwood honestly wished this was an argument he could lose.

"But if I started to bleed out, your powers could close the wound before I do, right?" Elwood felt shame that his powers couldn't get rid of the iron. After all, dead Fey was still Fey, and Fey tend to be useless against the damn metal. Relevard was silent, and Elwood looked up at the dancing sun motes and sighed.

"What are you planning?" Chais asked.

"You're going to chop my arm off," Elwood replied coolly.

"I'm going to *what*?" Chais's eyes grew comically wide. Elwood would have laughed if it didn't bring him pain. And perhaps it wouldn't hurt; his right arm and shoulder were completely numb anyway.

"I'm not going to make it to a place where I can get the iron removed in time. My natural Fey healing, along with Relevard's powers as a demon key, will keep me from bleeding out … probably," Elwood explained as he pulled out his bow and handed it to Chais. He hesitated for a moment before pushing it into Chais's hand. "It's sharp on the left end; make a clean cut." He pointed at the sharpened end of the bow, which was coated with drying blood. "That will need to be cleaned."

"I barely know you, and you're asking me to amputate your arm?" the half-human asked in shock, but he took the bow anyway, seeming by instinct. "How can you trust me enough? And 'probably'? That's not very reassuring."

"Don't worry about that part, I'm sure Relevard can handle it. As for your question, it's either trust you or die. And I promised my king I wouldn't die." Elwood gave Chais a lopsided smile. "Then again, I also promised to come back in one piece … I hope that was just a figure of speech."

That was the thing with Fey promises. They couldn't be broken, but if they were not carefully worded, they could be bent. It was the same with the whole dancing-around-the-truth thing.

"I'll have to take you further from the village then. If you scream we'd be given away in an instant." Chais knew he was buying time to think over the situation. He stared in the direction of the village as if he was considering going there anyway and risking capture. Elwood took the moment to lean all of his weight onto his companion, which almost pitched them both into the river. Chais hissed as the weight pressed against his ribs, and he glared down at Elwood, who returned the expression and added a gesture to it as well. Chais huffed in exasperation and hauled up the dead weight. They would have to come back for supplies after the messy procedure.

Once they got further downstream, they stopped at a relatively clean part with smooth, shining pebbles lining the shore. Both tried to mentally prepare themselves. The water bubbled and flowed rather quickly, and foams of white burst as the current ran around the river stones. The water was clear enough to see the bottom in the deeper, calmer areas. The sunlight left dots of white on the water surface. It was cold, a good sign, meaning it was clean and good for drinking. Clean also meant that it could be used to clean up the wound after the amputation.

Elwood knew that this was far from the ideal situation for surgery, but he really had no other choice if he didn't want to die or be captured by humans. Chais helped him shrug off his forest green coat, then slowly and meticulously folded the fabric to buy more time.

"Build a fire, and heat the bow to get rid of germs; I don't know how many people I've killed with that blade today," Elwood said and watched as Chais left to gather enough leaves and twigs to spark a flame. Using skills he undoubtedly honed on the war front, Chais quickly started a small fire and held the bow over the flickering flames. Elwood couldn't help but fidget nervously as the blade was heated. The blooming red and orange licking at the bow heated the blood into dry brown flakes that drifted into the open fire. The steel blade glowed with heat. Elwood tore off two pieces of his black, and slightly bloody, tunic with his uninjured left arm and watched as Chais approached with the hot blade.

"You sure about this?" the colonel asked. Hesitation colored his sapphire eyes. The Fey rubbed his fingers over the fabric he tore. The soft yet tough cloth caught on his nails, and he nodded.

"Let's get this over with." Elwood pushed himself up, bracing himself with his left arm and turning away from his right. This was going to hurt, a lot. He inserted the fabric into his mouth and tasted the bitter sweetness of blood on his tongue. The dry flakes made his mouth and throat parched, coating the inside of his mouth with a metallic taste. He passed the other strip to Chais and gestured for him to tie it above the bullet entry point. Elwood tensed as the fabric was bound and knotted into a tourniquet and a fresh wave of pain flared down his arm. He bit down hard on his cloth, but he could feel Chais wavering.

"Ge' i' o'er 'ith!" Elwood yelled through the piece of tunic in his mouth, gagging as the cloth pressed against the back of his throat.

"Shut up!" Chais growled and swung. Elwood felt the wind brush against his shoulder before the sharp faery steel cut through his upper bicep. He gasped as he felt the blade slice through skin and muscle, and the dull thud as it hit bone. A burn ran up through his severed nerves, and adrenaline roared through his veins.

"A'in!" Elwood choked out around the cloth. Although muffled, Chais got the message and tore the blade out of the limb. A horrible squelch, followed by a blade pulled free of flesh, sent a shiver down both their spines. Hot, warm, and sticky blood splashed against his face, dyeing his pale skin scarlet and his hair a dark crimson. The colonel then swung down again, harder this time, and Elwood both felt and heard the click as it sliced through bone; he prayed it cut cleanly through.

A sickening *shrink* echoed in his ear as the bow passed all the way through. The thick scent of coppery blood hit him like a warhorse, then the pain. Elwood clenched his teeth so hard he was sure that his teeth had cracked. He tasted blood as he accidentally bit his cheek. A strangled and muffled scream ripped out of his throat. He barely noticed the quiet thud as his limb fell onto the forest floor. Leaves turned red, and dirt became mud. Elwood felt like his arm was drenched in fire, licking at his bare bones and muscles. His vision flashed red, and black spots danced across the world. Despite the tourniquet, blood pulsed out at an alarming speed from what remained of his arm. Maybe he *did* miscalculate how fast he could heal. His breath sped up along with his heartbeat, and more blood poured out of the wound.

Deep breaths, Relevard reminded. *If you go into shock, you don't stand a chance.* His voice was strained with effort as he focused his power on regulating his host's breathing and warming his drastically cooling body temperature.

A sob tore from his throat, but he took a shaky breath as instructed. He barely noticed that Chais had ruined his coat to create bandages. Son of a bitch, that goddamned Feykin, Elwood thought. He loved that coat. Elwood shook the thoughts of shredded coats out of his head and concentrated on more pressing matters. He had to seal the artery, or he really would bleed out. Chais seemed to realize this as he quickly tossed the bow back into the fire and drenched a strip of his coat in the river. Chais began to clean Elwood's wound to the best of his ability, but Elwood barely noticed his companion's frantic movements. It felt like his arm had just been shoved into a vat of acid, as the cloth was roughly wiped over his exposed bone. Then, Chais picked up the bow that was now starting to glow red; he pressed the hot blade onto Elwood's wound, cauterizing the gaping hole where the arm used to be. The white-hot pain overcame his senses. The smell of burnt flesh sizzled from his arm.

Elwood's vision blackened, and when he opened his eyes, he was lying on his back with Chais hastily binding his stump of an arm.

"Fucking hell …" Elwood muttered. He turned to his side and spat out blood that came from the self-inflicted wound in his mouth. It was hard to think through the pain that still pulsed in his arm and up to his shoulder.

"For your information," Chais said, jerking the last bit of cloth into a tight knot, not even trying to be gentle with the wound, "We're even now."

"For what?" Elwood sighed. He suddenly felt very tired.

"You saved my life, and I just saved yours," Chais explained and slumped down next to him. Exhaustion made him look ten years older.

Elwood wiped some of the blood off his face and blinked, trying in vain to clear the mist that clung to everything. He glanced at the ground and noticed that the pebbles were slick with blood. How much blood did he lose? A halo of light rimmed Chais, giving him an otherworldly glow. If Elwood was seeing halos, then he had lost a lot of blood; his vision was blurred, and he felt extremely woozy.

Chais's messy hair drooped into his eyes. A hint of pride, however, was in his voice. Elwood guessed that Chais Nevermoon was someone who didn't like owing other people favors. He couldn't help but notice that there was uncertainty in his eyes. It was to be expected; the colonel was teaming with the very species he spent his whole life fighting. And, he was being hunted down by his own kingdom and being brought to one he probably had only heard bad things about. Chais stared into space, no doubt wondering what would happen to him now.

"Congratulations," Elwood snorted, coughing as the words grated against his sore throat. Just how long had he screamed? "I did it first though. Makes me better."

"I thought Fey couldn't lie," Chais grumbled as he gave Elwood a mocking glare. Elwood couldn't help but smile a bit. Almost dying had the remarkable bonus of creating fast friends. The tension in both their bodies unwounded slightly, not entirely comfortable in each other's presence, but not hostile either.

"I don't think opinion counts in the whole 'no lies' thing," Elwood murmured. The comfort of darkness pulled at him. "I think I'm going to pass out. Grab my bow, and drag my body somewhere secluded and safe."

"Don't order me around," Chais answered as he searched for the bow that he had thrown aside after sealing Elwood's wound.

Hadn't anyone taught him to be careful with someone else's weapons? Elwood grumbled and also started looking from his position for that familiar, silver gleam.

"Sure. Not used to doing what other people tell you, Colonel?" Elwood teased, gleeful to see the flustered look of the man's face. It made Elwood realize just how young he was—twenty? Nineteen? He was barely even an adult.

"I thought you were going to pass out," his companion said. Chais picked up the weapon, careful not to touch the still-hot left side, and brought it over. It laid within arm's reach of the tiring Fey.

"Getting to that." Elwood's voice was barely a whisper by now. Dulled green eyes scanned over his companion's body, lingering at his ribs. "How's your wound?"

"Healing surprisingly fast," Chais said. His eyes widened, as if surprised that the Fey would ask.

"Probably has something to do with the awakening ..." Elwood mused. His emerald eyes glazed over and started fluttering. Chais had just awakened, had just received his seal ... which meant that he must have just lost the parent that bore it before him.

"I ... I'm sorry for your loss," Elwood sighed quietly and glanced over to catch the colonel nodding soberly. He tried to read his expression, but consciousness was escaping him, and he felt himself slip into oblivion.

CHAPTER

SEVEП

CHAİS LEAПED BACK against the strong bark of the oak and scrubbed heavily at his eyes. In the area of Valport, although the region was still scattered through with forests, the trees grew taller and thicker as they approached the flattened hills. The leaves became darker and trunks wider. This made it an ideal spot for stealth—a first and foremost concern when it came to hiding from Gredian forces long enough to make it across the border.

Chais had chosen a more elevated ridge. The side facing the path was blocked with heavy underbrush. The trodden dirt path, worn over the decades, led toward what Chais assumed was the nearest village in Valport. On the other side was a stream much smaller than the one at the location where they first fell, but it was enough to provide a steady flow of freshwater. It was almost as if the place was made for tired felons on the run.

The day was drawing closer to evening, and though it wasn't finished, Chais felt heavily fatigued. Although the massive canopy of trees obscured the view of the sky, it cast spots of light onto the ground which glowed a darkened yellow-pink from the setting sun. There was barely any wind. The stream's quiet bubbling only added to the slackened atmosphere.

Chais felt a twinge of hunger. Weeks before, he hadn't even set foot through the Gredian gates before Adaric's men showed up, so the long trek from battlefield to capital didn't finish in a long shower and food like it usually would after so many years of fighting. Luckily, he'd found a few blackberry bushes, along the dried out clearing, when he'd first arrived. He popped one into his mouth and tried to ignore the undeniably sour aftertaste. But between being in the dungeon prison, almost being executed, and now running for his life, he hadn't eaten much lately.

Chais suppressed a yawn. If he whispered, chances of detection were little to none, even with the trail a few trees away. He just prayed that Adaric wouldn't think of unleashing the demons right off the bat.

"Aldridge, how far are we from Silvermount?" he whispered, softly enough that he could barely hear himself over the steady breeze. Silvermount—the capital of Gredian, the place he'd called home for the majority of his life. Now, well … now it was quite the opposite.

As much as he preferred to stay in one spot, wanted "criminals" couldn't do so for more than a day. Chais first needed to grasp the distance from where they started so he could come up with an idea of how long it would take freshly dispatched troops to travel.

I'm guessing between fifteen to twenty miles, which means you shouldn't rest for long. I can't exactly lend you all my power yet—I know it's difficult to remain on the move, but more speed would be quite beneficial ...

Aldridge sounded just as exhausted as Chais. The past day had passed in a blur of adrenaline and panic, battles and blood, and realizations of reality. Now, by the light of the setting sun, it took everything not to let sleep take him.

The ex-colonel cast a glance at Elwood's still body. The warrior appeared to be dead, but he knew better. He was thankful for the Fey's rapid healing.

Chais inhaled the scents of the forest—this one particularly reminded him of home. This was all that could remind him of Alryne; the smell of the wind and the trees were the only thing left of his childhood. Chais closed his eyes, but not to rest. Despite the calming nature of the light cast upon the ground, there was now something dry and bitter that had settled inside his stomach.

Traveling to Atrelia went completely against that which he had dedicated a large portion of his life. It was the home to the species he'd fought on the frontlines and the place where many Gredian soldiers lost their lives. Despite knowing Elwood personally—and that knowledge slightly altering his view of Fey—there was a nagging sensation that told him it wasn't over, not after what they'd done to the people he'd loved.

Forgive, it told him. Forgive, but *never forget.*

He cast an empty glance at the Fey on the ground. The makeshift bandages on his stump of an arm were soaked crimson. Elwood's breathing was steadier now, but Chais could still smell the strong scent of metal and blood. If Gredian dispatched those demons ...

"It's fine, Aldridge," Chais exhaled and ran a hand through his hair, in a way buying time for himself. He tried to see through the underbrush to the path, bracing himself for a pack of obsidian monsters to round the corner. How did this work? How could a Fey give powers to a human?

Chais recalled the conversation he and Aldridge had when they first met, deep within the Gredian dungeons. *You mean the humans and the Fey aren't* ... what did that mean?

He sat back. The world seemed to tilt as everything rushed to his head. Aldridge was dead silent.

"Aldridge," the colonel spoke carefully, "are my parents not ..."

Human? Not completely. There was a pause, as if the dead Fey general was letting it sink in. *I'll have you know that your father was a Feykin.* Half-Fey, half-human. Chais tried to recall anything, anything from Alryne that gave it away. From his family. From life before the tragedy. Had their ears been pointed? He had been too young to notice.

However, your mother was not a host, so I wouldn't know for sure. It seemed like there was some type of barrier that prevented anyone from observing her species; I could sense a Fey-like energy from her, but she—

She died before he could find out. Of course. Then, the aftermath ... Aldridge had seen it all through the eyes of his father, the seal host before Chais. He'd seen Chais grow up, had seen the days when he shed the most light, then watched as he burned, watched as Alryne fell, as Chais's father left for the army, all these years—until his host closed his eyes at last.

And now. Why had fate worked out this way?

Tucked away in a pocket within the forest, Chais let his head drop as he studied the ground. He brought his knees to his chest and looked back to the silent road.

Are you … okay? Aldridge asked for the second time that day.

Chais tried to blink the sleep away. The woodland was now cast in a darkened light, the nostalgic type that fell before dusk. "Yes, I—"

Distant footsteps. There. They were rounding the bend.

"I just need some time," Chais whispered. Another day, then. He'd think about his parents another day. He turned to make sure that Elwood was close, then palmed the single dagger he possessed. There was a faint breeze of conversation—male and female voices. To Chais, the words were muffled, as if spoken in water. He shook his head and wished for the prized Fey hearing that every warrior desired.

He could only watch. Aldridge's immediate gift of vision helped sharpen the details of the speakers. They were wearing silver, red, and black soldier gear: four people—two men and two women. Chais guessed they had been on patrol before being called to the chase. He scanned the skies. Good—no demons were present.

The dirt path snaked around a cluster of trees and dangerously close to Chais's hideout. Judging from the soldiers' pace, they weren't taking the job too seriously. None of them had been under his command either.

Chais gripped his weapon tightly and focused on staying still. From here, he could make out their conversation.

A woman was carrying the discussion. "… can't believe he's doing this."

"Watch your words. He's our king now," the soldier closest to her replied coldly.

She lowered her voice. "He sends us out while we're on our way back from the front, just to find a lieutenant colonel? I also heard he's going to use demons by morning light since the summoners are all away right now. If the demons are going into action, why do we have to?"

The man who was now nearest Chais groaned loudly. "I don't understand why the summoner freaks get all this luxury and we're forced to do the dirty work."

Their footsteps were now directly in front of him. Conversation cut off abruptly.

"Do you smell that?" the quieter woman asked. Her companions each took a sniff.

"Smell what? Wood?"

"No, it kind of ... I can't tell, but ... blood?" They made almost direct contact with Chais's eyes.

Chais stiffened, hoping that the shadows covered his hair. That damn, bleeding Elwood.

The Gredian soldiers lingered, not sure if they should keep going to the inn or conduct an investigation. Seconds passed in thick silence. Suddenly, Chais heard sticks cracking as boots recklessly covered ground. A soldier was climbing. Chais cast a glance toward the rest of the group, who had unanimously decided to leave. But this one man, climbing toward him ...

Chais braced himself as he listened to the soldier's steady scaling of the hideout. He heard fingers digging into every available ledge. An encounter would risk Elwood's life.

The man's fingers appeared a few feet to the left, then the top of his head. Chais raised his knife.

"Come on! We're leaving!" The voices sounded from further away. Chais narrowed his eyes. The man suddenly stopped his upward climb, as if he were debating his next move.

"Coming, coming," he finally responded. Chais waited for the *thunk* as the soldier hit the ground, dusted himself off, then ran to catch up.

Chais watched until the group disappeared beyond the trail before he exhaled, loosing a breath he'd unconsciously held. The colonel blinked several times and sheathed his dagger. He ran a hand across his eyes as a reminder to stay alert and awake.

By morning light. If they wanted to make it through alive, then they'd have to leave by morning light, when Adaric would supposedly send the beasts.

He closed his eyes to the familiar stinging sensation of exhaustion. Chais prayed that Elwood would wake up before nightfall so that the Fey could take over his watch.

"That was close."

Chais jolted out of his state and pivoted to face Elwood. Elwood was now alive, awake, and smiling, and he drew himself to a sitting position. Upon closer examination, Chais could tell that his wound was no longer bleeding and actually looked more or less healed. The Fey inside Elwood's head—what was his name?—must have dished out a large amount of power to lessen the pain.

"Don't do that," Chais hissed.

"Do what?"

Chais could tell that Elwood's throat was parched from his extended nap, so he tossed a canteen at the warrior's crossed legs. "I don't know, be a complete moron all the time?"

"Are we exchanging first impressions now? Now that you

mention it, we kind of skipped the whole formal introduction thing back at the capital." Elwood grabbed a blackberry from the pile in front of himself and popped it into his mouth; his features immediately twisted at the sour taste.

"I'm Elwood Zefire," The Fey said, still wincing, "and I think you're a grumpy ass."

"Thank you. I'm Chais Nevermoon," Chais returned, "and I think you're a moron."

"Good. Now that that's all said and done, Gredian's blackberries taste horrible." Elwood grimaced and downed a swig of water.

"They're wild blackberries. They taste tart."

"You're tart," Elwood whined. It didn't quite match up with the image Chais had of a battle-hardened Fey warrior. "Atrelia's are so much better."

"Stop complaining and eat," Chais said. While Elwood was busy forcing the sour fruits down his throat, Chais stood and retreated toward the stream to think.

I'm not sure you know who Elwood's seal is.

"Hmm?" Chais crossed his arms and he tried to sort through the day's newly acquired information. He hadn't expected Aldridge to cut in.

Relevard. Elwood's seal is named Relevard.

Chais might have been dreaming, but Aldridge's voice seemed softer at the mention of the seal's name. He recalled the flashbacks that Aldridge had somehow forced into his mind, the roar of fire, the crackle of electricity. Aldridge Fulmina and Relevard Oxidason—two renowned Fey warriors and demon seals.

"Was he a handful?" Chais managed a small smile despite their situation. He cast a pointed glance at Elwood.

Yes. Definitely, yes.

Chais snorted. He didn't know why he felt so in sync with this stranger inside his head. Maybe it was because Aldridge currently didn't have a physical materialization; he couldn't beat, abuse, or kill. Maybe, Chais thought sadly, maybe that was it.

In fact, Elwood reminds me of him.

As if on cue, the Fey sneezed, looked around, then swallowed another blackberry.

"Then they must be a good pair," Chais murmured. He let forth a massive sigh, which turned quickly into a yawn.

By the time Chais decided to switch watch shifts, Elwood was already standing with his faery steel bow clutched in his left hand. The Fey had already tried numerous times to conjure an arrow reinforced by his wind energy, but all that came to be were a few wisps of a distant breeze.

"Don't overexert yourself," Chais offered, deciding to some-what ease Elwood's nerves. He helped the warrior with water, but although he tried to suppress it, a second yawn still slipped from his lips. Elwood glanced at him, entertained.

"Look who's talking." The Fey grinned and lifted his bow. "I'll take over this shift." Chais was about to reject when all the fatigue and weariness from the past day, including the journeys from battlefield to battlefield, all the way back to the castle, hit him head-on. The static in his brain, exhausted from secrets that hadn't come to light in all of his twenty years, distorted and muddled his train of thought. Sluggishly, he found a spot at the base of a tree.

"You sure you won't pass out and doom us both?" Chais asked.

Elwood shrugged playfully. "No guarantee there."

Chais rolled his eyes and crossed his arms across his chest, slumping against the bark.

"Wake me up when it's my watch," he mumbled before he finally let the darkness take him.

THE KINGDOM WAS IN CHAOS—at least, more chaos than usual. But a Fey had interrupted a public execution and ran off with the prisoner. And not just any prisoner—he was the legendary lieutenant colonel of Gredian and the *murderer* of the king. She growled as her task list ran through her brain. Damn it, she hated not being in control. An emerald green vase, simple but elegant, appeared in her peripheral vision.

Don't break the vase. Don't break the vase. Don't break the va—

"Commander Merran." She turned to see a guard, face obscured by the shadows. Flickering torches were attached to the stone wall, and darkened silhouettes stretched across the hall. The man's head was lowered, and his posture was like any other, but she could tell exactly who he was by his voice.

"Eddas." Lynara cleared her throat. The well inside her simmered as she forced it down. "Report." The commander scanned the hallway. They were in a relatively quiet area of the castle, the route that she preferred to take to the council meetings. Oh gods, council meetings. Just thinking of her destination stirred up the beginnings of a headache.

"Commander, there is still no sign of the escaped prisoner or the Fey warrior. Most of the villages in Gredian have been notified of the situation." Lynara tilted her head back and let out a lofty sigh, checking her temper. The torches created small bursts of warm colors in her vision. Shit.

As Commander, Lynara Merran couldn't be blamed for her particularly hotheaded personality. She was in charge of quite a portion of the Gredian forces stationed at the castle, meaning she had power ... and too much responsibility. The recent events left her in an even fouler mood than usual, which was saying a lot, seeing that her troops were the ones mainly in charge of the search for Chais Nevermoon—the bastard. Boy, was that a familiar name.

"Dispatch more troops to the smaller areas. They wouldn't hide in the larger cities—" Unless Nevermoon wanted her to think that way. Both choices had reasonable logic. Larger areas provided more shelter and it was easy to get away from the guards; however, there were more small villages scattered across Gredian, and it would take a surprisingly long time to check them all. Lynara cursed loudly. She ignored Eddas as she paced the dimly lit hallway. The guard remained silent. For all she knew, he could be judging her, but she didn't give a shit.

"Target the remote regions. Mirstone, Shipton, Valport, all of them. You'd better return with an unconscious colonel and his Fey buddy by the end of next week, you hear me? That is an order," Lynara growled, and not bothering to wait for a reply , stormed down the hallway. Turning the corner, she flung open the oak doors of the council room and took her seat next to the empty chair belonging to the lieutenant colonel. She ignored the gawking stares of the other members already seated. It felt much more vacant, she realized as she analyzed the rest of the unoc-cupied leather seats of the room. Chais Nevermoon really had inflicted some damage. Even after all these years, the boy was still causing trouble wherever he went.

At the head of the long wooden table sat Adaric, his mouth set in a grim line. He still hadn't gotten over the escape of

Nevermoon. But then again, no one in this castle had. Lynara knew what Adaric had done, and how unfair the charges were on Chais's head. But she had no witnesses, and every member of the council leaned toward Amptonshire's favor. She had to think of some strategy, something that didn't involve the slaughter of the new king, and thus, more chaos and political frenzy.

"Major Vagish, report." Adaric was stoic, but there was an undeniable waver to his voice that hadn't been there before. The commander could easily detect the impatience in his tone, in the way he moved, how he tilted his head. An older man, seated near the middle of the table, cleared his throat. Lynara leaned back in her chair and exhaled loudly.

"There has been no progress at the frontlines, Your Majesty." He coughed, a sound closer to a hack of someone dying. Now that Nevermoon was ... absent, this unqualified major was in charge of the abandoned military unit left by Chais. If Vagish did well, then he would be promoted. Lynara Merran almost gagged at the idea—since Chais had shown up at the steps of the castle, young, bloody, and bruised, he'd been on a soaring trajectory that surpassed any of these old fools.

Lynara tried to remember the last time she had looked at Chais without jealousy. Before ... long ago, perhaps, when Alryne was still standing and the boy still had dreams instead of nightmares.

Vagish cleared his throat again. "It appears the Fey and our forces are currently at a standoff. Recently, we sent some men into the Fey kingdom to act as spies. Three out of four were killed or are missing in action."

"I see," Adaric stated blandly. With a man who desired war and power at the head of the table, Lynara saw no way they could progress toward peace. It almost made her want to seize control herself.

"Continue doing what you're doing," Adaric finally addressed the entire council. His golden eyes were hard. "Make sure Gredian is either winning or at a standoff with Atrelian forces."

A man spoke up. "But Your Majesty, if we desire a victory, we must launch a push—"

Adaric held up a gloved hand. "Our first priority, of course, is the war. However, considering the most recent circumstances," he cast a glance at Lynara, "capturing the lieutenant colonel is also a must. For the safety of the Gredian Empire, we cannot let him escape to enemy territory." There was a prolonged pause. "Now, we may continue with accounts on the condition of our nation."

Report after report filled the council room, and Lynara almost fell asleep. There were better things to do in Silvermount. Visiting bakeries and shops, talking with the kinder civilians, going to large events in the town square ... anything was more desirable than this. A part of Lynara wondered why she even considered pursuing this line of work, but it quickly faded away as she remembered. She'd always desired a break away from the dull life of the castle, but she had never really felt the push until Chais decided to join the army, and at such a young age too. Was it just jealousy? Buried dreams? The weight of expectations put upon noblewomen?

It was drawing near the fourth hour when Adaric took control again.

"To wrap up our council meeting, I'd like to hear any news from Commander Merran," the king stated with barely concealed hope. Lynara raised a brow but leaned forward, placing her elbows onto the table.

"There are no sightings of Colonel Nevermoon nor the Fey thus far." Lynara relished the disappointment in Adaric's eyes. "However, I've dispatched troops to the more remote villages since some of the more populated ones have been checked already. By morning light, I will have teams of summoners sent to cover more ground. My current plan is to accompany them with lugaires and reweraa for tracking purposes."

"Why not send a few high summoners? Their demons are of higher quality and can capture the criminals more efficiently," one of the officers cut in.

"They're fighting our war on the frontlines, and we're losing them by the dozen," Lynara said. "Just dispatching so many normal summoners is risky enough since many of them are close to being promoted. Besides, I trust in their abilities. Lugaires and reweraa are lower- to mid-level summons, and if they haven't learned it yet, then Gredian's summoning program needs some improvement."

Lynara pushed her chair back and stood. She was eager to be the first to leave. Some others sensed the end of her briefing and stood as well, but Adaric remained rooted to his chair, thinking of ways to get Chais back; a welcome would definitely not be in store for the colonel. Something painful tore at the edge of her heart. She wanted—she *needed* to do something about that. Maybe Adaric would let her be the interrogator this time.

"As of this moment, I will contact the summoning teams so they are ready to depart early tomorrow. They will each have a region to search, and with their summons, it should go flawlessly. Adaric ..." a few council members flinched at the casual address, "... has worked with me to alert most soldiers on patrol in the villages, and they will be searching until the demons arrive. I guarantee we will come back with Nevermoon in custody."

She met the eyes of every single person at the council. Fulvous flames burned behind her own. "In other words," Lynara strode to the tall oak doors as time ran out, casting her hand briefly over the carved material, "we have a colonel to catch."

CHAPTER
EIGHT

ELWOOD WATCHED as Chais fell into a slumber, the lines of stress and worry that had lined his face melting away like snow in the spring. In rest, the Feykin looked younger. He was unburdened by his duties and most recent adventures. Something about the sleeping form made Elwood feel a strange sense of protectiveness over the boy—no, man. Chais shifted slightly and moved into a more comfortable position, but the way he angled his body so his back was against the tree trunk and the river and open clearing were before him was not lost on Elwood. The young warrior was subconsciously placing himself into a protected position, a skill that was drilled into every soldier's brain the moment they entered the battlefield—never sleep with your back unguarded. It was almost sad seeing someone so young already living and breathing the rules of a warrior. But these days, with a war that felt like it would never end, it was expected. He wondered how long that peaceful expression would last.

Elwood closed his eyes, exhaled, and moved a few paces away. He looked down the small hill where Chais had dragged his unconscious body and saw the faint remains of footprints bending the grass at the sides of the path. The soft murmur of the retreating scouts' conversation was too distant for even him to hear. They were safe for now. There was no better time for him to assess his body's conditions. He would have to challenge the Feykin to a duel later, to assess both his own skills and his companion's.

His body took that moment to send a pulse of pain up his shoulder. Elwood grimaced; he was down an arm, and that was the biggest problem. He would have to use his weapon one-handed, and he needed to learn how to do it quickly. The Fey reached into the trickle his usual river of power had been reduced to. The aching feeling that accompanied the action warned him of his limits; he had overtaxed himself during the escape and amputation. Never one to be held back by supposed limitations, Elwood ignored the protests of his body and focused on the power within him. He focused all his concentration into forming a small funnel of wind to draw his bowstring.

The air warped strangely around the string, but before he could pour enough power into it to sustain it, it wisped away. Elwood cursed under his breath. He would have to wait for his energy to regenerate before he could try that again. Unless ... Holding his bow up again, he reached deeper within himself, tapping into the burning inferno of power that was granted to him through Relevard. He dug deep but found only a sliver left. It was mostly used up from healing his horrendous injury. It was like a raging bonfire had been reduced to dying embers. Just a tiny flicker of flame, bringing little to no warmth. Well, that wasn't very encouraging. He imagined himself carefully palming some of the still-burning coals, slowly soothing them into his own raw systems.

Be careful. Relevard's voice sounded strained as Elwood probed lightly at his depleted reserves, scraping up what he could without causing irreparable damage. It was one of the few advantages of being a host; the power reserves were both shared and separate. That created what was like a backup system for Elwood. It gave Elwood an extreme advantage for he had twice the amount of stamina, thanks to the deceased general.

"I know," he replied, resisting the urge to roll his eyes. This wasn't the first time he'd ever done this. Borrowing another Fey's power to heal was one thing, dissolving it into his own reserves was another. If done incorrectly, it could end with one destroying their own source of power. He knew better than to take too much or rush the transition. It could still strain their already frayed ties. Elwood could feel Relevard watching intently as he started to work, ready to step in should anything go wrong.

"Thanks for the vote of confidence," Elwood mumbled under his breath as he tried his hardest not to break anything in their power supplies. It's like threading a needle, he instructed himself. A peaceful mind was a steady one, after all. Imagine threading a needle with a gun to your head just waiting to unload a steel bullet into your skull after you missed the hole on the first try. A wisp of magic trembled in his mental grasp and sent a harsh burning sensation through his body. His arm twinged in echo to the pain.

I'm just taking precautions. If you are my vessel, and since you have no children, if you were to mess this up and die, who knows how long it would be before I could find a new host? Elwood could feel him flinch when he almost burned a hole through Relevard's power systems.

"Good to know you care," Elwood answered. He focused his absolute attention on his task now that he snagged and had a steady hold on the edge of the power, gathering it all while Relevard nudged any uncooperative tendrils back into place.

Gently tugging away a strand of the fiery energy felt like pulling a thread free from a piece of fabric. Elwood was careful not to snuff out the small flame completely. That would not end in the most desirable way. He took the wisp of what felt like a strand of fire and carefully channeled it through his body. The buffering winds within him slowed to a soft breeze. He could feel the foreign power, brightly golden-red against his own soft greens and yellows, like pollen scattering in the wind. He waited until it dissolved into pure energy before his breathing returned to a steady pace. The heat left a strange tingle where it passed, warm and comforting. It trailed from his heart to his stomach and back to the area where his powers were stored. Slowly, the heat faded and a warm breeze muttered as the last of the foreign power merged into his reserves. With just that little more in his reserves, he was able to pull it out and manipulate it into the wind energy he needed.

Elwood drew the bowstring. It was considerably easier now that he had the energy to do it, although he could still feel the deep, aching soreness from his raw reserves. He had maybe three tries before it was depleted again. Now came the hard part. The arrows he created required an immense amount of concentration:

the size, spin, and speed of the wind funnel needed to be just right; these arrows could rip a man's head off his body or simply ruffle his hair. By using a bow to shoot the magical projectile, he was able to focus his power wholly on the arrow without worrying about where it was going. Wind was not a stable element; it had a tendency to do whatever it wanted to, hurting everyone in its vicinity. The bow helped focus the tornado of power that roared within him. It directed the wind energy to a single target. However, now, if he wanted to continue using his preferred weapon of combat, he would need to form another cyclone of wind to draw the bowstring as well as aim it.

The air before him warped as he attempted to split his concentration to create the two items. A wisp of wind appeared where the arrow should've been. The moment it began to strengthen, however, the funnel holding the string sputtered out, and the string and arrow released with it. Elwood groaned as it slammed into a tree, not compressed enough to drill into it, not strong enough to do more than shake a few leaves out of the tree.

He tried again and was able to hold the string stable enough but ended up giving himself a demon headache that had pulsed with pain along with his arm when he started to speed up the counterclockwise spin of his arrow. Elwood was forced to release the premature projectile and winced as the tree before him splintered and cracked from the strength. It looked like someone hit the trunk with a carriage at full speed—not quite what he was aiming for.

He split his attention as evenly as he could with the last bit of foreign power. The string quivered with the unsteady wind that held it, barely strong enough to pull it back. A sad excuse for an arrow shimmered and faded, trying its hardest to hold its form. If he couldn't even do it in peace, there would be no mercy in battle.

Elwood yelled and let the last of his control slip. Both winds fell apart, sending a light breeze ruffling his hair in a sympathetic breath before disappearing completely.

He hated it. Hated this. Hated how foreign the weapon he had used for more than a century felt in his hands. Hated how difficult it was to harness the winds, his birthright. Elwood yelled again and slammed out his power in a ripple with himself as the epicenter. The grass around him in a two-foot diameter was ripped out of the ground, and he fell to his knees. Bone-deep exhaustion pulsed through him, his arm roared in agony and every part of him felt drained. He would have passed out if Chais hadn't been there to judge him if he did.

You need to calm down, Relevard murmured, a rare moment of gentleness in his usually commanding tone.

"Why?" Elwood growled back, even though he knew full well that it would help him concentrate better if he could rein his emotions back into control. He crawled under the shade of the nearest tree and lay on his back. Feeling the sharp grass poke through his shredded clothes, he closed his eyes. He simply didn't want to listen to reason right now; on the other hand, destroying the forest sounded *very* appealing.

Destroying the forest would not help you master your powers better, the dead general scolded, as if reading his mind—something that Elwood couldn't do, by the way. An insanely stupid and nonsensical power to lack, as they shared the same body! How was the mental communication a one-way thing? "Dad never had to speak out loud," Elwood thought glumly.

"It might make me feel better," Elwood sighed. He knew he sounded like a whining, ungrateful brat. He also didn't have the power to do so now, not after that childish outburst. Relevard had fallen silent, either tired of his complaints or just deciding to shut up. Elwood stared down at his hands and thought about just what kind of power ran through his veins.

Elwood's power was considered one of the strongest; too bad that power did nothing to save the dwindling family. Now there was no one, and he was left with a power he didn't understand and a bow he could no longer use. Thumbing the silvery material that made the bow, he couldn't help but feel guilty for the fact it was in his possession in the first place. The memory drained all anger that still lingered. Elwood stared up into the canopy of leaves and watched the spotlight as the sun streamed through. If he replaced the sound of the nearby brook with the deafening roar of a waterfall, he could almost convince himself that he was home. But … not really. The smell of blood ruined the illusion. Elwood shakily stood up and reached to brush his bangs back from his face. Instead, he winced as no hand came up. The stump at his shoulder only twitched.

If he didn't look at it, Elwood could have sworn his arm was still there, that his brain could still send a signal down his arm to move his fingers. Phantom limb. His brain hadn't caught up with the idea that his body now had one appendage less than it was used to. It would take some time to get rid of the feeling, and even then, it wouldn't be gone forever.

Dark red had seeped through the makeshift bandages. The wound must have split open again. That explained the heavy scent of blood, but there was something under the thick, coppery scent. If he was lucky, shiny and burnt scar tissue should grow over completely by the end of the month. And hopefully, Elwood would be home by then, with a Feykin in tow and a six hundred-year-old king to annoy. An irritation on his skin distracted him. It itched badly, especially around his right ear. Elwood reached up and felt his dried blood coating his face and hair. That was going to be a nightmare to wash out, but so much blood would make it far too easy for enemy trackers to find them.

Elwood stumbled rather sluggishly down the hill and sat by the stream. He dunked his face into the water and scrubbed his left hand roughly over his face. The cold water felt heavenly against his skin. Elwood pulled his face out of the water, brushing his dripping bangs back before scooping up a small handful to rinse out his mouth. He felt much better once his mouth no longer tasted like copper and his thirst was quenched.

Elwood stared into the calmer part of the water. He couldn't help but notice how bad he looked. His hair hung limply and soaked around his shoulders, and strands escaped from the tie that held it back. His normally shining green eyes were dull like emeralds that had lost their luster. He'd think being unconscious for most of the day would count as rest, but apparently, it didn't. In fact, he felt even more exhausted than before he had first fallen asleep.

But it was the flush on his cheeks that concerned Elwood. He felt far too warm. Infection. He could only hope that Relevard could stall the worst of it until they got the proper medication. A high fever now would be disastrous. Elwood looked beyond his face to the rest of the mess peering back at him from the still water. His tunic was torn and the right side was dyed a deep brownish-red by blood. The dried liquid caused the fabric to stick to his side, and his makeshift bandages were wet from leaking fluids. Flaking blood clung to his right ear and hair. They would need new cloth and bandages … and perhaps a hat.

With his arm bare and tunic ripped, one could just barely

make out a pale silver symbol tattooed on his left bicep. Curled leaves formed its base and wisps of petals twisted up from it, making the strange symbol look like a tulip: the seal of Atrelia, a symbol of his loyalty.

Only his duty as a demon key came before his duty to his kingdom, and sometimes, not even that. It seemed to shimmer and catch the sunlight, glowing in the dimming afternoon light. A physical proof that sealed his contract with the king, and his promise to be his daughter's personal knight. Elwood remembered when he received the brand. It wasn't long before the last of his family died, and a new voice appeared in his head: a new and very annoying voice from back when children didn't fight in wars.

Elwood closed his eyes and exhaled slowly. He tried to rid his mind of the cobwebs that tangled it, making clear thought impossible. He felt so *tired*.

But something felt wrong. He glanced behind him and realized that he couldn't see Chais. Elwood dragged his feet up the hill, trying his best not to leave tracks by stepping where the talkative scouts had left imprints. When did this hill get so high? Elwood panted as his vision swam. His right arm screamed as he kept forgetting not to use it to find purchase. And so steep? It felt like he was just one big bruise; every movement burned with pain and regret.

"I've made a horrible mistake," Elwood muttered to himself as he hauled himself onto the top of the hill. He crawled to the tree the Feykin was snoozing by. "Should have just stayed home. But no. Stupid. Seal. Business." He cursed; Relevard remained silent, but Elwood could swear he heard laughter.

Elwood immediately realized what was wrong as he approached Chais. The colonel's previously serene face was pinched and slick with sweat. Chais's eyes darted frantically beneath his eyelids, and his breathing became shallow and irregular. A nightmare—probably. Elwood knew the signs from soldiers he had shared sleeping space with, their dreams plagued with the horrors they'd witnessed. He also knew better than to wake the Feykin up, not with Chais's hand so close to his dagger. Waking him now could be dangerous. Instead, Elwood looked away. He didn't wish to intrude.

Chais's dreams were his own, and Elwood felt he had no right to watch him in this moment of weakness. He kept an ear on his movement, though, in case he tossed and turned his way too close to the road, or if he went for his blade, or maybe impaled himself with a branch or something. Elwood was charged with the task of keeping Nevermoon alive, after all.

As the cold breeze stirred across the forest floor, Elwood struggled to stay awake. He tried to ignore the nagging feeling of homesickness. It was just too quiet. There was nothing for him to do but drown in his thoughts. He missed the magical forest of Atrelia, the lazy evenings in the sun, the horrifying and hideous creatures that would leap out at you from the waters and shadows. He even missed the familiarity of the war zone; at least things were constant there. Elwood chuckled lightly to himself. This generation was really a strange one, that its youth would long for bloodshed.

CHAPTER
NİNE

CHAİS JERKED AWAKE.

He scanned the clearing as he caught his breath, a cloud of numbness still pulling at the edges of his brain. A slightly hunched figure was sitting on a rock, and dirtied bandages were wrapped around the husk of something that had once been there. The moonlight gently brushed the edges of his form. Somewhere near him, the brook bubbled almost silently.

Chais cursed softly and leaned back. He closed his still-tired eyes. At least Zefire didn't kill him in his sleep, although Chais knew he wouldn't go down that easily.

Dream?

"Call it a nightmare. They're closer than you think."

Well, at least you got to rest.

Chais chuckled lightly and shook his head. Elwood seemed like he was in some sort of stupor; he focused only on the trees. He seemed so different now. It was as if the bright and lighthearted persona had never existed. The Fey's hair was much longer than Chais had realized, now that he could get a closer look. Of course, being immortal probably led to a decrease in motivation for such trivial aspects of life … hair maintenance included.

"If reliving an event in my gods-damned past could be called rest, I suppose you're right," Chais whispered at last. He tried not to break through Elwood's musing. Sometimes thinking could hurt more than battle wounds, however. Maybe the reason Elwood always wanted someone to talk to was because silence could be hell.

Chais knew how that felt.

Chais brushed off his blood-stained pants and quietly approached. Although he made sure his steps were light, there was still a purposeful crunching of dirt beneath his boots. Before he reached a distance that the sharpest of human ears could hear, Elwood's head tilted slightly toward the colonel. His face was obscured partially by the shadows. Chais scanned the perimeter briefly. Habitually.

"Hey, Stumpy," Chais said. He was still adjusting to the darkness of midnight. Zefire flashed him a lopsided grin that didn't seem like it had been forced at all. He must've had years of practice.

"Hey, Grumpy," the Fey replied, but did not make any move to stand. Elwood still clutched the bow, its limbs stretching toward the sky and the ground, two complete opposites. It was a well-crafted bow, better than anything in the human realm. It reminded Chais of the two species' conflict. The war had been going on for much longer than Chais's lifetime. He didn't remember a single day without it. It was a shame, really, that the concept of peace could be so hard to understand.

Chais took a seat next to Elwood. The slightly damp grass tickled the skin that peeked out from beneath his ripped clothing. In front of them, the stony brook gurgled along, a never-ending rhythm. Other than that, and the chirping of crickets, the forest was silent.

"What's on your mind?" Chais asked softly, noticing his reflection in the waters. It was a familiar sight: dirtied and matted hair littered through with flakes of blood. Scars, both new and faded, crisscrossed his skin, although the fresher ones were almost completely healed over. His clothes were in a similar state, shredded and stiff where blood had dried. In the faint moonlight, the two golden rings on his left ear shone dimly.

Elwood shifted. "Stuff. You don't need to know." Although Chais barely knew the Fey, had even battled his kin, the shift in personality truly worried him.

"I could always …" What? Listen? Chais trailed off. Why? When he barely knew Elwood? Why was he opening up so easily to someone who he had considered an enemy for his entire life?

Elwood seemed to have read his mind. He searched the ground as if he could find an answer there. Chais glanced at the Fey's expression—he'd seen it before, even just now when he had looked into the stream at his own reflection. Chais sighed.

"Do you ever … miss it? Miss them. Even if you're not gone for long?"

Elwood looked up suddenly, surprised. A few heartbeats passed. The Fey slowly narrowed his eyes suspiciously at Chais.

Chais narrowed his eyes right back. "What?" He was beginning to regret having said anything.

"I want," Elwood's brightness was returning to him now, but Chais wondered at what cost, "to know more about you."

Frank, as usual. What a weirdo.

"We can trade," Chais heard himself offer. He secretly hoped to uncover whatever confidential matters this immortal had compiled over all these years. And maybe Elwood knew something about ... him and what kind of blood ran through his veins.

"Well ..." Zefire sat back, debating whether or not it was a reasonable deal. "Fine. What do you want to know?"

"Tell me about Feykin."

"Well ... I don't know much, but Fey and human are two separate species that can interbreed." The faintest smile pulled at Elwood's mouth. "Feykin are sort of like ... the mules of humanoids. The main difference between humans and Fey is the organ that allows us to do stuff like this." He waved his hand and a soft breeze rustled through the undergrowth. "Depending on whether a Feykin's magic organ is dormant or not, they can appear as either human or Fey. Questions?"

"Yes—" As the seconds ticked by, Chais noticed Elwood's progression in body language. Elwood's eyelids were only half-open, he was resting his chin on the palm of his hand, and even his pointed ears seemed to droop. Chais stood and took a step away from the brooding, partially awake man. "Never mind," he said. "Goodnight, sleep tight." Maybe he could get some information out of the warrior some other time. On one hand, a sleepy talker was an honest one. But, on the other, even immortal warriors who could control the wind needed their rest. Chais didn't want to force Elwood awake just for his own selfish reasons.

"Wait ..." Elwood interjected weakly and mustered his remaining strength to crawl toward the nearest tree. The moonlight flickered through the leaves, shaken by a phantom wind. Ominous shadows danced across the clearing. The silence suddenly seemed almost suffocating.

Chais coughed. "What is it now?"

Elwood found a relatively comfortable spot, wiggled around a bit, then settled down. Chais wouldn't be surprised if the Fey passed out again.

"It's a trade, remember? Tell me a story."

Chais frowned. He blamed the odd request on Elwood's lack of sleep—it seemed that was what made him so delusional. Upon second glance, however, the Fey appeared stone serious. Not even a hint of a foolish grin was present on his features. Chais paused, suspended between the decision of walking away or complying.

He exhaled irritably but sat down anyway—comply it was, then.

"Why are you like this, anyway?" Chais interrupted his own train of thought. "Isn't a warrior like you supposed to act his age?"

"You try living for hundreds of years and see where it takes you. Smile, have a little fun! Life's too long to brood and act like you don't have any emotions," Elwood said. "Now please, continue with the story."

"If it will make you shut up, sure." The ex-colonel found himself searching his mind for fairy tales. Gods, this was so childish.

"Once upon a time, there was a Fey princess who had extremely powerful—"

"I've heard of that one before. Remember, immortal?" Elwood rudely interrupted. Chais rolled his eyes.

"Fine then. Once there was a summoner who—"

"That one too. Try again." The Fey warrior yawned but didn't seem any closer to falling asleep than before. Was there a story that the immortal had never heard before? Chais desperately tried to recall all the tales he'd heard.

"There was a—"

"Nope."

Chais growled. Staying with this Fey certainly wasn't helping his temper. And he thought he'd mastered concealing his emotions.

"Just make one up," Elwood offered and shifted slightly against the tree. Chais understood that Elwood had wanted him to create a tale all along.

"Let's see ... once upon a—"

"Don't use that starter. It's boring." There was a tiny smile on Elwood's smug face now.

"Isn't the whole damn point to get you to sleep?"

"Just don't use that starter."

"Legend says—"

"Not that one either."

"Would you just shut up and let me tell my story?" Chais felt the familiar tick in his brow as the Fey got to him. Again. There was a moment of silence as the ex-colonel pointedly made sure the Fey didn't offer any snarky remarks. Elwood didn't, and instead obediently slumped against the bark. Satisfied, Chais turned to the brook.

"Once upon a time, there was a family of ..." Chais paused, "... lions." Even out of the corner of his eye, Chais could sense the Fey's sarcasm and protest about to spill out. The glare that Chais shot him shut Elwood's mouth, and he nodded at Chais to continue. It was darker now. The silhouettes of spindly trees surrounded them with illusive safety. Shadows danced on the ground, fading away where the bright moonlight beamed. Without demons to plague the sky, dark blue and black swirled together around the cloudy moon, adding a hint of orange light to the horizon.

"The adults in the pride were stronger than any other predator in the territory, so none dared attack. In other words, they lived in paradise: plentiful food and fresh water ... however, they were surrounded by enemy prides. Even with so much power, the family knew that they could not survive if all the rival lions decided to strike."

Chais cast a glance at Elwood. The Fey was bracing his head on his one good arm, and his eyes danced like lights shifting across the forest floor.

"Then there was a territorial dispute, another pride invaded, and in the midst of it all, the mother was killed. The father and son fled." Chais could imagine the thick scent of corpses and ash clogging the air. Fire, blazing hotter than the sun. Burning. Buildings collapsing. Yellowed blades of grass crushed under bloodied boots.

At this point, he wasn't even pausing to see where the story was heading. He just let the first words he could think of fall out of his mouth.

"The fathers don't stick with the cubs, you know," Elwood helpfully piped in. His tired eyes were glazed over with a bit of curiosity.

"Shut up. It's just a story." Chais cleared his throat, irritated, but at the same time relieved for the break. Elwood opened his mouth to reply, but it quickly turned into a yawn.

"Anyway ... after the father-son pair fled the scene, they faced starvation since there wasn't enough food in the wastelands." Chais stopped to think, "Now that the previous momentum had been cut off, it would be better if he just ended it here."

"Desperate to survive, the father ate the son ... and no one knows what became of him." Realizing that his voice caught on the last sentence, Chais stood and turned away from Elwood so that his expression was hidden in the shadows. He ran a hand through his hair, filthy against his fingertips. "The end."

Elwood blinked. "Well, that escalated quickly." A pause. "Tell me more."

Chais looked over his shoulder at the Fey. "No. You look horrible. Be quiet and sleep." Dull light seeped into the clearing, barely noticeable, even though it hadn't been long since Chais had woken up. There was much to do, now that a new day had begun. However, even a Fey needed rest. Having an overly fatigued travel companion, immortal or not, wouldn't be good for progress. Elwood didn't complain as he allowed himself to sink into a light slumber. He really did look like he was passing out every time he slept, Chais noted with a hint of amusement.

Chais lingered for a few moments before he palmed his dagger and began to check the camp's perimeter. The early morning chill found a place in his bones and settled in. A shiver ran down his spine.

Valport's nearest village was visible over the treetops, if a person found a high enough rock to stand on: a silhouette residing on the hill. Its land covered half of the massive forest, and the rest was rolling rises, dried out from excessive farming in the past. Because it did not possess any precious metals or goods, the living conditions were less than ideal, but then again ... there weren't many affordable provinces with a good environment in Gredian. Not anymore, not after war destroyed the surface and blood had stained the ground for generations.

Chais looked around and tried to picture the land as green as it was over thirteen years ago when Valport was just half a day's trip away from Alryne. He willed the trees to grow, and for the people to live again, and for the sky to return to a dazzling blue, and for the birds to come back. Where did the stars go? Ever since Alryne fell and the Fey forces moved toward Valport, where had the stars gone?

The world hasn't changed, even after all this time.

Aldridge's voice was sad, nostalgic. It pulled at Chais's heart. How much longer would it be until the world learned to love?

Chais shook his head. Now wasn't the time. It had been too long since he had last trained; he could feel the strain in his muscles and the exhaustion in his breath. If he didn't want a tragedy like that to happen again, he'd have to prepare ... so that if there was a next time, he would be able to protect those he loved instead of watching them die.

The colonel aimed for a barely noticeable blemish in the bark of a tree and chucked his blade. It missed by a few centimeters. It seemed the dungeons hadn't been enough to refine his skills further, not with the slippery walls and the lack of weapons.

So? Are you going to answer your own question?

Chais walked over to the tree, confused. "What do you mean?" He grabbed the dagger and tried again.

Do you ever miss them? Even if you're not gone for long?

Chais paused. He thought first, heartbreakingly, of Alryne, but then understood what the demon key meant. Gredian—all those memories, people, places. The castle that took him in when he couldn't find anywhere else to stay. The dead king and the jealous sister—He opened his mouth to assent but found that he was unable to reply.

CHAPTER

TEN

ELWOOD STIRRED AS THE HAZINESS started to fade; the warm heat of the sun irritated his skin. He groaned and shifted into a more comfortable position. The spiked grass that tickled his palm and the rough bark behind him gave him some insight into his surroundings. Elwood frowned lightly. Where was he? He didn't remember falling asleep. The wood didn't smell quite like the Emera Forest, and the sound of the Orphic Falls was … not there. He could hear a bubbling brook nearby but it was too shallow to be the Mannagrass River. Elwood eased open his eyes. The world momentarily spun in a kaleidoscope of colors, painfully bright. A gaping yawn brought a crack to his jaw as he took in the landscape. Oh. Right. He was currently resting somewhere in the Gredian Empire, nowhere near his usual napping spot.

I was wondering how long it would take you to get your bearings, Relevard mocked. Apparently, a few hours without tormenting his host was too much.

"Give me a break." Elwood gave an exasperated sigh. "I was tired, half unconscious, and probably feverish for most of yesterday. What did you expect?"

Speaking of the fever, I've dealt with the infection to the best of my abilities, but I am no miracle worker. You still need to get proper antibiotics. All the work I've done to keep your fever low won't last. An edge of exhaustion still lingered in his tone, as if he hadn't paused to rest since Elwood's amputation.

"Since you're awake, do you mind getting off your ass so we can move?" A new and just as infuriating voice interrupted his conversation. Elwood looked up and was met with the sight of a very unimpressed Chais. What did he do this time? What did he do to deserve such a wakeup call? Elwood tilted his head. Despite the ex-colonel's disdainful look, he seemed more relaxed. It could be the sleep, but ... Elwood had a feeling it had something to do with the conversation they had before he had passed out, a conversation that regrettably would take a little digging to unearth. Memories made while in a half-awake state of mind were like that.

"I don't know," Elwood replied slyly. "I'm feeling a little woozy, why don't you carry me?" He spread his arms, as if waiting for a hug. The slight tick in the Feykin's temple was a satisfying reward.

"Then you can crawl after me," Chais answered with an even tone. Elwood expected as much. People couldn't survive for so long during a war and not be able to keep their temper. After all, many commanding officers tended to have an uncanny ability to get on some nerves. 'Must be a requirement,' Elwood mused. Chais had certainly mastered it.

Elwood grunted and forced himself onto his feet, stretching until he felt his spine pop and his arm twinge with pain. He muffled a yawn and blinked up at the sky. It was brilliantly blue, with a rolling sheet of clouds approaching from the west. The evening would undoubtedly bring a spring storm. But, for now, the sun was just approaching its apex. Its blinding light, unhindered by clouds or mist, watched over the forests and towns below. While the heat from the sun would be annoying, at least a clear sky meant they could see the flying demons coming from miles away.

"Where are we going?" Elwood asked.

"To the nearest village, Valport," Chais replied. He was heading back the way they came. "That village where we were going to get a doctor before you decided to chop your arm off." Chais gave him a glare that flickered toward the missing arm. Guilt burned in the gaze. Why he appeared so distraught was beyond Elwood; after all, if the colonel had not done the task, Elwood would be dead by now. But then, from what he had seen, the Feykin seemed like the type of person who could blame himself for everything.

"Hey, but a one-armed warrior is cool as hell," Elwood answered in an attempt to distract Chais. If the rest of this trip is going to be this way, we are going to have some very interesting and distracting conversations, Elwood thought to himself. He was unsure if that was a good thing or a bad thing. He needed the distraction too.

Hell isn't supposed to be cool, Relevard kindly pointed out.

Chais lightened up slightly before bullying Elwood as well. Why couldn't Chais just be nice for once? Although Elwood did feel rather accomplished in succeeding at pulling the Feykin out of his brooding.

"Keep telling yourself that, Stumpy," Chais snorted. "Whatever makes you feel better."

"So, is that like my official nickname? Stumpy?" Elwood asked once the silence became uncomfortable and unbearable. He reached up to snag a leaf from a low-hanging branch and ran his fingers over the pale veins.

"Absolutely." The Feykin nodded gravely as if considering the idea. His azure eyes sparkled with light humor. "They probably have wanted posters on us by now. I can see it." He waved his hands grandly before him.

Elwood 'Stumpy' Zefire, Relevard decided to helpfully give his input. Wasn't the bastard supposed to be resting?

"Elwood 'Stumpy' Zefire," Chais said at the same time, as if he had heard Relevard's comment.

Bastards. Both of them. Elwood tore the leaf in half and tossed it into the river, watching as it lazily tumbled downstream.

"Both of you, shut up," he growled without any real threat or anger.

Trudging through the undergrowth, Elwood couldn't help but feel like something was not right. He paused for a moment and realized what it was.

"What's wrong?" Chais asked, feeling the Fey warrior's uneasiness. He slowed his pace, and his hand drifted toward his weapon. The green-eyed Fey felt his own hand inch to his bow.

"It's too quiet," Elwood whispered. Even the leaves didn't seem to rustle, as if the whole forest was holding its breath.

An eerie howl echoed in the distance, one that sounded far too familiar.

"Lugaires." The colonel visibly paled. He had seen the power of the demon dogs before. Their sense of smell was five times more powerful than that of a mortal mutt.

"Why would there be summoners so close to the capital?" Elwood hissed. He reached out with his right arm to grab Chais before remembering that he no longer had it. "I thought all summoners were at the war front!"

Depending on how many there were, there was a chance they could take them out. But with the Feykin armed with nothing but a dagger, and himself still in such a sorry state, the odds were hardly in their favor.

"They should be! They're too rare to just keep around at the capital. Only trainees live there, and none are supposed to graduate until next month!" Chais sounded just as distraught as Elwood.

"We have to find a way to get rid of our scent!" Elwood was just babbling now. He took a deep breath and forced himself to calm down in order to think clearly.

"No kidding, genius," the Feykin growled and grabbed Elwood's wrist before he could even blink. "The river should lead us to a small village downstream. It should keep them busy for a while."

"Wait!" Elwood cried as Chais dove in, dragging him with him. He gulped a large lungful of air a moment before his head was completely submerged into the biting cold water. The calm current suddenly felt a lot more violent. The current ripped and tore at him; his clothes whipped around him. He peered through the murky currents. The howls of dogs echoed across the forest, the sound muffled by the rapid waters. Elwood could see the warped shadows of the onyx hounds above. They were followed by eager outlines of mortals. Chais pulled them down deeper, still submerged and gripping the thick root of a tree, watching and waiting. The soldiers stopped directly above where they were. If Elwood reached out of the water, he could grab their boots.

The soldiers in question were yelling orders at each other, and Elwood could feel his heart rate increase. The hounds excitedly yelped and howled. Something had caught their attention. Elwood glanced at his abused, numb limb and saw the swirls of scarlet drifting downstream. The lugaires were following the scent. They bounded downstream and ripped through the undergrowth. A few doubled back to their hiding spot, spinning around and confused, before reluctantly following their masters and brethren back downstream. If they weren't underwater, Elwood would have sighed in relief. He felt a shred of respect for Chais. The hounds, their summoners, and the soldiers continued down the river, trailing a false scent.

Now that the danger had passed, his body's need for oxygen was making its demands known. A stream of bubbles escaped from his mouth. His lungs were burning like iron bars pressed against his ribs. Elwood forced himself out of Chais's grip and kicked toward the surface. He surfaced in a loud splash and floundered, grateful for the miracle of air. Elwood sagged on the solid ground, hacking.

He heard a splash and saw Nevermoon emerge from the river to sit next to him. Everything sucked. His vision was swimming, his brain felt like it was trying to break its way through his skull, his lungs still felt drowned, and his missing arm would have hurt less if he had submerged it in boiling water. Not only that, but the risk of further infection had just increased. He pushed himself up on his elbow and glared at the Feykin.

I am going to murder him in his sleep, Elwood thought before slumping back down, ignoring the mud and grass pressed against his cheek. His feet were still in the water, but he did nothing to move them out.

"You are absolutely *fucking* insane," Elwood gasped once he had managed to get enough air into his oxygen-deprived lungs.

"It worked, didn't it?" Chais sounded somewhat relieved that his plan had worked. It was something Elwood wasn't very comfortable with.

He isn't even winded, Relevard noted. Ask him. Elwood groaned softly and sat up, wringing bucketfuls of water out of his soaked ponytail. Chais was dumping out his boots.

"How are you not out of breath?" Elwood asked, deciding to humor Relevard. He was a bit curious himself. Chais twisted around and looked at him, midway through putting his boot back on. Elwood wrestled off his own boots.

"I'm not?" The ex-colonel sounded genuinely surprised. He paused for a moment in his shirt-wringing to check his breathing. Strange.

"Well, not important," Elwood decided. He shoved his feet back into his shoes and stood up. "We'd better go before they come back." He retied his hair, flicking droplets of water off his fingertips.

"We need to rebind that arm," Chais pointed out. The stump was currently oozing blood. If they moved, it would be leading a trail right to them. Elwood frowned and looked down at his tunic, trying to find a piece that could be used. A light sigh interrupted his search, and he glanced up. Chais held out a strip of his dirtied and still damp uniform, maybe the remains of a jacket. Elwood nodded a thanks and examined the fabric. It was coarse but comfortable, lightweight—training gear perhaps—well made too. Shame it was completely ruined—served the mortal right, destroying his coat. Elwood ripped off the bandages and tried not to be too bothered by the healing flesh. It didn't look infected, and he didn't feel like he had even a low fever, but he didn't know a lot about medicine—better to just trust Relevard on this. He tightly bound the wound. Hopefully, they could find proper bandages soon. Wet fabric couldn't be good for an open wound. He gestured for Chais to lead the way; standing around would get them nowhere.

Elwood walked behind the man. The hellhounds tracked by scent, but humans could track by sight. They could afford to provide neither. Elwood picked up a snapped twig and tossed it into the rushing waters. Why did a simple rescue mission have to end up so complicated?

Soon, Elwood saw the first few clay-brick structures of the village. They were small and rundown. Most had wooden doors and clothing hung to dry in the back. Some had strips of meat hanging out to dry, easy for stealing. Elwood noticed the uneasy expression on Chais's face. It was to be expected; this was a man who fought on the battlefield for years to protect these people. Now, here he was with the very enemy that he used to fight, to steal from the people he used to protect. Fate loved messing with people, whether they deserved it or not.

"Let's just get this over with," he heard Chais mutter to himself. Cautious not to be seen, they snuck behind the nearest house with clothing out. Chais reached out and grabbed a worn tunic that looked about his size, then tossed another one at Elwood. Elwood blanched at the shirt's color—a nasty yellow, washed out and faded.

The sound of footsteps distracted him. Elwood spun around and saw a young man, maybe around Chais's age—perhaps twenty? The man donned a gray tunic and pants. A hunting knife was strapped to his deer leather belt. The lingering smell of pine and blood told of a recent hunt.

"Who? What?" the man stuttered. His gray eyes flickered from Elwood to Chais and then back. The man noticed the blood splattered across their clothing, and then the slender, pointed ears. Fucking dammit.

"You're a real unlucky fellow, aren't you," Elwood smiled and threw his hand out, still holding the tunic. The fabric rustled before a large blast of air knocked the poor mortal off his feet. His body slammed into the clay wall of the building, and he slumped over, barely conscious. Elwood turned toward Chais, who was looking at the man guiltily, and shoved him forward.

"Move. Grab that meat while you're at it." Chais spared a second to glare at Elwood but leaped up and snagged a string of what looked like rabbit meat. Elwood darted inside. It was a modest-looking house—despite the town being small, they were clearly well-off. A carved wooden table sat next to a kitchen and fireplace. A wall separated the area from what he assumed were the bedrooms. No one was in the house, thankfully. Elwood tore open cabinets before finding a half drunken bottle of liquor; it wasn't antibiotics, but it would have to do.

Before he left, he snagged a bruised apple from the cutting board and shoved it into his mouth. The lady of the house must have left it there while she went to the market to gather the rest of the ingredients for her baking project. Elwood flung open the door to see Chais pacing, a string of dried rabbit in hand. The colonel raised an eyebrow at the apple but did not comment. He left once they made eye contact, not even looking back to make sure Elwood was following. The Fey warrior jogged after him but stopped once more at the back entrance. He grabbed another tunic for bandages, in case they couldn't find real ones.

Elwood juggled his many items and tried his best not to drop the liquor bottle as he wrapped the extra tunic around his neck like a scarf.

The duo raced through the town and slipped behind a small tavern. Elwood tore off his dark gray tunic, wincing as the dried blood pulled at his skin. He shrugged on the yellow shirt and rewrapped his makeshift scarf. Dark stains still splashed across his pants, but hopefully, no one would notice. He tore the tie out of the tangled mess that was his hair and allowed his dirty black locks to tumble down his back. He arranged it so that the strands hid his Fey heritage. He looked like a homeless man who lost a wrestling match with the mud. Chais had also changed, his hair dimmed slightly by the mud and blood but still a distinct metallic gray. Elwood knelt down and grabbed a handful of muddy sludge, then reached up and smeared it onto the startled Feykin.

"Now we match," Elwood chuckled to himself. They would need to find hair dye later.

"What the hell?" The ex-colonel jumped. He shook his head like a mutt, flinging mud everywhere.

"Hair color," Elwood deadpanned with his mouth still half full of apple. Before Chais could reply, a shout for help rang across the village. Someone must have found the hunter; leaving without attracting attention was *apparently* too difficult for two well-trained warriors. Hopefully, they could blend into the village before law enforcement—or worse, the king's men—arrived. The forest was probably already swarming with them, spreading out to every village like a plague. In any event, getting out was going to be a lot of trouble; at least if they went by common roads they could pass as traders. If caught in the woods, there would be a lot more explaining needed.

Elwood turned to tell Chais of the plan but instead saw a small group of children staring at them in shock. The shouts to find the intruders had masked their footsteps.

"Ah. Hell," Chais groaned. He scanned the crowd of small humans, frozen by their large, curious eyes.

That about sums it up, Relevard sighed. One of the pigtail-wearing girls screamed for help.

"I recommend we stop standing here," Elwood pointed out and was helpfully met with the Feykin's exasperated moan.

CHAPTER

ELEVEN

THE TRESPASSERS ZIGZAGGED TOWARD the general direction of the common roads, careful not to knock over any obstacles in order to hide their getaway route. Shouts drew closer, bringing with them more people—whether or not those people belonged to the village or the capital still remained a mystery. Chais kept his eye on the road and searched for anything or anywhere that could give them some chance of escape.

"We have to hide! There's no way we can outrun them in our current state!" Elwood hissed. His eyes darted rapidly back and forth. Amongst his other items, the Fey was still juggling his stolen apple, the fruit now eaten to the core.

There was no time, however, and Elwood was speaking the truth—Fey were swift and dexterous, but when transferring their power toward keeping them alive in a near-death situation, they became much slower. He could tell that much from Elwood, who was struggling to keep pace. Chais himself was also feeling weak and out of breath after the Gredian dungeons failed to provide enough food, sun, or room for exercise. He couldn't complain; compared to the slums, the conditions were almost acceptable.

Dodge right! Aldridge's voice broke his thoughts.

An iron bullet shattered a doorway next to Chais's head. Sharp chunks of wood flew across the street. Chais didn't waste a glance back, but instead grabbed a merchant's cart that was parked at the edge of the road and dumped its contents behind them. Gods, he hated doing that, but it was necessary. Now that there was a crowd chasing them down—judging from the noise, they were a fairly medium-sized bunch—they couldn't risk a race against the odds. Chais was avoiding obstacles before, but it was useless now that the village had so obviously seen the runaways.

"Give me these," Chais said and grabbed the alcohol and tunic that Elwood was desperately trying to hold on to, now that he was short one arm. He held the neck of the bottle with his left hand and forced the cloth and meat into the same grip so that his right arm was free for knocking objects around. There was no way he was taking the spit-soaked apple core.

If there was an iron bullet, chances were that the soldiers had caught on. Commoners in less populated areas such as this one didn't often have guns—they usually fought and hunted with knives or bows. Luckily, it didn't seem that this group of king's men, probably patrolling the area beforehand, had any creatures of the dark. Those normally went to the frontlines or the cities. However, knowing the Gredian forces—and the lugaires he and Elwood had so barely managed to dodge—there was no doubt that word had already gone to the capital and the demons in the form of animals would be sent soon. He and Elwood had to come up with another plan.

Chais spilled the components of another cart onto the street and looked toward the rooftops. Many of the village houses had a flat roof and large barriers that prevented an accidental fall. Perfect, for the short term, at least. Elwood seemed to notice also, and it was silently decided where the two runaways were now headed.

"Throw them off!" Chais said. He ducked around a corner as the window next to him exploded. A sharp pain blossomed in his shoulder, but adrenaline mostly numbed the sensation. They dodged through the small number of alleyways that the village had to offer in an attempt to lose the pursuers.

"I have—the perfect idea—for that!" Elwood announced, despite his state. As they turned a corner and the pursuers rounded the one a few feet away, the Fey twisted and drew his arm back, still holding the apple core.

"What are you—" Chais began. His breathing was choppy and foreign. It seemed Aldridge was still working on transferring Fey speed to him. The process of gaining Fey powers was apparently a slow one.

If Elwood had a right hand, Chais was fairly certain it would be pointed at the rapidly approaching soldiers as they passed from building to building. Elwood closed one eye, stuck his tongue sideways, and hurled the remains of the fruit at a villager near the front.

It slammed into the villager's face, briefly discharging a shower of water. Stunned, the inexperienced man jolted backward. His momentum shifted toward the rest of the crowd.

By the time the duo turned another corner, the group was lagging behind and had now significantly decreased in numbers. Chais shot a look at Elwood that consisted of surprise, confusion, and shock.

"How did that work?" Chais breathed. All Elwood did was shrug and grin. Astonishment was written over his own face, and he was clearly surprised that an apple core could have such an impact.

They're far enough. You should climb the next house—I saw a sign about a hairdressing salon, Aldridge offered, bringing the two distracted escapees back on-topic. Chais took the next turn and hastily wrapped the alcohol bottle inside the tunic. He gauged the distance to the top. There was a small chance of it shattering if he threw it right since the houses here were barely high enough for some headspace.

Chais tossed it over the edge, followed by the string of rabbit meat , thankful when there was no sound of breaking glass—and then he quickly scaled the building. The rough material of the house dug into the skin on his fingers, breaking it and chipping his nails. Crevices enabled him to find good hand and footholds. Chais hoisted himself over the barrier and leaned over the side of the roof to help Elwood, whose single arm severely hindered his climbing ability. Even with the handicap, the Fey warrior's heritage shone through in the way he moved, swiftly and efficiently.

They dropped low. Chais listened to the thundering sound of heavy footsteps drawing nearer by the second. There was a brief scuffle below their hiding spot, and a few yells rang out over the crowd. It appeared the townspeople and the soldiers were debating where the intruders had headed. Chais remained still as stone, as did Elwood, until the pursuers went raging down a separate road. Thank the gods the lugaires weren't here.

Chais exhaled and scanned their surroundings. Sure enough, they were on the roof of a hairdressing salon—typically, the villages in small regions wouldn't have one, but this village wasn't exactly poor. It seemed a bit too lucky that such convenient disguises would fall right into their hands, even after he and Elwood managed to escape from Silvermount in an otherwise impossible situation.

The flat rooftop was lined with clothes that were out to air and a few broken supplies that seemed like they were intended for hairstylists. A wooden trapdoor led down to the first floor. Several used hair dyes were stacked next to it.

"Hey, Grumpy," Elwood whispered. A slight breeze stirred his bangs. "It won't be long before they have lugaires. Remember, if we're caught, you be the dog chow while I run for the hills." Chais rolled his eyes and made his way to where the hair dye was. Although the trapdoor was wide open, a glance down the ladder ensured that the house had no occupants. He grabbed the blonde dye and some clothes, then turned and tossed a new tunic, cloak, and cap at Elwood. No doubt someone had seen them. Why not switch disguises while they could?

"There's a stream near here, I think. We can clean up there." Chais peered over the edge. The yelling had gone down significantly, but it wouldn't be long before the soldiers began to check individual houses. He gathered the wrapped bottle and rabbit meat.

Elwood examined the tunic with the manner of a fashion critic. Once it was certain that the coast was clear, they quietly climbed down and headed toward the stream, which was nestled beyond a patch of woodland. The dying echoes of voices followed them until they gradually faded into the wind.

Chais took a moment to gain his bearings before continuing in the direction of the river. The forest pressed relatively closely on one side, while the other provided rolling hills ideal for a hideout. He didn't dare initiate conversation. The Gredian forces could be close. Although Chais Nevermoon was deserving of his title of lieutenant colonel at such a young age, there were many others, both in the capital and out, who could give him a run for his money. Elwood seemed to realize this too. He trekked behind the ex-colonel with lethal grace and silence. If he hadn't known any better, Chais would've believed that there was a ghost at his heels.

At the stream, and after a surprisingly peaceful but short journey, Chais made sure there was no one around. Elwood also checked the perimeter. It was something like second nature, even more so now that they were the most wanted fugitives in Gredian.

Chais quickly changed into the new tunic. Its edges were slightly frayed, but the quality of the clothing was better than the previous ones. The minor glass wound that he'd received during the chase was easily cleaned out and was already healing. He noticed that Elwood had already changed. His long hair was now tied up and hidden beneath the trader's cap. A few locks slipped out, in order to better hide his delicately pointed ears. Chais also noticed a marking that appeared to be a teardrop with two semicircles cradling it, on his left arm, before the cloak covered it: the symbol of Atrelia.

It reminded him bitterly of Gredian. The arrow with a key crossing it horizontally—it symbolized a place that was no longer his home. There was that fleeting sensation, the sensation of never again belonging anywhere. Gredian had been his lifeline, the lighthouse in the foggy distance. But now that it was gone, Chais found himself wandering in the darkness, not knowing where to go or who he was. And no one else was there. He was hopelessly, desperately lost.

Chais dunked his face into the cool stream. Dirt and mud from Elwood's idea of do-it-yourself dye clouded the water and swirled off into the current. He hastily colored his hair with the dye that he'd "borrowed" from the village house, silver hair once again masked by a sort of strawberry blond.

Chais unwrapped the alcohol bottle and took off the cap.

"Time to rebind," Chais said. He pushed his thoughts of Gredian to the back of his mind and swished the alcohol in a circle so that the liquid inside lazily smacked the glass. Elwood groaned but moved his cloak back so that his stump of a right arm came into view. The most recent bandage material was stained with blood but not enough to drip. The wound needed some disinfecting.

Although Elwood flinched rather violently at the contact with alcohol, it was apparent that the freshly bound arm made a world of a difference. The Fey took the bottle, which still had some liquid in it, and raised it as if he were at a ceremony and making a toast.

"Want some?" He smirked.

Chais glanced at the small amount remaining. Even that much could throw him into a drunken frenzy.

"No, thanks."

Elwood narrowed his eyes. A smug grin was still plastered onto his face. If this was his sober state, Chais couldn't possibly imagine how the Fey acted when he was drunk. "Can't hold your liquor?"

"Does now look like the right time to drink?" Chais snapped, snatching it from Elwood's hand and tossing it into the river.

"You're no fun," the Fey grumbled. He took the old tunics and positioned one on a sharp branch. Elwood tore a piece of the cloth in one swift movement and dumped the rest of the clothing into the small river. As soon as it disappeared with the current, a piercing howl sounded in the distance. Chais judged that the lugaires weren't close enough to be a major threat, but soon they would be, with their keen sense of smell that stemmed from their demonic origins. Elwood leaped across the stream and Chais joined him. The hard ground ensured that no prints were left behind.

"The common roads are through this small stretch of forest," Chais noted as he started at a brisk walk. The road was not exactly bustling with merchants and traders, but the occasional person passed every few moments.

"What's the stop after Valport?" Elwood pushed his cap down to shade his eyes. The ground rustled, barely audibly, beneath their feet. It was likely that many traders were having lunch since there was a tavern further up the road. The area was a popular place for commoners, but no one was ever alert and the security was less than satisfying.

"Hmm ..." Chais surveyed their surroundings. They were still in Valport. Their destination was west toward the border with Atrelia—even though Chais still hadn't completely made up his mind about joining the enemy. One Fey he could be on good terms with, but a whole kingdom of them? They probably despised him ... although the same could be said for Gredian, However, much pain it caused to admit. Atrelia and Gredian weren't exactly the only kingdoms on the face of the planet either,

Chais reminded himself, so maybe there was somewhere else he could go. After this whole ordeal, that is.

Chais searched for the empire's map in his memory, for an area that was further west of Valport. West of Valport, west of Valport …

"I believe Mirstone is our next destination. We can stop by villages in Valport if it's necessary, but we'll have to be more careful." Elwood glanced behind them. His eyes narrowed just slightly as the sound of lugaires drew closer but still not close enough to quicken the pace. Both of them had been careful not to leave any tracks behind, whether that referred to sight or scent.

"How far away is Mirstone?" The Fey's remains of an arm twitched as if he were reaching for his bangs, and Chais noticed that there was also a strand of hair hanging stubbornly in front of Elwood's line of sight. Phantom limbs.

"Well, I'd say …" Chais said, trying to mentally calculate the distance. He drew a blank for a couple of seconds. "A little more than ten miles."

They arrived at the fringe of the forest. Chais checked both directions before stepping onto the road. Across from them, among other structures, was the tavern, its interior bustling with activity. Drunk shouts and the sound of glass shattering emerged from the building. Chais dawdled alongside the road, appearing to all the world like a carefree trader who had already sold enough and wasn't in any hurry to get home. Elwood put up a spectacular act as a talkative rookie merchant—were there theaters in the Fey kingdom? The Fey could be a great actor.

The large oak door slammed open, almost bursting off of its hinges. A ragged man, probably in his late thirties, stumbled out with a beer mug clutched in his beefy hands.

"And don't come back!" said another male voice before the chaos of the tavern was dulled by the forceful shutting of the door. The two "merchants" kept their distance and made false conversation as their eyes trailed the drunkard to his cart. They watched the trader undo the lock on the wheel, then the cover to count his goods. The security of merchant carts had gone up recently, but it was still normal for a thief to slip in and steal away some items. Locks were easily undone by those with the skills to do so. Cursing loud enough for everyone nearby to hear, the man's hand flung up to his mouth, and he frantically disappeared into an alleyway.

Seeing his chance, Chais walked as fast as he could without appearing suspicious. The drunk's cart was in one of the building's overhangs, so anyone further into the village wouldn't suspect a thing. The locks were already undone, so all they had to do was wheel the goods out and away. It made their disguise much more believable, and who knew? Maybe there were some valuable things in there.

Chais despised the idea, but he grabbed the handles of the cart anyway and tossed his strip of rabbit meat inside. It didn't take much effort at all to get the cart to move. It was obvious that there were still things in there that hadn't been sold. The duo rounded the nearest corner and wove between a few buildings before coming out on the other side, exchanging small talk. By then, the angry shouts of the man near the tavern had faded into the background. His drunken state had prevented any further pursuit.

The particular road that they were on would likely lead to several different areas in Valport, so blending in was key. The forest was probably infested with Gredian forces by now. Chais felt a strange pride he was worth so much effort to obtain.

"My ears hurt," Elwood said passively as he grabbed an apple from the merchant's cart. Another one? Chais looked into the cart, curious. It only had fruits, not including the meat he'd thrown in, but food was always welcome if you were a runaway criminal.

"That's great." Chais eyed the stiff hat on the Fey's head. It did seem a bit painful, as it sat harshly atop Elwood's pointed ears.

The Fey smirked. The cloak covering his absence of a limb rippled slightly in the breeze.

"Why don't you—"

"No."

"You didn't even hear what I had to say."

"Whatever it was, it wasn't going to be good. I had to cut it short." Chais sighed. Who knew a seasoned Fey warrior would be such a handful?

"Short ... like your height?" Elwood sputtered, holding back barely contained laughter.

Chais would've punched the idiot if they weren't passing a commoner on the road. It was a fairly wide path and designed to accommodate the busier days. Of course, before the war, the streets were almost always flooded with people of all different backgrounds and purposes, appearances and cultures, or at least, that was what he was told. Compared to that idea, the modern-day Valport seemed like a ghost town.

"Just so you know, you colossal dimwit," Chais growled, momentarily dropping his mask as the commoner continued on her journey, "it's only by an inch. Putting up a high ponytail doesn't make you any taller."

Elwood shrugged. He was still struggling to hold back laughter.

"An inch is an inch. I'm taller, and that's a fact."

"Only by," Chais rotated his hand so that the palm was facing down and drew an imaginary line from the top of his head to Elwood's forehead, "one inch."

Elwood finally let go of the laughter that he'd been trying so hard to restrain.

"Tiny, Grumpy Chais, do you need help reaching the apples?" Elwood tossed one of the fruits at Chais and sprinted out in front, possibly avoiding a fist to the face.

Chais rolled his eyes. A part of him was stunned at the endless chasm of energy this Fey possessed. He cast a glance behind them. There was no one trailing them, and no sound of soldiers or creatures of the dark. They were safe.

For now.

CHAPTER

TWELVE

"GET OUT OF THE CART. I know you're not sleeping anymore," Chais said from somewhere behind him. He panted heavily as he pushed Elwood and the cart up an incline. Elwood grinned softly and pushed the hat he had over his eyes back to its proper place. The wooden roof of the cart was peppered with small holes, allowing thin streams of sunlight into the rather cramped space. His legs were folded awkwardly and pressed against the walls, but despite the awkward position, he had slept rather well. Elwood yawned wide enough to crack his jaw and smiled to himself.

"But, Grumpy ... I'm injured! I need to rest!" he whined mockingly and rested back on the small pile of blankets they had found while taking inventory of their new trader's cart. By now, all the fresh fruit had been demolished by a very happy Fey and only the dried goods and cloth remained. Just as he was rooting around the cart for the small bag of caramel candy he had found when they first acquired the cart, the vehicle came to an abrupt halt, slamming Elwood's forehead into the side of the wooden cart. Elwood chuckled lightly and leaned back against the wall. He plastered a smirk firmly on his face as footsteps came around the cart and the roof was cracked open. Vivid blue eyes glared down at him.

"Get out," Chais threatened, looking ready to drag him out by force if necessary. Elwood wasn't sure if he should be scared. At least the Feykin's head blocked the setting sun's light and gave his eyes time to adjust.

"You've let me ride in here this long! Why not a bit longer?" The Fey stretched and felt his back pop. Now that he was moving, his body felt sore from his sleeping position; the hardwood scratched against his skin.

"I never let you, you idiot!" Chais said. "You just yawned, crawled in, and passed out! I even dragged you out and kicked you around for a bit. I swear, if I didn't know better, I would have thought I was dealing with a corpse! What the hell is wrong with you?"

"Wow. You're even grumpier than usual." Elwood blinked. He stood up and smoothly vaulted over the side of the cart.

"Of course I'm grumpy. I just pushed you around this country for three hours." Chais glared and leaned against the stolen vehicle. Elwood landed softly on the ground and faced the Feykin. While Chais still looked ready to explode, his fists were no longer clenched, a sign that he was calming. The colonel exhaled loudly and brushed his foreign-colored hair out of his eyes.

"Ahh ..." Elwood took off his cap and ran his hand through his hair, trying to ignore the snags in the strands. He gathered it back into a loop at the base of his neck and slapped the cap back on. "Sorry, but hey, I figured you needed the exercise."

"... I really hate you," Chais said as he turned around to close and relock the cart. "You're on cart-pushing duty from now on. Have fun, Stumpy." Elwood pouted but did not complain; he simply grabbed the cart and fell in line with the Feykin, who walked ahead. He noticed the roads ran smoother and were wider as well; the earth was packed and hardened by many years of travel. Many paths split off from the main road, and recent footprints and tire tracks littered the area. Elwood could see a village not too far behind them with higher, whitewashed buildings. While over the last few days of travel the roads had grown in size along with the population, in the last three hours he had spent asleep, they must've passed the invisible border between Valport and Mirstone. And, in the last few days, there had only been one significant incident. But it had left its mark.

While they were staying in a shady inn in a smaller town, royal guards and a summoner had appeared. Their lugaire had tracked them down. The results were a frantic bolt for their cart, multiple false trails, and a banished demon. Neither Elwood nor Chais sustained any injuries, having broken the demon's neck with a chucked vase and a very hard wall and losing the guards during a terrifying game of hide and seek with bullets and crossbows. However, in the hectic scuffle, an unfortunate civilian was caught in the crossfire. A crossbow bolt had buried itself deeply in her shoulder. It left her writhing on the ground in pain. The terrible look of guilt and horror in Chais's eyes at the hurt of the innocent woman was worrying.

Elwood couldn't help but marvel at the deep dedication Chais had to his people. Despite the deeds that the Feykin must have witnessed and committed on the frontlines, he still had a caring heart. Elwood had seen too many of those die. Seeing one still so vibrant, this battle-hardened, yet young colonel, was truly a rare sight to behold. It was really sweet and naive.

Elwood also noticed that Chais became tenser and tenser as they passed the larger towns. His shoulders were tight, and his hands were clenched. His eyes darted from citizen to citizen, settling on children with guilt heavy in his eyes. Elwood knew that Chais was concerned that every time they were in one of the villages, they were putting the people at risk. If a fight were to break out, there would be unwanted casualties. Also, whenever they traveled through a village with royal guards already stationed, Chais's gaze darted from face to face in search of former comrades. It was honestly kind of heartbreaking to see his face fall whenever he recognized someone—a former friend now hunting him down.

Elwood knew he was brooding and could see that the silence caused Chais to brood too. The shadows thrown onto his face by the setting sun seemed to dull his bright eyes. They both needed a distraction, so Elwood did what he did best and let his mouth move.

"What did you do?" Elwood asked, wincing slightly at the inconsiderate question. Maybe he shouldn't have let his mouth open after all. But still, he was curious. He had heard the rumors and the long speech before Chais's execution, but he wanted to hear the story from the ex-colonel.

"Apparently, I killed the king," Chais replied. His monotone didn't stop bitterness from leaking through. Elwood frowned; if he were to guess, he would guess that Chais was innocent. He had seen how these people loved King Havard. It was a fresh change from the psychopath who had started the war. Havard had started to mend the wounds that the past king had torn into their country; with a few more years, maybe a peace treaty could have been signed. And, unless Chais was one of those war fanatics who supported the first king's bloody ways—which wasn't likely considering his age, as well as his protective personality—there was little chance of the colonel being guilty. That, along with the genuine sorrow he had witnessed at the execution? It didn't make sense that he would kill Havard, the best ruler the mortal kingdom had had in a while.

"So … did you?" Elwood finally asked in hopes of figuring out the true story. He wanted to know what kind of person he had been forced to befriend. It was strange—as a Fey, long lives taught him to never befriend anyone until he knew them almost better than he knew himself. The web of lies that many wove to entrap and ensnare were plentiful. People tried to earn a favor from high-ranked officers. On the battlefield, most didn't have time for such petty entertainment. When people faced life and death together, respect was quickly earned. Comrades were common, but true friends were rare.

Elwood had grown up with his two best friends—they knew each other inside and out, sometimes better than they knew themselves. When one of them died, it had been devastating. Bonds meant something much more when they could last forever. And since promises couldn't be broken, friendships, based on an unspoken oath to always have each other's back, was something not given out lightly. So, the fact that he was now viewing this near-stranger as a friend was strange indeed. Perhaps it had something to do with the sense of familiarity and protectiveness he had whenever he looked at Chais.

"No! He ... he was this country's best hope. I knew that." Then, almost too quiet for even Elwood's sensitive ears to hear, "I knew that better than anyone." Chais looked away, but Elwood could see the glassiness of tears filmed over blue eyes and fists clenched so tightly the knuckles flushed white. Elwood remembered in a half-exhausted blur that Chais had told him some weird story. He sounded far too invested with the characters. A character whose father had ... eaten him? Elwood glanced at Chais and wondered what that could mean. Nothing good, that was for sure. He pushed away all thoughts of pity; the Feykin wouldn't appreciate that. But ... clearly, his love for the king was real, and more than just the love of a soldier for his king.

"Do you know who did kill him? Because whoever did royally screwed up any hope of peace in your lifetime." Elwood voiced the question lightly. He knew the train of thought wasn't a pleasant place for Chais, but he still wanted to know, needed to know. Even if he only wished to use the knowledge to destroy the man who was causing Chais's distress. That strange protective feeling washed over him again before he shoved it aside. The Feykin could take care of himself.

"Not really. Maybe Adaric?" Chais was hesitant but there was an undertone of certainty. Adaric. That golden-eyed man at the execution and the same one Elwood had sent launching like a catapult. Elwood snickered at that memory. "He and I ... I would say never got along, but that feels like an understatement. A better way to state it would be we hated each other and secretly plotted the other's assassination from the moment we met."

"Yeah, he seemed like a real goblin," Elwood commented, earning an enthusiastic nod of agreement. A small smirk pulled at the edge of Chais's lip, and a matching one formed on Elwood's own. "If you still want him assassinated, I would be happy to help. My rates are very reasonable."

"You do assassin work? I never pegged you for the type."

"What? You don't think I can be subtle?" The Fey tried to sound indignant, but his wide smile gave him away. "I would have you know, I am very good at it!"

"Are you sure Fey can't lie?" the colonel asked as mischief twinkled in his eyes. One day, Elwood knew that tongue was going to get the Feykin into big trouble. Maybe it already had.

"Why you little—" Elwood pulled his hand back, ready to release a burst of air just big enough to knock the smug, young Feykin onto his ass when a jolt of fear and anxiety ran down his spine. He froze and reached for his weapon instead. Chais also stopped, his own hand drifting for his dagger.

Demons are near! Relevard warned. *Listen!*

Elwood opened his mouth to reply that he didn't hear anything, but he suddenly realized that was what the dead Fey ex-colonel was talking about. Considering they were still traveling near the woods, the harmony of a thousand avian species had become constant background noise. Demons had a tendency to scare away all natural lifeforms, so it was a good heads up to potential attacks. Elwood squinted into the dimming skies and caught the dark wings of large birds. Their feathers glistened against the array of reds and purples like onyx stones in a sea of rubies and amethysts, dark with a hint of bad intent. The wingspans were too big to be regular crows or ravens, stretching an impressive six feet.

Rewaraa. The raven-like hawks of the underworld were the ideal scouts for the battlefield, and they were often used for ambushes as well. They blended in perfectly with the only other fowl that existed in the desolate wastelands of death and destruction. Reweraa would circle their targets like any other bird of prey, only to swoop down, revealing burning eyes and razor-sharp talons, ready to tear through metal and flesh alike.

Elwood cursed their luck and reached to grab Chais, only to feel a spasm of pain. He hissed lightly and waved away the ex-colonel's expression of confusion and concern.

"We have to find cover, now," Elwood muttered. "How long before we get to the next village?"

"Ten minutes. Three if we run," Chais answered, and his eyes widened. He cursed. "Rewaraa?"

"Yeah, and we need to find shelter before they decide to attack us or alert their summoner." Chais nodded and gestured for them to start moving, striding with purpose and speed, yet cautious not to break out into a run. The Fey followed silently, still pushing the cart while using his powers to slowly block all of the cracks in the wood but one. He started to forcefully push air into it, increasing the pressure, being very careful not to act too suspiciously. The demon beasts weren't the most clever creatures—they followed their summoner's orders perfectly. It was the price of being allowed into this world. If Chais and Elwood ran, however, the birds would definitely notice, and they wouldn't have time to reach the village before the hawks swooped in to attack.

"Why would battlefield-level summoners be here? Surely that fool would care more about the war effort than the head of an ex-lieutenant colonel," Elwood heard Chais murmur under his breath. Elwood flinched as a low caw echoed through the dusk air, and he couldn't help but wonder which gods they had offended. The demons, previously circling from a distance, had flown away from them toward the direction they had come—and presumably, toward their summoners and warriors.

"You can wonder later. We need to run. Now!" he urged Chais. The Feykin momentarily rested his hand against the small dagger at his side. Comfort, perhaps, from the touch of a familiar weapon?

"Don't order me around," Chais said and took off at a speed that would make mere mortals wonder if the man was human. To Elwood, however, it was to be expected of the half-Fey. He kept up best he could while pushing the cart. Elwood tried to ignore the concerning rattles as he continued to force air in.

"Ditch the cart, idiot!" Chais called back and slowed down to wait for him. Elwood shook his head. He was concentrating too hard on keeping the cart together to reply. The Feykin hissed in annoyance but came to help him push. No longer bothering to hide their tracks, they raced toward the village, praying that they would reach it before the summoners called in lugaires.

They were not that fortunate. The village was already in sight, and the white walls of the buildings were washed purple in the sunset. Just when they were beginning to believe they could make it and throw off their pursuers, the dogs attacked. Their owners were still far behind but getting closer every second; the hounds held them. Elwood released the cart and took a step back. He paused to boot the nearest beast as hard as he could across the road. It landed with a pitiful whimper. Before Elwood could congratulate himself for his small victory, the rest of the demons leaped. Chais swiftly drew his blade and tried to fend off the fangs and claws that aimed for his chest and legs.

"Lead them to the cart, then on my signal, drop to the ground!" Elwood yelled as he twisted away from a lunging hound. The Feykin threw him a confused look but nodded. Chais slashed his dagger over his palm and raised the bloodied hand. All the demons turned and attacked him with renewed vigor, drawn toward the cut. Elwood drew his bow and used the bladed end to drive away the few still after him.

"Any. Time. Now!" Chais yelled. He slit the throat of a demon and turned away to pry the teeth of another off his leg before the demon had even managed to finish disintegrating back to shadows.

Elwood released his hold on the winds tightly bounded in the cart. "Get off the cart!" he warned, and the flash of blonde leaped away in response. Elwood let the winds explode as soon as his friend was out of harm's way. The cart combusted. Shards of wood flung outward as a shock wave of wind slammed the nearest lugaires into trees. They disintegrated. The deadly shrapnel of jagged wood impaled the demons, returning them to their realm. Elwood silently mourned the loss of the caramel candies.

"Come on!" Elwood ran to Chais and threw his arm over his shoulder. The colonel grunted in pain as he placed weight onto his injured leg but did not complain. The paralysis poison that laced the hound's teeth was obviously taking its toll on Chais. Elwood winced at the small shards of wood embedded in Chais's back from the explosion.

No more than ten steps later, a demon tackled them from behind. Both men cried out in shock and pain as they impacted the ground. Elwood shoved Chais aside and twisted onto his back. He kicked the lugaire off. The dog snarled, long and looping saliva spinning from its jaws. Blood red eyes glowed with horrific malice. It growled and Elwood growled back.

Elwood rolled to the side as the beast charged. He slammed his boot into its side and scrambled to his feet. Elwood gripped his bow and swung. The blade cut through the demon's thick fur, and it exploded into shadow. Chais had gathered his bearings and was standing unsteadily on his feet. His dagger was out, and he eyed the recovered lugaires warily. There was a low bark before everything descended into a chaos of fur, claws, and teeth. Elwood stepped next to the colonel, covering his weak side while presenting his own for the Feykin to protect. He slashed a demon midway through its lunge but failed to notice another beast attacking from behind. Hot, burning pain bloomed in his back. Claws ripped into his muscles, and the beast's teeth sank into his shoulder.

Chais plunged his dagger into the hound's skull and defended Elwood while he struggled to recover from the wound. Elwood pushed the pain aside and returned to guarding Chais's side, but at a significantly slower and less successful rate. They both began to stack up on injuries. The soldiers caught up as they struggled to reduce the demons to smoke. The screech of blade against blade penetrated the evening sky, and the sound of battle rang in Elwood's ears.

Elwood parried a sword back and riposted with a swift glancing blow to the shoulder. The fabric tore under his sharpened blade, but it was not deep enough to form more than a thin line of beaded blood. The soldiers continued their relentless barrage of attacks, and Elwood felt himself losing ground. Snarling forms of large dogs continued to nip at his heels. A wall of fur ebbed and flowed between barely blocked strikes of iron blades. One sank its teeth into his leg. Elwood stumbled from the pain and swiftly beheaded the beast. Adrenaline and willpower helped him ignore the wound and concentrate on the much more threatening weapons aimed at his vital points.

None of the warriors drew their crossbows or muskets in fear of hitting a comrade. Relevard pointed this out, and Elwood was careful to keep at least one opponent in a position where they could be potentially hit by a comrade's ranged weapon. He took note of at least twenty warriors between himself and Chais. Half of them were focused mainly on the Feykin. Three summoners stood at the further distance; their demonic creatures aided the soldiers' battle. Dark energy pulsed off of them, residue from the summoning of monsters from another dimension.

Elwood staggered back. He realized that the careful blade-work of his opponents had moved him far from his companion. A pulse of panic ran through him. He had to get back to Chais. This amount of enemies wouldn't have been easy to take down even if he was at full strength, which he was not. By their sword-play and spears strapped to their back, Elwood knew they were skilled. These men were all prepared to fight, unlike the men at the execution. That, in itself, made a world of difference, now that he had experienced both.

Elwood hoped that Chais would be able to subdue his attackers and turned his attention back to his own. He barely dodged a fatal blow to his neck. He was careful not to allow the iron weapons to even graze him; this, however, had opened him up to the hounds. The deep claw mark across his back burned and rippled at his every movement; this and the bite mark pulsing angrily at his thigh reminded him to pay attention to the demons as well. Every injury could lead to an iron weapon slipping through his defenses and pulling him out of the fight for good.

Elwood released a shockwave of wind, pushing as much power in as he dared. Three of the men were flung into the air and landed with a sickening crunch. They did not get back up. The remaining five soldiers were pushed back, giving him a moment to breathe. Elwood panted heavily. He shoved a column of air at one of the attackers but fell to his knees from the exertion. The world swayed. Elwood looked up, trying to focus, but the soldiers were too fast and he couldn't make himself move.

BLOCK IT! Relevard roared. The command pounded through his skull, and Elwood raised his bow by instinct. The strike reverberated through his body, and he clenched his teeth in pain. Through the pain, he could hear something snap. The soldier's body was impaled upon his bow. Elwood pushed the body off and dug his bow into the blood-soaked ground, using it as leverage to rise. Before he could, one of the remaining soldiers charged and shoved his spear through the Fey warrior's back. Elwood coughed as blood flooded to his mouth. He barely recognized the pain as he fell limp.

"... not ... kill him! ..." Elwood heard through the haze, but couldn't find the energy to act on it. Blackness was eating away at his vision, but he could see Chais's bright hair flash against the dark sky. The colonel's eyes met Elwood's. Chais's blood-streaked face paled, and something changed. Elwood swore he was hallucinating, but the Feykin's eyes suddenly gained a wild, uncontrolled aspect, a burning blue fire. Tentacles of water formed from the humid air, swaying and grasping around Chais. They smashed the man that attacked Elwood into a tree, and the water coated his head. Just as the *creature* turned its attention to the rest of the men, the unnatural power faded from his eyes and he fell limp. Elwood's own vision faded completely, and his other senses started to flee him as well. He could only stay conscious long enough to hear the soldier nearest to him speak. The man's voice was trembling slightly.

"H-hurry. Tie him up before he—it—does *that* again."

CHAPTER
THIRTEEN

SOMETHING WASN'T RIGHT.

Lynara knew from the moment Adaric had been crowned king that *something wasn't right*.

Aside from Chais and the general drama that the kingdom was in, of course.

Suspecting people had always been her forte, and at the moment, her senses were tingling. That didn't matter though. She would just have to put it aside for now—there was work to do, and a lot of it.

It seemed like the capital was always alive and bustling with activity. Merchants and traders always flooded the streets, as well as commoners, the wealthy, and the not-so-wealthy. Silvermount was a perfect city for the crowd-loving person, as bakeries, restaurants, and shops offering all types of services seemed to never run out of stock. The spectacle of the botched execution that had just occurred a few days ago seemed to have completely left the minds of the people. They strolled along the cobblestone paths on a routine shopping route, baskets on their arms. Children dashed through the swarm of legs, laughing and clutching stolen fruits as merchants shook fists at them. Everything was back to the customary, normal happenings that Silvermount had always experienced. It almost seemed too expected too unperturbed—as if something demonic was headed for Gredian any second.

Lynara shook her head clear of the thoughts—it wasn't good to think so darkly on a bright day such as this one, where the white clouds hung serenely amidst a backdrop of vivid blue. It reminded her of Alryne and that business trip that she had embarked on with her father to find dealings in Gredian's busiest trading center.

Lynara was visiting Silvermount alone today. The head summoner's directions occupied her brain as she rounded a corner and ducked under a particularly low rooftop, its surface gray and water-stained. Before she came within a couple of blocks of her destination, the delicious aroma of various bread, pastries, and cakes flooded her senses. Lynara didn't bother to apologize as she bumped shoulders and stepped on feet. On such a busy day, no one expected an apology from anyone.

As Lynara strolled into the bakery, she briefly scanned the streets and rooftops for any followers, but all she saw was the usual throng of civilians and the signature gray tiles of Silvermount. The glass door opened with a cheery ring of a bell. Immediately, a wall of air conditioning slammed into her face. It was not too crowded today, but what "not too crowded" in Silvermount meant to someone from Shipton was a whole different story. Without her uniform on, the commander didn't receive any glances filled with fear or respect—it was usually one or the other when she visited the city. Lynara looked average, with a medium height and build, as well as regular auburn eyes—a bit *too* red to be completely normal—in her opinion—and scarlet hair. If the capital wanted a high-ranking, skillful soldier to be their eyes on the city, she would be the perfect pick.

Lynara made her way carefully through the line of civilians, as well as the occupied wooden tables, and approached the side of the counter. From here, she could see all the desserts through the glass, drenched in oozing chocolate and topped with smooth, thick cream. The bread on the other side of the shop, fresh out of the oven and gleaming a healthy golden brown, looked much better than the sweets, in her opinion.

One of the bakers, already notified of Lynara's ... *appointment*, strolled over. She leaned an elbow with a rolled-up sleeve on the counter, dusted lightly with flour.

"Here for the consultation?" the woman asked quietly. Her voice was barely audible over the buzz of the shoppers. "Consultation," Lynara thought, "that could work instead of appointment."

The commander nodded and raised a crest with her right hand so that the shop's customers wouldn't be able to see.

The baker examined her identification briefly before gesturing toward a gated hallway. Lynara followed. They rounded a few bends, where the walls changed from the warm yellow of the bakery to a royal red as they approached the end. At a set of stairs leading down to yet another door—this one painted pitch black—the baker stopped.

"Don't take too long," she said before returning the way they came. Lynara descended the steps carefully. She pulled out a pocket watch to make sure she wasn't late.

Lynara easily noticed the fading symbol on the door. It couldn't be entered without identification, and the key laced through an arrow told her exactly who could go in. The commander flashed an identical symbol, etched into the same crest she'd shown at the front. There was a quiet, barely audible clicking sound. Lynara slipped in. The door shut itself.

It took a few moments for her eyes to adjust to the gloom. The wide hallway stretched before her was adorned with dimmed lights, spread evenly along the wall like wisps leading into the darkness of the forest. The place was not nearly as depressing as the dungeons beneath the capital, but it still held that same musky odor. There were more side rooms than she could count. Each entrance was sealed until whomever had the room wanted to exit or enter. Scarlet rugs, silver accents, and darkened—almost black—wooden furniture: the colors of the Gredian Empire.

Lynara had never set foot in this place before, although she'd heard many things about it. The Convexus ... As far as she knew, this was its only location. Even as commander, she had no right to learn more about the top secret area that the empire hid from mostly everyone. She didn't even know what its purpose was.

She approached the third door from the entrance. Its surface was imprinted with strange markings that curved and twisted over each other like snakes lunging for one another's neck. Lynara reached down for the doorknob, only to grasp air. Confusion flickered over her as she searched the door for a way in, occasionally casting nervous glances at the foreboding entryway she'd gone through. This hallway gave her the shivers, and not in a good way.

Finally, Lynara resorted to an awkward "Neveah?"

Silence.

Lynara opened her mouth to try again when a familiar voice, smooth and mellifluous, seemed to fill the Convexus.

"Commander Merran, I have been awaiting your arrival. Please, come in." The door vanished, and Lynara lingered only for a second before stepping through. She threw a careful glance behind her and noticed that the door was back. Huh.

The first thing that Lynara noticed were the leather couches, the polished wooden walls, the fact that someone was here, and the fireplace that was crackling in the corner. The heat wasn't needed at all—it was nearing the temperature at which a normal person would sweat. The second thing she noticed was the bowl of steaming hot soup with a side of baked potatoes. Its savory scent filled the entire room, and Lynara inhaled it almost greedily. In one of the chairs was a very recognizable figure. Even without the light of the strangely ominous fire, Lynara knew who was before her.

"Neveah," Lynara said. The woman looked up, odd but striking silver eyes sparked by the flames. A hint of a smile tugged at her lips as she spoke.

"Commander Merran. You're here." She drew herself up slowly, as if she had all the time in the world. The movement portrayed power and elegance.

"We've already talked about this, Neveah. There's no need for the professional address."

"I dare say you've heard about my policy for more ...

businesslike exchanges." The other woman motioned with her left hand. She drew imaginary circles in the air as she spoke. The heat from the fireplace caused her dark skin to glow almost heavenly.

"Adaric had some personal matters that he had to attend to, so I'll be relaying the information to you. And yes—" she continued when she saw Lynara open her mouth, "I left another summoner to momentarily take my place. The search and the frontlines are secure from our perspective." A smile. "Don't worry, Commander."

"Neveah, I don't mean to come off as rude, but ..." Lynara tried to find something to do with her arms, and in the end, decided to cross them, "... why you? You're the head summoner, and you usually don't get any breaks from the castle."

The woman laughed lightly. "Why not? I just wanted to see a friend is all."

When Lynara didn't look convinced, Neveah sighed.

"I pulled a few strings to come out here; only because you've been a bit busy at the other side of the castle. I enjoy keeping tabs on all of my familiars so I can be there for them when the time comes." The head summoner's silver eyes were difficult to keep contact with, so Lynara exhaled and looked at the fire.

"Well ... thank you. Frankly, I'd much rather talk to you than with one of those messenger lunatics." They both shared a laugh. It was common knowledge how most of the runners had qualms about basic communication.

"But in all seriousness," Lynara pointed at the door that now looked as solid as ever, "no one can hear us, right? Gods forbid one of our messengers pass by while we're talking."

Neveah shook her head. There was still a smile on her lips. "That's why Gredian officials prefer the Convexus over private rooms at the castle. Although it's a short walk, it's also quite a scenic route. Furthermore, the rooms here are sealed with ancient magic similar to that used in the dungeons. The conditions are much more preferable."

The head summoner gestured toward the soup and potatoes on the table. "Speaking of which, why don't you have a bite? The bakery doesn't only produce bread and cake."

Lynara nodded and sat. The leather was oddly cool, even when it made contact with her clothes instead of her skin. It still seemed like a bother if Neveah herself had come; the information she was about to relay was either highly important or ... or what? The commander lifted the bowl to her lips, silently brooding until the delicious flavor of the broth snapped her out of it.

"Quite the delectable treat, isn't it?" Neveah said as if she could read Lynara's mind. The summoner took a seat across from the commander.Lynara could only nod as she finished the soup. She would have basked quite enjoyably in the delightful aftertaste, had there not been a high-ranking official in the same room. A question suddenly came to mind as she set the bowl down lightly.

"If the Convexus is so popular, how come I've never been here before?" Lynara asked. She stabbed her fork through a slice of potato.

Neveah tapped her chin lightly, pearlescent eyes drifting toward the corner of the room. "It's normal. Many court members still haven't learned of it yet, and they've been there for longer than you have. The Convexus's dark facade may also appear ..." She waved her hand around again as she searched for the right word, "... arcane. Dismal. Austere to many. Thus, it's not often brought up in conversations regarding meeting places.

They would prefer the sunlit offices of the castle, despite the risk of eavesdropping."

"And despite the remarkable food here," Lynara added as she swallowed the potato and poked another. "If soup and potatoes are this good, I can only imagine what the fancier dishes offer."

Neveah chuckled. "But the Convexus isn't what I came here to tell you about, of course. It's mostly about the search for Colonel Nevermoon and the Fey."

Lynara nodded. She was eager to hear whatever news the court wanted Neveah to relate.

"In terms of the search mission," Neveah crossed her legs and clasped her knee elegantly, "the court of Gredian has decided to exclude the Fey from operation objectives. In other words, once the soldiers secure Colonel Nevermoon, they need only return to the castle for the interrogation. Whether or not the Fey is eliminated during the capture is not of the empire's concern."

"What about information security?" Lynara asked as she ate another potato slice. "Chai—Colonel Nevermoon wouldn't have disclosed any Gredian war plans, would he?"

"I'm quite certain he hasn't. Colonel Nevermoon isn't the type to grant his trust to a mere stranger, nor is he the variety to hold a grudge against the empire, even after an attempt at execution."

Lynara nodded. Of course. She silently scolded herself; Lynara of all people should know the colonel the best.

Neveah shifted, balancing her chin lightly on her hand as she faced the fire. The flames drew patterns across the summoner's skin.

"Additionally, there have been recent sightings of the pair on the border of Mirstone and Valport. Mirstone's not a very large area, so I recommend you alert the troops there."

Lynara crossed her ankles and stretched, excited by the prospect of soon catching the fugitives. "May I borrow a few of your forces for a quicker capture?"

"I've already prepared a few of my summoners. You may use them for the reweraa and lugaires. You'll find them in the west summoner wing of the castle."

Lynara stood and checked her watch. If she didn't leave now, she'd be late for the next meeting. "Thank you, Neveah. If that concludes our meeting, then I'd best be on my way."

The summoner stood as well, easily a head taller than Lynara. She held out her hand and Lynara took it, noticing briefly just how cold her skin was. Neveah smiled.

"I enjoyed our discussion today, Commander Merran." The summoner let her arm drop to her side. "If time allows, I have one more thing to add."

Lynara raised a brow.

"Once you're finished with your private business, maybe during the afternoon, why don't you meet me in the courtyard? There's something else I'd like to tell you." Neveah still had time? It struck Lynara as fairly odd since the woman didn't usually offer personal encounters, due to her hectic schedule. Lynara thought perhaps it was the summoner's day off, but then she realized there hadn't been one as far as she recalled. Maybe she just wasn't paying enough attention to her friend's endeavors.

Lynara smiled. She slid out the door as it immediately dissipated into thin air before her very eyes.

"Of course."

"ALERT TROOPS at the border of Mirstone and Valport—send some reweraa too. Apparently lugaires aren't enough."

The summoners nodded. Their darkened robes disappeared with them into the building.

"Commander, the messengers just have to get their rides, and then we will be ready to depart at your command," a slightly plump woman said. A pair of glasses sat atop her head.

"Use the kymatis. They're the quickest option that we have right now," Lynara ordered. The woman rushed off to relay the information to the summoners.

The only reason Lynara Merran was chosen amid the pool of other commanders was because, out of them, she knew Chais Nevermoon the best. Plus, as she was the commander of the Steelwing Squadron, they had a higher chance of finding the runaways, due to the Steelwings' skillfulness in tracking and espionage. Lynara sighed. She had known Chais well before, but that had since worn out. She tried to shove the guilt down and return to the task at hand.

The messengers would oversee alerting the troops near Valport and Mirstone so that the capture would be more effective. It wouldn't take long, and it was drawing near the evening. Chais and his Fey friend couldn't keep moving forever. She glanced at the door leading into the castle, the place where the on-call summoners had disappeared into. The Gredian soldiers and their renowned summoners worked hand in hand. No force had more authority than the other, and they often fought together on the battlefield. Although the soldiers were greater in number, the summoners generally beat them in individual strength, so the powers were balanced. However, the empire was beginning to see change. There was a continued usage of demons and an influx of summoner apprentices. The number of humans who depended on monsters from another world had been increasing dramatically since the fall of the previous king. Transportation now relied heavily on demon creatures. With the war having dragged on for years, there was no guarantee that the demon seals, wherever they were, were safe.

The quiet was suddenly disturbed by an ear-splitting shriek. Lynara instinctively looked to the darkening skies overhead. With a wingspan larger than the average crow, the cluster of demon hawks almost blocked out the setting sun. Their wings left behind tendrils of residual darkness, and their eyes glowed murderous scarlet. Lynara could never stop being impressed at the sheer power that not only these creatures held, but every demon that the summoners could take control of. One slash of those razor-sharp talons or beak could easily leave a human torn in two. Thankfully, reweraa were somewhat easier to control than some other demons—it all depended on the skill level of the summoner.

The aerial predators flew in wide, lazy circles. Each beat of the wing unleashed a muted but powerful force. They were probably following the orders of the summoners, as the reweraa weren't the only thing being brought out from the demon world. Their masters would be out soon. The summoned usually didn't stray too far from the summoner—with a few exceptions.

As if on cue, the raven-like demons stopped circling and shot out like a flash of light toward the west. Lynara pivoted on her heel to see a group of massive beasts. Their dark aura ate up the air around them. The horse-like demons approached like imposing giants, their willpower connected to whichever person had summoned them. Messengers climbed onto their backs, one human for every demon.Kymatis. A demon species discovered earlier on. Lynara had seen the beasts in action, and their piercing sharp teeth and hooves created a very formidable enemy. The kymatis were larger than an average draft horse and could reach much higher speeds than a racehorse. As the summoners climbed onto their own mounts, Lynara kept her distance from the kymatis. Only those riding were relatively safe from the creatures.

"We're all set. Remember, the colonel is our first priority." Lynara gave the captain summoner, a spirited warrior named Anwarah, a salute from her position by the entrance to the castle. After a few brief moments, the messengers set off first, leaving Anwarah and her summoning troupe. Summoners often stayed behind or in the middle of an army, but depending on the summoned demon, it could be better to command from the frontlines. With reweraa and kymatis at their disposal, small groups of attackers wouldn't do the mission much harm. Summoners were a vital part of battle for a reason.

"Commander Merran!" Lynara turned to see Anwarah standing next to her demon. Darkness radiated off of the horse in waves. Anwarah waved animatedly, freckles spilling over her tan cheeks like stars. "Don't worry! We'll get him back for you!"

"What are you going off about?" Lynara hissed playfully. The Steelwings were always a better squadron to command, compared to some others that she had the "privilege" of overseeing for a mission or two.

The summoner laughed and swung onto the kymatis with practiced ease, despite it being so tall. She gave Lynara a two-fingered salute before signaling the rest of the group. Men and women alike called out their farewells as the creatures set off. The herd of kymatis stormed forward. Lynara could see their blood-red eyes and knife-edged fangs as they tossed their heads back.

Like a shadow made quicker by the sun, the demons glided out of sight, leaving behind wisps of what appeared to be blackened smoke. The darkness dissipated within seconds.

"Uh, Commander Merran?" Lynara turned. She didn't recognize the voice, so she knew it wasn't one of her soldiers. The person who called was a young man, definitely in his teens. He was wearing an apprentice summoner robe—so that was why she didn't know who he was. But why was he here?

"That's me."

"Miss Neveah wants to, uh, meet later in the evening. After … after dinner," the apprentice said.

"Oh. All right. If that's all, you may go."

Odd, she thought to herself as she watched him scurry away. Neveah typically didn't alter appointments, whether they were casual or not.

AS THE MEETING with Neveah drew closer, Lynara paced her room nervously. Dinner had already finished, although it was a very unpleasant one—meeting with important figures from places outside Gredian and Atrelia was always quite boring. Adaric had been at the head of the table as always, jabbering away about topics that had already been addressed or ones that were being confronted. Dinner didn't worry the commander though. It was the fact that it had been hours since the Steelwings set off—and she still hadn't received word. The first time that Chais and the Fey escaped from her clutches, she was pissed, but a second time? Lynara hated being outdone, again and again. It was all she ever knew when she was growing up in Silvermount.

Lynara glanced at the clock one last time and decided to go meet Neveah. It still puzzled her as to why the summoner wanted to converse, but she hoped it would prove to be a good break from all the drama that was happening in the castle.

Lynara drew her coat tighter around her shoulders before treading toward the courtyard. Clouds of frigid breath floated before her face. It didn't take long to locate the powerful summoner.

The silver markings on Neveah's face were easy to spot, as they had a natural glow to them. She still had her summoner robes on. Dark cloth flowed to the ground like a midnight waterfall. Although Neveah had added a white fur collar, it still seemed too cold outside for her choice of clothing.

The tall woman fell into step with the commander and took the directional lead.

"I'm still surprised you can do that," Lynara said.

"Do what? This?" Neveah's face dimmed, then lit up, brighter than before. She chuckled. "I'm not even sure how. It's like controlling a new limb. You just … know."

Lynara nodded and stuffed her hands deeper into the warmth of her pockets. Spring was just beginning to make its way to Gredian, so she wouldn't be surprised if more snow fell that night. They followed the neat cobblestone path for a while in comfortable silence; Lynara hoped Neveah would begin the conversation first, but when she didn't, Lynara decided to take charge.

"So, why'd you call me? You usually don't have much free time, what with the war going on and all."

Neveah surveyed their surroundings—a bit too cautiously, Lynara thought.

"I just wanted to check in with you, see how the search is going. You seemed agitated during our meeting today, and I'm quite intrigued as to whether or not it's turning out to be a success."

But Lynara knew, somehow, that it wasn't about the search. Well at least, not entirely.

"I haven't gotten word back yet ..." Lynara began, keeping an eye on Neveah's peculiar behavior.

The head summoner cast a glance into a darkened part of the courtyard. The place was usually deserted at this time, so why was she checking? For someone, or ... something?

"—But I'm sure they'll catch Nevermoon this time," Lynara finished. She was wholly aware that Neveah was more on edge than usual.

"Well, ever since I've known you, whenever you say you're sure, it's a certain outcome." Neveah smiled. "So, I'll trust you on that."

Lynara was just about to reply when a strange scraping sound escaped from the passage to the left of them. The summoner grabbed Lynara and drew both herself and the commander to relative safety. Noticing that Neveah was now staring past the bend of the wall, into the passageway, Lynara followed suit. Her breath caught when she saw what was happening.

Dark shadows manifested themselves into an indistinguishable form, red eyes prominent against the night. The very sight of it, whatever it was, sent shivers down Lynara's spine. Its aura poured across the passage, flooded with darkness and evil. It didn't take a genius to see that the foreign creature, or entity, was powerful. Extremely powerful. And *enormous*. The demon seemed to make eye contact with Neveah, and a glowing smile stretched out across its remains of a face.

It took Lynara a few moments to locate a figure slumped before the mass of corruption, his eyes closed.

Adaric.

CHAPTER

FOURTEEN

THE SMELL OF BLOOD clogged the air. Rebme wrinkled
her nose and pulled her scarf up to cover the lower half of her
face. What happened here? She approached the area cautiously
and narrowed her eyes, trying to make out the vague shapes in
the dim moonlight. Were those bodies? Violet eyes widening,
Rebme rushed over; the soil was still wet. Whatever occurred
was recent. The moonlight glinted off the bodies, reflected by the
armor they were wearing. They must have been soldiers. Dread
pressed heavily against her ribs. Rebme kneeled next to the nearest body and pressed her fingers against its neck, searching for a
pulse. Her fingers came away wet with blood. She braced herself
and rolled the body over. The symbol of Gredian was printed

on a red handkerchief hanging from his belt, the arrow and key blotched with blood blending it in with the background.

Rebme moved onto the other bodies. They had the same armor, all except one. A young man, maybe eighteen years old, tall and lanky in frame, wore a dark robe with thick leather armor beneath it. Inky tendrils of smoke curled in wisps off the ends of his robe. Rebme recognized it as residue from recent summoning, which meant that the boy was a summoner. The only reason so many soldiers and a summoner would be out here in the middle of Mirstone was the fugitive ex-colonel and the Fey, Elwood Zefire, who helped him escape in the first place. Chais and his companion were nowhere to be seen. They had either successfully evaded the guards or were now being dragged back to the capital—back to Adaric—in chains.

Rebme sighed. Great. If *she* found out that the boy-colonel and his little Fey friend were captured in her area, she was never going to hear the end of it. Rebme considered lying about it, but a shiver down her spine warned her just how much more terrifying the woman could be if she found out Rebme had lied to her. She unconsciously rubbed her arm, where goosebumps had risen. She could already feel *her* metallic gaze pinned on her, a ghost of a smile gracing *her* lips. Creepy lady. Rebme tugged irritably on her scarf and prepared to give her employer the news.

Dark wisps of smoke started to gather before her in an inky mass, a pitch blackness that seemed to swallow even the dim moonlight. The shape twisted and spun lazily. It stretched out into an onyx orb that pulled at her core. A single black demon materialized on her outstretched arm. Red eyes watched her expectantly, washing its beak in a hellish crimson light, as if the bird had dipped it in fresh blood. The reweraa ruffled its smoke-like feathers and waited. Wisps of pure darkness curled off it, spinning away hypnotically.

"Go tell Master that Nevermoon is probably on his way to the capital. The Fey is most likely dead—" Rebme stopped. She strained her senses toward the faint groan that had broken the otherwise silent evening. Her reweraa stood statue still, ruby eyes locked onto the source of the disturbance. "Go check it out." She ordered and reached for the whip curled by her side. Her power spiraled inward, in case she needed to summon something bigger. The large bird fluttered toward the noise. It landed by a body that she hadn't noticed until now. The body's dark hair and clothing had shielded it from sight. Rebme knelt carefully by the body and rolled it gently onto its side. A pale, young face was revealed, his features too fine and sharp to be completely human. Under the glow of the moonlight, he seemed to shimmer with unearthly beauty. The slight flutter of hair against his face proved he was still alive. Rebme reached out and carefully brushed a blood-crusted strand of hair back. She inhaled sharply as she took in the slender pointed ear. A Fey.

"I take that back; the Fey is alive. I'll bring him to the meeting point as soon as he is well enough to travel." Rebme spoke out loud, knowing her summon would relay her message. Summons were good at following simple orders, and reweraas specialized in communication. However, she didn't trust most summons to send important messages—two summoners could theoretically summon the same creature and order them to replay all the messages they'd ever received and sent. Her rewearaa was different in the sense that only Rebme and her master could use it. It was essentially the most secure form of communication in the country.

Rebme reached down and unbuckled her leather satchel. From it, she pulled out some gauze and bandages, in case she needed them. Zefire's eyes fluttered open as she stripped off his outer coat to assess the damage. Emerald eyes gazed at her, clouded and unfocused with pain. Rebme's normally steady hands stuttered at the sheer amount of blood that had seeped into his shirt. A wooden shaft ending in the iron tip of a spearhead jutted from his navel—if it hadn't plugged the wound, the Fey would have bled out. A bandaged stump where his right arm should be was completely hardened with blood. Carefully, she peeled away the dirty bandages, feeling the dried blood flake beneath her fingernails. Ugly purple scar tissue stretched thinly over bone. Pus and blood oozed from multiple areas. The healing skin must have broken during the fight, and the time spent in the mud definitely hadn't helped. Rebme pulled out her water canister and cleaned the wound as best she could. The moment the cold liquid hit his shoulder, Zefire flinched violently, eyes still hazy with pain and confusion but much more lucid than just moments before.

"Don't move, I'm an ... ally of Colonel Nevermoon." The Fey seemed to have heard her but continued to struggle against her grasp. If he had been in even slightly better shape, she would have lost the fight without question. However, in his weakened and most possibly feverish state, she was able to stop him from breaking free.

"Listen, if I wanted you dead, I would have killed you already. Instead, I'm helping you." Rebme grunted and pressed the immortal against the ground. "So stop moving, and try to be grateful." Her words finally seemed to get through, as her opponent stopped struggling. Either that or the movement had exhausted him, and he had passed out from exertion.

His eyes fluttered closed as his body fell limp. Rebme cleaned the wound, applied her herbal medicine, and wrapped it. She could stitch him up later, hopefully in a more sterile environment. Bandaging a few lacerations, she smeared gauze over the larger wounds—long gouge marks down his back and deep teeth marks that appeared to have come from lugaires. Those would need stitches later as well. Incredibly, some of the smaller scratches were already closing. There was no longer any doubt who this Fey was; with such powerful regeneration, he had to be a demon seal. But even with such incredible regeneration, Rebme could tell that the spear wound was serious. Slowly healing iron burns lined the edges of the wound.

Rebme grabbed the spearhead end of the weapon and snapped off the head. The barely conscious Fey growled as it jolted into his body. She then pushed him onto his side and ripped the shaft out, feeling the wooden body slide through flesh before popping out. Rebme tossed it aside and wrapped the wound as tightly as she could. She would take care of the rest when they were in a cleaner environment.

Rebme sank her focus deeply within herself and pulled at the dark pool of power that pulsed right below her heart. A form twisted before her, the same as when she had summoned the rewerra. Only this time, it didn't stop once; it was the size of a large hawk. The air continued to expand and shimmer as the otherworldly substance ate away at her strength. Once it had reached a good nine feet tall and eight feet wide, it started to take form: a long, curved neck leading down to powerful muscles, muscles that flowed seamlessly into its hindquarters and legs, hooves that glimmered as if dipped in steel and then sharpened dug into the blood-soaked earth, ruby eyes glowed dimly as it snorted, baring sharp, needle-like teeth.

As the kymatis solidified and the servitude bond snapped into place, Rebme positioned herself as best she could to slide the Fey warrior's limp body onto the beast. She half dragged, half carried the man onto her summon, trying not to upset his numerous wounds. After she was sure he was secure, she scavenged through the dead soldier's belongings. After all, the dead didn't need possessions. A beautifully crafted bow made of a strange silvery material lay on the blood-soaked earth. It undoubtedly belonged to the Fey warrior. She would return it later.

ZEFİRE WAS STİLL ASLEEP, and Rebme feared that if he didn't wake soon, he might never wake up at all. His wounds had healed nicely, and the fever had passed in the few days he had been under her care. The spear wound was the biggest issue. While all the other wounds healed at unnatural speeds, the iron slowed down the healing significantly; she would need to tap the depths of her medical knowledge to keep him alive. Thank goodness her master had forced her to learn and perform simple surgeries on people before.

Rebme yawned and stood up from the hardwood chair she had been occupying for hours while keeping an eye on the Fey's recovery. She left the room to clean up and make herself a poor excuse of a breakfast before going back to tend Zefire. Rebme entered her small bathroom and washed her face. She tried not to look at her reflection; she knew exactly what she would see: a girl with messy honey brown hair that tumbled down in curls that brushed her shoulders. Her amethyst eyes glowed against her bronze skin. They were not the features of Gredian—the empire's people had skin ranging from pale to a slight tan, while Fey in Atrelia had pale to golden skin. She did not have the features of any bronze-skinned race either. The continent of Xilan held people with tan and bronze skin, but they had wide upturned eyes of pure amber, rounded faces, and small noses. This girl had hooded eyes of the sharpest purple: the features of Pixies—the island people.

Rebme brushed her hair behind her ear and tugged her white hood over her head. Her eyes were cast into shadow. Just as she was about to leave the bathroom, she heard a painful thud, followed by a string of curses in multiple languages. Zefire was awake, it would seem. Rebme adjusted her scarf and reentered the bedroom, where the Fey had rested for the last three days. The scene that greeted her was wholly unimpressive. Somehow, he had managed to tie himself inside his blanket and bedsheets, fall out of the bed, *and* rip at least three of his stitches … if the blood slowly staining her sheets and floor said anything.

"Good, you're awake. I thought you were going to slip into a coma," Rebme said. Her finger traced the fraying edges of her scarf. Zefire stared at her for a moment before starting to frantically untangle himself. When he only succeeded in worsening the situation, he gave up and leaned against the side of the bed, looking very calm and composed for someone tied up in blankets and bleeding on a stranger's floor.

"Who are you? What happened?" the Fey asked. His green eyes were piercing as they met Rebme's. A puzzled expression graced his face as he took in her features and compared them to the database of races he knew. He found no match. She could see his suspicion grow.

"Rebme Luxdare. As for what happened, I'm hoping you would tell me," Rebme answered lightly. She walked over with painfully deliberate and causal steps, projecting each move beforehand, so as not to startle the Fey even more.

"I—" Elwood frowned. "Why should I trust you?" he asked instead of answering. His eyes narrowed.

"My … master wishes to help the colonel. And since you are his companion, I would guess he is probably on his way to the gallows as we speak, I suggest you let me help. Start by telling me what happened and how long your recovery time will be." Rebme needed more information before she could start planning for a Silvermount castle-dungeon break-in.

"Well, we failed to evade the soldiers," Elwood answered. He shrugged with his left shoulder. "And at the moment, I really don't know—maybe two or three days before I can use my powers to their full extent. So, a full week before my wounds are 100 percent healed … apart from the arm. I can't regrow limbs." Rebme watched him coldly.

"Zefire, I am going to untangle you from this mess you made, so I would appreciate it if you didn't struggle," she said. Injured patients, especially warriors, needed to be handled with care. Zefire watched her for a moment before nodding his assent.

"Call me Elwood. Zefire makes me sound old." Elwood wriggled out of the blanket at last. "I'm guessing your master told you my name?" Rebme hummed in confirmation and gestured for him to get back onto the bed. When he paused in confusion, she sighed heavily. He was one of *those* patients.

"You tore my stitches, and your wounds need to be cleaned. So I need to you take off your top and do exactly as I say." She moved to the medical cabinet by the bed and pulled out rolls of fresh bandages, gauze, a needle, thread, and matches.

"I'm good. I swear. I'd rather not have a stranger stick a

needle into me." Elwood slowly backed away, frantically searching for a quick exit.

"Get on the bed and sit down, you imbecile," Rebme growled. Her eyes glowed a bright purple, and a dark summoning residue surrounded her small form. "You are my patient. That means that you either do what I say or I put you under and do it anyway."

Elwood stared for a moment before quietly plopping himself back onto the bed. He eyed her warily.

"Thank you." She allowed the aura of shadows to retreat and walked to his bedside, ready to start working.

"So … you're a summoner, huh?" Elwood asked after far too many moments of him sitting shirtless while Rebme probed him with gauze. She nodded and heated her needle, sterilizing it before threading it with practiced ease.

"I'm going to stitch the bite wound first, so don't move." She leaned over, wiped off the blood with a warm towel, and started to piece the broken skin and muscle back together.

"So, who is your master? What is her relationship with Chais?" Elwood hissed as the needle entered but didn't move. Many scars littered his body, and there would definitely be more when these healed.

"They worked together. And they have a mutual … friend," Rebme explained as she tied and cut the last stitch. "That one's done. Once I'm finished, I want you to keep sleeping. You'll need your rest if we are going to storm the capital."

"Yes, doc." Elwood flashed Rebme the cheekiest smile she had seen since Anwarah. This was certainly going to be interesting, now that the Fey was conscious.

CHAPTER

FIFTEEN

DON'T YOU EVEN THINK *about telling them anything!*

"Damn it!" Chais hissed. He struggled to see his interrogator through the spots that flooded his vision. Aldridge's constant reminders to stay quiet didn't help, and frankly, he was offended that the dead Fey saw him as so mentally weak. His sweat-soaked skin felt feverish against the cold wall behind him; his wrists and ankles burned.

Another scream ripped from his throat as pain, simmering like molten fire in his veins, flared throughout his body. Frigid fingers tilted his face up, but all Chais could see were blotches of scarlet, like blood. The voice cut through the fog in his brain.

"Who is the Fey, and why did he help you?" Lynara Merran pressed. A tone of impatience ghosted behind her every word.

Elwood. Was he okay? What happened? After the lugaire poison had hit, Chais could only recall blood, screams, fear, and …

When Chais didn't reply, she glanced quickly at the door behind her, then back.

"Answer me, dammit!" Lynara said loudly, much louder than she needed to. Chais gritted his teeth. Her voice made his head ache.

"I wouldn't tell you, even if I knew!" he spat and glared at the kaleidoscope of color that was the commander. Lynara stared into his eyes for a few moments before backing up. Chais barely registered the light prickle in his arm, and then a brand new wave of agony completely overwhelmed his senses. Ropes dug into his wrists as he strained against them. A strangled sound escaped from his lips. Lynara leaned in again to ask for information when the door swung open, revealing a figure cloaked in shadows. Something told Chais this person had been outside all along.

"Amptonshire," Chais's interrogator stepped back and addressed the ruler by his last name, her tone suspicious.

"Merran. I see the colonel—former colonel," he corrected himself, "hasn't talked yet." Chais groaned at the voice, feeling too distressed at the moment to deal with the king. He trembled as the pain began to gradually die down. Adaric stepped closer and gestured toward the exit. "Step out for a moment, Commander Merran. You have other duties to attend to." Lynara lingered for a few seconds, then snorted and left the room.

The king's fingers instantly closed on his throat. There was nothing Chais could do, as his air supply cut off. Adaric's eyes were wild in the dim light of the chamber.

"You have something to hide, don't you?" His grip tightened, and Chais felt his face heat up even more from the lack of oxygen. He tried desperately to free his bound limbs; black veils began to claw at the edges of his vision. "There's something different about you, isn't there, Chais Nevermoon?" There was an ominous light dancing behind the king's eyes, something Chais knew had always existed there, no matter how hard he'd tried to hide it. The king was not a person to mess with, and no matter how many enemies Adaric managed to create, he always had the vote of the people. The masses loved him, that cunning politician. Something about his appearance, or rather how he presented himself, manipulated the population of Gredian to favor him.

"Let," Chais gasped as the ruler already began to loosen his grip, "go."

Lost air rushed freely into his lungs as Adaric stepped back. The features of his face were shadowed by the candlelight. Chais coughed and greedily drank it in, feeling the pulsing of his head begin to fade away.

I ... I might have just ...

Aldridge's voice was only a thin whisper. Chais glanced up, only to see that the king had turned around. He was oddly silent.

... Never mind.

"If you don't talk today," Adaric studied the table of syringes, "then you will soon." He approached, and his eyes burned with an internal fire. "Because now that the secret of how you murdered the king is out, you still have *so* many more mysteries to uncover."

There seemed to be something he wasn't saying. Did it have to do with the capture? Chais tried to remember what happened, but the details wouldn't come.

"I didn't murder the king!" Chais snarled. "You of all people should know—" His head snapped sideways. Only a hair's breadth of distance prevented it from colliding with the wall. Stray stars began to appear in his vision

"The hell?" Chais managed to say as soon as he recovered.

"I've always wanted to do that," Adaric sneered as blood began to drip from Chais's nose to the ground.

"Do what? Punch someone who can't counterattack? Congratulations, Ricky Boy."

The king paused, obviously angered by the comment, but he managed to ignore it as he headed for the exit. "Have fun hanging there until I send someone down."

"I will, thanks," Chais grumbled as the door closed yet again. He tilted his head back to catch the blood, not caring if that could result in sickness. Losing too much blood, especially in the case where he didn't have access to his hands, wasn't good. Torture could always get to the point of permanent wounds. His job was to not lose too much blood before that happened. The spot on his cheek where Adaric had punched him began to pulse—that would definitely be a bruise. The metallic taste at the back of his throat vanished in a few moments, something Chais owed to Aldridge. Now, to brace himself for yet another round of torture—and death. That would be the outcome of all of this, anyway, if he didn't find a way out. Chais tested the ropes. They were too thick for him to bend his wrists and too tight for him to free himself. He couldn't reach them with his teeth ... And he'd been unconscious when they tied them up, so he hadn't been able to pull any tricks there.

Someone's coming, and it's not Adaric.

The door clicked open. The first thing that Chais saw was the red hair. Lynara?

That's her.

The commander checked the hallway and silently closed the door. Lynara fixed Chais with a look, as if she wasn't impressed with something he had done.

"... Ricky Boy? Are you fucking kidding me?"

"Language. And, in my defense, it pisses him off easily." Chais hesitated. "What was that for, Nara? First time we've seen each other in years, and you respond by torturing me."

"In my defense, Adaric was waiting right outside the f—"

Chais raised both brows.

"—reakin' door."

"Why not just let me scream it out?" Chais said. He began to feel vulnerable as he hung onto the wall. Rampant thoughts ran in circles through his brain. Where was Elwood? Was he okay? Where was Elwood? Was he okay?

"Because we both know that you are a complete wreck when it comes to acting."

Chais groaned. "What are you trying to do, then?"

Lynara took a few steps toward him and placed her hands on her hips. She was contemplating something. "I'm here to get you out."

"Get me—what? I don't see how that benefits you." The commander began to untie the thick ropes on his left wrist. He and Lynara had grown apart over the years, and a part of him suspected that jealousy was the villain. This woman who he'd seen as his sister for a good portion of his life ... she was now a commander. That was a well-deserved title that she didn't need to throw away for a prisoner who had drifted out of her life many years ago.

"Let's just say that I believe you more than Adaric, and I think you're telling the truth." Lynara untied the rest of the restraints.

Chais inhaled in both pain and relief as the ropes fell to the floor, exposing the tender, abraded skin underneath. He held onto the back of a chair for support. There would be much worse—and permanent—forms of torture if he stayed any longer.

But how could he escape the castle? Even with Lynara's help, soldiers were at every turn. Unless they had some extremely convincing disguise, which they probably did not, a smooth getaway was impossible.

Well, no one said it had to be smooth.

"Stay here. There's someone I know who can help us." Lynara was already headed toward the door.

"Why are you risking yourself for me?" Chais stretched his limbs, which were quickly regaining their capabilities. The reddened skin where the ropes had dug in were already beginning to heal, although it was a relatively slow process. He would probably have to take a look at it some other time.

That is, if he made it out.

Lynara turned to face him. She had already palmed a couple of fighting knives. Her auburn eyes narrowed just slightly.

"After everything you've done for the empire, I'm sure you deserve better." She tossed Chais the knives in her grip and drew another. Then she was gone.

'Because I see you like family.' Chais sighed—what did he expect?

Weighing the blades that were now in his possession, Chais found a spot near the entrance to the chamber. He rested his fingers against the cool stone ground, muscles taut, and waited for whomever Adaric had sent to interrogate him.

A key. Chais was a demon key, a Feykin who didn't belong to any kingdom, yet he was part of the reason why the world hadn't fallen from a species that had taken so long to seal. What was waiting for him in the future? If he actually escaped, where would he live? Atrelia was the only place he could think of. Staying anywhere near Gredian was a gamble, with its power-hungry nobles who wanted nothing more than to get their hands on the keys and use that strength for their own twisted plans. Not that he knew anything about Atrelia either. The story of the five keys was well-known, but every version seemed different. Chais had only heard of the tale that favored the human race and cast the Fey in a monstrous light—creatures who only allied with humans for their own selfish desires. As for the real story of the five keys and the history of the two species, he'd have to do more research on it.

The muted scuffle of boots against stone drew him back to the matter at hand. Chais tensed and lifted the fighting knives, checking the rhythm of his breaths. Light. The footsteps were light. They possessed a hunter's stealth that a typical human couldn't achieve—someone trained to fight. Just as he'd expected, whoever it was halted before the door. A few moments passed in silence, as if they were listening, as if they knew something was wrong. There was a sound of metal sliding against leather. The door slowly creaked open. Just a couple more seconds ...

Not even a whisper of sound alerted Chais to the throwing knife that shot through the door's gap. The only thing that allowed him to register what happened was the *thunk* as it pierced the wall behind him after tearing through his shoulder. Chais darted out of the way and tried to see his attacker. Warm blood flowed down his shoulder blades. A glimpse of metal. Another stab of pain across his chest. Air rushed out of Chais's lungs as the stranger plowed into his abdomen, slamming him against the wall.

"Gods, I don't even know who you are!" Chais wheezed as he flipped his knife and ducked under his assaulter, who seemed to have momentarily frozen at his voice. Chais swiftly rammed the hilt of the blade into the attacker's throat. An elbow to the stomach, then the nose. A blow to the wrists. The clatter of weapons hitting the ground. Chais pinned his assailant. The smell of blood and sweat made him want to gag, and the gash on his shoulder pulsed with every exhausting breath. He pressed a knife to the stranger's neck, finally getting a clear view.

"Sovan?"

The man pinned to the floor seemed as surprised as Chais was. His expression faded as quickly as it had come, though, replaced with a cold mask.

"Go to hell, Chais," Sovan spat and grabbed the knife hand with shocking strength. A swift twist caused the blade to plummet to the floor. Dark eyes flashed as the man lunged for the weapon and swung it toward Chais's skull. Sparks danced for a second as Chais blocked the blow with his other knife. He grunted as he forced his body weight into it.

Sovan stumbled back and growled in frustration. Noticing that the door was wide open, the man seized the opportunity and sprinted out of the room and into the hallway. Chais staggered to his feet but cut off his chase when Sovan—or anyone else, for that matter—couldn't be seen. Chais cursed lightly and gripped the only blade he had left. This could be a massive problem.

Maybe Sovan truly believed that Chais killed Havard Avington, but that seemed like a stretch for someone like him. Sure, there were heated arguments in the past, but the warrior trained in torture never hated Chais. The blow that Chais deflected was lethal: an intention to kill.

Did something happen during the past few days? Or even before that?

"Chais!" A harsh whisper came from the end of the hallway. Chais whirled, knuckles white against the knife, then realized that it was Lynara. Her foot was on the first stair, as if she were prepared to run from an invisible disaster down the passage. Behind her, deeper into the stairwell, was the lead summoner of Gredian—Neveah.

"We don't have all freaking day," Lynara hissed. She turned as Chais began to catch up. "Did you check the surrounding area?" the commander asked Neveah, who nodded.

"The entire route to the meeting place is clear for at least the next ten minutes." With an impressive speed that outmatched many soldiers, the powerful summoner scaled the rest of the stairs. Chais followed. He applied pressure to the wound on the muscle of his shoulder, which was now bleeding profusely. The time limit made sense, seeing that the Gredian castle occupied a large area of land. To the average commoner, navigating the long halls of the castle proved to be a near-impossible challenge. Ten minutes should be enough. It depended on where Neveah was planning on taking him. However, what came as a shock to Chais was how the summoner had managed to create such a period of time where guards weren't patrolling and the citizens weren't flooding the courtyard. It must've been an alternate route. Chais hadn't lived in Silvermount for as long as some other members of the court had, so even he didn't know half of the secret places and passages that Gredian had to offer.

"Follow me," Neveah told both Lynara and Chais in a hushed tone. Her footsteps were light, almost as light as Sovan's, but she wasn't trained in combat as he had been. The summoners of Gredian faced harsh training as well, as was expected with their line of work, but it was in a completely different field than the warriors and soldiers. Where warriors trained physically, summoners trained with their minds—pulling out that dark power that was brooding from within and shaping it into a creature beyond their world.

Chais had a vague idea as to where they were located in the castle, but that didn't make the journey any less confusing. Blood leaked out from between his fingers. The pain was still there. The injuries reminded him just how easy dying was—how enemies existed, how at any given moment, the tables could violently turn.

The distant chattering of royals, or at least assumed-to-be royals, reached his ears as they neared the dining hall. There were usually guards on patrol, especially near the court members. However, with the twisted paths that Neveah led them through, there were no fatal encounters yet. The lead summoner, the commander, and the ex-colonel made for a pretty formidable team. As long as they didn't run into a large group of soldiers, they would be fine.

Almost. Almost fine.

Chais heard the lugaires before he saw them. The mass of razor-sharp teeth and glowing red eyes nearly filled the hallway that led to what he assumed was the back of the castle. Their panicked howls pierced the air as they scrambled over each other and toward the awaiting prey. If the guards hadn't heard before, then they definitely had now.

Damn, it must've been all the blood.

Get to the exit. You don't need to kill off every single lugaire.

Aldridge's voice remained calm. Chais still had the single knife.

Lynara rushed forward first and tore a wide gash across a demon's throat. Dark matter poured out of the wound. Behind

173

them, Neveah's eyes glowed a brighter silver than usual as she focused on summoning ... or was she? Nothing was being created, but something was definitely happening to the demon hounds. It slowly ate them up from the inside.

Something tells me that Neveah has the situation under control. Or, at least, she will.

"Are we supposed to meet someone outside?" Chais asked Lynara as he ducked under a swipe.

"Yeah. Your stupid ass Fey friend is still alive, which means our soldiers need a lot more training," Lynara grumbled.

Chais had no time to celebrate, however. He shifted his weight forward and plunged the knife into the hound's skull. With a sickening crunch, he pulled out the blade and faced the continued onslaught of lugaires. The wound in his shoulder was bleeding down his back, mixing with sweat that glued his tunic to his skin. It made him a beacon for bloodthirsty demons.

He instinctively brought his guard up as a demon rammed into his side, catching him off-balance. The cold marble floor came as a shock. The lugaire was on him now. Spit dripped onto his tunic. A sharp stab of pain shot across his arm. It took a few moments to realize that the hound had sunk its canines, laced with poison, into the flesh of his forearm. Chais cursed as he felt the effects begin to take place, first in his arm and then gradually throughout the rest of his body. Smelling blood, other hounds were beginning to bound toward him. Almost lethargically, Chais summoned the last of his energy and pulled the lugaire off of him before slitting its throat. His breath came in shallow gasps. The sound of drums echoed in his ears.

A group of lugaires suddenly stopped their pursuit. Their darkened forms shuddered in the long pillars of light from the windows. There was a flash of silver. In a heartbeat, the hounds had disappeared. Not even a hint of shadow residue lingered in the battle-soaked air. Neveah's eyes were now completely silver, and her arms were extended in front of her. Even more of the demons disappeared.

"Run. I'll take care of the rest," Neveah ordered as shouts from castle guards began to approach from the other hallway. Chais gave her a single nod and headed for the exit, following Lynara. She seemed to be signaling to someone outside, but it increasingly became less and less clear where she was as the poison obscured his vision. His entire upper body was going numb. The poison was easily removable, but it worked fast.

I've blocked the poison at your waist. You should be able to run for a while before it spreads.

Chais whispered a quick word of thanks to the Fey warrior in his head. He stumbled outside and squinted against the blinding light, trying to locate a group of silhouettes. Elwood. Was Elwood there?

Sorry I couldn't do more.

A screech of metal, seemingly distant, sounded from behind him. Chais listened for more—words? He couldn't hear anything behind the fog in his brain. They sure weren't here.

"Elwood! Lynara!" Chais yelled. He tried not to be too loud. The poison was already starting to slowly but surely move to his thighs. "Elwood, Lynara," he tried again, softer this time. Gods. The pounding headache was really getting to him. His vision began to distort, only adding to the nausea.

Hang in there. I'm trying to locate them.

"Hey Aldridge, I think I might pass out," Chais murmured as he found a stone wall to lean against. He had no idea where he was, but something was better than nothing.

A few more seconds. That's all I need ... hold on, I found them—

"Damn," Chais managed before the world went dark.

CHAPTER
SIXTEEN

ELWOOD *saw* Chais collapse. The colonel fell like his strings were cut, eyes dull and unfocused. Three days. Three damn days of travelling with a stranger who refused to disclose her ancestry, trying to teach his body to function again, just to save Chais. He sighed and smiled fondly. How the man survived this long was a mystery.

Elwood cut down a lugaire—where were they coming from?—and stepped toward where Chais was sprawled. The palace garden was swarming with the demon hounds. Yet, not a single summoner, apart from the one he had come with, was within sight. Nor, strangely, was a guard. Wary to avoid the teeth, Elwood tore his way through them as he tried to clear a way to the fallen colonel. He pushed through the swarm of hounds, ripping through any that got too close with a flick of his bow. Elwood kept an eye on Chais the entire time. He blasted away any dogs that neared the colonel in hopes of keeping him in one piece until Elwood could reach him. However, at the speed he was going, Elwood doubted he'd make it there before one of the lugaires got lucky and tore out either his own or the Feykin's throat. There were simply too many of them.

Rebme, seeing his predicament, held out a hand toward the pack of lugaires closest to him. Her eyes glowed faintly. Pale purple light illuminated her face. A dazed look seemed to glaze over their eyes and make them appear like dyed glass. The lugaires stumbled back before regaining their senses and turning on the remaining hellhounds. The summoner was still a mystery, but at least she was proving herself useful.

Neat trick, Relevard commented. He sounded interested in this new power. *Now, stop staring and go help the Feykin.*

"Yes, sir." Elwood rolled his eyes. "Can't you try to be nice for once in your life?" Relevard ignored him. Elwood side-stepped a lugaire but almost walked straight into another. He spun to prevent any further limb loss, resulting in its teeth tearing through his empty right sleeve. The Fey wanted to kick himself. He still wasn't fast enough, wasn't strong enough. If only he could heal faster.

"Dammit! Stupid mutt. I just got that!" Elwood frowned and beheaded the hounds with a flick of the wrist. He sighed and poked the ruined fabric lightly. He would just have to steal another one from the next village.

Elwood kneeled next to the fountain where Chais collapsed and assessed his situation. A streak of red on the wall behind the colonel gave a warning that he was injured. He pulled up a wall of air that would alert him to anyone who entered its radius. Elwood leaned down and positioned the unconscious colonel on his back like a sack of potatoes. Using his single hand to maneuver the man into a more comfortable position, he searched the chaos for a small, curly haired woman.

A streak of fur and claws came barreling at his face instead. Elwood barely ducked fast enough to avoid horrible scarring. The stench of smoke and blood clogged his senses for a moment as the hound brushed past. Its claws dragged deep gouge marks down the side of the fountain. Elwood gagged and stumbled back, miscalculating his balance with Chais draped across his shoulder and landed in an ungraceful sprawl. The hard marble ground slammed into him, and he gritted his teeth.

A head of bright red hair loomed over him. Piercing eyes glared down.

"I heard that Fey were graceful," she muttered. Her tone oozed displeasure. Were all of Gredian's people so unpleasant? Not one had given him a normal, friendly greeting so far. The lugaire he had avoided earlier skidded to a stop. It snarled and charged at them again.

"Sorry, Sweet Cheeks. I happen to be a bit lopsided at the moment. Tends to mess with your balance," Elwood grinned, watching as pure fury blazed in the woman's eyes. The sheer amount of force the soldier used to rip the dog apart caused it to combust into a cloud of smoke. The lady knew how to use those blades—he wondered what she was doing here. Was this the redhead who Rebme had talked about? The one who would aid them in their escape? She certainly matched the fiery description he had received.

Elwood choked on the foul air and couldn't help but laugh as his body tried its hardest to throw up his lungs. Tears blurred his vision as the smoke stung his eyes and his laughter and coughing irritated his spear wound. If the lady was planning on joining them, the trip back to Atrelia was going to be even more interesting than it already was. When his eyes finally stopped watering and the smoke dissipated, she was already gone. The lack of any lugaires in his immediate vicinity told him that she was probably just letting off some steam on the poor creatures. Elwood braced himself against the fountain—still bubbling cheerfully as if to mock him—and picked up the unconscious colonel again. He hoped the whole process hadn't bruised Chais too badly.

By the time Elwood found Rebme, more than half the lugaires were gone, at least a quarter were under her control, and three kymatis stood next to her. Her whip was raveled and latched onto her belt, and her purple scarf trailed down her back and rippled in a phantom wind. Hair fell into her eyes as she climbed onto the nearest horse. Her slight frame seemed even smaller upon the huge beast. Dark hooves pawed anxiously at the ground, leaving deep marks in the dirt. Elwood grimaced at the thought of what those could do to flesh.

Elwood shifted Chais onto the nearest mount and climbed on behind him. He winced as his still healing spear wound pulled painfully in protest of the movement. Elwood couldn't help but wonder what was keeping the guards or demons from overwhelming them at this very instant. In fact, there weren't even any guards to be seen, only faint echoes of boots against marble floors and shouts for order hinting at them being present at all. The summons not under Rebme's control attacked at random intervals, but they mostly wandered around in a daze, growling at anything that moved. It was almost as if their master had summoned them and had given them no clear purpose other than to wander.

"Master is keeping them muddled." Rebme's cold, flat tone answered his unasked question. The woman was perceptive; Elwood could respect her for that.

"And the guards?" he asked, curious as to just how much power over the king's army this mysterious "Master" had.

"That would be my doing," a familiar, irritated voice responded from behind him. Elwood glanced over his shoulder and saw the woman mount the steed behind his. So, the lady did have a play in this. Her garnet eyes were eerily similar to those of the demons—while theirs were red as flowing blood, hers were the dried remains. Elwood grinned at the obvious rage that simmered beneath the surface.

"Nicely done, Dewdrops! You coming with us?" He gestured for Rebme to get the steeds moving and eagerly watched as the redhead's face morphed into a livid plum, teeth bared and eyes flashing with anger. It was almost too easy!

"Why, you pointy eared bastard! I ought to rip—"

"Quiet." The woman's cursing and ranting were cut off by Rebme. Her expression was as stoic as ever. "We are about to leave castle grounds. Master has caused a distraction; as long as we don't draw attention to ourselves, we can leave the city easily." Elwood sighed reluctantly. Well, he could mess with the redhead later.

... You actually stopped talking! I didn't know that was possible. Relevard took the moment to declare himself in all of his bossy-ass glory. Why couldn't the dead spirit ever just be quiet and stay quiet? Or at least say something nice whenever he did decide to talk?

The kymatis trotted through the panicking city at a steady pace, slowly picking up speed as they cleared ground faster than any mortal horse. The shrieks of fear seemed to rise from every building. What kind of chaos did Rebme's master create to cause such commotion? The summoner didn't even bat an eye when a door blew open and a group of people tumbled out. Each scrambled to climb over the others. The growl of some unseen beast echoed from within the shop. A small stand with dyed clothes was thrown haphazardly into the middle of the street, adding to the clutter of panicking people and spilled goods. Their kymatis leaped and wove through the area without slowing down. Fruit crunched under their hooves. The rest of the city was in similar disarray. Guards were too busy trying to comfort noblewomen and fend off the beasts that frightened them to even notice the three steeds racing through the streets.

Elwood used the opportunity to check Chais for the source of the blood. With his one hand, he struggled to remove the dirty, shredded tunic. It offered little protection and would just serve to hide wounds that might require immediate attention.

Elwood tucked the shirt into his belt and awkwardly locked the unconscious man in place with his knees. He carefully examined him for injuries. Small lacerations littered his body, most already clotting. A nasty bruise curled around his neck—he was choked. A bruise on the cheek. Nothing to worry about unless it jarred loose a tooth. The more serious wounds included a row of teeth marks, a knife wound on the shoulder, and a thin slice across his chest. The last wound didn't seem too deep, but it was bleeding far too much to be safe. It would probably need some medical attention. Shame that his own medical knowledge ended at 'stop the red stuff that is pouring out of the hole in the body.'

He really didn't know how bad the wound was, other than the fact that it was bleeding a lot. It didn't smell infected, but that didn't mean it wasn't at risk. Good thing they had someone with them now who could pass as a medic.

Scars, both faint and white with age and new and flaming red, crisscrossed his chest and back. Nothing less was expected from a soldier, especially one that probably spent the better part of his childhood in the war zone. Considering the man's former rank as a colonel, and despite the fact he couldn't have been more than in his twenties (and even that was stretching it), he had to have started at a ridiculously young age. What kind of parent would allow that? Elwood glared at the scars, as if they could tell him the story.

"You should really stop using your body as a shield," Elwood muttered. He eyed a thick knot of scar tissue that slashed across Chais's stomach, as if someone had tried to gut him. His own gut wound twinged in sympathy.

Elwood continued his check for injuries. A number of recent burn marks, probably from whatever interrogation he was put under once he had been recaptured, stood red and ugly. The skin was curled back and blackened. At least burn wounds didn't bleed. The very method kept them clean and cauterized; some salve and herbs and they would heal over well. Rebme was sure to have some.

Elwood shifted Chais slightly and looked at the wound causing the majority of the blood. A deep bite mark pumped blood. It also explained the man's state. Lugaire poison was not deadly, not unless the dosage was incredibly high. However, it acted fast and caused paralysis and eventually a loss of consciousness. It worked slower on Fey and required a higher dosage, but a bite mark as deep as the one on Chais's arm was more than enough to knock a man out. And despite Chais's position as a demon seal and the Fey blood that ran through his veins, he was still partly human.

After a few rounds in the bloodstream and a lot of water, the poison's effects wore off. The Fey warrior knew from experience—both on the battlefield and just recently on that road in the forest—that the colonel would wake up with a headache and numb fingers, but those would wear off sooner or later. It left no permanent effect on the body, except for a scar where the poison had entered the flesh in the first place. Looking at the man, however, Elwood felt that it wouldn't even be noticed. It would blend right into the patches of scar tissue that painted his body.

Elwood tore the tunic into uneven strips—it was hard with one hand and on a moving horse—and bound the chest wound first. He wrapped the cloth tightly and staunched the blood flow as best he could. Chais flinched under his touch but didn't awaken. The man's brain was too busy trying to keep his heart and lungs moving to notice much else. Elwood took his water pouch and dumped a generous portion onto the colonel's bite wound. The summoner would scold him for using so much of their water, but they would just have to get more. Swirls of liquid dripped from the arm resting on his lap; the angle at which it was bent looked very uncomfortable, but it was the best Elwood could do at the moment. He checked for the number and severity of the bite wounds before tying the cloth so tightly that Chais's skin turned white from the lack of blood flow. He'd get Rebme to stitch it up later. The injuries looked a lot worse than they were—mostly just a lot of blood. The flesh wasn't too ripped, nor were any major arteries punctured. For now, Elwood would try his best to keep the man from bleeding out.

Death by exsanguination was a rather horrible way to go—the feeling of not having enough oxygen to feed your starving brain while still breathing. Elwood took Chais's weight off his numbing legs and wrapped the arm around his waist, holding the colonel upright and trying his best not to think of how awkward the position was. He instead focused on the shoulder wound that was now completely ruining his coat. Elwood used the last strip of relatively clean tunic and looped it over and around the arm. He tied it with a jerk of his head and his teeth.

Elwood looked down at his handiwork and felt a trickle of doubt sink in his stomach. Blood was still leaking out from beneath the makeshift bandages. It stained his fingers, drying under his fingernails and crusting. In fact, the amount of blood still seeping out was rather worrisome. Surely it shouldn't be bleeding this much, not if Aldridge was doing his job and healing him. Maybe Elwood could help out with the process, just in case the seal key was too exhausted to use his powers.

"Hey, Relevard?" Elwood said quietly, not wanting the ladies up ahead to hear him talking to himself. He didn't trust them enough yet to reveal such an important part of his existence, even if he strongly suspected that Rebme already knew. They had long since passed the gates, seeing as the guards hadn't even been there to stop them. The soldiers had all been swarming into the city to control the mayhem.

Yes? Relevard responded, *And before you ask, no, you can't heal the Feykin. Even if I do lend you my power, you don't have any previous knowledge about transferring power. You've only ever done it with me; even then, it was me transferring to you. You were merely receiving it. Giving is drastically different. You have poor control over your own powers to begin with. And without his consciousness to receive you on the other side, you can risk burning yourself out or overloading him.*

"You could've just told me that I couldn't do it," Elwood said under his breath, annoyed at the not-so-subtle insult from Relevard. He glanced down at Chais and hoped that the quickly darkening bandages looked worse than they were. "No need for a lecture."

I apologize.

Elwood blinked. What? Did the bastard just say he was sorry?

Knowing your stubbornness, I assumed that unless I gave you a detailed reason as to why you wouldn't be able to accomplish such a feat, you would just try it anyway, with or without my power to aid you.

There it was. He should have known better than to think that Relevard would apologize. Maybe Elwood's brain was still fogged by the inhalation of demon smoke from earlier. It would explain why he even considered that his soul's roommate—Body-mate? Brainmate?—would have regretted the action. Of all the keys he could have gotten, why was it the one with the bossy attitude who hated his guts? How had his father dealt with the general for over a good five hundred years without going insane? He had received the stupid spirit just a few years ago, and he didn't know how much longer he could stand the thing.

The trees were beginning to thicken, Elwood realized, and he smiled as the scents of pine, grass, and dirt flooded his senses. He inhaled deeply. He could feel any remaining adrenaline settle as the scent soothed his mind. The only thing missing was the smell of cinnamon. Elwood shifted Chais slightly and let his tense muscles relax, now that he knew they were in relative safety. The Feykin's injuries could be taken care of by the summoner and healer; there was no point in fretting over something he could not fix.

The horse beneath him galloped across the narrow forest path as if it were an open field. Elwood had lost track of how long they'd been moving, but the sun was no longer where he last saw it. Soon they were going to have to dismount. Even demon horses couldn't travel through forests for long. Elwood sighed as he leaned against the Feykin and thought of the long journey ahead. The warmth radiating from the colonel was actually quite comfortable. Elwood enjoyed silent laughter at the thought of how Chais would react when he woke up in this position.

As if his thoughts had reached the man, Chais stirred. A faint moan escaped his lips as his eyes cracked open, glazed blue eyes staring without seeing at the road in front of him. His hair fell into his eyes as he swayed in rhythm with the horse. Elwood released his death grip on the man and watched him with interest. Chais certainly was something to have shaken off the effects of the venom so quickly. He also had good riding instincts, better than good if he could ride through sheer muscle memory. Elwood wondered how good his other instincts were.

Ignoring every logical warning in his mind, Elwood leaned forward. The colonel smelled thick with blood and stress still radiated off of him, but under that, Elwood could catch a faint wisp of the ocean. His lips nearly brushed the Feykin's ear—he still hadn't noticed his presence!—and Elwood whispered as lightly as he could.

"Morning, Sleeping Beauty!" The result was immediate. Chais's sapphire eyes cleared. Confusion and fear flashed across his face. Without even identifying whatever threat might be near him, he lashed out. An elbow to Elwood's stomach left him reeling, and his wound burned and boiled as he choked out a scream of pain. His eyes widened. He had not expected such a fast and violent reaction. Before Elwood could recover, a solid mass slammed into his cheek, and he felt himself falling. Dammit! The Feykin just punched him off a horse! he thought in a voice that didn't belong to Relevard. Elwood tucked into a semi-graceful roll when he hit the ground and pulled himself to his feet. His single arm braced his stomach.

"Dammit," he cursed as Chais and the others disappeared. Elwood spat out blood from his mouth—whether it was from his tooth cutting into his cheek or something much worse, he didn't know—and prayed that the elbow to the stomach wasn't hard enough to rupture something. "Dammit."

You deserved that, Relevard stated in a perfect monotone. It only pissed Elwood off more. He sat down and gently probed his cheek, checking to make sure all his teeth were still in place.

CHAPTER
SEVEΠTEEΠ

THE FIRST THIΠG that Chais felt when he came to was the wind.

There was way too much for it to be normal, he decided, as goosebumps began to rise on his arms. He was moving—that was for sure—and at a speed which made the forest blur into a colorful palette. Dark matter beneath him. Solid, but at the same time not exactly there ... a kymatis, then. Last he remembered, the metallic smell of his own blood had been—

"Morning, Sleeping Beauty!"

Panic instinctually flared through Chais's system at the unexpected presence. Without thinking, he felt the muscles in his arm react until his elbow connected with an object. He twisted and drove his fist into the relative head area. When he was sure there was no one else with him, he began to relax. The brief burst of adrenaline died down as quickly as it had begun. Chais's poison-muddled brain didn't process a single moment of the encounter.

Gods, everything was numb. Everything. Aldridge might as well have been dead; not even a whisper of his voice slipped into his mind. The seal was probably exhausted from all the energy dispelled to keep Chais alive until he could be healed. How Chais got onto the demon in the first place was unknown to him. Chais secured his place on the back of the creature and checked the wounds on his forearm, which were bound. With his tunic. Come to think of it, the wind felt awfully cold on his bare chest and shoulders. He suppressed the urge to immediately cover up and tried to connect the dots in his clouded brain. So, why was he riding a demon horse in the middle of a forest, half-naked?

Suddenly, pain plowed into his skull. It spread slowly to the rest of his body as the numbness dissipated. Chais cursed and doubled over, which lessened the agony. Not by much, but at least a bit. Ahead of him, he could spot ... Lynara? Her red hair and Gredian outfit was a dead giveaway. Riding on a kymatis near the commander was a woman—summoner, judging by the curls of smoke flowing out of her form—who had a more slight figure than Lynara, but Chais could tell that she had some tricks up her sleeve to overcome that. Speaking of which, where was Elwood? Hadn't Aldridge detected the Fey warrior before Chais passed out?

Ah ... That wasn't good.

The kymatis charged forward, their minds set on one command; however, demons were creatures of instinct. If they so much felt a prick of pain, they wouldn't hesitate to lash out. With those sets of teeth and hooves, no one in their right mind would mess with a kymatis. Their shadow-like way of moving didn't allow for much vertical disturbance for the rider. It was something Chais was thankful for.

"Lyn ... Lynara," Chais strained. His voice was only a cracked whisper as pain continued to lace through his body. He couldn't feel his fingers, and his arm was suspiciously numb, but any other place on his body was currently bursting with a sharp, volatile pain that ebbed and flowed in unpredictable patterns. He tried again, his muscles weak.

"Lynara!" Chais yelled, louder this time. It seemed to do the trick.

She turned her head, and her eyes widened as she realized they were now missing a member.

"The hell, Chais!" Lynara growled. Her eyes were shadowed by the trees, casting her in an even more threatening aura. "Rebme, we need to turn back now!" she hollered at the summoner riding a little ways ahead. With the hood pulled over, Chais couldn't tell what her face looked like. There was no sign of acknowledgment or indication of action from the woman. He stabilized himself as the kymatis suddenly slowed. It would have thrown him off the front if it weren't for the demon's colossal barrier of a neck. The kymatis turned—by Rebme's command—back in the direction they had come from. Now that he was in the lead, Chais scanned the passing forest fringes for a Fey. Every second they were searching, the danger became more prominent. It would take the capital a while to recover from the second escape of their "colonel," and then Adaric would be back to initiating search perimeters. Without

Lynara there to guide them, Gredian would need to find another skilled commander from the court. That wouldn't be too difficult. It would be a mistake to underestimate their forces; Chais knew that every soldier put their blood, sweat, and tears into their missions. Now, if there hadn't been a war going on, Chais doubted he would've been able to escape with his life. The empire's main focus wasn't a runaway soldier. It was a conflict that could be escalating by the day.

Chais didn't have time to analyze their surroundings, but the brightness of the day gave him an idea of how long they'd been riding. The previously cold sensation of wind on his skin died down as he grew used to their slowed pace. It was sluggish enough to expose the warm climate of the region. Sweat dripped into his eyes, a result of the oddly sweltering sun near the beginning of spring and despite the wintry nights just a few days ago. Wiping it off with his forearm, then wholly regretting it as blood mingled with his sweat, Chais wondered just how angry Elwood would be when they reached him.

There. A bundle of green, sarcasm, and attitude lounged by the side of the trail. The Fey stopped muttering to himself when he saw the shadows of monumental beasts approaching at an alarming speed.

"I see him," Chais announced. He braced himself for a torrent of verbal abuse. The kymatis decelerated until it came to a perfect stop right next to the Fey. Chais extended a hand toward Elwood. The action sent a spark of pain running up his arm, but he tried his best to ignore it. The warrior glanced at Chais's outstretched arm, then at his face.

"Hey, Elwood. Uh, sorry about that," Chais said as he forced a smile. "Instinct sucks sometimes."

"You suck sometimes too," Elwood growled jokingly, then paused as he took Chais's hand.

"Make that *all* the time." The kymatis began moving as soon as Chais hauled Elwood up.

"The feeling's mutual," Chais said. He expected the Fey to reply with some other witty comment. Something about Elwood's expressions seemed familiar, and he realized that that was because they were so much like the people he'd dealt with in the past. Although Elwood held back on the verbal attacks, Chais knew from experience that there was going to be some sort of payback in the future.

Elwood remained quiet, something that, Chais had to admit, worried him. He wouldn't be surprised if the Fey was angry at him; after all, Chais had been caught, and as a result, so many people went through the trouble to get him out. Maybe there was something else though. Three days had passed since the attack in Mirstone. Similarly, years had passed since Chais last saw Sovan; years had passed since Lynara carried on a conversation instead of walking past him without a word. People could change so violently in the smallest amount of time. Chais knew that all too well.

Chais took a deep breath and tried to focus on the fresh air to clear his head, but his thoughts didn't go away.

Without Elwood's constant teasing remarks to occupy his mind, he lost himself.

ELWOOD STARTED SPEAKING again once they couldn't ride the kymatis any further. The forest had gotten too bumpy. Its trails faded and tree roots stretched out so that they met in the middle. Rebme had hastily tended to Chais's wounds so that the pain numbed, but once they pitched camp, she would take a closer look. With Lynara leading them and a summoner at hand, the situation seemed much calmer.

Chais trailed the group with Elwood. He inhaled the familiar scent of the forest. An occasional bird passed by overhead and interfered with the spotlights cast on the floor. The trees didn't crowd as much. It allowed for easier defense against any incoming attacks. Shadows of calculating predators appeared in the distance, but they rarely approached groups of travelers. Individuals were so much easier to pick off.

"Tell me about yourself," Elwood pressed for what seemed like the fifth time in the past minute. Chais closed his eyes in annoyance, but a part of him was conscious of the fact that he couldn't go without them—these interactions. Maybe these past days, not quite occupied with battling on the frontlines or the countless war plans, had gotten to him. Maybe facing the abyss inside him was too much to process at the moment. Later. He'd deal with that later.

"I said no, Elwood." A leaf crunched under Lynara's boot. Chais watched with faint amusement as the commander cursed colorfully and tossed the evidence into a pile by the path. The ground was still littered with dead leaves from the hard winter. Green appeared here and there, a result of spring arriving in Gredian. Gods, he didn't want to think of winter and what horrible events it had brought ...

"Come on, you owe me after punching me off of a fucking demon horse." Elwood took a deep breath. "Relevard didn't help much afterward either," he added quietly so that Lynara and Rebme wouldn't hear.

"That was partially your fault. But sure, I'll take the blame."

"You and Relevard keep saying the same things. I swear, things probably would've been better if we switched keys," the Fey scoffed and shook his head. He still managed to keep his voice low. His hair fell into bangs, and the areas where his eyes shown through were chopped off haphazardly.

Chais snorted. "I'd feel bad for Aldridge then."

I'd feel bad for me too.

Chais jumped at the seal's sudden entrance. Gods. He'd have to get used to that.

If Elwood noticed, it didn't show. "I feel bad for him right now," the Fey said, "since he has to keep you under control."

Chais rolled his eyes. "Speak for yourself. Aldridge doesn't need to."

"Aldridge, do you?" Elwood whispered. His eyes were alight with mischief.

... No comment. Aldridge tried to hide a smile, but Chais could easily detect it in his voice.

"He says no." Chais wondered whether or not he should give in, just to lift the Fey's spirits a bit more.

"Whatever, we don't need his confirmation. Need I remind you," Elwood grinned, "that you're the only baby among us, so naturally we'd have to keep an eye on you, even if Aldridge doesn't want to."

Right. Lynara was six years older than Chais. He didn't know about Rebme, but she seemed even older than the commander. And Elwood, well ... Elwood was self-explanatory.

"I'd watch your words," Chais growled. Although the subject of age hit just shy of a sore spot, he'd long since ignored it.

"I'd watch your face. It doesn't look like it's having a good day," Elwood said, out loud this time.

"Neither is yours. In fact, it's never having a good day."

"Both of you, shut the hell up." Lynara sent the colonel and Fey a death glare, which seemed to do the trick.

Chais cast a glance behind them. It was impossible to cover every single trace, especially in messy terrains such as this one. Their best bet would be to eliminate all obvious signs. Plus, Lynara was supposedly on a mission to follow the group of escapees. With her tracking skills, the capital didn't have to put as much energy into retrieving Chais and instead could focus on the war at hand. Gredian knew Chais had something to hide, especially after an unnamed Fey arrived to stop his execution.

If he truly wanted to make it to Atrelia and stay there, he needed to become stronger in order to survive among the powerful immortals who resided there and who would undoubtedly detest his presence. Physical training had a limit. Chais had no magic aside from what Aldridge offered.

Chais took the time to check the bandages on his forearms. Not bleeding anymore, which was a good sign. The pain had died down a bit too. His chest wounds were bound, thankfully—it made him feel less vulnerable. Rebme hadn't specified when they'd pitch camp; Chais didn't feel like asking. There was some kind of commanding aura that surrounded her, similar to Lynara's, but somehow different.

Elwood reached back and tightened his ponytail with the aid of the wind. His delicately pointed ears brushed his arm. "I'll see if I can annoy Lynara," he whispered and made his way up to where the commander was currently walking.

"I'll come to your funeral," Chais called and let his hands fall comfortably to his side. He made a quick scan of their surroundings, once again unsure of where they were exactly. He'd tried to ask Lynara, but she didn't know either—only the general direction of the Atrelian border. Forest stretched beyond them. Chais could catch the ragged mountains of what he presumed to be Scarlet Pass above the tree line. Its peaks faded as they intersected with the clouds. Scarlet Pass could usually be distinguished by its towering, red summit. It was a result of a certain type of plant that grew among the rocks. However, since the fog grew thicker in the mountains during spring and winter, Chais could only assume its existence. The forest looked the same all around, so that didn't offer much of a clue. As they continued, he realized that Rebme was drifting closer and closer with each step. She would slow her pace for a few moments, shortening the distance between her and Chais, then proceed at a normal gait. By the time the summoner was within arm's length, Elwood had gotten numerous death threats but surprisingly no beatings. Although, with Rebme approaching by the minute, Chais had other things to worry about besides how Elwood was getting along with Lynara.

"Rebme, was it?" Chais decided to start the conversation. He realized that they hadn't had a formal introduction yet, but then again, those weren't the first priority on the battlefield. Rare moments of rest were when armies usually bonded, even though fighting alongside each other certainly sped up the process. However, as he sized her up, he couldn't help but observe her foreign skin tone and features. Bronze skin and purple eyes? Chais didn't know any continent with people having those attributes. Was she even human?

"Mmmm," she replied, "Rebme Luxdare."

"Chais Nevermoon," he said cautiously, but something told him she already knew. If the summoner was from Gredian, then she must've gotten wind of the recent events. Chais scanned her face for any emotion. There was none.

She had a whip latched onto her belt—an odd weapon, even for a summoner. The sight brought back unnecessary memories, and a painful tingle raced up his spine.

"Is something wrong?" Rebme asked without any indication that she cared. It contradicted the words that came out of her mouth. Chais raised a brow. No way she could've seen that.

"What do you mean?"

Rebme glanced sideways with half-lidded eyes. "You flinched."

She was quite perceptive; reacting to such a small motion was not something normal people could do without intense training on micromovements.

Chais reached down to brush a crushed leaf off of the trail. No one on the front line used whips, so it had been a while—not including Adaric's warm welcome before the murder trial, of course—since he'd last been so close to one.

"Just the wounds."

Rebme stared at him for a moment too long, but nodded and dropped the matter. "Do you know Neveah?"

"The head summoner of Gredian? I know her," Chais replied. Why would she bring up Neveah?

"Master told me to speak to her." Rebme paused. "Neveah noticed that something was happening with the demons ... and the seal. I need to let you know." She seemed slightly on edge, but maybe that was just the light messing with her features. "The seal that keeps the demon world separate from ours is weakening. We need to find the other keys and reinforce it, or else—"

A tree snapped in two. Wood chips and leaves sprayed as it collided with the ground. Chais immediately reached for the dagger that Lynara gave him in the castle. The forest suddenly chilled and fell into a numb quiet, as if it had plunged into water. With a low rumble, a cloud of shadow spun into a tornado, easily towering over the treetops. The skies darkened as the twister slowly took form. Multiple crimson dots blinked into existence.

Elwood clutched his bow as wind energy began to pulse around him.

The Fey gulped. "... Shit."

CHAPTER
EIGHTEEN

"HEY, TIGER LILY!" Elwood greeted Lynara. Her fists immediately clenched, and her muscles were taut as he fell in line next to her. He cupped his hand behind his neck and threw her a cocky grin.

"What do you want?" she asked. Her eyes burned with unconcealed fury, and her voice carried an undertone of hate that promised pain if he pushed her.

"Well, you see," Elwood started, ignoring the waves of annoyance pulsing off the redhead, "you seemed rather jealous watching me and Grumpy chat. So I thought I'd come and keep you company!"

"I was not jealous!" she said. He could practically see the steam pouring out of her ears.

"Could've fooled me," the Fey warrior grinned, "Snow Blossom." Behind him, he could hear Chais talking with the creepy summoner lady. Elwood kept an ear out for their conversation. His grin widened as Lynara's face turned a livid purple and she reached for her knife. With her hand around her blade's worn, leather handle, she seemed to deflate. Her posture relaxed, and her form unlocked itself from the tight coil it was in moments ago. Lynara took a deep breath and looked Elwood straight in the eye.

"Keep pushing, and I will end you." Her voice was hard, but he could hear just the slightest hint of a tremor. The threat was real. There was still a fair amount of pushing, however, that could be done before she acted upon the threat. He made it his personal goal to find that line and play with it.

"Really?" Elwood pouted. He schooled his face to resemble that of a kicked puppy as he sidestepped a cluster of leaves. "That's not very nice."

"I'm not a very nice person," Lynara replied, trying her hardest to control her temper. But there was an amused spark deep in those burning eyes. Her hand still rested on the hilt of her dagger. She eyed the patch he had avoided and stepped around it too. A hunting trap, not sure for what, but big enough for deer.

"Cinnamon!" Elwood cooed. His eyes danced with restrained laughter. The beams of sunlight danced across his hair, giving him an almost wild look—born and raised in the woods, and most comfortable in them too—*most* powerful. "That's just sad. Is everyone in your pretty empire like that?"

"Stop talking," Lynara sighed in an attempt to act indignant, but Elwood sensed her anger begin to fade as she realized the Fey was only joking to get a rise out of her. She was still wary, but she was moving closer to an interest in the man's behavior and further from an urge to behead him for mocking her and her kingdom.

"So, they are? Why? You people are all so grumpy. Can't you just try to be nice?" Elwood cocked his head to the side, feigning confusion. "It's not that hard. Try smiling." He grinned wide and pointed, as if showing her what a smile should look like.

"I will permanently cut a smile onto your face," Lynara said. She squirmed as Elwood summoned a small gust of wind that brushed against her skin in an attempt to force a laugh out of her. Ticklish, he noted, filing that information for later. Maybe a wake-up tactic. Her grip had left her blade, and if Elwood wasn't mistaken, he'd say that quirk at the edge of her lips was a smile.

"Thanks for the offer, but I think I'll pass ..." He paused. The hairs on the back of his neck stood up. Something wasn't quite right. Lynara had frozen also. Her eyes darted from shadow to shadow. Shadows ... the shadows were too dark, and they were turning darker by the second. They seemed to converge and twist in a towering pillar of black ink. The shadows seemed to pass through the trees as they spun into the air. They didn't rustle a single leaf. Piercing red points stared at the surrounding area, lusting for destruction. It was still not solidly formed, like smoke—a tower of black smoke.

"... Shit," Elwood whispered. "Is it too much to ask for a break?" His fingers curled around his bow, the smooth material familiar beneath his touch. Elwood glanced back at his companions. He saw them draw their own weapons as well. Rebme's form warped as she drew on her own abilities. All of them looked terrified. Looking back at the swarm, Elwood decided that he was too.

"What are they?" Lynara's voice no longer carried anger or amusement, but awe and fear instead. The lady must have never fought on the frontlines. Elwood recognized the species, rarely seen because they were so hard to control. But whenever a summoner appeared with the skill required to both hold open the portal and rein in so many minds, the Fey forces scattered faster than most could blink.

"Molecus," Rebme growled. It was the first sign of any emotion, apart from disapproval, that Elwood had heard from the summoner. And it was fear. Maybe with a touch of respect and interest, but heavy with fear. She knew what they could do, had probably used them before. She was very familiar with what they were capable of.

"Their spit is acidic," Rebme said. She remembered the melted remains of those unfortunate enough to get caught in the whirlwind of death, tattered tunics hanging off of bleached bone frames. Black sludge smudged the bodies and the areas around them, a sharp contrast to the red and white of blood and bone. And the smell, sharp and painful. Eyes watered from the melted flesh and burning remains of acid, mingled with fear, pain, and despair. The wind picked up. Their clothes and hair whipped around them. Elwood subconsciously pulled up a shield, allowing them refuge from the flapping of a thousand insect wings. If their wings had solidified, they would be ready to attack soon. Question was, who was summoning them?

"How acidic?" Lynara eyed the column. Her eyes seemed to glow with the same ghastly red light.

"Acidic enough to melt off your pretty face, Fairy Wings." Elwood turned toward the redhead and gave her a mocking smirk. He was glad for the momentary distraction.

"As entertaining as it is to see you push every single one of her buttons and attempt to dodge whatever she ends up throwing at you," Chais interrupted before things could escalate further than a clenched fist and gritted teeth, "We need you in fighting shape."

"... You mean running shape ... right?" Elwood hoped the colonel wasn't as suicidal as his comment indicated.

"No. I mean fighting," Chais replied. His eyes were still fixated on the swarm.

"Why!" The Fey warrior groaned. If his hand wasn't busy holding his bow in a death grip, he would have slapped some sense into the Feykin. Instead, he settled for a bewildered look with a hint of: 'I can't believe the sheer amount of stupidity you just vomited out, and we are all going to die, thank you.'

"Even *I* wouldn't dare challenge a molecus storm with only four people!" Elwood said. "Are you absolutely insane? We'll be reduced to bare bones!"

"Have you noticed?" Chais continued in his infuriating monotone voice. He was still staring into the storm cloud of monstrous bugs. "They aren't attacking us. Do you know why?"

"Oh. Do tell, wise one," Elwood mocked. He ignored the looks their female companions were sharing.

"Rebme, Lynara, can you tell where we are?" Chais asked. Both blinked in surprise, one more apparently than the other.

"Is this really a good time to be taking geography lessons?" Rebme replied. She raised an eyebrow, and her violet eyes bored into his sapphire ones.

"There is a village there. We need to protect it," the colonel answered his own question, eyes hard as the swarm organized, facing away from them and toward something hidden by the trees. The rage simmering in his eyes was cold and frightening. Even when his people abandoned him, he could not abandon them. Elwood felt his respect for the Feykin rise further.

"Why would a summoner attack its own village?" Elwood muttered. Rebme and Chais shared a look. They knew something. Elwood didn't know what, but for now, he was too focused on trying to convince an idiot to be reasonable. Which, now that he thought about it, seemed to contradict itself.

"We'll just be killed with them!" Lynara argued. At least not all of Gredian's people were completely shitting insane.

"Rebme, if we get you close enough, you can find the swarm mind, right?" Chais asked. Lynara opened her mouth to argue but was silenced by a raise of Chais's hand. The Feykin now looked every inch the lieutenant colonel Elwood knew he was. The weight on his young features tugged at his heart.

"Yes, but it would take time ..." Rebme trailed off as she connected the dots. Her eyes widened, and a flash of doubt crossed her face before it disappeared.

"There really is no stopping you, is there?" Elwood sighed. Running a hand, bow included, through his bangs—the cold silver felt nice against his forehead. He met the Feykin's eyes. "What the hell. Let's do it."

"Thank you," Chais whispered and rushed toward the village. The rest of the group followed close behind. Chais needed this, Elwood realized. After everything that happened, he needed this. He needed to feel like he was still protecting the people he had signed his life away to keep safe. He had to try. And Elwood was going to help him the best he could.

"Rebme!" Elwood called out as his military instincts took over in the situation. Orders flowed smoothly from his mouth and tactics were formed and discarded in his mind. Rebme's eyes filled with worry. "You just focus on finding the mind. I'll shield off the village as best I can for as long as I can to buy you time. Chais, you take down any that slip through, and watch Rebme's back. Make sure nothing distracts her. Lynara, find the summoner behind this; find out why they are attacking a village—why they are here in the first place. While you're at it, herd all the civilians to one place, preferably somewhere at the center of the town. Chais, help her with that first before defending Rebme." He paused.

"Oh, and don't die. Dying is not as fun as it looks."

You sound like a general, Relevard commented as the little band of fighters nodded. Elwood had already pulled a thin shield around the village's general area. Hopefully, it would hold long enough for them to get there and set up proper defenses.

"I am one, you know," Elwood whispered back. He kept an eye out for Lynara and Rebme. They were following close behind, keeping up remarkably well considering the two men had Fey heritage. Any attempt to hide their tracks was abandoned.

I keep forgetting. If you acted like one more often, you might actually get things done. Elwood gritted his teeth.

"I hate you. So much."

"Talking to yourself again?" Chais had slid into a comfortable pace beside Elwood. He stared straight ahead and looked from molecus to molecus, as if he could count how many of the vile creatures there were.

Elwood almost sighed with relief as they broke through the undergrowth. The slight distortion in the air around the village indicated that his shield, although crudely made, still held. He could feel the heavy tension and fear in the air; the mortals had already retreated to the center of the town. Smart, and also less work for him.

Elwood collapsed the shield behind him as he ran. He could feel the first of the swarm brush against it. The smaller the area he had to shield, the stronger it would be.

"Gather the citizens as closely together as you can. I don't want to waste energy on surface area." Chais and Lynara immediately ran to the nearest homes and businesses. They knocked down doors and rushed people toward the largest building. The town hall—perfect.

Elwood created the densest dome he could and stood his ground. The bright afternoon sun was completely blocked, casting the village in a shadow. It was like night, but the stars glowed a menacing red, and the air was filled with the buzzing of wings. Rebme had retreated into the windshield as well. Her eyes pulsed as she fought and searched for control. The two Gredian soldiers had emerged from the dome. Their hair was tousled, and their clothes were ripped from the ferocious winds. Lynara met Elwood's eye, then left. She was searching for a summoner that Elwood's instincts told him would not exist. Chais had drawn his blade, staring at the oncoming storm with the determination of a dying man.

Quiet sobs and the bitter smell of tears wafted from the house behind Elwood like thick syrup. It made his thoughts sluggish. Elwood took a deep breath and let out a shaky laugh.

"I bet I can kill more than you," he taunted and ran a trembling hand through his bangs. He drew his bow. He wouldn't be able to use arrows, not if he wanted to maintain the shield behind him.

"In your dreams," Chais humored him, needing something to distract him from his beating heart and too-fast breaths. The air seemed to still, and the buzzing intensified. Thousands solidified. They dove.

Their wings screamed as they tore through the skies. The first few that struck the shield, eager to feed on the two creatures standing against them, immediately fell out of the sky. They landed on the ground with a wet smack, their wings torn. The demons dragged their disintegrating bodies a few more feet before evaporating into smoke. But far too soon, the bugs began to get through the weak defense.

Elwood swatted at them with his blade. He growled with annoyance when they just nimbly avoided it. Chais wasn't doing much better. Their deadly spit sizzled on the ground as the two fighters dodged the small spittles aimed for exposed flesh. Elwood concentrated more power on the section directly ahead of him. He accelerated the wind speeds and couldn't help but feel proud as the next dozen exploded into smoke before ever reaching them.

Elwood coughed from the putrid smell and knocked another molecus out of the air. Despite their best efforts, they were being overwhelmed. Elwood saw only determination in Chais. The lunatic. Elwood looked back at the swarm, and his heart sank as the insects pulled back and regrouped. The bugs formed a solid, spear-like mass and drilled forward.

The shield was cracking. Elwood dropped his bow and fell to one knee. His hand was outstretched as he desperately tried to keep the dome from shattering. He was aware of Chais killing the few that slipped through, but soon, they would all come. And he was powerless to stop them.

A pulsing headache was forming. This was putting too much strain on his recovering body. Elwood had connected himself too deeply with the shield, pouring more than just his magical energy into it. He had subconsciously poured his mental energy into it as well. The structure's integrity was connected to his own mental strength. It fortified the winds but left him more vulnerable than he would like to have been. If the dome broke, he knew without a doubt that it would hurt him mentally as well. A burst of pain, like a strike of lightning, streaked through his concentration.

He felt it shatter.

It was so much worse than he thought it would be. It was as if a thousand glass shards were shredding through his mind. The shield was down. They were going to die. Elwood prayed that Rebme would be able to stop the molecus before they reached the townspeople and that Callum would forgive him. Never would he have suspected that a promise to come home alive would be so difficult to keep.

Elwood heard screaming. At first, he thought it was his own, it hurt so much. Then he realized that the bug demons hadn't melted his flesh off yet. Doing his best to reorganize his scattered thoughts, he glanced behind him. Chais had dropped his weapon and was screaming as if his very essence was being ripped from him. It took Elwood a moment to realize that it might be true. A great tidal wave of water surged toward the insects, drowning them before they even hit the ground. It tore their bodies apart.

Chais had awakened his ability—this wasn't his first time either. Elwood could barely remember the moment in a haze of pain, but the last time the Feykin used his magic, he had drowned a man. This time was much worse—untrained as he was, Chais was using too much, too fast. His body couldn't handle it. He was dying. It was as if a man had never deep dived in his life, then decided to go all the way to the bottom of the ocean as fast as he could. It was amazing that the colonel's body didn't instinctively stop like it did the first time. In not doing so, he was hurting himself.

Elwood stumbled to his feet and rushed to Chais, hoping he could stop or at least slow down the torrent of energy flowing out of the Feykin.

He grabbed on to Chais and did the most reckless thing he could think of. Elwood reached out with the sliver of power he had left and sloppily connected it to his energy system. He ignored Relevard's warnings as he found the main output and forced it close.

Chais collapsed—his eyes staring sightlessly at the ground. The water suspended in the air obeyed gravity once more and crashed to the ground. Elwood spat water and helped Chais back to his feet, grunting at the weight.

Elwood looked back at the swarm. They were disappearing. He glanced at Rebme to see her practically hovering in her own torrent of black smoke. Her bright purple eyes shined from the depths of the cocoon. She'd done it. He released a relieved chuckle and sat down, dragging the half-lucid Chais with him. Elwood rested his still pounding head on the colonel's unresponsive shoulder and laughed again, not quite believing they were alive. But they were. They didn't die a horrible, gruesome death.

"Yay," Elwood whispered. He felt unreasonably happy and proud, but then again, Chais had just created a hurricane and saved their lives. Elwood just hoped that the unholy unleashing of dormant power wouldn't leave permanent damage on Chais, considering the Feykin's lack of visual Fey biology. But with that show of power, that might've just changed.

The feeling was slowly returning to his limbs as the adrenaline faded, and his missing appendage ached with a burning fury. Elwood gave the arm a wary glance and groaned at the weeping burn wound.

EIGHTEEN

Rebme was going to kill him.

CHAPTER
NINETEEN

"IT'S GETTING WEAKER. Soon, the seal won't be able to contain them." Rebme broke the silence. Her voice was grave.

Lynara peered at the summoner. Even Elwood was quiet; although she despised mostly everything about him, the atmosphere felt too tense. "Is there a reason?"

Rebme leaned back with a short sigh, but her expression didn't change. "Neveah didn't detect any ... It must have something to do with the age of the seal. The molecus just now didn't have a summoner, which is near impossible for such a complex species ... If the seal let those out, more could be coming in worse forms." Rebme seemed like she was trying to convince herself. The space between her brows creased with concentration. During the molecus scare, her hood had fallen off. There was time to put it back on, which was something Rebme would normally do, but she left it off. The situation at hand proved more dire. Dark brown curls tumbled over the folded fabric.

"There's no doubt," the summoner said as she concentrated on the ground, "these demons are wild. Their minds aren't connected to anything, or else we would have found someone in that village."

There was a pause. They had retreated again to the forest, which was darkening as night fell. Lynara poked absentmindedly at their fire. This was another soldier-free zone, which she knew only because of Adaric's slightly sloppy search plan. While wandering the village searching for a summoner, she recognized the village as being in Valport.

Rebme glanced at Chais, who was silently brooding away from the camp. The colonel's hair stood in stark contrast to the dark shirt on his back. It had been offered by a villager to the group of warriors who saved their lives. The place where Chais and Elwood were first spotted after their escape was south from the molecus attack, so chances were the villagers didn't recognize the party. None of them had raised alarms, thankfully.

Somehow, Chais's blond dye had washed off during the attack, although Lynara hadn't been there to witness it. Both he and Elwood had been drenched to the core when they regrouped, and Chais was barely conscious. Rebme had taken a look at both of their wounds, given them each an insane earful, then rewrapped the bleeding injuries. If Lynara hadn't wasted her time looking for a summoner, she'd feel a lot more useful—and a lot less in the dark.

"How do we reinforce the seal then? Before, you know, they come back?" Elwood's right sleeve lay empty on the ground. His hair was a mess, but with the energy used on the shield, he didn't bother to fix it.

"Find the rest of the seals, which are spread throughout Gredian and Atrelia. Thank the gods they didn't wander any further," Rebme explained. "Then take them to the place of the original binding. The summoners will handle the rest."

"How would we do that?" Lynara asked. The talk of demons and summoners cast warning lights in her brain. She tried to find what memory they were pointing at. She vaguely recalled a flashback to the Gredian courtyard. Neveah was there, wasn't she? Why was the memory so murky and disorganized?

"Chais and Elwood are already headed toward Atrelia. They'll probably be safer there," Rebme reasoned.

"Then Rebme and Lynara can stay in Gredian to search," Chais cut in for the first time after the attack. Surprised, Lynara looked up to see that the colonel had approached. He was now standing with his hands stuffed into his pockets. Light cast ominous shadows over his not-quite-human features.

"How will we know though? If someone is a seal?" Rebme's tone was puzzled, but her face remained devoid of emotion. Chais threw a lazy glance at Elwood. The Fey paused his fiddling with the faery steel bow.

"We'll figure that out later. There's got to be a way," Chais concluded smoothly. Rebme stared at him—she was probably suspecting Chais and Elwood of something, but Lynara didn't know what. Lynara also reminded herself to approach one of them after the first watch about the Fey-Human War. It was something she'd glossed over at Silvermount, so she had some information gaps that needed filling. Rebme? No ... Lynara didn't trust the summoner. It also appeared Rebme wasn't from around here, although she could be wrong. Chais? That conversation would probably quickly redirect itself toward "family" matters. Plus, he didn't seem so well right now—Lynara wondered what had happened during the molecus scare.

Elwood it was, then, no matter how agonizing the idea seemed. He was, after all, the only immortal among them, and had seen the war with his own eyes.

"We'll sleep on it then. Any idea where we are?" Rebme asked. She scanned the woods around them. The trees pressed in on them. It gave Lynara an uneasy sense of claustrophobia. Sounds she'd never heard before echoed in the distance. She wondered how the rest of them could sleep in this nightmarish place. Upon further examination—Elwood's half-lidded eyes, Chais's relaxed shoulders, Rebme's comfortable posture—Lynara realized she was an outsider.

"Lynara said it was Valport," Chais offered. Then he twisted to point at a barely visible peak jutting out of the fog. The night air seemed to have cleared it up. "And that's Scarlet Pass."

"Which means we're heading the direction west, right?" Elwood concluded. "I mean, west, the right direction?"

Chais raised both brows in mock surprise. "Looks like Elwood's been studying his geography."

Lynara looked around. Hadn't anyone else notice his odd speech pattern just now?

And then she remembered. Demons, summoners, kings, and royalty. It triggered something that had strangely been pushed back in her memory: Adaric and the … the *thing*. Neveah trying to find the mind of the demon but not strong enough to do so, running and—

Waking up the next morning?

Lynara squeezed her eyes shut and forcefully diverted her attention to reality. Memory didn't work that way. Seeing the new king of Gredian in front of a demon so powerful that not even Neveah could control … that wasn't something that could be repressed so easily. But if Chais and Elwood were heading to Atrelia, then chances were this matter didn't concern them. Once they parted, she'd talk to Rebme.

Rebme stood. Although she was shorter than everyone, Lynara felt a strange energy coming from her that made her seem just as tall, if not taller. Well, probably not to Chais or Elwood because of their experiences, but to Lynara the summoner felt almost … superior.

Ah, not that feeling again.

"I'll take first watch," Lynara cut in shakily.

"Aww, look who decided to stay up for all of us," Elwood said. "Pretty—"

"Shut up, or I will do it for you," Lynara warned before the Fey could call her anything else.

"Elwood, she'll murder you in your sleep," Chais said.

Rebme turned to catch Lynara's eye. "I'll fill you in on the whole backstory tomorrow," the summoner offered, "you seem like you need it."

"Is that an insult?"

"Not unless you make it one." Rebme held her in a stare for a good five seconds before she yawned and backed away. Chais took an area far away from her but still in the camp's perimeter and crossed his arms comfortably across his chest. A barely noticeable shiver rose through the thin fabric covering his torso. Upon closer examination, Lynara realized that the colonel was unusually pale. His form seemed fragile against the towering tree that served as a background—weak, even. Where had his energy gone?

"Looks like you're stuck with me, Princess."

Lynara groaned as a familiar figure strolled in next to her. He still hadn't fixed his hair—with one arm it would be relatively difficult for a human to even tie their hair back up, but Elwood was a Fey who controlled the wind. She guessed the molecus were quite energy draining. On another note, although Rebme offered her the story, she just couldn't pass on this opportunity ... Even though she completely despised Elwood and all Fey in general, she told herself it was for the information only. It was also better to get an idea from all three of them—"Yes, that could work," she told herself. She'd ask Chais afterward, then Rebme.

"Could you tell me about the seals?" Lynara worded carefully. Her hopes for a calm conversation sunk when Elwood grinned.

"Oh, a story, huh?"

"Yes," Lynara rolled her eyes. Fey.

"From *me*?"

"Yes, from you." Idiotic creature.

The Fey sat back as if he were judging her from afar, which could be exactly what he was doing. She leaned against the bark of the tree. The roughness dug into her shoulder blades. She felt the dried-up grass beneath her feet and smelled the earthen scent that sprinkled the air. So unfamiliar, this world. It surprised her, really, just how a person could get used to ... this ... in the midst of a bloody war. In the midst of anything, really.

"Before this one, there was another war between the humans and the Fey." Lynara focused on his words. "There was always tension. Even I don't know what exactly sparked it. Humans wanted a level playing field, Fey wanted a different kind of balance."

"So four people—"

"Five." He grinned.

"… Five people," Lynara blinked hard, "were fed up with the war and decided to use their combined powers to end it?" Elwood began to nod but flinched lightly and pressed a hand to the back of his head. The darkness made it impossible to see if he had sustained any injury. Lynara took a hesitant step toward the Fey. His next words stopped her as her boot touched the dusty ground.

"… But I'm guessing that part of the story's not what you're looking for." Elwood faced the space to her left. His attention was directed casually at something in the forest.

"I just need to know about the seals …" Lynara waved a hand in front of the Fey's face, "and how they … work."

"The seals? Oh right, the seals." Elwood scratched the back of his neck. "Three of them are human, two are Fey. They bound the demons to their own world by combining light and dark magic— oh, also, more seals are human because dark magic comes in smaller vessels than light magic—and using a few elements of nature, plus the draw of summoning skill. Oh, I forgot to add, the Fey weren't just amateurs, they were masters at their craft. I think, uh …" He trailed off and tapped his left finger against his chin. "Well, they weren't Zefires, that I know for sure …"

Lynara raised a brow at the Fey, who seemed to be avoiding eye contact. She snuck a glance at the forest behind her, where Elwood was looking. Nothing. The commander decided to continue. Her senses stood on high alert. "How do they work?"

A brief pause, during which Lynara heard a rustle from the camp—probably Chais. "I'm not one hundred percent sure because I don't know too much about the seals," Elwood said, "but I learned that they hear a voice. It awakens when the host dies, which is when it passes to one of their younger relatives. Then the seal supplies heightened abilities—for Fey seals, they provide increased physical and light magic capabilities, and for human seals, they add less to physical attributes but more to the dark magic pool." The Fey frowned. His attention was now directed to a spot above Lynara's right shoulder.

"I think I left something out ... right, if a summoner strong enough possesses the power of the seals, they can control the portal between this world and the demon world. The strength of the portal depends on the bonds between the host and the ..." he waved his arm in an almost frantic motion, "the uh ..."

"Keys? Seals? Warriors?" Lynara offered.

"Right." Elwood pointed at her shoulder.

Lynara waved again. "Elwood, I'm right here." The Fey redirected his line of sight, but even then, he wasn't focusing on her. Clearly, this wasn't working. However, the information he painstakingly supplied was useful and filled in her knowledge gaps well enough. She resolved to ask Chais for clarification, no matter what issues their past brought up. Only time could tell whether or not this group of untrustworthy soldiers would bond in the end. For now, though, she patted Elwood's shoulder.

"You seem tired. Let's get you some sleep." Lynara guided the Fey to a tree and set him sloppily against its trunk. In an instant, Elwood passed out. She'd never seen anyone sleep so suddenly before.

Without anyone else awake to keep her company, Lynara grabbed her dagger and clutched it in front of her with white knuckles. An unearthly howl echoed in the distance. She flinched. Even backing up against a tree didn't feel safe. Shadows fed at the pit of her stomach. Distorted figures danced in the light of the dying fire, magnifying them to the woodland beyond. Tree limbs stretched spindly fingers toward the midnight sky and painted a ghostly, supernatural image. Alien sounds altered their distance—one moment, it would sound like something was a mile away; another, it seemed like it was a foot in front of her. Lynara resisted the urge to wake someone up. She was already the most useless of the crew—if she revealed that she was horrified of the night, then that would only make matters worse. She ignored the cold sweat that built on her palms and forehead and forced herself to endure it.

It took far too long for Chais to stir. When the colonel blinked awake, Lynara resisted the urge to hug him. Gods, what a hellish watch; and it had only been an hour too. She loosened the grip on her blade. Lynara hid the darkened crescents on her palm and wiped away the perspiration on her brow. Chais gave a quick, practiced scan of the woods before walking over to Lynara, who tried her best to appear relaxed. From the odd look he was giving her, however, it was clear he knew she wasn't.

"How was the watch?" Chais asked. Clouds of frozen vapor appeared from his mouth. Now that he was up, the air had dropped in temperature, although it wasn't a large change. Or maybe she was just imagining it, but with his eyes and oddly colored hair, it seemed winter left too quickly in the forest.

"It was fine. Nothing out of the ordinary." Lynara couldn't help but avoid eye contact as a tense quiet fell.

"Look, I'm sorry for ..." she attempted to break the ice.

"... Interrogating me?" Chais made a sound that resembled a snort. "It was for the plan, even if it didn't work in getting Adaric to leave. But ..." he started but paused, as if he was unsure whether or not he should tell her. There was still a thin veil between them, one that held the history of a strained relationship. Lynara didn't know when it first started; maybe it was when he joined the army and she was sixteen. It was just fleeting jealousy, she decided.

So then, why was she still feeling it?

Lynara let out a short breath. The creatures of the forest suddenly seemed like a muted backdrop. "These past years, I—"

She couldn't say it. Chais watched her for a few seconds, then looked away when he realized she was unable to speak. Lynara saw a flickering image of a younger brother before it faded away.

"It's fine, Nara. It's been nine years. You don't have to tell me." Lynara could detect the slightest tremor in his voice, but his eyes said otherwise.

Lynara bit her lip. She desperately searched for another topic.

"Would you mind telling me about the seals? Elwood was a bit ..." she cast a glance at the passed out Fey, "... sleepy."

"I learned the Gredian version, which is a bit biased ..." Chais frowned, seemingly forgetting about their tense exchange just a few moments ago. There was something different about his appearance that didn't quite match the Chais she'd known before the execution drama. Something, but she didn't know what. "What did Elwood tell you?"

"I think he said something about the different magics and how the seal works. Bonds, voices, a bit of history." Lynara tried to decipher the fatigued Fey's words from her memory. Chais nodded.

"What do you want to know?"

"Just clarification. How the seals work, the history of the Fey-Human War."

"I'll start with the seals since they had some information on them in the Gredian Library." Lynara raised a brow but motioned for him to continue.

"They're passed through bloodlines, unless there aren't any relatives to pass on to—then it finds another capable human or Fey. Seals don't stick to their own species; a Fey can go to a human host or vice versa. The keys have a lot of power stored in them in case it's ever needed, but the host can't borrow that hidden power unless it's an emergency. They also can't remember much from their past life, excluding information about the war that's required to run a seal."

"Gredian has this much on demon seals?" Lynara asked. She recalled the infinite shelves of leather-bound books in Silver-mount.

"Believe it or not, yes, they do." Chais didn't seem like he was lying. There was still some hurt in his expression, but he had smoothed it over with indifference. Lynara decided that she would tell him another time ... a time when she no longer felt envious of him.

She suddenly realized just how much colder the night air was than before. Lynara crossed her arms and tried to trap her body heat. Deciding to get closer to the warmth of the fire, Lynara shuffled to the side, just a bit. Chais was casting a glance off into the forest so that the side of his face, including his ear, was visible.

Oh. Oh, gods.

"Actually, That's all I need to know at the moment," she managed and turned away from him. "Have a good watch."

Lynara left a somewhat confused Chais and took a spot on the ground. She faced the opposite direction. It must've been her vision, or she was more tired than she thought because it wasn't possible.

There was no way Chais was Fey.

A WELL-AIMED PUПCH sailed at his head. Chais raised his arms to block it, only to be knocked back. Sharp wind grazed his cheek. Elwood leaped. The air moved seamlessly with him, and he drove a kick toward where Chais stood. Chais ducked and grabbed the Fey's leg in an attempt to gain control. Elwood lashed out with his only good arm. Chais deflected it and sent a counterattack. A parry. More counters. The fist connected with the foot, expelling both fighters from each other.

"Break," Elwood half panted and threw a breeze against his own face. He sat, glancing at the direction where Rebme and Lynara went to talk. No one trusted Rebme enough to fully believe her story about the seals, but the molecus without a summoner served as good evidence that the seal was breaking. So, maybe she wouldn't kill Lynara and dispose of her body in the river, although none of them knew where she had come from. They stayed on edge anyway.

Elwood propped his foot up onto a rock. "Hey, Chais, some water right now would be great."

"For the last time, I don't know how to control it." Chais ran an errant hand through his hair. In the past few hours, Elwood had been passive-aggressively urging him to touch deeper into the "system of power" that he supposedly should feel by now. Nothing felt different though. Nothing magical or otherworldly—just complete, utter exhaustion.

It's there, you just need to ease open the blockade. Aldridge spoke for the first time since ... well since the escape. Chais couldn't help but flinch at his sudden entrance.

"And how would I do that?"

"Aldridge?" Elwood guessed. "Welcome back to the party!"

"He's happy to see you too," Chais deadpanned.

I can take care of it, but I might need some of Relevard's help. Elwood's careless sealing luckily didn't damage your system. It's a difficult process, though, to open it up again. And, Aldridge added, *for the record, I'm not happy to see him.*

Chais contained his laughter. "Stumpy, I need your help."

"What kind of help, Grumpy?" Elwood sprawled across the rocks, as if he were getting a tan from the hot midday sun; in reality, his pale skin would probably stay that way for a while.

"Tell me about the power. How does it work?"

Elwood groaned and shifted to a more comfortable position. "Do I have to?"

Chais exhaled. He cast a glance toward the sky. "Well, if Rebme really is telling the truth, wouldn't having a water-wielder really help with saving the world?"

The Fey fell silent, shadows disabling Chais's ability to see his face clearly. Finally, he hoisted himself up into a sitting position.

You should probably listen to this, Aldridge advised as Elwood shot him a half-grin..

CHAPTER
TWENTY

"SIT DOWN, THIS COULD TAKE A BIT," Elwood
said as Chais stepped forward. The colonel's lips tugged downward and a slight wrinkle scrunched up between his narrowing
eyes. Elwood gestured for him to sit, patting the slightly damp
grass at his side. A few leaves clung to his palm, leaving wet
imprints on his hand. He wiped it off on his trousers. The dark
patch faded, and the fabric slowly stiffened as it dried. Chais gave
him a wary glance before he eased himself onto the rock, nudg-
ing the Fey's two leather-bound feet to the side. Elwood grunted
indignantly and tucked his feet more comfortably at his side.

"So, what exactly is your problem?"

"You've only been telling me to dig deeper, but I don't know what I'm looking for. The molecus incident was the first time I've ever used … this power. And I was barely conscious during it," Chais sighed. The Fey warrior traced a crack on the rock and decided not to tell the Feykin about the first time he had used his powers; it wasn't important anyway.

Rebme looked up from her history lesson with Lynara and offered her own input. "Try tucking your consciousness in. Whenever I summon something I sort of … dig into myself. And I find … some kind of energy that pulses there. Is it the same with Fey magic?"

"Uh …" Elwood considered it; it was similar, but while summoners tapped into a single point of power derived from another world, the Fey's magic was closer to blood vessels or nerves, all connected to one main system but expanding throughout the body—only it wasn't physical. "Kind of. But … more heart and blood vessel-ish?"

"How am I supposed to … how did you two phrase it, 'focus my consciousness inward'?" Chais said after a minute of attempting their suggestions. His eyes were screwed shut in concentration. He opened them and glared at an innocent patch of grass. If he was an Oxidason, it would have caught on fire. Rebme shrugged and returned to her previous conversation with the fidgeting redhead.

You are being a horribly inconsiderate teacher, Relevard pointed out. *Fey children are born with the natural instinct to use their powers, to spiral their consciousness into themselves. This Feykin, however, has just awoken these powers, powers he didn't even know existed within him. And after such a violent explosion, it's changed him.*

"Changed him?" The Fey quickly searched his friend's

features. Elwood inhaled sharply as details that had previously escaped his muddled mind registered. During the few hours after the molecus attack, his thoughts had been scattered and disorganized, resulting in a very confusing conversation with Lynara and many missed details. His head still hurt a little, but he now noticed what Relevard was referring to. A low, delighted chuckle escaped his lips.

"What is it?" Chais asked. His ignorance only made Elwood laugh harder. Apparently, pushing a recently dormant system so hard had its consequences—Grumpy's appearance had been altered as well. His ears, very human just a day before, were now pointed and definitely Fey. While his face hadn't changed too much, there was an inhuman essence to it too sharp and ageless. His sapphire eyes seemed timeless, deep enough to drown in. How had he not noticed sooner? And why didn't this occur the first time? He would have to do some research once he got back home.

"You're Fey," Elwood breathed, his smile widening as he drank in the details. When he looked a little longer, he noticed that while the ears were indeed longer and pointed, they were not nearly as sharp as Fey; many of his other features were also somewhere in between. But they were absolutely obvious for anyone that bothered to look. "Well, not quite. But there's no more doubt about a Fey lineage."

"What?" Chais's hands searched through tangled, dirty hair and gently, almost hesitantly, traced his ear. The locks twined around long, calloused fingers that trembled as he reached the top, feeling the too steep curve and foreign folds. He might have made a musician with those hands in another time.

"How?" he whispered letting his hands drop back onto his lap. Chais stared at them, as if he wasn't sure they were his.

"It's the power system. It works like your blood vessels, but instead of pumping blood through your body, it pumps energy. With that energy, we can then expel it and shape it to suit our needs," Elwood said. He could sense the rising fear bubbling upward from within Chais. It was already showing in Chais's eyes, a deep, rearing darkness. "It's also the biggest difference between a Fey's anatomy and a human's. And after straining a previously ignored organ so badly, I'm guessing your body just changed to better adapt to the new energy flowing through you." Elwood spoke slowly and calmly in hopes of keeping any fear from growing.

"But why can't I feel it? If I've suddenly awakened some power great enough to change my physical appearance, why can't I feel it?" Chais's voice crackled with panic, and his breath hitched. He leaped to his feet, his body unwilling to stay still a second longer, needing something to *do*, to fix whatever was causing the distress. Chais's hands were balled up into fists at his side. It was as if he was holding on to something he didn't want to lose. His knuckles flushed white, exposing crisscrossing scars—small tally marks counting each battle.

Elwood watched him. He felt his heart clenching with worry, yet he didn't know what to do. Maybe Rebme would know—she was a medic after all. But no, this was not her business. Chais wouldn't want a total stranger to see him in this state; Elwood was pretty sure he was also overstepping his boundaries. Someone had to calm him down though ... might as well be the one who caused the problem in the first place.

Elwood discreetly pulled a small shield between his group and Lynara's, blocking any sound. They were too occupied with their talk to notice the colonel's growing panic attack anyway.

"Chais ..." Elwood stood. He took a cautious step toward Chais and met his blue eyes. They darted, unwilling to make contact, searching for a way to run, to fight, like cornered beasts. Elwood was unprepared for such violent reactions. He understood shock, but this, there had to be a cause for such fear. Maybe it was just the thought of being the same as the enemy he had fought his whole life? Then why was he so calm about learning magic? Nothing made sense.

"I don't—I can't," Chais muttered, but not to Elwood—his gaze was distant, listening. He was talking to Aldridge. Elwood took a step back to allow the panicked colonel's companion to calm him down.

"Okay ... I'll try ... I'm sorry." Chais's eyes closed, and when they opened again, the fear was buried. But Elwood could still see it, a gold coin glimmering at the bottom of a well.

"You all right?" Elwood asked as he carefully eased back into his relaxed position. Chais's fists clenched. Little crescent moons were imprinted on his palm, small divots of white against soft red flesh. Elwood dropped the shield once he was sure that Chais wasn't going to start screaming.

"Please, Elwood," Chais said, "help me understand what has happened to me." Chais clasped his hands behind his back to hide the shaking. He looked so young. His normally confident aura was gone as he hung his head and folded into himself. The colonel, who had seen more death in his few years than some men do in their entire life, stood afraid. It took Elwood's breath away.

"Okay," Elwood whispered, "But ... can you tell me why you freaked out so badly?" Elwood winced at the tactless question. He looked down at the grass, unwilling to look up and see Chais's reaction. With his head down and his hand tightly wound in his coat, he felt like an ashamed child.

"I—" Chais's voice broke. Elwood felt the colonel's body slide down on the rock. "I can't, at least not now. But I have it under control now. Trust me, it's under control. And before you ask, no, it's not because of … of all those years fighting your people." A pause. "You told me before—that the dormancy of the Fey organ determines the physical appearance of a Feykin. Is this … is this normal?"

"I'll try to explain what you are …" Elwood leaned his head back onto the rock. He ignored the bump digging into his neck and prepared himself for a long monologue, eyes never leaving the cloud-peppered sky.

Elwood told Chais everything he could remember about half-Fey. How most didn't ever gain powers and some were born wielding it. Never had there been a Feykin that awoke his power so late in life. He explained how most were outcasts, being of neither and both species. Those who could hide one half of their lineage normally did, those who proudly announced to be both were some of the most powerful people he knew, and those who couldn't choose often became bitter. He tried to describe the feeling of searching through those veins of energy and tugging at them. How to him, it felt like he was walking through storm winds, their power pulling at his very being and how he would grab it. Seize the wind like one would hold a favored blade, gentle and firm, to meld himself into that wind, to become it and yet not let it blow him away. Elwood explained how the cold winds bit at his cheeks and nose and blinded him with strong gusts. The freedom of submerging himself in that chaotic order, of never-ending swirls of power. He had always felt it, and now, he was going to teach Chais.

"Take my hand." Elwood's eyes met the colonel's. Chais slowly placed his hand on the Fey's. The nail marks were red and deep, ugly marks on his battle-worn hands.

"Thank you. Relevard, take us in," Elwood said.

You are the most idiotic, reckless, and annoying host I've ever had the misfortune of meeting, Revelard ranted, but Elwood could feel his powers rallying. *If you live, you'd better thank me.*

"I know." Elwood grinned, far too cheerful for what he was about to do. Before Chais could even question what was about to happen, Relevard, with the help of Aldridge, pulled both of their minds into Chais's system.

Elwood could feel Chais beside him. He was floating, weightless in the calm of Chais's center. He had unlocked it before they had begun training, but he could still sense the heavy weight of the leftover chains.

His friend and owner of the body they were currently in was screaming. Well, not exactly screaming since they didn't have a physical form (and therefore, didn't have a mouth or vocal cords).

Calm down! Elwood projected the thought to his panicking companion. Their surroundings were a rippling field of blues and greens. The faint scent of sea salt and breeze spun through the space.

Where are we? What did you do, you idiot! Chais growled, sounding much more like his usual grumpy self. At least there was that.

This is your power system center. Elwood introduced him to … himself. It was really one of the stranger things he had done in his twenty-five decades.

But how? There it was, the question Elwood was looking for. *And why?*

Skilled Fey can link systems and share energy, and energy can be linked with your thoughts too. You've seen me power a shield with the aid of my will, an extension of my consciousness. With some help from Relevard and your key, I bound a fraction of my consciousness to some of my energy and connected our systems. I may have also grabbed a handful of yours too, the Fey warrior explained.

As for why, it's to get you to know your own systems better. Just to see them so you have something to visualize when you dive into yourself and try to gather this energy—so you can feel what it's like to focus in.

Elwood gestured around them at the ever-changing hues of blues and greens. Small, almost unnoticeable golds streaked like shooting stars and Chais took it all in. Elwood could feel the sea-tinted power surrounding them pulsing to the Feykin's increasing heartbeat, dull drums playing in the distance, yet the rhythm sank into his mind.

This is what the power system looks like? Awe crept into Chais's projection as his presence took in the scenery.

Well, this is what the center looks like. You'd find the branches to be a little more chaotic. The Fey laughed—whenever he took the time to meditate and enter his own center in this way, he was always taken aback by the feelings and the colors. It was truly something beautiful.

Where does this come from? Why do your—my kind have it? While panic was still lingering around the Feykin's consciousness, it was quickly fading as the calming colors of his own core put him at ease.

I don't know. I would think it's kind of like the humans' ability to summon. They have something similar, I believe, but theirs is a power to open a rift in our world—and to draw that power in to chain a creature to their service. Elwood did the best shrug he could without shoulders, which wasn't really a shrug so much as a ripple of wind energy. The small strands of white danced like seafoam before disappearing beneath the sparkling, gold-flaked waves.

Seen enough to get a decent picture? Or do you want to play with the storms?

I ... I've seen enough. If I had a stomach, I'd probably throw up or faint. Chais's projection did sound rather strained. Elwood sent him a mental pat on the back and released the death hold Relevard had on their powers. He felt himself yanked back into his body.

"Damn," Chais reeled. His pupils were dilated so only a thin band of blue wrapped around the yawning black center. "Do you see that every time you use your power?"

"No—most of the time, it's just a flash of the rapids. I only feel the center's calm when I'm rallying something big—like a tornado, or a dome of wind large enough to shield a village, or when I meditate."

I can't believe that worked.

"What do you mean? Of course, it worked!" Elwood laughed.

You both could have died there. One small mistake on my part and you would have been lost in the raging waters of his power. Elwood's overprotective mind-mate was on a mission, and his lecture hammered each syllable into his brain. *You're lucky Aldridge was smart enough to guess what we were going to do and receive us from the other side.*

"So good to know you care. Besides, you don't make mistakes," Elwood replied.

I suppose you are right in that sense, his seal preened. Elwood almost felt the ridiculous, smug smile on the dead Fey's face. It was like a cat, and he had never liked cats.

It was still awfully reckless of you; then again, I should have expected as much.

"Mind informing me what's happening?" Chais still sounded slightly shell-shocked, but certainly calmer. He then wrinkled his nose, a rather cute expression. "It doesn't have anything to do with why Aldridge is now muttering curses under his breath, does it?"

"Probably, don't worry about it. Just an argument with dear old Relevard. It has been resolved. So, are you ready to try diving into that pool of power yourself?" Elwood asked. He brushed off the question, eager to see whether the risk had been worth it.

"Not really," Chais admitted. A small laugh broke through his lips. The smile—just slightly fearful, but a smile nevertheless—made him look younger, not a war-hardened colonel but a young boy, barely into manhood yet. It was rather endearing; it sounded like chiming bells trickling from his lips.

Chais finally slumped down. He seemed to slide down the rock until he rested his head on the forest ground. With the afternoon sun casting halos of light over his prone form, he looked ancient—a true Fey, more elegant and older than mortals could ever hope to be. It was odd how one man could look so young one second, then so old the next.

"We can start another day. First with the calm core since it's easier to control. We can jump into small tricks later," Elwood said and flashed a smile that lit his emerald eyes so they seemed to glow. He settled down next to Chais and let his eyes wander, eventually settling on the two women. One was a whirlwind of loud, wild gestures, blood-red hair, and a hot temper; the other a stoic mystery of caramel curls and bronze skin from a land she refused to admit to. Neither even glanced toward their general direction; they were too occupied with their own conversation. Lynara seemed to have warmed up to Rebme. Her previous wariness and distrust evaporated like morning mist. Chais closed his eyes as his breathing became even and calm. Elwood used this time of quiet to reevaluate his female travel companions.

Lynara had an innocent look about her that told stories. A sheltered childhood, never having seen war, only hearing tales of glory and conquest from the rich, stuffy nobles who surrounded her. But she was determined, too, eager to prove herself as a woman without the aid of summons. She had managed to climb to the rank of commander in her castle and her own division. She had worked harder than any man in her position—her disdained glances toward people of power showed that. Her temper helped keep lusting men away, and now she had been thrust into a world bigger than anything she thought she would ever see. She hid her secrets behind red-tinted glass walls and loud, rage-filled retorts. It was all in those bright eyes. She would need to learn how to hide it or she would risk losing it all. The world was much more dangerous than she was prepared for. Maybe this budding friendship with Rebme could help her learn, either that or leave her bleeding out. Elwood hoped it wouldn't—he found the woman fun, not to mention she was someone important to Chais. He could tell from guilty glances and a tenderness that could only be from family.

Rebme looked old; she carried too many secrets on shoulders too narrow to hold them all. Burden and loneliness were etched into her essence, but all emotion was closed behind a heavy fortress armed with iron and creatures from another world. She was so small, not even reaching his shoulder, and older than Chais, but still young. But she was also powerful—he had seen the darkness she wielded. He had never seen a summoner so young with such precise control. And he didn't even know who or what she was; those eyes gave away nothing. She still needed to do a lot more to prove herself. By giving so little, not even a continent of origin, it was impossible to truly trust her. Elwood's lips pressed into a thin line, and he looked away.

"Hey, Chais," Elwood said. The colonel hummed in acknowledgment, almost drowsily. "We've certainly gained two peculiar allies."

"I don't think normal people could handle us," Chais responded, causing Elwood to chuckle. It was an odd group he was traveling with. But maybe, just maybe, they could make it work.

CHAPTER
†WE∏†Y-O∏E

CHAIS PLAN†ED HIS FEE† on the soggy ground and closed his eyes.

Focus on your surroundings. Take in everything you feel, and channel that through your system. Aldridge's voice seemed sharper. Clearer. An ocean of waves spread across his vision. They shifted and blended into each other, a breathing mass of blue and green shades. They twisted and spun, colliding and breaking apart, releasing sparks of gold.

Chais metaphorically inhaled with ease and practice. He forced his beating heart to slow to a crawl. Fluidly, as if he had been a master of this power for centuries, he picked out his exterior senses. With Aldridge's Fey abilities, he could hear the light breeze, smell the scent of wood and blood ... With a calm equivalent to that before a storm, he gently eased his power through his entire body, to his fingertips, his mind, his veins. Gently, gently—

A deafening roar snapped Chais out of his system center. He stumbled back as the river water surged upward and spiraled forward with no leash. In a panicked attempt to rein it in, he stretched his arms toward the source. The magic within him gathered into a tornado. A tree collapsed. Dead leaves were sucked into the coiled force, immediately disintegrating. An arch of pain shot through his heart. Chais collapsed. He clutched onto his chest and released any attempts at control. The pillar of water finally obeyed gravity. It crashed down upon the forest and thoroughly soaked everything it hit, including Chais. And, well, a couple of unfortunate companions.

"Chais!" Lynara approached at a worrisome pace. Her clothes and hair clung to her, and her face was burning the shade of the plants that grew on Scarlet Peak. If Chais could harness his powers and throw some water at her right now, she would probably have vaporized it with the heat from her face alone.

"At least direct it *away* from us?" Elwood offered with a half chuckle, peering through drenched bangs. He pulled a small fish from his hair, stared at it in disgust, and threw it back into the emptier stream.

Chais exhaled, wringing his hands. There was a wisp of panic inside his throat that threatened to crawl out. Not today. "I'm trying, I swear."

"Try harder then!" Lynara growled, her stern, sisterly side showing through. Rebme brushed aside a curly strand of hair that hung in her eyes—she seemed strangely unaffected. Her clothes were dry.

"I think he's doing fine. Powers such as these don't develop so quickly." Rebme glanced toward Scarlet Pass. It was a larger silhouette in the fog now that they had moved on from Valport. The closest town was still far—otherwise, Chais wouldn't have tried with the whole soak-a-forest act.

Chais sprawled onto his back and felt his muscles relax now that they didn't have to support him. He summoned the little energy he had left to unstick the thin fabric of the tunic from his chest. A strand of anger flitted through his consciousness, and he decided to let it out.

"I don't get it," he managed, despite the lack of compliance from his jaw muscles, "I'm calmer than I've ever been, yet I still only create tidal waves and hurricanes."

It's not just a matter of calmness, you know.

Chais sighed. He didn't bother to answer since Lynara and Rebme were within earshot. He stared at the sky, which was slowly bleeding to orange. Harmless creatures as small as a hand floated about. The sun set their feathers and scales on fire. No stars, as always. They seemed to be nonexistent now, at least in this part of the empire.

"Do you know what other factors there are?" Lynara asked. She was still trying to avoid the fact that Gredian's former colonel—someone she had regarded as a brother—was more Fey than human. He had the power to harness the water element, and she had been too ignorant to know. But now she did, and, like him, she would have to find a way to accept that.

"Elwood said that he only saw a flash when he was summoning something small ... I think I have to move to the branches. Or visualize something smaller ..." Chais, filled with a new type of determination, pushed off the ground. A swarm of black spots immediately flooded his vision. He felt Lynara's hand on his shoulder as he shakily adjusted. It was familiar, yet foreign.

"You should rest." Rebme crossed her arms. Her dark brown curls framed her face, one side shadowed as she turned away from the slowly setting sun.

Suddenly, a scream pierced the air. Chais pivoted to see Elwood holding ... something; its source appeared to be Zefire's hair. The Fey spiked the pitch-black blob onto the grass and backed away quicker than the wind he controlled. The shape, which was the length of an entire arm, writhed on the ground. Its furious red eyes and yellowed teeth were the size of a finger.

"Is that what I think it is?" Elwood extended his arm, prepared to kill it with wind energy.

"I ..." It was the first time Chais had seen Rebme so uncertain. Her eyes darted rapidly across the creature's body, as if she were trying to figure out what it was. "I ... don't recognize it."

"It's a demon, isn't it? Shouldn't you know the different species of demons?" Lynara had her dagger out and was now speaking through the side of her mouth. Her deadly gaze was locked on the fish-like creature of darkness, which had gone still.

"There is a world of demons that even the most powerful summoners don't know. I've never seen this one before." Rebme pressed her lips into a thin line. Her whip was in her hand—its fairly new edges catching the slight breeze.

"Is it dead?" Elwood whispered. He approached the creature, which was as still as a stone. He looked like he was about to prod it with an imaginary stick.

"Oh, gods. That's not good." Chais pointed. Elwood turned to the riverbed, where Chais was looking, and cursed colorfully.

A flood of what seemed like oil rose from the stream in a torrent of writhing fins and teeth. Pinpoints of red, eerily similar to the eyes of the molecus, stared up at them. Each demon bore at least ten. A low buzzing sound escaped from their mouths and through the empty snap of six-inch teeth. As a single entity, the demons slithered at breakneck speed toward them.

"Run!" Elwood yelled, and they all scattered like pawns on a chessboard. The demons followed and snapped hungrily at Chais's heels. His muscles screamed for rest, and his lungs burned with the extra effort; it wouldn't take long until collapse. He felt a sharp prick in his left arm. One of the massive creatures dangled painfully from his skin. In one motion, he decapitated it. The head fell to the ground with a wet splat. Dark blood, the smell of metal and sewage, coated his torso. Chais was still moving, but the trees were a blur of greens, yellows, and browns, mixing with the onyx wisps radiating off of the demons. Don't look back, just go. The breeze danced alongside him as he picked up speed. It was so easy to run now. He didn't feel a strain in his legs or sweat dripping down his back, just wind. Wind and ... water?

Water droplets appeared beside him as he ran. They didn't seem to move—as if they were frozen in time. As if they were waiting for his command.

"There are too many! They must have a source!" Lynara cut down a beast, but not before it took a bite out of her too. She winced and grasped her thigh. Red blood mixed with black ooze that dribbled down her skin almost lazily. Chais instinctively reached out for her, but she was too far away.

"The river," Chais realized; then louder, "We have to circle around to the river!"

He saw Elwood and Rebme nod, but Lynara was too busy nursing her wound to hear what he was saying. Rebme grabbed the commander by the sleeve and dragged her after Chais. He was in front now. Thrashing shapes leaped at him, but he managed to sever his way through. There was a distorted crunch under his boot, then another prick of pain on his calf. He barely had time to register the fact that the dead demon fish left its jaws behind.

The riverbed was nearly pitch black now, a sea of shadow and infinite red glowing dots. There was no way they could make it through without getting overrun.

"Cover me!" Chais yelled and backed up. He felt a sharp wind against his cheek, then sticky warmth. Chais watched Elwood take a few more out with his bow; they exchanged a nod. Chais closed his eyes.

You need a tidal wave. We're not working on control right now—it's your lives on the line.

"Got it," Chais whispered. His eyes snapped open.

Magic. It seeped through his lungs, mind, heart, and blood. It pulsed with an ethereal presence and chilled his fingertips and breath, causing a tingle to race up his spine. An image of his system center, with its beautiful blues and golds, flashed in his mind before he let go. At that moment, he could do anything.

A tidal wave soared over his head. It didn't spill a single drop until it crashed upon the bodies of squirming demons, obliterating them in one fluid, breathtaking motion. It spread like a blanket across the forest floor and brought with it the ancient scents of the trees, mingling with the rotten odor of corpses. He caught a hint of the bubbling brook before the wave was sucked back into the river. Clouds of murky shadows sprung to the surface, but nothing else climbed back out.

But it kept going. Spiraling, twisting out of the river, hungry for more. Chais was tempted to fight for control, but the job had already been done. He dropped his arms and snapped out of his center. Now succumbing to nature, the water slid back.

Why was it so hard to control, but so easy to let go?

The silence was enough to kill. Chais blinked, and all of a sudden, the world was back to its dull color scheme, not the otherworldly brightness at his center. The magic which had once tingled in his veins was absent, as if it had never appeared. He no longer felt immortal.

"Your eyes glowed, you know," Elwood breathed. His face lit up even under the shadow of the trees. "And for the record, glowing eyes make people look cooler."

Chais managed a weak smile. The exhaustion hit him like a brick and blew out any fire that had been inside him before. The wound on his arm and calf didn't help much either, although the pain was just a dull throb.

"I have to learn to do that more consistently though. And," he glanced down at his trembling legs, "to use less energy at once."

That'll take time, but we can learn.

Learn a foreign power he had just discovered. Despite every instinct in his brain telling him to panic from the information overload, Chais forced it down. Seeing the calm of his power center seemed to have made everything at least a bit more tolerable.

"Do you know what that meant?" Rebme was pacing. Her eyes were dark beneath her hood.

"The seal is breaking. We don't have much time if something Rebme doesn't recognize crawled out of the river," Lynara cut in. She avoided eye contact with Chais. A thin layer of sweat coated her forehead, and the dark red liquid seeped through her fingers. Rebme rummaged through her leather satchel for medical supplies and worked quickly to stop the bleeding and bind the wound. As she tended to Lynara, Chais could only put pressure on his arm—the familiar sting raced throughout his entire body, reminding him strangely of the magic he'd felt just moments ago. Elwood cozied in. He was covered in demon blood that smelled like the sewage-filled slums Chais had grown up in. Chais tried to ignore the warm liquid that was still on his cheek. This demon's blood seemed to last longer than others such as the reweraa or the kymatis. That was one thing he preferred about killing demons over humans; demon blood didn't stay on your skin—or conscience, for that matter. They were just creatures from another world, but killing humans, or even Fey ... created a special type of feeling. Murdering someone who looked like him ... it just had a haunting aftereffect that demons, no matter how formidable, couldn't match.

"Hey, look on the bright side," Elwood grinned. Chais raised his brows—even that took too much effort.

"If your injury gets worse, we could always chop off your arm and be twins!"

Of course. Of course, only Elwood would say that.

"The wound's on the wrong arm. That wouldn't make us twins."

"Then we could be halves of a whole." Elwood's eyes lit up. "Imagine that—I couldn't go anywhere without you and you couldn't go anywhere without me because ..." He grabbed one of Chais's hands and brought it close to his chest. "... because you make me complete."

"Stop it already, you idiot."

Then the pain hit.

Suddenly, as if he'd been struck by lightning, it ripped through his body and caused his vision to go blurry, as if he was back to the tearing agony of the whip. Over and over again, two opposites raced through his veins until he doubled over and screamed for it to disappear.

In his peripheral vision, Chais could spot movement. Screaming ... not him, but Lynara. Chais barely registered two pinpoints of violet light. The pain heightened tenfold. A strangled gasp escaped from his throat as something within him writhed, slowly being pulled up through his esophagus. To his throat. His mouth. And finally ...

He inhaled sharply; the pain dissipated as quickly as it had come. Vision spinning, Chais vomited into a bush and tried to gain his bearings. Lynara seemed to be cured as well, though she was passed out. Whatever it was, it must've been from the demons.

"It's out of your system now," Rebme murmured. Her violet eyes flashed. "I had to force it through your mouth—you'll probably taste something foul for a few hours."

Chais blinked hard. He could already taste the sewage-smelling blood on his tongue, but other than that, there were no immediate side effects. "What was it?"

"A special type of residue from only a few species of demons," Elwood answered for the summoner. The teasing light in his eyes was now gone. "Damn, was it unsettling to watch shadows pour out from your eyes."

"Yeah?" Chais said, out of breath.

Lynara's breathing returned to her. She started to draw herself up, and a low cough escaped from her lips. Rebme immediately rushed to her, waiting for a moment before explaining her and Chais's condition in a hushed whisper.

"I'm just surprised those demons exist." Chais scrubbed at his face, as if trying to purge any remaining residue out. As a colonel on the frontlines, he'd seen his fair share of both demons and—well, more disturbing things, to say the least. Normally, he wouldn't be concerned if he didn't recognize a demon species, but if Rebme, a powerful summoner, couldn't tell ... that was something else entirely.

"Well, at least you won't have to worry about being my twin," Elwood said and gestured toward Chais's arm wound. It was already beginning to scar, and the black blood was gone. The wound on his leg was only a dull throb.

A sudden piercing shriek echoed through the valley—a reweraa—its figure blocked by the canopy of trees. Chais instinctively dropped low, and he felt Elwood do so as well. The demon bird circled lazily around the patch of small woodland between Mirstone and Valport. Its glaring eyes flickered back and forth before it set off with a couple of powerful wingbeats. It had been too high to pick up their scent; if it had been a bit closer, they would've found themselves at the mercy of Gredian's forces once again.

Looks like you'll have to be more alert now. Even I can't detect reweraa too well when they don't want to be detected.

"Well, ship me to the Vlyth," Lynara muttered, referring to the large, rugged mountain range that ran a span longer than Gredian itself. "Now Adaric is after us? I told him I'd take care of the search situation, so shouldn't he be off our tails?" Her face was still pale. Her thigh was wrapped, and a few clouds of blood surfaced on the gauze, but it was red and nothing else.

"He's after *us*." Elwood jerked his chin toward Chais. "He doesn't know about you two though. Maybe he thinks Candycloud's progress was too slow, so he decided to step in like the controlling freak he probably is."

Lynara grumbled at the nickname, but Rebme prevented her from leaping at the Fey's throat.

Chais nodded and forced himself to his feet. "As long as we stay on the move and as a group, we won't be his first target." If Adaric was smart enough to have been an advisor to Havard, chances were, he wouldn't waste precious resources on a search expedition. The war had been going on for more than fifty years now, and neither side had shown signs of stopping. The remains of destroyed Gredian cities plagued the front range of the empire. Alryne was one of them. It served as a flag in the ground; the Fey-toppling Alryne had brought economic devastation to Gredian, despite the many other ports along the southern Ashwood Sea.

Which was also why Chais was against going too far north from Valport or Mirstone, toward the Embercain Sea. His home city's ruins stood like graves in the dying sunlight, shaming him for its demise. He shuddered inwardly. No way was he going back.

"Let's get going then," Rebme said as she neatly packed the rest of her medical supplies into her satchel. Chais helped Lynara up, offering support when her leg fell out from under her. It wouldn't be long before they'd have to stop again to take another rest, what with the recent injuries and Chais's utter exhaustion. A reweraa had just flown over; it would probably come back to double-check. They wouldn't want to be here when it did.

So, they were back where they started, Chais realized, except now they had two more strong warriors to assist them. In Valport, he'd heard about Adaric's reignited quest to find the travelers, but some were against the newly crowned king. They didn't believe in his tendency to send soldiers out who had never seen battle before, and frankly, Chais didn't either. It wasted too many Gredian lives.

Something like sadness sprung into his heart when he thought about his father dying out on the devastated landscape. Chais wondered if the man had regretted abandoning an eight-year-old son on the streets or if the son's life simply wasn't a part of his anymore.

Chais supposed he would never know.

IT HAD BEEN A WHILE since Lynara Merran killed.

Sickening thoughts flashed through her mind as she twisted the blade—hearing the wet crunch of skin, flesh, and bone—ending a life. Just like that.

She perched on her haunches for a few moments and peered at the mess of blood that marked the remains of a boar-like creature. She studied its open eyes, devoid of ... anything. Its elongated tusks that tapered off into a sharpened point mirrored the zigzagging of faint brown markings on its hide right above its open stomach. Since the rest of her companions had killed not only animals but people, she'd better get used to the sight.

Lynara stood, grabbed the animal by a tusk, and made sure not to spill any blood on the way back to camp. The woods seemed to sway, but she ignored it. Forests didn't startle her nearly as much as before, not since they'd been on the road for a while. The bloody cliffs of Scarlet Pass stretched toward the sky. It wasn't in front of her anymore. Now it was to her left, providing a momentary distraction from the ruined landscape ahead.

As the sound of the crackling fire and low conversation approached, Lynara felt herself disappear, only to be replaced with a scowling image of a woman that no man would prefer over the street services. Gredian was harsh. Over the years, she'd finally developed something, some sort of facade that would draw thirsty soldiers away and keep untrustworthy people at bay. Her companions hadn't gotten to the point of bringing that wall down yet—not even Chais.

"Brought dinner," Lynara announced and set the creature down. She quickly washed its blood off in the stream. Elwood raised a hand in greeting while Chais and Rebme set to work preparing the carcass.

"Sugarplum! Glad to see you'll be joining us," Elwood greeted in a singsong voice. His eyes gleamed with a flame of orange from the campfire.

Lynara scoffed. "It's not mutual," she said. Elwood pretended to pout. She resisted the urge to laugh at the Fey's expression and instead took a spot on the dried-up grass across from the warrior.

"We're approaching the ruins next to Quelf," she informed them. "Beyond that is The Unknown. It's not that Gredian hasn't explored it yet; it's just an area where no one likes to live."

"Also, where the main war is being fought," Chais said as he rotated a chunk of meat over the fire. Lynara averted her eyes.

"He's right. I've never been out there before, but I've heard it's not very nice to your sanity."

Chais's silence only confirmed it. She didn't risk glancing at his expression, although Rebme probably got a good look.

"I went through a quieter place when I first …" Elwood cast a glance at Lynara, "… politely entered Gredian."

"You invaded us," Chais snorted, catching himself at the last word, "the empire."

"Politely entered."

"Invaded."

"Boys, cut it out," Lynara interjected. Men.

The savory smell of roasted whatever-it-was filtered through the darkening skies. Elwood's thin shield was enough to keep hungry creatures—and demons—from attacking, and the area was quiet enough so that Gredian soldiers wouldn't be on regular patrol. It granted their group some calm time with a fire. The animal, although small for its species, gave them enough for the night. She took a bite and swallowed before deciding to discuss the plan. Rebme beat her to it.

"We'll accompany you on your journey to Atrelia until about halfway through the Unknown," Rebme said. She looked at Chais for confirmation.

"Where the Embercain Sea ends," he added. "If we travel west from here, then the end of the sea will be marked by a tower—a watchtower. It'll be hard to see since it's so far away, so keep your eyes peeled."

"Then Grumpy and I will proceed toward Fey Wonderland, and we can train while searching for the rest of the seals," Elwood chirped, drawing all eyes toward him. There were a few heartbeats of dead silence, where the Fey's gaze flickered between each person.

"What? 'Atrelia' sounds too formal."

"Sure, sure," Lynara yawned. Rebme was already searching for a more comfortable place to call it a day. Elwood stood, extending his one arm in a half V-shape as he stretched.

"I vote Grumpy for first watch," he said.

"Then I vote Stumpy for the rest of the night afterward,"

Chais replied. Lynara still couldn't get over the delicately pointed ears that barely poked through his hair, but she decided to accept it for now. At least, until the full truth of reality could hit her square in the gut.

"No fair," Elwood grumbled, but retreated to his corner, knowing it wouldn't happen. The commander had to marvel at the sheer beauty of Fey, not only in their physical appearance but also the way they moved. Elwood walked on the wind. He had feline steps that would catch anyone by surprise, and they wouldn't even realize it when a Fey slit their throat. He'd killed before. There was something about his cheerful aura that felt too ... positive, happy to be true. She could also tell Chais's heritage in his features and movements. Hell, even the signature Fey glow that Elwood possessed was beginning to show on Chais now. And to think that all this time, Gredian had never found out. Lynara vaguely recalled the life he had led before coming to the castle, but she clearly remembered when they first brought him in. It was something she'd never erased from her memory.

Lying there in the dark, with Chais's silent promise to keep them safe, Lynara thought about their situation—it seemed too ... easy? Was that the word she was looking for? She couldn't help but feel that there was something bigger about this, that it went beyond just finding the seals and reforging the gateway that linked the demon world to theirs. Something ... but she couldn't put her finger on it. That was the thing about late-night reflection—it blurred her ability to think.

Chais's back faced her. It wouldn't be long before he would resort to pacing the perimeter. His chin rested on his hand, and although she couldn't see his face, she could tell he was deep in thought. He was now a far cry from the boy she'd grown up with, although his quietness remained the same. Before Alryne's end, he was a completely different person; running up to her on her business trips, a bundle of sunshine.

Nostalgia. It was heavy, an indescribable feeling that clung to her heart. Lynara listened to the still night air. If it was this quiet, then Chais was bound to—

As if on cue, the colonel stood. A gentle tune escaped from his mouth as he began to pace, and she recognized it as one of those folk songs that the village mothers would croon to their children. Lynara closed her eyes. She listened to the warmth of his voice and the barely audible scrapes of his boots on the ground.

There were a few cries of birds in the distance, but Chais continued to hum, his voice getting increasingly soft until the night air's silence pounded in her veins. She wondered how he looked now—lonely? Heartbroken?

Somehow, she could sense a lost presence about him, as if it was just him and the stars and nothing else—a soul that could never find his way.

CHAPTER
TWENTY-TWO

REBME WATCHED with growing amusement as her male travel companions sparred. Despite Chais's obvious exhaustion from another morning of creating tidal waves and Elwood's occasional imbalance, they moved with sure and confident grace. The first few days, she had noticed an uncomfortable hitch whenever Chais used his back muscles in his movement. Now the tick was gone. Every inch of him moved perfectly in sync. He lashed out and blocked hits without the slightest hesitation. Sweat shined on both of their brows as they exchanged blows. It was like crystallized drops that gave their features an unnatural glow in the sunlight as if their skin was shimmering. The solid beats acted as a percussion to the symphony nature provided them. Soaked grass bent beneath their feet but with a feather lightness she could not comprehend; their mud-coated boats never snapped a single blade. The sun cast spotlights through the leaves, giving the two fighters the lighting of a stage performance. It only brought another layer to the already unearthly dance.

Rebme idly ran a finger down her whip. The cool, polished acacia wood was smooth under her fingers. She traced the little animals carved into the handle, their outlines faded from use. The snouts pointed downward, and she let her fingers follow them. Small clouds of smoke and the tight sealing that wrapped around the handle where the heel knot was and the leather began. Cords of braided dark leather, strong and worn down, wrapped around the belly of the whip by her own hands. Four-seam plaits in an intricate but practical design snaked down the belly of the whip. Coil after coil. Hours of work and many sleepless nights. Ending with strips of unbraided leather, oiled and cared for and made to tear through skin effortlessly. She had seen the same beauty and love on Elwood's bow. Even now she witnessed him polishing it every night, wiping away dirt and grime under the moonlight. It was a shame he would probably never be able to use it to its full potential again.

Her attention was drawn back to the fight as they both sped up to a signal she didn't catch. Rebme's eyes followed every Fey-speed movement exchanged between the two. Elwood ducked beneath a blow and slammed a fist into Chais's ribs. His opponent took the blow and retreated a step, absorbing the blow without flinching. Then he smoothly stepped back from a second punch, aimed to drive him further away, and swung his leg up for a kick. Elwood instinctively twisted so his right side was faced toward the oncoming blow and grounded himself. Rebme noticed the slight lift of his tunic sleeve. Shock and dismay colored his youthful features. Elwood was trying to block with his right arm, an arm that he no longer possessed. Chais seemed to realize it too and pulled back his kick, but momentum sent it slamming into Elwood's shoulder.

And Elwood fell. His face twisted with pain as he knelt in the mud. His hand cradled the stump as blood seeped out between his fingers. Chais's pale features turned pasty white, and his hands were clenched at his side as he stared at his fallen friend.

Rebme and Lynara were moving immediately. With gentleness the summoner did not know the commander possessed, Lynara placed a hand on Chais's shoulder and led him away before he could do anything rash. Chais struggled for a second before following Lynara away from Elwood. Worry and guilt were clear in his eyes.

Rebme knelt next to Elwood, unconcerned with the cold mud pressing against her legs and soaking her clothes. Leaves stuck to her cloak, along with grass and whatever else was in the slug. She focused on her patient. She watched warily as his eyes cleared. His wet breath gasped as he tried to calm his heartbeat. Rebme's fingers brushed against her leather pouch. The material was a warm brown that Elwood seemed to focus on, drawing a sense of peace from the leather and grounding himself. Its surface was soft and worn smooth from years of use. She unfastened the knot of cracked leather straps.

As slowly as she could, trying not to startle her patient, Rebme removed Elwood's hand from the wound. The blood was already crusting. It began to harden around the edges and seal the wound from the elements. Elwood healed faster than any Fey she had ever met, but that also meant that the rocks and mud that worked into the bloody wound were not removed. She didn't care how well Elwood could fight off infections; Rebme didn't want to risk it.

She pulled out a cloth and carefully wiped away the dried scab. A steady stream of blood flowed again. With one hand pressed against his collarbone for support, she used her other to pull out a small branch of pale yellow flowers from her bag, smaller than the tip of her pinky and smooth as the silk cloth. Rebme brushed the plant against the Fey's wound. The blood soaked into the petals and dyed them red. Rebme could feel Elwood's muscles tense beneath her other hand as the cleansing properties of the flower pulled the debris out of his cut. She looked up to see his eyes clear of pain and confusion. Good. She no longer had to play "kind doctor."

"You are an idiot," Rebme said as she smeared gauze onto the cracked and bleeding remains of skin on Elwood's right shoulder. "I told you to avoid using it, and yet you insist on sparring with that bullheaded half-Fey every chance you get! And, as if that's not bad enough, you seem to insist on using your right side to take hits!" She wrapped a new layer of cloth over the strong herbs and ignored the startled yelp of pain her patient gave at the unexpected roughness.

"I need to get used to working with one arm! It's already hindering my movement, so I need to learn how to work around it!" Rebme gave him her coldest stare, hardening her eyes to shards of amethyst. Elwood had the nerve to look innocent. "What?"

"If you don't let your body heal properly before you strain it, you may end up with a permanent imbalance in your fighting style." Rebme tried to explain that even after the body had accepted the missing limb—if it ever did—Elwood would never fight the way he did before. He would have to develop a new, completely untested form of combat or retire from battle entirely. And judging from what Rebme had seen in their time together, Elwood would never put down his blade. His willingness to fight, despite knowing he was at a great disadvantage, was proof of that statement.

"You think I don't know that?" Rebme heard the voice of the general that appeared on the day of the molecus in the deadly calm of his tone. She always knew his happy-go-lucky attitude was like the soft snows of winter back in her forgotten home: kind and seemingly gentle … until someone stepped on it and found it falling away beneath their feet, into a chasm of unimaginable depth, its walls lined with ice and wisdom and its darkness yearning for comfort where it would not be found. Elwood was hiding more than just a capable leader beneath his mask, but he had been kind enough not to pry into her past, so she could only return the favor.

"You are doing a remarkable job at appearing ignorant about your current wellbeing," Rebme said. She was careful to keep her voice static and her eyes dull. Her hands, never idle, gathered her supplies and tucked them neatly back into her bag where they belonged.

"I know. I know perfectly well that my body is not happy with the strain I'm putting it under. But if you hadn't noticed, All-Wise One," he sneered, a trickle of genuine malice coating his words as his shining eyes glowed, "we are on the run from an empire that would very much like to see me dead. Preferably to display my head on an iron spike. I need to keep in shape, no matter what my body may think the limits are. If I don't try to break them,

I never will. I might as well just cuff myself with iron and greet the next patrol with a sign around my neck saying 'Free Fey.'"

"Better than having the next patrol group find you dead in a ditch from infection," Rebme bit back. Her hand was now tightly wrapped around her whip, just in case the Fey got aggressive. She could never be too sure—injured, angry people lashed out. She had a scar to remind her of that.

"I don't know. It's how I always wanted to go, you know?" And it was gone. She felt herself relax as well. His humor-sparkled eyes seemed almost dead compared to the ancient glow that had resided in them not moments before. It was as if his eyes now were merely emeralds, when before they held the very life essence of the forest. Rebme took this as a cue to hand Elwood back to Chais.

"You two kids have fun." Rebme walked away. She was so focused on keeping a straight face she almost tripped over a root. Those two boys wouldn't know how to make a proper conversation if it slapped them. Not that she could admit that she was much better.

Lynara was perched on a stone, hands clasped over her lap and back rigid straight: the posture of a lady raised in the court. Rebme joined her, draping her cloak over the slightly damp rock. She reached up and rearranged her hood to ensure that it didn't fall off if the cloak snagged on a branch when she rose again. Once she was certain the white fabric was secure, Rebme observed the interaction between the men.

"Sorry about …" Chais attempted and gestured hopelessly at the rebound appendage. Rebme resisted the urge to slam her forehead into the nearest tree. Had no one taught the boy basic communication skills? It almost felt like, apart from the occasional snarky comment—more often than not at the wrong place and time—everything that left that poor boy's mouth was just there to show his social ineptness. Then again, he was young, very young to be a lieutenant colonel, meaning he started young. Maybe he really was never taught communication skills beyond relaying and giving orders.

"Grumpy, please," Elwood sighed and lay back into the mud, unconcerned about the filth seeping into his hair. The summoner applauded herself for using waterproof gauze as the dark liquid stained the new bandages. "I don't want you to get all mopey again because you feel like you now owe me or some shit."

"I don't get mopey."

"Sure you don't."

Rebme tuned out the conversation and focused on the fidgeting Lynara by her side. Her usual confident face disappeared as the two men headed back to the river. Rebme felt a strange urge to yell at them to be careful. The faint splashing of water reached her ears as Chais and Elwood started their afternoon practice.

"Rebme …"

The summoner carefully took in her body language. Lynara's shoulders were tight and drawn inward. Her lips were pursed into a thin line, and her eyes latched onto her shoes. She was nervous, but Rebme couldn't tell why.

"Yes?" Rebme decided she didn't wish to waste time guessing what Lynara was so reluctant to tell her. She would talk, or she wouldn't. It didn't matter to her either way. Well, maybe it mattered a little, but not enough for her to be gentle about it.

"How do you do it?" A whisper that caught her off guard. Seeing the flash of confusion, the commander elaborated. "You always know what to do, you're always so …" She frowned and bit down lightly on her lip, trying to find the right word to use. Rebme waited. She shocked herself with the interest she felt in Lynara's declaration.

"What?" Rebme pushed when Lynara's face dusted with a light pink. The summoner suddenly felt so old, staring at the commander.

"Useful."

"Does no one here know how to make a proper conversation?" The words fell out before Rebme could stop them. In her defense, it was both amusing and irritating, how apparent the lack of basic communication skills was.

"We're traveling with idiots. I've gotten used to dumbing down my language for their benefit," Lynara said.

Rebme could tell it was instinctive and developed from years of being beaten down. The commander was far too used to using anger to shield herself from ridicule. Her arms wrapped around her waist, as if she was comforting herself.

"One of them has been learning our language for longer than you've been alive," Rebme pointed out in an attempt to lighten the mood.

"Yes, and I don't think I've heard a single intelligent word come out of his mouth in the few days we've traveled together. And the only time I don't hear him is when he sleeps." Rebme hummed, neither agreeing nor denying the claim.

"The Fey *is* rather loud," Rebme finally said as she adjusted her bag from where it was scrunched against her hip. She diverted her piercing gaze from Lynara, hopefully easing her nerves a little.

Lynara sighed again. "That's what I'm talking about. You're always so calm and composed!"

Rebme remained silent. Lynara was still avoiding the real reason she started the conversation—Rebme could see it now.

The question about her attitude and confidence was just the redhead probing the surface of what she wanted to inquire about. Her fingers constantly brushed against the areas where her daggers were hidden. Her eyes darted from the summoner's purple ones to her whip and back. Rebme suddenly felt she knew what the commander wanted, but she would wait until Lynara asked before deciding if she was willing to offer it.

Lynara continued talking about nothing and everything, but she never made eye contact. Rebme watched her until her rambling died down and she returned to gnawing on her lip. Finally, she met her eyes. Lynara took an audible breath.

"I want to learn."

"About what?"

"I want to learn how to act like a leader. I'm a commander, but I know it's just a fancy title. I've never seen true battle—my squadron is tracking and information-exclusive. And ... and I'm scared." Lynara expelled the words like she couldn't get rid of them fast enough. "I'm so, so scared. This—this is way more than what I signed up for. I don't know how you handle it so well, but I want to also."

"I'd be happy to teach you what I know. But, for details, you would need to ask the general," Rebme warned.

"I want to at least know the basics before I ask," Lynara murmured. She was clearly ashamed by her lack of knowledge.

"Then I'll teach you." Rebme wasn't sure what made her promise to aid Lynara. But the genuine smile she gave was enough to banish any lingering doubt she had about the lessons. So she gave one back. "But ... to be honest, I'm scared too."

Lynara's head jolted up. Her eyes were wide with surprise. "What! But you seem so ... calm."

"Practice. I can teach you that if you want as well. So, you don't have to hide behind anger." Rebme tugged her hood further down in an attempt to hide herself. From what, she wasn't sure. The commander remained silent, at a loss for words, waiting for her to explain.

"I ... as a summoner, I can ... *feel* the demon's intent. The thought of them being free scares me more than almost anything else," Rebme whispered. Most of her instincts were screaming at her for exposing a weakness, but a small part of her felt relieved. In a world of demons and magic, it was easy to forget that not everyone was an enemy.

"Don't worry. We'll stop it. We've got two insane Fey on our side." Lynara gave her a hesitant, but real, smile.

For a moment, Rebme felt like she had a friend. Maybe not a close one, but perhaps someday.

Then, that second of tranquility was shattered.

"Shitting hydra hatchlings!" A startled voice, unmistakably Elwood's, rang out from the distance. The two women shot to their feet and raced toward the racket. Lynara had instinctively unsheathed her daggers, and Rebme summoned a lugaire to follow at their heels.

When they burst into the riverbed, they were greeted with an odd sight. Elwood was sitting in the river. He was thoroughly soaked, while a giant black bear sat on top of him. Dark tendrils of smoke trailed behind the great beast and gave the monstrous creature shattered wings upon its back. Its eyes, four pinpricks of bloody red nestled above a snout, glowed with an other-dimensional power. Its giant head rested contently on Elwood's head, almost burying his skull in fur. The bear yawned, and the maw stretched open to show lines of yellowed teeth growing from a jaw strong enough to break bones like toothpicks. A rough, pink tongue dashed over its leathery nose before disappearing back into its mouth. Claws, longer than her forearms, were carefully placed so they wouldn't shred the unfortunate Fey trapped under his thick, coarse fur.

Once Rebme took it all in, she realized the scene didn't make any sense. The Fey was, as far as she could tell, being snuggled by a black demon bear. She only knew one person who could summon such a creature—a creature from a species so rare that it hadn't been given a name. It was her, and she most definitely did *not* summon it.

Chais was momentarily frozen. He seemed to be extremely conflicted between helping his friend or enjoying the scene. He stepped back uncomfortably, unsure what to do while Elwood continued to wrestle the bear demon. His dagger was out, but apparently, the sight of a demon cuddling his friend was enough to stun him. Chais saw that the beast wasn't hurting Elwood, so he simply stood back and waited for the summoner to arrive to sort things out. Rebme knew that the moment Elwood appeared to be in real danger, the blade in his hand would strike fast and true.

"Diad?" Rebme walked over, thoroughly baffled by the appearance of her personal summon.

"Who is Diad?" Elwood asked. His voice was muffled by the dark fur. Despite his position, he seemed perfectly content and let his hands roam through the bear's thick fur. Chais had shed his blade and approached Diad as well, his hands wandering through its coarse hairs.

"The demon bear thing," Rebme gestured. She motioned for it to get off Elwood before it accidentally crushed his ribs. Diad huffed and blew Elwood's hair out of his eyes, but the animal shuffled off him. The movement nearly knocked Chais over.

"It's yours?" Chais bent down to examine its enormous claws. "Would have been nice if you gave us a warning. I nearly decapitated the thing before it started rolling around like a large puppy."

"How did it end up on Elwood?" Lynara asked. She was staying well outside of the bear's reach but was certainly curious about it.

"I wanted to pet it," Elwood answered, rubbing the back of his head and chuckling softly, "Not my brightest moment."

"So, what is it doing here?" Chais stood up once more and walked to Elwood's side. The two always seemed no more than a few feet away from each other. "Why did you summon a bear?"

"I didn't summon it ... apart from me, only Master would be able to summon it. And she's busy keeping the guards distracted from our path, so she couldn't maintain it this far." Rebme reached her hand out to feel Diad's aura for the signature tug that would lead her to its master ... only to find that the connection stretched out and faded to a frayed end—like it had been cut.

"How odd," Rebme muttered and felt her own energy. But it belonged to the lugaire she had summoned earlier, now sitting quietly and docilely next to a dripping tree. She felt nothing for the beast before her.

"Is it possible ... that it came out on its own? You said that it's a personal summon, right? So it must be different from regular summons? More obedient and loyal?" Lynara stood and stared at a puddle at her feet, deep in thought. "Is it possible that it, uh ... sensed your anxiety and came to protect you?"

Rebme tried to hide the proud smile threatening to spill onto her lips. The commander was far more clever than she realized.

What she said certainly made sense; some of her personal summonses had almost summoned themselves in the past. With a weakened seal, they might have just been able to do it. But they had never tried to summon themselves when she was emotional, only when danger was approaching—a warning.

"No … Diad didn't come to soothe me. It's warning me of something." Rebme eyed the surrounding forests. She dismissed her dog summon and forced a bond onto the bear, tying it to the frayed end she found earlier.

"Something is coming. We'd better get going before it gets here."

CHAPTER
TWENTY-THREE

"GET ON A KYMATIS," Rebme ordered. Her voice was deadly calm. She reached for her whip, and her fingers trembled from something other than the cold. Shadows hovered midair, seeming to feed on the shade of the trees as they fused into more distinguishable shapes, followed by hazy, nebulous manes. Traces of violet residue lingered on the demons' coiled muscles, a result of haphazard summoning.

Lynara rushed to one of them. Her boots threw up minuscule dust clouds. Their need to get moving pressed down heavily on her shoulders. Chais watched as she attempted several times to mount the creature that was nearly twice her size.

"If you wanted help, you could've just asked," he said and

weaved his fingers together as a makeshift step for the commander. She took him up on his offer and swung onto the horse with ease.

"Says you," Lynara murmured before Chais found another kymatis. At a staggering nine feet, the horse-like demon towered over him like a barricade. He reached in for his power when he realized that he still hadn't learned to control it yet. A short jet stream of water would be near impossible.

Jump. Your body is part-Fey now—you'll make it.

Chais backed up a few steps. The muscles in his legs tightened as he eyed the wispy image of the demon. Lynara and Rebme were ahead, already starting at a walk, while Elwood seemed to be watching with faint interest. Chais leaped. His arms reached out for the horse's shoulder as he vaulted above. He almost, *almost,* overshot.

His left leg caught the side of the kymatis, and he bent his knee so that he wouldn't make a fool of himself by completely missing the horse. It felt so natural, so ... light. Every movement was fluid; he could run so much faster, fight so much easier, and—if the current situation was any indication—jump so much higher. It was as if there was an infinite expanse of physical capability, and he had just unlocked it.

"I was almost inclined to help you," Elwood said, "but I decided against it because it would be amusing to see you tumble over a demon horse."

"I'm delighted that my pain serves as your amusement," Chais snorted as they set off at a breakneck speed. The duo rapidly caught up with the women ahead. Rebme still hadn't given up control of her demons, but maybe it was from something other than issues of trust. Her bear summon—Diad, was it?—ate up the shadows of the trees with its silhouette. Although the demon had seemed clumsy and a bit lethargic when it wrapped Elwood into a hug, it certainly wasn't that way now. Diad kept up with the kymatis next to it, gait for gait. Its tongue hung to the side as it ran. No wonder it was a rare summon; it seemed to have many tricks in its arsenal.

Listen. What are you running from? Aldridge asked, his voice grave but serene at once. It sounded more like the Aldridge who had trained him mentally during his practice sessions with Elwood, the Aldridge who had guided him through each Fey ability as they came, helping him get used to the enhanced sight, smell, hearing, and movement. It wasn't the Aldridge who threw rare snarky comments at Relevard or the quiet Aldridge, who did more dreaming than seeing.

Chais's Fey senses sharpened. All of a sudden he could hear his breathing, his heartbeat—then, as he focused, the distant pounding sound of hooves on hardened forest dirt and the deadly sound of swords sliding from their sheaths. So many soldiers—armed to the heel and back, toiled beneath their own blood and sweat, people he would undoubtedly recognize—

Chais steeled himself and forced the power within him to swell until he could feel it at the tips of his fingers, no more and no less; he kept both Aldridge and Elwood's words at the back of his mind.

Control. *Control.*

With each beat of the kymatis's hooves, he moved to its unearthly rhythm. Chais twisted to face the trees. The ghost of his element began to tickle his fingers, and the cadence of his heart sped up with the demon beneath him.

"Time to test your aim!" Elwood Zefire yelled. His pupils danced with a vivid light. The Fey's hair was everywhere now that they were both riding backward on the kymatis, whipping around his face and nearly obscuring his view.

The weight of the dagger at Chais's waist acted as an anchor.

Remember how we trained. Aldridge's voice was serious. *If there are too many, you can create a shield. Don't tire out.*

Of course, the word "shield" was a term best used lightly. These past days, including just now by the riverbed, Chais had been working on forming some type of barrier with his energy; sometimes it worked, sometimes it didn't. He prayed it would be the former this time—but he was so tired—overexerting his reserves due to lack of experience, creating tidal waves and explosions without a shred of control ... It exhausted him in a way that sparring with Elwood couldn't.

"Thanks, Aldridge," Chais whispered, genuinely, right when the forest cracked open.

Trees split at their trunks. Sharp wood chips scattered in every direction. The simultaneous thud of the first layer of trees was loud enough to shatter the silence for minutes. Dirt sprayed, coating the surviving trees in a layer of grime. And the soldiers ...

There were too many—easily a platoon. Their crested sashes gleamed even under the shadows, and their iron swords formed a wall of lethal stakes. Enemy kymatis bared their needle-like teeth. Their muscles rippled underneath their coat as they launched themselves forward, scarlet eyes screaming death. Their manes disobeyed gravity. Shadows reached spindly fingers out to the sky.

Gredian's intention of capture or kill was obvious.

Chais scanned their faces, each one twisted with killing intent. Reweraa. Had they used reweraa to find them? Did Adaric lay low, watching their movements, until he decided to strike? He suddenly recalled Rebme's words from earlier. Why had her master let the guards through if she was busy keeping them distracted? Elwood fired the first shot. With bow in hand and plenty of space between them, the Fey warrior harnessed the infinite energy roaring around their ears, concentrated for a heartbeat, then sent a blast of honed wind shooting forward in a wide arc. Men fell, and order fell with them.

Chais blinked. A flash of golds and blues crashed against the edges of his fingers in a wild attempt to break out. Behind—far, far behind the soldiers, over the bellows of war-driven men, over the untamed fury of Elwood's wind energy, he could hear the faint bubbling of a stream. A stream—

The sound of bowstrings rebounding at once drew his attention. With a rush of wind, a few arrows pierced the air. Their red flags caught the dying light of the sun. There were too many demons, too many creatures that swallowed its rays for the daylight to survive.

Shield!

An arrow struck him in the shoulder, and the force drove it through and out. Blood splattered behind him and landed on the mane of the kymatis, narrowly missing its head. Chais choked back his immediate cry. Warm blood poured down his right arm. It pooled into the crook of his elbow. The arm hung limp, a useless appendage so early in the battle.

Chais pushed the hurricane within himself down, instead hauling out a thin, controlled line of power. His hand was shaking—almost as much as that day by the river, over ten years ago. There were still arrows hung midair, as if pulled by a divine being. A shield. He had to make a shield.

Chais struggled to focus as he attempted to recall the training. He wove the lines of power into a sloppy half-dome of protection, and it glowed a supernatural blue, nearly transparent. It shuddered, weaker through the pain that throbbed on his shoulder. Tawny veins swayed methodically back and forth on its exterior.

The arrows almost shattered it. Jagged cracks exploded across its surface. Forcing his heart rate to slow and clenching his teeth against the wound consumed by fire, Chais wove layer after layer of water energy over it and built a thick security against the attack. From beneath, large wolf-like demons charged forward and drove their fangs into the enemy kymatis' necks. Rebme. She had summoned lugaires.

Soldiers fell, but too many remained. Chais scraped desperately at his drying reserves and molded his energy into a core of pure power. He tried to remember the day when he'd created a tidal wave, crushing the sea of slithering demon fish—tried to remember that feeling of magic, of beauty, of poise.

He could spot the outline of a shield in front of Elwood. The ends of both their barricades provided shelter for the companions riding ahead of them. Chais searched the fringes of the bloodied forest. His shield trembled, so weak next to Elwood's, as each layer cracked and broke under the onslaught of projectiles.

"Make a tornado!" Chais shouted over the wind. Exhaustion was slowly settling into his bones now. He grabbed his arm in an attempt to staunch the bleeding. Pain, dulled by adrenaline and Aldridge's aid, laced through his muscles.

Elwood shot him a look, and worry flickered briefly over his features. He cut down an enemy lugaire midair with a practiced swing of a bow, and the hound violently crashed at high speed into the forest ground before dissipating into darkness. Elwood was untouched, clearly, or else he would've been doubled over in the agony that resulted from iron poisoning. He would have to be even more careful this time.

The howling of high-speed winds created a pillar of spiraling energy. Its size grew larger and larger with each heartbeat. Gredian soldiers relentlessly charged, some paling at the monstrosity, some undeterred. A cry sounded from behind, and a few lugaires went up in smoke. Air whistled by Chais's ear as a dagger—its hilt a polished silver and red—flew forward in the direction of the soldiers. A man toppled. Lynara had another dagger in her grip now, not pausing to realize that her shot had been successful.

Chais inflated the core of his power until it once again touched his fingertips. Electricity sparked. It thrashed as if it were a wildfire fighting for a taste of freedom. And freedom he would give it. The stream—that would be his source.

In one surge of strength, he catapulted his energy forward and let go of control.

They didn't see it coming.

A tidal wave reared behind the Gredian soldiers, as if it were a monster and the soldiers had entered its cave. It pulsed with an unearthly essence. Lightning—white-hot daggers of water energy—throbbed in the water beast's heart. Sharp prongs protruded from its body. Silently, like a predator stalking its prey, it rose. It built. And built. Higher and higher, until its monstrous shadow was blatant as night, until the soldiers realized just what lurked—a second before their deaths.

Chais didn't allow himself to scan the faces of his enemies before it crashed down.

Blood swirled through the liquid in ribbons, dyeing the clear surface a murky red. Darkness sapped into the clouds as kymatis dissipated. The ebbing screams of men who were not given a swift death echoed endlessly through Chais's eardrums. Familiar.

But even that wasn't enough. The water, thin and weak from Chais's fatigue, still left three-fourths of the platoon charging. Their course was redirected away from the vortex of high-speed winds in front of them. Bodies of dead soldiers swept up in the tidal wave's path, which headed straight toward Elwood's roaring tornado.

Chais cursed under his breath as the wave shuddered and shrank in size. The bodies that were once swirling in its depths were violently thrown to the side, leaving a glass wall of watered bloodstains. Chais stretched his left arm out as if he could grasp that line of power and tried to reel in what was gradually spiraling out of control. Sweat dripped down his forehead. If he could get the twister at the right place ... if the water energy was strong enough—

The world seemed to pitch onto its side as wind and water collided. A low rumble vibrated the rock particles on the earth. Blinding energy exploded outwards, only to be replaced with something new, something entirely different.

"Holy shit," Lynara muttered.

It was a pillar now—a pillar of ice-cold river, of gale, of strength and dynamism so intense it froze the air. It didn't reach the skies—barely even touched the trees, but the power—

Gredian soldiers scattered. A majority were launched into the hard bark of surrounding trees, dying on impact. Others were sucked into the hurricane and shredded in seconds. Only a handful were still alive now. The others were victims of the collision. Chais could still feel that burning ember in his system, power that would take time to regenerate, power that he didn't know he had. Rebme's kymatis hurdled on, their muscles propelling them away from the hurricane, away so that it shrunk, in size, and in strength. Smaller. And smaller. A soul dying of exhaustion in a bitter, death-ridden landscape.

But something wasn't right.

Chais scanned the dying red hurricane and tried to differentiate water from wind. There. His wave. It was moving through Elwood's twister. Droplets wriggled midair, as if unsure where to go. It was moving *through*—toward them. And Chais didn't feel a whisper of magic in his veins when it broke free.

It lurched dangerously. Gold shot outward like strokes of lightning.

Then it was off, careening at a speed that not even the greatest demon horse could match. The wave spread its wings. Trees toppled. It had a mind of its own now, and Chais was absolutely helpless to stop it.

"Chais, stop!" Elwood was shouting now. A bead of sweat made its way down his temple. Strong winds began to build a thick wall in front of them, stretching to accommodate the sheer size of Chais's magic.

You've lost control of the reins—you can still get it back, just calm down—

Chais barely registered the speed of his breathing. It was ragged, as if his magic had punctured his lungs. His heart was beating at an inhuman pace. What had once been flowing through his system was gone, as barren as the ruins of Alryne. He tried letting go, tried dropping his arms like the day they fought the demon fish, but it was no use. There wasn't a single shred of control.

He could see Elwood, teeth clenched in focus, as he threw up wall after wall of wind defense. The colossal tide slowed but still

274

shattered them, one after the other, spilling wisps of zephyr back into the air. Chais could tell the Fey was tiring at a treacherous pace. He reached toward the surge of water with everything he could muster.

Stop! His mind screamed in a voice that wasn't Aldridge's. Stop it, dammit! Before—

Before it happened again. Before he killed a friend because he couldn't control it.

As if it struck a wall, the surge of water reeled back. There it was—magic, coursing through his body again. It buzzed with an electricity that made his hairs stand on end. Powerful—the force of a dying lion.

And ... control. He only felt it for a fleeting moment, a scrap that was swirling away in the receding tide, but it was there. It was there.

"Thank the gods!" Elwood flung his one arm into the air as the wave retreated. Chais tried his best to turn back around on the kymatis, which was beginning to slow down. He was drained, depleted. What had only lasted for a second, ephemeral in nature, was now dried up and spent. There was now a fuzziness at the back of his head that could only mean the edge of consciousness.

"You almost killed us," Lynara hissed. Her tone was reprimanding, as if she were speaking to a much younger Chais. He didn't bother to answer, but beneath her angered tone, he could tell it was fueled mostly by breathless relief and adrenaline.

"But he didn't," Rebme said, winded, "and we're still alive. That's all that matters."

Yes, they were still alive. A group of ragtag adventurers had just herded off a platoon of Gredian soldiers, and they had survived for another day.

The demon horses had braked to a walking pace, and flakes of shadow parted from their skin, as if they couldn't hold themselves together. Rebme took her hood off as the kymatis stopped. When she turned, Chais could see the exhaustion clearly in her violet eyes before she spoke. "We're moving on foot from here." The summoner suddenly seemed ages older. "I can't maintain control on the kymatis."

She waited a few moments for everyone to dismount before the demons dissipated into ebony smoke. The walk through the ruins was laced with thick silence.

Chais stepped over the crumbled remains of a building, where wildflowers barely managed to sprout among the stone. Wreckage. What was once a village had been reduced to nothing but slabs of rotting wood and cobble. Occasionally, the deathly white surface of bones peeked out from beneath. The carcass of a tower coated in fog seemed to sag from its weight. It was nothing but a graveyard now—the only thing that kept Chais walking was the fact that these ruins looked nothing like Alryne. Compared to that, this destruction was minuscule.

Chais raised his chin. The blood that had been flowing from his shoulder was now stopped, a result of Rebme's quick medical skills and Aldridge's handy healing. It felt odd; there was a confusing mix of pain and numbness pulsing in his right shoulder. There really was no way to describe it. Rebme had also been nicked by an arrow, but it wasn't as bad—a few unique medicines from her worn leather pouch fixed it in no time.

"What stopped you?" Elwood's voice was suddenly close to his ear. Chais flinched. A small smile spread over the Fey's face, as he probably planned to use it against him someday.

"What?" Chais said.

"You know." Elwood kicked a pebble. He was unsettlingly radiant in such a desolate landscape. "What stopped you? What caused the magic to flow again?"

Chais ran a hand through his hair as he looked the other way. He finally realized how unsteady his steps were and how much his eyes wanted to close. It was a different kind of tired, not the kind that he was most familiar with—physical exhaustion, from fighting too much, from pushing himself too far beyond his limits. He'd been told that that was one of his fatal flaws. But this was different. Magical exhaustion.

"Nothing," Chais murmured. He remembered the bitter rain soaking into his skin and the smell of the earth and her face—but that was a memory that he pressed down, again and again, until it didn't come back. "It was nothing. Just the urge to save all of you, I suppose."

Elwood didn't seem convinced.

Suddenly, an explosion rattled the deserted land ahead. Chais squinted. Lightning?

It feels familiar. Whatever ... aura ... is coming from over there. Aldridge's voice was laced with curiosity. *You should look into it. I don't think it's hostile.*

"Wait," Chais muttered and picked up his pace. His hand was already by his knife. As he passed Rebme, the summoner's whip was in her grasp. Her wrist twitched, and in that small movement, Chais flinched. It seemed he still hadn't gotten past the trauma of whips yet.

"Chais, you're too—" Lynara warned.

"It's fine. I'm just taking a look."

He set off at a brisk pace, gaze flitting between the collapsed buildings of what remained and the minute details that signified life. A rustle of grass here. A flutter of wings there. Amidst the destruction, something still remained. Amidst the bleeding and misery and sacrifice, something still breathed with vitality.

Another eruption brought his attention back to the matter at hand. The dry wind picked up whatever had been unearthed from the loose soil and sent it his way. Chais brought a hand to his brow in an attempt to shield the dirt particles. He was further out than he'd expected to go, yet the explosion should've been somewhere around—

The air shot out from his lungs as a mass collided with him and sent Chais and his attacker to the ground. Not wasting a second, despite the pain that heightened tenfold in his right shoulder, Chais felt the reassuring leather hilt of his knife against his palm. Dirt obscured his vision as he blocked a blow to his arm. His heart increased in tempo. Breathing was the same as choking: no air could get through.

With a surge of energy, he managed to kick his attacker off. It only took a few parries and counterattacks for him to fall again. His knife was knocked far away and the bone of an elbow pressed into his windpipe. Chais almost slammed his head against the hardened dirt ground in frustration. Damn. Damn that annoying agony in his shoulder. Damn this magic exhaustion.

"State your business," said a female voice with an accent that wasn't native to Gredian. Chais blinked away the dust in his eyes and was met with ones not unlike the golden flashes that flowed through his system. Her black hair, shimmering a slight brown under the light, hung toward the ground in the form of a braid. Loose hairs caught the sun and turned flaxen.

He swallowed. The pressure from her elbow barely allowed him to breathe. The woman had pinned him, expertly at that, and the lack of strength in his muscles only reminded him of his fatigue. If he tried to reach into his power system, all that came out was a faint headache and black veils pulsing at the edge of his vision. Chais could hear Rebme, Lynara, and Elwood nearby, still searching for him. The clouds of dirt messed with their senses. They were behind a mostly intact structure, after all.

"Why don't you state yours …" He noticed her pointed ears and caught the slightest whiff of Fey. Not only Fey, but human as well. "… Feykin," Chais said, hiding his surprise, "this isn't Atrelia."

"You're one to say that," the Feykin grinned. Her golden eyes flashed. Chais struggled briefly beneath her, but it was utterly in vain. He was drained, and her Fey strength—no doubt honed during her elongated lifespan—was too much for him. "If you must know," she said, "I'm looking for someone. From Atrelia."

Chais narrowed his eyes. Not a scout then, but why did he care? Gredian wasn't his home anymore. Could it be … Elwood? If she was indeed looking for Elwood, then that was beneficial, right? If they were heading toward Atrelia, injuring her now— not like he could do anything in his current situation anyway— wouldn't be a smart move.

She looked up, keeping Chais in her peripheral vision so he wouldn't do anything stupid. She sniffed once, and a smile broke out over her ethereal features.

"Something tells me my mission from Atrelia is going to end right here," the Feykin said. A barely contained web of excitement coated her every word.

A brief pounding of boots on dirt sounded next to them. Elwood appeared, his bow clutched in his left hand, prepared for whatever jumped out. The weapon lowered as he noticed the two Feykin sprawled on the floor and seemingly at peace.

"Uh," the Fey laughed nervously, "am I interrupting something?"

Chais welcomed the air into his lungs as the pressure of the woman's elbow disappeared. He coughed twice and stood to dust off his pants. The other Feykin pulled a tie out of her hair and began to braid it again. She was concealed by the shadows of the ruins that shrouded her appearance. There was still a knowing grin painted onto her face, as if she was waiting for the newly arrived Fey to put two and two together.

Elwood's eyes suddenly widened, and he pointed at her.

"Wait—" he began.

Elwood was cut off by the woman's hug, and his breath escaped from him as quickly as the wind. Chais picked up his knife from the ground. He winced at how bone-crushing the embrace looked. Whatever this reunion was, he had to give the two warriors some space; so he resorted to leaning casually against the toppled structure.

The Feykin let go and opened her mouth, as if she was going to chastise the Fey, but Elwood beat her to it.

"Don't randomly explode the ground with your lightning. It attracts unwanted attention!" he said in a scolding manner, one that Lynara had often used on Chais in Silvermount. Chais nearly snorted at the irony of his statement.

"Sorry ... I was just training and thought that no one was around ..." she murmured guiltily. The woman seemed to notice his stump of an arm. Her expression immediately darkened. In a flash, quicker than Chais could blink, she delivered a swift kick to Elwood's shin. It connected ... and definitely sounded like it hurt.

The Fey cried and stepped back, cradling his leg.

"What was that for?"

"We thought you were dead! Callum—I was—" She exhaled in exasperation. "And your arm is gone! How the hell did that happen?"

"That's, ah ..." Elwood laughed awkwardly, scratching at the base of his neck, "a long story. I'll tell you later."

Chais turned to Rebme and Lynara as they approached. They stopped dead in their tracks at the sight of the newcomer, who was talking to Elwood as if she were his sister. He hoped Lynara wouldn't impulsively throw a knife at a complete stranger.

"Don't mind me," Chais said, striding up to the Feykin. She turned, casting a suspicious glance at the women behind him before realizing that they, too, were a part of Elwood's small band of bizarre travelers.

"What, do you want another battle, dunce?" she asked. That wicked smile appeared again.

Chais nonchalantly pointed the dagger at her and glared into her eyes. "Not unless you want a blade at your throat, dolt."

"Oh no, there's two of them," Elwood whispered, but thanks to Fey hearing, he was met with the molten glares of two Feykin, blue and gold. If looks could kill ...

"Are all Feykin this rude?" Elwood asked.

"I don't believe we've formally met yet." The woman ignored Elwood and picked up her own knife. She flipped it in the air a few times before sheathing it.

"Chais Nevermoon," Chais said. He extended his hand.

She grinned, shaking it. "Lilith. Lilith Fulmina."

CHAPTER
TWENTY-FOUR

"LILY ..." Elwood said and flashed the newcomer a cheeky grin, still rubbing his sore shin. The Feykin could kick *hard*. He had to hold himself from strolling over and ruffling her hair. The long braid usually snaking down her left shoulder was loose from the earlier scuffle and dusted white and brown from their tumble in the dirt.

"Stop flirting in front of me; it's making me uncomfortable," Elwood pouted mockingly and put his single arm onto his hip. He didn't miss the worried glance toward his empty sleeve. That was not going to be a fun story to tell.

"I'm not flirting, airhead," Lilith scoffed and crossed her arms. Chais had shaped his face into an expression that conveyed shock, embarrassment, amusement, and confusion, all in one. Elwood didn't even know it was possible to do that. He was mildly impressed.

"You have a lot of explaining to do," she growled and glared at him with hard golden eyes.

"So do you. What do you think you're doing here? Did Callum send you to babysit me? Because you can tell that old piece of—"

"He was worried about you. And no, he did not send me. I took matters into my own hands when vines started strangling the guards stationed in front of his office. That and when he crushed a part of the throne in a fit of worry." Lilith stared back, unfazed, instead looking at Elwood as if it was all his fault.

"Awww, it's so nice to know you care! You sweet little thunder cloud." He leaned against the nearest crumbling wall and slapped his happy-go-lucky mask back on, although his eyes were still darker than normal. He ignored the fine layer of stone dust that rose and settled around him. It was as if powdered sugar was sprinkled on his hair and coat.

Lilith's hands halted from their work, her hair half done. The indignant and outraged gasp at the old nickname nearly made him choke on his suppressed laughter.

"Just how well do you two know each other?" Chais asked. He ignored Rebme's mutterings as she rebound his arm.

"Far too well," Lilith said. She watched Elwood, daring him to elaborate. Not one to turn down a challenge, Elwood's grin widened.

"This little halfing here, you see, was taken in by Callum's family about fifty years ago, just before the war started. Then, she was just the cutest little girl. Called me—correct me if I'm wrong, but—didn't you use to call me Cuzzy Elwood?" He grinned and tilted his head to the left, silently baiting her. All the things they would have to address later were pushed to the back of his mind. He was allowed a little fun every now and then.

"No … " she said as she gave up on a larger knot and swept it into her braid. Small flakes of white dust fluttered from her hair. Lilith blushed furiously and looked away. "It was Cuzzy Elly …"

"As I said. Such a sweet child," Elwood sighed and put his hand onto his chest, a faraway look in his eyes. He gave an exaggerated sniff. Lynara looked so confused she almost broke character … almost. Chais, on the other hand, was most definitely enjoying the show.

"As nice as this reunion must be, why are you here?" Rebme asked. She inspected the off-white bandage one last time before collecting her supplies off the small slab of what might have been a roof. She dusted off dirt, mud, and a powered rust substance that smelled suspiciously of blood and tucked the rest of the bandage roll into her leather satchel. Fingers smoothly tied it closed.

"To make sure that Elwood gets back alive so *I* don't have to deal with a grieving Callum," Lilith grunted and sat down on the nearest piece of rubble, a large stone chunk that looked a little scorched on the back side.

"Who is Callum?" Lynara walked almost hesitantly forward. Her eyes traced Lilith's pointed ears before darting between her golden eyes and hands, as if expecting electricity to be dancing over the long, slender fingers. Slowly, as if approaching a wild animal, she sat down next to where Chais had decided to sprawl for his medical checkup as well. Chais eyed her for a moment but then scooted to the side to give

Lynara space. Rebme took a seat on the slab she used previously. Now that everyone was settled, it looked like they were going to have to answer some questions.

Lilith froze, realizing that if she said any more she would be giving too much information to a stranger. She glanced at Elwood before plastering a false but very convincing smile onto her face. Elwood would have been fooled if he hadn't taught her that smile himself.

"He's a powerful and temperamental Fey who also happens to be our adopted brother." Powerful and temperamental summed up the king of Fey pretty well. "You two are siblings? Then why did she call you 'cousin' when you two were younger?" Rebme's eyes narrowed, her hood throwing a shadow across her face. Violet slits darkened to black. The questioning had certainly started. Elwood felt something twist in his gut.

"My family was close to Callum's ... and uhhh ... they died, so Callum's father invited me into the family. This was about twenty years ago, so Lily grew up knowing me as a cousin, not a brother." Elwood copied Lilith's smile and ran his hand through his white, powdered hair. Stone dust rained down into his eyes, and he used it as an excuse to blink rapidly. He rubbed the back of his hand across his face, and it came away wet. Stupid dust. Elwood wiped his hand on his coat and focused on the streaks of white on the dark fabric.

Rebme nodded. She clearly noticed the holes in their explanation and the false smiles plastered across their faces. A sad smile seemed to pass over her lips as she decided to respect their secrets.

That woman is way too observant for her own good, Relevard scowled. Was that a compliment or a threat? Knowing the dead general, it might have been both.

"You here to take me back then? I was on my way, you know." Elwood forced the subject out of the minefield. He could play there later. "It wasn't very smart of you to come into enemy territory alone and without permission."

Lilith shrugged off the last part with a grin. "I was fine. Who needs permission anyway?"

"Don't you 'who needs permission anyway' me. This was a very stupid decision, and we both know that. Callum must be panicking about both of us! Now I'm almost afraid to go back," Elwood lectured. He ignored the looks Lynara and Chais were sharing.

"Someone had to come to make sure you stayed on track and got home some time before the war ended," she said. "Knowing you, you'd stop by the nearest Gredian camp and dye all their uniforms some ridiculous color, just for the sake of it."

"I'd need dye for that," he said, but tucked that idea away for some other time. It certainly could be interesting.

"Well, then you'd stop by a tailor, rob him blind, and *then* go dye the nearest Gredian camp's uniforms a ridiculous color."

"You make it sound like you wouldn't be right there acting as lookout," Elwood shot back. His eyes gleamed with child-like glee. The banter between the two Atrelians was familiar in this daunting and foreign situation. He wondered how Callum would react when he delivered the news of the failing seals.

"You're off-topic again." Chais's voice was so dry Elwood thought it was Relevard for a second. The disappointed amusement was a perfect imitation of the dead general. "Lilith, what are you planning to do exactly?"

"That is none of your business, Bubbles." Lilith flashed Chais a shit-eating grin that looked eerily similar to Elwood's. Then again, he did pass on a good number of his own mannerisms to her, so it only made sense for her to pick up some on her own.

"I would say it is. After all, I'm coming back with you. Don't know how I'm going to put up with you for the entire journey."

"That makes sense, I suppose ..." Her eyes narrowed to slits, then widened as she connected the dots. "You're the reason my idiot family member left Atrelia while on leave?"

"Leave?" Chais blinked. He looked at Elwood and chuckled. "I thought you just abandoned your post to come after me."

"As if I'd commit treason for you." Elwood rolled his eyes and pushed himself off the hard stone wall, stretching hard enough to feel his spine pop. Dust spun around him like glowing will-o-wisps as the motes caught the sunlight.

"No, you care about me much more than that. You gave up vacation time to save my ass," Chais said as he got to his feet as well. "I might as well give up trying to pay you back. Nothing I could ever do would equal that."

"Huh. I like you," Lilith said. "Elwood, we're keeping him." She tied off her braid, whipped it over her shoulder, and walked toward the Fey. Without even thinking, he ruffled the freshly braided hair, ignoring her indignant squawk.

"Cool. I kinda like him too. He can be a real sourpuss, but he has his moments," Elwood agreed. He enjoyed the shocked and offended expression that twisted Chais's features.

"I'm not some kind of ... pet," Chais said, waving his arms to express his opinion about the situation.

"Of course not," Rebme agreed, stepping into the rapidly derailing conversation. Something similar to amusement flickered in her eyes. "Lilith—can I call you Lilith?—what is your plan? I can speak from experience that these two are quite the handful."

"We have two options: go around the battlefield or through it." Lilith squirmed out from beneath Elwood's arm. "I came around, and I'm guessing Elwood did too. On foot, it takes a while unless you can fly, but it's much safer than the other option."

"We have a rapidly approaching deadline. I'm guessing it took you the better part of two weeks to get here?"

Lilith nodded.

"With Gredian's soldiers on your heels, you'd never make it on foot. And I can't keep kymatis summoned that long," Rebme said.

"What do you propose then?"

"If we go through the center, we could be lost in the fray," Elwood said. "Just a few Fey soldiers and the occasional Unknown-bred monster ... it's risky, but at least we won't be facing a squadron with demons focused on our capture and our capture alone."

"Risk isn't anything new. If this way we have a better chance of avoiding capture, I say we take it." Chais leaned against the edge of a crumbling wall, positioned to get up the second danger was present but allowing himself to rest while it was more or less peaceful. He was clearly tired, but restless nonetheless.

"So, are we going to camp here tonight?" Lynara stood and stepped out of the corner she had previously been desperately melting into, finally comfortable with the new company.

"No—we may have avoided the soldiers for now, but they will regroup and be heading here fast. We need to at least camp off the main path," Chais sighed and rubbed a hand over his eyes, their blue dulled with exhaustion as any remaining traces of adrenaline faded away.

"We have a plan then. We're splitting up in the morning. You will continue through the Unknown. Lynara and I will return to the capital," Rebme nodded as she spoke, running the facts through her mind. "Spend one more night to rest for the long journey ahead of you before leaving."

"I guess this will be our last day in each other's company." A shadow of a smile flickered on Elwood's lips. He was unsure if he was disappointed at that notion. He had become quite comfortable with the girls watching his back.

"Good riddance," Lynara said, and Elwood laughed out loud. Trust the redhead to efficiently halt any conflicting thoughts.

"Don't say that yet. You still need to suffer a day with us." Chais's voice had an almost tender tone to it. It was drastically different from the way he had spoken to her at the beginning of their journey. The glare the commander sent the colonel had a spark of kindness in them. Her blood-red eyes didn't burn with the same guilt and regret they used to. Had they finally come to terms with what was eating at them? Or was this more of a silent agreement to let the past stay in the past?

"Let's get moving. The sun is not slowing down for us." A small, almost regretful sigh left Rebme's lips as she headed toward the woods again. Her cloak billowed behind her while the long violet scarf snapped in the wind. She provided a welcome splash of color against the shades of whites and grays in the deserted village. Her small frame cast a long, dark shadow behind her.

Elwood sighed and walked after her, following her shadow. Chais silently stepped to his right, Lynara slipped to his left, and Lilith hung back. She saw the underlying sadness in their conversation. They had become close over their travels, and now they were going to split apart, each heading into a different danger.

They followed close to the edge of the Unknown, not wanting to lose the progress they had made but still sticking to the shadows, alert for the sound of soldiers. It wouldn't do to get caught when they were so close to getting home. One more night at the edge of Gredian, then a few days across a battlefield.

Their march was eerily quiet. It was a stark contrast to the loud, boisterous conversations that took place just minutes before. Only the whispering of leaves pierced the dead air. Even that seemed to dim as the sun lowered, gently wrapping them in a different layer of silence. The whole area felt devoid of life, but the occasional chirping told of life remaining despite the ruined landscape. The forest here at the Unknown was drastically different from the woods they had ventured through on their way here.

The previously thick canopy of trees had been reduced to charred stumps and broken branches, leaving a poor cover of leaves over their heads. But small saplings were already pushing their way through rubble and dust ... Someday, the corpses left from the war would be buried under this landscape. The scars would still be found under twisted vines and animal dens, but someday nature would seal all the wounds. Elwood wondered which battle had brought the Fey forces so close to the Gredian empire. He also wondered what could have driven them so far back. The invention of guns? The sudden and unexplained increase of summoners? Or was it something else? He almost barreled over Lilith in his musing. He chastised himself for losing focus in such a dangerous place.

Elwood quickly took in his surroundings. The sun was kissing the edges of the horizon and washing the sky in hues of orange and purple. They had been walking for hours. The setting sun's rays washed over the remains of what might have been another village. Moss and flowers had already started to crawl over the rotting wood and poked their way out from between cobblestone. It must have been a very small town; there was a small twisting path leading out from the buildings, but it was no road. Such a small place, sitting in the middle of nowhere … its people probably had no involvement with the war. Yet, here was the corpse of their home.

The fact that there were no signs of death helped ease his conscience. Maybe they had all left before Fey forces came in and razed their houses to the ground. Elwood knew better though—he had seen villages like this in Atrelia as well. While Fey lived in the capital, the rest of the empire was the land of many small species. Some were allied with the Fey; others stayed neutral in the war. The fact that they were neutral did nothing to protect the settlements from destruction when the Gredian forces neared the Atrelia border. When people visited those areas, there were never bodies; surviving family took them and laid them to rest, leaving a hollow and torn village in their wake.

"Are we camping here?" Elwood asked. He was unwilling to keep thinking of the consequences of pride and ambition brought to these peaceful settlements.

"Yes. This village isn't plotted on any map. Even the old ones. It was too small, and now it's not even a village anymore. No one would suspect us stopping here, and we've covered our tracks well enough that no one can find us before morning." Lynara sounded confident sharing the information. She probably studied Gredian's maps more than any of them, so he decided that if she was so sure that this was really a nameless settlement, it probably was.

"How do you know about this place?" Lilith asked. Her eyes still scanned the wreckage, as if expecting a soldier to pop his head out of the cracks.

Lynara's face flushed bright red. Oh, so there was a story here. A mischievous grin crossed Elwood's face. "What is it? A special someone brought you here? Seems a little bit too 'in the middle of nowhere,' doesn't it?" Elwood leaned forward as Lynara struggled to keep her composure.

"He was a friend, a soldier. He was fighting on the frontlines, and I happened to be at a nearby village for business matters. This was our meeting place," she said. A strange look flashed over Chais's face; he muttered something about the perimeter before dashing off. Lynara watched as he walked away and slid an imitation of Rebme's mask over her own features. The summoner had clearly been giving the redhead lessons. Elwood moved to help Chais scout the perimeter.

"Are you okay?" Chais asked the moment they were out of hearing range. His eyes were piercing in the darkening atmosphere. They glowed with his Fey heritage, seeming to wash his face in pale blue light.

"Uh … yes? Why do you ask?" Elwood wasn't expecting the question; in fact, he was about to ask the same. He blinked, then smiled and tilted his head slightly, looking like a curious dog. "Is Chais worrying for me? Awww, wittle Chaissy is so sweet."

"No," Chais growled and looked away. "It's just that you were really quiet. I've never seen you silent for longer than an hour before. You even mutter in your sleep. I was simply wondering if it was going to become a regular thing."

"Aww … so you do care!" Elwood feigned delight and patted him on the head, ruffling his mess of silver hair. "Don't worry, I promise I will never not talk again!"

"What have I done?" Chais groaned and looked up at the painted skies. Whatever the expression Elwood had caught previously was nowhere to be seen, so he didn't probe for information.

What has he done? I finally had some time to hear myself think, and that Feykin just ruined it.

"Relevard! Where have you been? It's been hours since your last snarky comment! I thought you died or something!" Elwood held up a hand to Chais's questioning look.

I can't die, you imbecile. I was just trying to find the other keys, gauge their opinions on the weakening seal. I can't tell if it really is failing, so I was hoping one of the others might.

"Couldn't you have told me before going silent?" Elwood asked. "I mean, we share a body. It could have been as simple as: 'Off to research, be back later.'"

I was still here; I could hear everything you said and see everything you did.

"That's not creepy at all," Elwood snorted. He propped an elbow onto the nearest waist-high piece of rubble and stared toward the burnt husk of a house in front of him. He wondered if the people that lived there had children.

Shut up, I just need some time to concentrate on those connections. You had finally shut up, and I was going to take advantage of it. Telling you would have just caused you to start talking again. He sounded more pissed off than usual.

"Did you find anything?" The Fey felt like he already knew the answer, but he wanted to hear it.

No. I couldn't contact a single one of them. He expected as much.

"Care to fill me in?" Chais interrupted. He looked a strange mixture of amused and upset at being left out of the conversation.

"Relevard was trying to find the other seals on our way

here. Said he found nothing and that he hates my guts," Elwood summarized.

Not just guts.

"I hate you too," Elwood responded. He pushed himself off the wall and traced a line in the soot from the house's window sill. It came off thick and dark on his fingers.

"Aldridge?" Chais questioned, addressing his own seal. "Yeah, I figured. He's got nothing. None of the seals are responding, and he can't obtain the concentration to find them."

"Why can't he obtain the concentration?" The Fey warrior wiped his soot-stained finger onto his empty sleeve and turned away from the husk.

"He says you're too loud."

"Fuck you, too, Aldridge," Elwood said. He walked back to where the girls had set up camp, not bothering to see if Chais was following. No fire was built—in fear of detection, but they had found a cozy little hole to burrow into. Two slabs of stone leaned against each other in an upside-down V with tangles of plant life wrapped around the bases and connecting points. Lilith was distributing small rations of smoked mystery meat, and Rebme had found some wild berries. Lynara was sipping from her water flask as she tackled the tough jerky.

Lilith seemed to fit with the two girls perfectly, pushing Lynara hard enough that she reached playful annoyance, but never further, and chatting quietly with Rebme. With some time together, they could become close friends.

Rebme had taken off her scarf. She folded it and tucked it neatly away in her bag, but she left her hood on. Frizzy curls popped out around her neck, no doubt irritating her skin as she mindlessly pushed them aside. Once again, the question of why entered Elwood's mind. He really wanted to know, but he had to respect her secrets. She respected his, after all.

Elwood dropped himself down next to the girls and moved the loose sleeve of his most recently stolen coat so it didn't drape over Lynara's lap. The clothing never seemed to last long. It felt like he needed to swipe more every time they stumbled upon a new village. Elwood could just cut it off so it didn't get in the way, but he found it kind of cool. After all, if you can't look cool with a missing limb, what was the point to losing said limb in the first place?

"What kind of meat is that?" Elwood snatched the strip out of Lilith's hands. She grabbed wildly at her stolen food, but in her sitting position wedged between the rock and Lynara; she could do nothing to save her meal. With narrowed eyes, he sniffed the meat and stuck out his tongue.

"A teakettler? Seriously? You couldn't have caught a normal creature?"

"I was in a rush! In case I didn't make this clear, Callum was tearing apart the entire. Damn. Capital! I swear the walls were coming apart! I left without grabbing anything but a water pouch and some daggers, came upon a migrating group of teakettlers, and decided it was better than nothing, okay?" Lilith glared at the stone across from her as electricity crackled through her braid. Lynara flinched back as the flashes got too close for comfort. The female Feykin immediately reined in her anger and apologized under her breath.

"What's a teakettler?" Chais asked. He laid a gentle, reassuring hand on Lynara's shoulder and slid down next to Rebme, then leaned back against the rocks. His face was hidden by the shadows of the overhanging stone.

"One of the creatures in Atrelia."

"Just how many creatures are there?" Rebme quietly tugged on the straps of her satchel. Her fingers ran up and down the fraying leather edges.

"More species than you have here. You've got your bears and dogs and deer, we have those too. But we also have our dragons and griffins and unicorns," Lilith explained, not seeing the harm in warning some Gredians about the land they were trying to take. "Too bad none of them really care for the war. They could be a real asset." Elwood thought about the boulder-sized scorpion creatures that lived in swarms of up to a hundred and was inclined to agree.

"Do any of the species help?" Lynara scooted forward. She was eager to learn more about Atrelia, the country that was just days away, yet unknown and mysterious.

"Mostly just to provide supplies," Elwood said. "They don't really want to lose their homes, but they don't want to get too engaged in the battle either. They have their own tribes and most live nomadic lifestyles. Only the Fey have a real city form of government. The bigger monsters tend to live alone and eat anyone that gets too close. We just leave them to do what they want. We don't rule over them, just like you don't rule over your bears."

"Only instead of a bear, think thirty-foot-long, talking, fire-breathing lizard." Lilith nodded sagely. "Giant, talking, fire-breathing, gold-hoarding lizard."

"I'm not sure I still want to go to Atrelia if wildlife has a tendency to be five times larger than you," Chais said and took a quick swish of water from the pouch Rebme handed him.

"Don't worry. Unless you go looking for trouble, they

normally just keep to themselves." Lilith leaned contently against the moss-covered stone. Her hands undid and rebraided her hair.

"That normally would reassure me, but considering I would be traveling with Stumpy here, I feel like he would drag me toward trouble and then throw me at it." Chais glared at Elwood, daring him to deny it.

"Okay ... so there may be some truth in that," he laughed sheepishly.

"Chais is completely right. How many times have you tried to swim with kelpies?" Lilith asked. She poked Elwood in the ribs, and a wide smile spread across her face as he squirmed away from her finger.

"You both suck."

"At least it's good to know you two won't be having a vacation in Atrelia while Rebme and I go hunting for demon keys and avoid capture," Lynara said bitterly. Her eyes dimmed as she looked down.

"I'm sure you'll do fine. You've dealt with us for a week, so beating up soldiers and finding seal keys should be a piece of cake after that," Elwood said as he nibbled at the teakettle. The dried flesh had an almost herb-like aftertaste.

"Yeah, sure. Try to get some work done in Atrelia? Don't just play with dragons and whatever other terrifying beasts there are?"

"No promises, but we'll try," Elwood grinned, grabbing the pouch of water Chais threw him and downing a gulp. Chais had accepted a piece of teakettle jerky and was examining it with narrowed eyes. After a quick sniff, he shrugged and shoved it in his mouth, slowly taking in the flavor.

"We'll be fine, Nara, and you'll do great too. I know it." Chais smiled softly, and Lynara nodded, eyes set and confident.

Elwood once more wondered what their relationship was as he nibbled on his jerky.

Rebme, ever the nagging mother, ushered everyone away as Lilith got ready for first watch. She reminded Chais and Elwood to change their bandages before they slept and told them not to disturb the girls' rest.

Elwood laid silently with his back pressed against a stone slab. A wooden beam rested just by his head, and a small iridescent beetle scuttled its way up the plank, the rising moon's beams dancing over the shining shell. The soft breathing of Lynara was just behind him, on the other side of the slab.

Chais listened to the calm and leveled breaths of their traveling companions for the last night.

CHAPTER
TWENTY-FIVE

HE AWOKE TO THE SOUND OF RAIN.

The first drop, wet on the tip of his nose, stirred him. But he decided not to open his eyes, despite every fiber of his being aching for him to do so. Chais kept his breathing even. Scents, magnified by his Fey heritage, drifted through the air: Earth. Blood. Dust. Something long lost. He could feel Elwood beside him, hear the Fey's heartbeat, a steady rhythm with the rain. It was warm, a warm rain. There hadn't been one of those since the end of last summer, when not even the shade could provide shelter from the heat—when so many people, innocents, breathed their last breath.

Slowly, Chais cracked open his eyelids. It was still dark, yet no chilling wind swept over the cold stone. He inhaled. His vision was tainted with the blur of early morning, but that didn't bother him as he picked out the scents again. Earth. Blood. Dust. Something long lost. Lost—

Chais was on his feet in a heartbeat. He scanned the slab of stone that Elwood was propped against, and where Rebme and Lynara were supposed to be. And Lilith, she was gone too. The Fey at his feet shifted, and Elwood yawned. Chais heard his jaw crack from lack of use.

"They left," Elwood explained, his voice laced thick with sleep, "Woke me up in the middle of the night to tell me they were leaving."

Chais sighed and ran a hand through his hair. He glanced at the empty patch of land that was supposed to be Lynara and Rebme. A slight shadow, cast by the slab catching the first few rays of daylight, convinced him that they really weren't there anymore.

"By 'morning,' I'd thought it would be a little later," Chais said. After his shift, the leftover weariness from the battle had pulled him into a deeper sleep than usual. He blinked a few times and stretched his right arm before realizing the bandages were still there. It didn't hurt anymore; regenerative healing really was a plus these days. *Especially* these days.

"Where's Lilith?" Chais asked. He could feel some energy in them, in the droplets, and he suddenly registered how alive he felt, despite just waking up. The magical exhaustion was gone, then.

Chais strained his hearing and could barely make out approaching footsteps. Light, feline. Speak of the devil.

He turned back to Elwood. A drop of rain landed on his arm. "Why did they leave so early?"

The Fey tossed Chais a water pouch, and he gratefully caught it. "I'm guessing it's because they wanted to avoid a tearful departure." Elwood chuckled, almost to himself. Chais took a few generous swigs of the water, then wiped his mouth with the back of his hand.

He wouldn't say it out loud, but a part of him felt relieved that he wouldn't have to see them off—relieved that he wouldn't have to watch their backs until the white robe and Gredian leathers disappeared, knowing that he might never see them again.

"Morning, Sleeping Beauties," Lilith cut in. Her words and tone were eerily similar to Elwood's. Chais could barely make out her features under the shadow of the trees and the dim light that the day had to offer.

"Morning, Lily." Elwood propped an elbow against the lowest chunk of the slab. His eyes were half closed and his hair was a mess. The battle must have taken a toll on the Fey, too, Chais realized.

"Morning, Knucklehead," Chais said, forcing a bundle of mixed feelings away.

"Elly." Lilith pointed her chin at the Fey. "Numb Nuts," she addressed Chais with a grin. He snorted.

"Let's get breakfast started." Lilith rubbed her hands together. "Chais, we should hunt while Elly over here struggles with waking up."

"What were you doing just now then? I'm surprised you even found your way back." Elwood scrubbed at his face in an attempt to get rid of his sleepiness. It seemed a far cry from the normally vivacious Fey they all had the misfortune of seeing. Or fortune. It depended on who was speaking.

Lilith pressed her mouth into a thin line. "Just went for a walk. And give me some credit. I don't get lost *that* easily." She picked up an extra knife, which had been sitting in her pouch.

The metal gleamed briefly as she spun it dangerously in the air. Before Elwood had the chance to do anything, Chais felt Lilith nudge him, beckoning him to start walking. He looked at the sky, only to be greeted by a couple more drops of rain, warm and wet on his face.

"You just stay still, Elly," Lilith assured, "We'll be back with some delicious breakfast in a few." Elwood stuck his tongue out but decided not to follow. They entered into a denser patch of forest, a brief flair of wildlife before the tragedies of the battle-field came into view. The occasional flutter of a butterfly's wings stirred at the edges of Chais's Fey hearing and disrupted the distant chirping of birds. He couldn't hear the relaxing bubbling of a stream anywhere near here, but they had already filled up the pouches with plenty of fresh water. The rain was starting to fall at a steady pace now, although the canopy of trees shielded them from the thick of it. How was Elwood faring? A shield of wind, probably.

"We're not actually hunting, are we?" Chais whispered once the Fey was out of earshot, something that took a while with his inhuman hearing.

"Was it that obvious?" Lilith whispered back. Her golden eyes blended perfectly into the color scheme of the forest. The fact that she hadn't killed him during his ... recovery ... meant that she was more or less trustworthy. She seemed to be thinking the same thing, from the way her body language had opened up some. Just a bit though. This was just everyday amiable banter, not a talk between future close friends. It appeared there was something holding her back, despite her cousin-slash-brother confirming Chais's harmlessness.

Which, frankly, sounded more offensive in his head.

"Are you going to answer all of my questions with another one?"

"We each say one line, and you're already convinced?" Lilith returned. The forest, normally darkened and foreboding from the unlit morning, seemed to glow with the Fey-like aura from the two Feykin.

"Well, I'm a decent analyst, so what can I say?"

Lilith rolled her eyes. "Hypocrite."

"Speak for yourself." Chais smiled and stepped over a root. "Where are we going?"

"A clearing," Lilith replied. Her golden eyes flitted back and forth, as if searching for something. She wasn't messing with her braid anymore—it must have been idle behavior. "I found a pretty large one ... somewhere around here."

"Are you sure you know what you're doing?" Chais asked. Elwood had mentioned something about her getting lost.

Lilith cut him a glance, feigning offense. "Of course! I've navigated plenty of times before."

Chais allowed a brief pause to hang between them as he followed close on her heels, making sure not to trip over anything. "So, are you taking me to this clearing for round two?"

The female Feykin looked back as if he had grown a second head.

Chais sighed. "You know what I mean."

Lilith laughed and faced forward again to move an overlapping layer of leaves. "We're here," she announced as she stepped into the clearing, "for round two, but not the type you were thinking of."

"You were the one thinking dirty," Chais growled.

Lilith cocked her head to the side and sized him up. She flipped her ebony braid over her left shoulder and unsheathed the knife she'd grabbed earlier from camp. Chais took out his own, and they simultaneously sank into battle stance.

The first blow, metal against metal, created a sound softer than he'd expected. It chimed dully through the air, only to be stopped by the mossy trees surrounding them. Chais knocked her arm aside and attempted to wrench the blade from her grasp. Lilith's dark braid flew as she expertly avoided it. She ducked under. A kick to the chin then. Chais felt the muscles in his neck twitch in reaction, dodging her left leg as quickly as she had sent it. He aimed for her stomach. A blow. Just a blow to buy him time.

Lilith saw it coming. She grabbed his fist and replaced it with her own, barreling in the opposite direction. Chais barely side-stepped it. A counterattack to the jaw ... no, the knee. Parry. Swipe. Feint. Her movements were unpredictable, but then again, so were his.

Chais blocked two swipes of the knife and kicked her back, giving him room for his magic. He felt his reserves, depleted just hours ago, come alive with blues and golds. They glimmered brilliantly from the warm-up. Chais reached in just enough so that his pupils began glowing a faint blue and watched Lilith through the screen of supernatural luminosity. Her eyes, even more golden now, widened for a brief second before her front foot dug into the ground, propelling herself toward him with breathtaking speed. There was something like alarm, anxiety, flashing across her face as she reached an arm out to stop him.

The world returned to its somber state as Chais dodged to the side. Lilith hurtled past, the cloth at her waist fluttering behind her like a flag. He seized the opportunity to tackle her as she slowed and sent them both tumbling. Taking advantage of Lilith's momentary shock, Chais pinned her and knocked her knife to the side. The blade landed with a muted skid and thud. He brought his own weapon dangerously close to Lilith's throat.

"Dammit. Dammit, dammit, dammit!" Lilith protested, trying to wrestle free. "I should've known you wouldn't use your magic when you haven't mastered it yet!"

Chais smiled. "Glad to know you care enough about me to stop me from draining myself."

"It wasn't for you … Let me up—if Elwood stumbled across us right now, he'd be getting ideas."

"You're the only one right now who's getting ideas." Chais rolled his eyes and stood. As Lilith took his hand and followed suit, he saw a lightheartedness in her eyes that was somehow different from Elwood's. He couldn't pinpoint how.

"Well, now we're tied." Lilith grinned and dusted herself off. Particles floated through the air around her, visible through the sun's rays; it only just occurred to him that the rain had gone. It had left dewy leaves and grass, the surfaces brimming with a clear liquid. Lilith began to walk, but Chais stopped her.

"We're not going to wander for another ten minutes again," he said and set off in the direction of the camp.

Lilith pouted. "But I can make it back!"

"With an extra ten minutes, maybe." There was a pause, then Lilith decided to start following him.

"Touché," she murmured.

The forest was brighter as the sun climbed up the sky. Overhead, orange and pink faded to blue. Chais could hear the distant chirping of birds and the quiet sound of wind combing over the treetops. As he picked his way back to camp, he noticed the soggy forest ground in contrast to the dried areas, having been protected by the shade. A few moments of surprisingly comfortable silence passed. Lilith's boots scraped softly against the roots of trees.

"Why did you hesitate at first?" Chais asked, realizing just how vague and off-topic the question sounded.

"I was ... wondering whether or not I could test something out," Lilith said. Had they been thinking of the same thing?

"Test what out?"

"Lightning and water. I heard it's a really powerful combination, so I wanted to take the opportunity ..." Lilith shrugged when Chais cast a glance over his shoulder, "... but then again, it could have destroyed the forest and alerted Gredian soldiers in a who-knows-how-many-miles radius, so ..."

Chais registered the subtext in her words, suddenly recognizing the reason why she hadn't tested that combination in her fifty years.

"Which family can use water?" he asked, intrigued.

"Nimphz." Lilith had gained ground and was now striding beside him. Her tiny smile seemed forced.

"Well then," Chais said in hopes of lightening the lightning-user up a bit, "they remind me of Gredian councilmen—snobbish and racist."

She laughed. "You included?"

He growled and kicked at her heels. "I don't count. I haven't even met them yet."

Lilith's smile was real this time. "Come on, don't be such a grump. Once we make it to Atrelia, we can be the Feykin Duo!"

"Great. Do you have a motto for us?"

The female Feykin put a finger to her chin and acted deep in thought. "Kicking ass upon arrival?"

Chais couldn't help but laugh at that.

Look who warmed up. Aldridge might as well have been screaming because Chais flinched. "The hell, Aldridge?" he hissed. Lilith kept walking. She respected the conversation he was having with the warrior, but he caught the corner of her mouth twitch up. In fact, she must've had her fair share of them in Atrelia with Elwood and Relevard. She'd known Chais was a seal because Elwood had told her during the twilights of their journey.

Apologies, Chais, just making remarks. The dead Fey hid a smile in his voice. *On another note, Elwood's approaching. Same with the battlefront, which is closer than it's been for a while.*

"Right. The war," Chais muttered. "After we reinforce the seal, we'll have to do something about that."

Seems like the Fey are gaining ground. You won't have much time if you want to get both tasks done before either side destroys the other.

"No pressure."

Chais heard the light tapping of boots on the forest ground. If it had not been for his Fey hearing, Elwood could've been a ghost. The Fey warrior burst into the clearing. Cold wind surrounded him on all sides. He looked from Lilith to Chais and back.

"Hunting, my ass!" the Fey said, a hint of humor lighting up his words now that he could see that they were both safe and weren't running from anything. His hair was dry, but that was to be expected of a wind-user during the rain.

"Don't worry Elly. We were just 'training,'" Lilith assured him with air quotes.

Chais shot Lilith a glare.

"Training, huh?" Elwood laughed. He turned and parted the last layer of leaves that blocked them from the camp. "Don't get *too* cozy. Makes me feel like a third wheel."

The trio emerged from the forest and settled down for breakfast.

A brief, pleasant silence swept in as they snacked on teakettler; they were just a group of travelers with different motives— one who wanted to return home, one who had no place else to go, and one who was just returning from a mission.

Chais looked down and realized that the arrow wound had almost completely healed overnight, to the point where a fight like the one with Lilith wouldn't tear it open again. After all, it was the Fey healing that allowed him to survive the two weeks in the Gredian dungeons. As if on cue, the scars on his back seared with dull pain, a sick kind of art that someone decided to paint. The king—Havard—had been killed that day, and Chais had only since repressed the memory; he knew that Havard deserved better than to be buried in a colonel's muddled thoughts, along with the rest, and Chais swore he would give his late adoptive father the right amount of attention, but ... not today. He tried not to recall those days when the man had still breathed the same air as him, when conversations pulsated with joy and belonging. He tried not to recall the feeling of acceptance, of warmth, of ... love. But even when he wanted to feel those radiant emotions, he came away empty.

Chais glanced at Elwood, then Lilith; the Fey's pale skin made it difficult to see whatever damage his skin had gone through, but it was there. Centuries of living, only to bring more agony and permanent reminders. Lilith was more tanned by the sun, hours of training outdoors, playing with electricity and sharp objects as if they were toys. Her scars stood out. Tissues crisscrossed each other around her arms, as if she didn't care how much people stared at them. It instilled an emotion that Chais couldn't put a name to—seeing the stories that everyone carried.

Him? He kept to himself a bit more when it came to his scars.

"We should start moving before the sun gets any further up the sky," Chais said. He finished the last bit of the teakettler and stood. Elwood and Lilith followed suit, and within a few moments, they were on the road again. The ruins were behind them, and the war was ahead.

Out here, it was becoming more and more prominent that Gredian's many biomes were giving way to a healthy mix between Atrelia and the empire. Occasionally, some pixies would flit by, wings catching the rays of sunlight, before heading back the way they came. Chais also caught a glimpse of gemstones between the long blades of grass.

The sun was now larger than it had ever been. Its cerise surface was paled by the wisps of clouds that obscured it. There was nothing but the fields of grass, blossoms, and a looming mountain range in the distance. Chais raised a hand to his eyes. Sweat dripped down his temple, and he took a sip of water. Damn—back to this feeling again, of walking into battle, where death was a compromise.

"I hear it," Elwood spoke first. His voice was as dry as the lakes in the Unknown.

Chais strained his hearing. Nothing. Lilith didn't seem to hear anything either.

"We have to get closer," she said. Her eyes were hard. It contrasted with her previously luminous features. The mood had sunk into a state of preparation for what was to come. What images of death and destruction would await them once they got far enough?

They walked onward for what seemed like hours, faces set, mouths pressed into thin lines.

The sky was the color of ashes and the grass the color of dirt when Chais first heard the sounds of battle.

It was an explosion, barely even there, but an explosion nonetheless.

"How far away are we?" he whispered to Aldridge as he forced his heartbeat to slow. They were going through the frontlines, where his friends were and where he had been for so many years, experiencing the relentless toll that war had on an empire.

Death. Desolate, corpse-ridden landscapes.

Not very far. Aldridge's voice was stern. Despite his vagueness, Chais decided not to reply.

Lilith was ahead of them. Her long fingers played with the ends of her braid in anticipation. The torn fabric at her waist stirred, as if it were slowly losing life. The ebbing wind carried the scent of rotting carcasses and blood, of smoke and dirt and murder. Screams—shouting of orders, wailing of the dying, short shrieks of the slaughtered.

Chais felt his entire body jolt when he heard—*felt*—the guns go off. It reverberated through his core, striking his bones and spine. But he'd done this before. He'd fought in this war.

So he steeled himself, painted a mask on his face, and descended headlong into chaos.

CHAPTER
TWENTY-SIX

THE BREAK FROM FOREST TO WAR ZONE was sudden and stark. The growing trees were razed and grounds leveled for armies to reside in. Thousands of mud-splattered tents peppered the ground, their inhabitants fewer than a mile away, fighting for their kingdom and their lives. When Elwood was last on the frontlines, they were nowhere near as close as they were now; this had to be the furthest they had gotten in decades. If the main fighting force had made the same amount of progress ... this sent a shiver of glee up his spine. They were winning. Maybe this war could end at Chais's generation.

But one look at the colonel's grief-stricken face made him pause. It was surprisingly easy to forget that the man standing next to him had fought on the other side—that if circumstances were a little bit different, they would still be trying to kill each other. If true peace was to be achieved, a simple victory in war wasn't going to cut it—the treaties would have to be perfect, or they would simply be thrown into another war. Elwood wondered how they had stayed in relative peace for thousands of years if the idea couldn't catch on for a single one.

"What would happen if Atrelia won?" Chais asked. His eyes were locked on the horizon.

"We negotiate peace, I guess—take land, exchange prisoners, establish new trade, and try to deal with the backlash," Elwood said, knowing it wasn't a satisfying one. But it was all he had to offer.

"I don't think Adaric would allow that. He would have all our people die before surrendering to the Fey," Chais said. A small, insincere smile graced his lips.

"And if Atrelia surrenders?" Lilith asked, counting her knives before sheathing them and counting them again. She had already braided her hair five times, and this was her third time counting her weapons.

"I would have answered the same as you back when the old king ruled. He didn't want to push it too far, he just wanted this …" Chais gestured to the bleak, cold, and graying landscape "… to end. To fix his predecessor's mistake. Now, I don't think the king would let you surrender. I think he would wipe you out. I mean, if the cause of the problem no longer exists, then there will no longer be a problem, right?"

"He doesn't care at all about the casualties, does he?" Elwood sighed before heading toward the edges of the abandoned camp. He stuck to the shadows and ignored the thick scent of despair and old blood. His mind easily filtered and discarded the information, returning to its wartime habits.

"What I'm hearing is after you two solve the key bullshit, you'd just be returning to a never-ending war. What's your plan?" Lilith asked. Her breath was shallow as she tried not to show the toll the odor was putting on her. The smell was something you just needed to get used to; weeks out on the war front was usually enough, but Lilith hadn't been in many major campaigns since she started training to be a king's advisor.

"I'm going to commit the crime I was sentenced to," Chais replied without an ounce of hesitation. He threw Elwood a wide grin that made him look younger, or maybe his real age. "Would you like to join me?"

"If we make it out of this alive," Elwood returned the grin and stuck out his left hand, "gladly." Chais grasped his outstretched hand; his thousand-watt grin made his eyes glow.

"Normally, I would judge you for bonding over a murder conspiracy, but honestly, it's unexpectedly noble, so I'll allow it." Lilith shook her head. She shaped her expression into that of an exasperated parent, but the small quirk at the edge of her lip ruined the image. "But right now, let's focus on getting to Atrelia alive before we make any big plans, okay?" Elwood was prepared to answer with a snarky comment that would most likely result in a very painful physical retaliation when the first line of slaughter entered his sight.

Any humor leached out of them.

They hadn't passed the tents yet, but the battle was clear on the horizon. Red-tinted armor shined as it clashed with green. Chais threw Elwood a hesitant glance and subtly gestured at the large broadswords the soldiers were wielding, then at his own rather small knives. Suddenly, Elwood's plan of charging headfirst into the fray seemed like a bad idea. Lilith seemed to agree as her feet stumbled to an immediate halt, stirring up dust.

"So ... there's no way we're just going to run into that ... right?" Her voice seemed strained as her hand found her knives. Once again, counting. "We have nothing on us that will help identify us as either friend or foe. Doing this would be suicidal!"

"What, do you not trust me?" Now that his dearest cousin was doubting him, he couldn't back out. "We'll be ..." Elwood paused, trying to find a word that would honestly describe the most likely result of the charge without straight out spelling their demise. "Well, don't worry about it."

"You fill me with so much confidence," Chais murmured. He seemed to regret the decision of letting Elwood plan their escape from Gredian as well. This only made Elwood more determined to go through with his initial strategy. He was a general after all—he could form and execute a plan.

"I'll make it work! You'll see," Elwood assured them before muttering, "I'll do it just to spite you and your stupid doubting asses."

Your immaturity never ceases to amaze me. How do you even know the general will be here? You could very well be sending this group to their deaths, said Relevard, the ever helpful and supportive shitstorm.

"All of you, shut up and stop wasting time. Just follow me. If we can't find Finly, I'll eat my boot." Elwood waved away their concerns and drew his bow. He was probably not going to need it for ranged attacks, but it would help to save his magic for close combat. They just needed to make it to the frontlines and cause enough of a ruckus that the Fey wouldn't kill them on the spot.

You know you can't back out of a promise, right? Relevard had the nerve to sound worried. He was absolutely silently praying for the opportunity to see his least favorite host try to eat a shoe, especially one who had been struggling through Gredian forest for the last week. Deciding not to grant Relevard an answer, Elwood instead bellowed a war cry and ran into the more loosely knit and squishier side of the human forces. Chais and Lilith had no choice but to follow, the latter with a bit more enthusiasm than the former.

Elwood crashed into the flank of the back lines. And despite only being one man, his charge was apparently mind-boggling enough to cause many of the men to hesitate. After all, Elwood assumed it wasn't every day that a crazy, grimy, one-armed Fey without armor attacked an army from the woods. Their surprise was completely justified, but it would be their downfall.

Elwood used the precious moment that the shock cost them to release an unfocused but powerful pulse from his body, sending every person within a ten-foot radius flinging back. The wind was nowhere near powerful enough to injure any of them or even knock them off their feet, but it cleared the way. He moved forward and used the swinging motions of his bow to release more concentrated blades of wind. The waves rippled the air as they slammed into the still stunned soldiers.

Elwood could feel his comrades at his back, a reminder to be cautious with the wind or risk their safety. With an almost sadistic giggle, Elwood cleaved the way through the warriors. There was the occasional clang of blade against blade as Chais and Lilith protected his exposed back. The sounds of clashing armies was getting closer as he moved through the ranks of Gredian soldiers. Trampled mud sucked at his boots. Shit. If they failed, he would have to eat one of those. He could only hope that they at least made it halfway there before the troops reorganized and dealt with the new and unexpected threat. A burn sliced pass his ear, and his adrenaline roared at the echo of the gunshot. That had been too close.

"Fucking dragon shit …" Elwood laughed and ducked as another bullet flew overhead. "Grumpy! Lily! Duck!"

The two Feykin dropped like stones. They hit the ground without hesitation as Elwood held out his bow. Time slowed as he entered a battle calmly, spiraling into his essence and shaping his power. He released a slow breath and then allowed the attack he was forming to burst from him.

A circular blast of air, compressed to a thin blade, rippled outward with him as the epicenter. It easily cut through armor and sent bodies flinging, injured but not dead. He used the seconds the attack bought him to release another blast. The charging soldiers were knocked further away. They took a step back, shields raised as they watched, wary for another attack. Elwood just laughed again. He sagged a little from the display of power before straightening again, then moving with speeds impossible for a human to replicate. If the humans didn't have larger numbers, iron, and creatures that were literally ripped out of another dimension, they wouldn't stand a chance.

Elwood leaned down and dragged Lilith to her feet. He bolted forward, trusting Chais to take care of himself. Both Feykin looked like they had been drowned in mud.

"You are insane! Any one of them could have shot you while you …" Chais paused his ranting to parry a blade aimed for his neck. "… while you stood there gathering power!"

"It worked, didn't it?" Elwood whooped and kicked the knee

of a man who was charging him with a mean-looking ax. The crunch of a shattered knee cap and howl of pain was like music to his ears. "We're almost to the frontlines! I can feel it. Just keep an eye out for Finly, okay?"

"I hate you!" Lilith cried from his left as she ducked frantically under a spear. Her braid snapped from the change of direction, whipping around her head. She swung her dagger up and sliced through the still-extended shaft, then launched herself forward and landed a devastating right hook across the attacker's cheekbone. He had lost his helmet during the battle, and the punch snapped his head hard enough so that Elwood could hear the crack as the man's eyes rolled into his skull and he slumped over.

Elwood quickly returned to his own fight. He slid aside from a man's wild swing, sheathing his bow with the same smooth motion and stepping back into his guard with a quick shift of momentum. He placed his hand on the human's battered chest piece. The soldier had the time to look terrified before the Fey launched him into the sky with a quick pulse of air.

"Did you see that! Look how far he flew!" Elwood cheered and knocked a few bullets out of the way with a quick shield of air. With a slight growl, he unsheathed his bow once more to block a close-range fighter. He could hear a very familiar voice shouting out orders and moved toward that direction. Finly was definitely here—he just hoped they would be alive when they got to him.

"I feel like you are enjoying this far too much," Chais growled. He disarmed his opponent with a quick flick of his wrist but was careful not to kill him. Stupid softie.

"We all need to get our fun somewhere." Elwood was just

about to engage another man when a familiar prick on the back of his neck warned him of a dangerous attack. "Scatter!" He screamed and dove to the side. The two Feykin quickly followed his example. And not a moment too soon.

A roar of flame burned toward them, a funnel of fire fueled by multiple Oxidasons. The mud dried and cracked against his skin. The flames tore a path through the ranks of soldiers. Its heat melted their armor and fused it to their skin. Screams of agony and the thick scent of burnt flesh filled the air. Elwood scrambled away from the torch of the flame with his hand over the lower portion of his face, trying to ignore the blackened bodies that fell away from the fire. The corpses were covered in twisted metal as spiny burnt bones reached outward and yellowed teeth gaped from charred skulls. Thick fat oozed and bubbled beneath the flames. Lilith was being pulled to her feet by Chais; she looked on the verge of losing her teakettler jerky, eyes wide and fixated on the gruesome remains of people.

The fire died down and a barrage of bullets replaced it, ripping through Fey ranks. The Oxidasons rose a wall of flame in hopes of melting the iron bullets before they touched flesh. The carnage was breathtaking. On the bright side, they were on the frontlines, and once the shield was dropped, Elwood saw a mop of mouse brown hair and bright orange eyes. The man was screaming orders. His blood-coated hands flashed signals to the officers under his command. Long, slender ears poked out from beneath the shaggy gore- and mud-stained locks. The tall form and distinct growl were unmistakable.

"Finly!" Elwood screamed and blasted the soldiers in front of him away with a draining pulse of wind. He felt his body stumble but forced himself to focus. Now was not the time for a power drainage. "Finly! Hey, you damn Morfern! Look at me, dammit!"

Citrine eyes locked onto him and widened comically. "Zefire? Aren't you supposed to be with the 'battering rams'?"

"I'm on leave! Been since last month. I was supposed to be back like … last week." Elwood grinned. He began to push through while keeping an eye on his two Feykin. Lilith looked mentally scarred, and Chais was still half carrying, half dragging her. Neither looked hurt, and Elwood trusted his cousin to snap out of it and deal with the shock later.

"So then, why are you here?" Finly bellowed back. He cut his way toward the trio with a large battle ax that had been previously strapped across his back while he gave orders. Finly managed to look both confused and exasperated, an expression Elwood was far too familiar with.

"King's orders," Elwood said. As a former bodyguard of the royal family, the orange-eyed general could be extremely nosy when it came to the well-being of the royal family. "The three of us happened to be around this edge of the Unknown, and I needed a favor."

"Favor?" The general's eyes narrowed into glowing slits. His mouth and neck were coated in dry blood. "What kind of favor?"

"A small one," Elwood almost squeaked. The man could be very intimidating. It was hard not to be when you were built like a grizzly bear.

"Get to the point, Zefire. In case you didn't notice, we are in a war zone."

"I need help getting back to Atrelia—can't fly, you see. And let's say that this far north of the battering-ram region, I'm a little lost." Chais took that moment to shove Elwood to the ground as another barrage of bullets hit the Fey ranks. Those who were hit fell and did not get up. Their bodies were soon trampled as the two armies pushed for an advantage.

"Get over here. We can talk after the bullets stop flying," Finly groaned and pushed back his brown locks, smearing them with blood and efficiently slicking them back. Elwood nodded and returned his attention to his surroundings, only glancing back to see Finly morph into a brown wolf and eat a man. Gross.

The next few … hours? passed in a blur—a constant clashing of weapons and cries of wounded, moving through the crowds of soldiers and the flash of steel, always moving, for a still target was a dead one. Elwood was still high on adrenaline when the ceasefire was called and both armies retreated for much-needed rest. Dark shadows hung beneath every eye as troops staggered away. They held up the wounded and carried their dead.

Finly had disappeared to talk to his men, so Elwood led his small party to the one tent in the center of the camp with a flag planted outside. He entered the general's personal tent in a daze, barely noticing the two Feykin following him into the shade of the fabric. Elwood slumped down onto a chair. He leaned back and allowed his body to unwind. The hard wood dug into his back but he didn't pay it much mind, instead thankful for the strain it took away from his body. Two twin *thunks* and the creak of springs told him that both of his companions had taken over the general's cot.

"How in the world did that work?" Chais breathed, breaking the silence with a bewildered laugh. "And look at us! We're barely hurt." He was right; although Elwood was completely drained of magic and on the verge of passing out, he had nothing more than a few already healing scratches. Chais shared the same amount of cuts and bruises but nothing that pointed to an immediate need for medical attention. Lilith still looked slightly shell-shocked. While she had participated in battle before, it was probably the first time she had been so close to a victim of the Oxidason family's infamous flame column. Her eyes seemed to shine less, but a slight nudge from Chais jerked her out of her thoughts.

"To be completely honest, I was ninety percent sure we were going to die," Elwood threw his head back and slumped down in his chair. When did his hair come untied? It was probably all covered in blood and mud by now. Elwood reminded himself to take a bath the first chance he got. "There was no reason that should have worked."

"I'm glad you know that." A familiar voice greeted them as the tent flap opened and Finly stepped in. His lower face was still coated in a layer of blood, and his hair was slicked back with gore. He looked like he had fallen face-first into a carcass, then rolled in it like a dog covering itself with the scent of its prey.

"That was probably the dumbest plan I've ever seen you pull off." Finly's voice was rough from whatever nasty substance he managed to swallow and vomit. He glared at the members in his private tent and sat in the only other chair in the room, raising his hand to wipe off the blood from his face. His huge hands were coated in the same substance, however, and only served to smear the scarlet liquid around a little.

"What about the Merfolk one?" Elwood shot back, happy to see the general relatively unharmed, if slightly green from the taste of human interiors. He was quite proud of that particular endeavor. If it hadn't worked out so well, the former Fey king might have had him hanged. Elwood sighed happily as he remembered the look of complete and utter fear in Callum's eyes when Elwood had shoved him in and jumped in right after. Finly might have gone into a state of shock, considering he had stood still for about five seconds before turning into a goldfish. It was magnificent.

"I thought we agreed to never speak of that again." What little of Finly's face was visible beneath the mask of blood blushed a cherry red, obviously remembering his little flop session as a fish on dry land.

"Do you know *everyone*?" Chais said from the cot. His gaze darted between the two Fey generals before him.

"Oh, right. Introductions. Chais, this is General Finly All-You-Can-Eat Morfern. Finly, this is ex-Colonel Chais Grumpy-Ass-Hat Nevermoon."

"Can we focus? Please? Before I end up kicking all of your asses?" Lilith interrupted. She rolled her eyes at their antics. Elwood frowned. Normally, she would be encouraging or even engaging in this kind of behavior. He would have to talk with her later, when there was time.

"Of course. Lilith is right, we need to focus." Finly straightened and tried to look as dignified as possible, despite being covered in blood and specks of who-knows-what.

"Zefire, what in the name of all that is good are you doing here?" Finly asked. His eyes narrowed as he focused on the loose sleeve on the Zefire's right. "And what is the story with that? His Majesty is going to be very pissed off."

Elwood laughed nervously and tugged at the empty sleeve self-consciously. It still hurt. "Long story. Anyway, I told you, I need help." He shrugged, diverting the conversation to more urgent matters and avoiding an awkward story time session.

Elwood continued. "I know the battering ram well, and a few leaks, but not this one. I need help getting back to Atrelia—can't go around, it's too easy for Gredian soldiers to find and follow us straight home. But, knowing the Unknown, without a guide or at least a map, walking through unfamiliar territory would just result in me falling into a quicksand pit, stumbling onto monster breeding grounds, or something worse." Elwood leaned as far back in the chair as he could. The wooden furniture creaked as he stretched back.

"Couldn't you have picked any other leak? We are so close to breaking through this one! And you show up and decide to cause a ruckus ... because, of course, you do. Zefires." Finly released a rather animalistic growl. He was trying to sound annoyed, but Elwood caught the slight hint of appreciation under the rough accusation. After all, their entrance served to distract the enemy and helped aid in Fey advancement. "Fine. I'll help you. It wouldn't do to get his Majesty's favorite idiot lost in the Unknown."

"Yay!" Elwood cheered. He decided to ignore the 'favorite idiot' part of the comment and focus on the help they were going to receive. Not that he really doubted they would receive it or anything; Finly just gave off an uncaring vibe. Elwood's muscles were beginning to ache, so he let his arm fall away from where it previously was—draped over the back of the chair—and let it drop limply at his side. He was sorely tempted to throw his hand up in victory but he felt too exhausted to do much more than cheer softly. Maybe some other time. "You know you're my favorite leak general, right?"

"Wasn't your favorite Nikan Sprintide?" Lilith interrupted. Chais's eyes darted from Atrelian to Atrelian, searching for context, clues, and answers.

"No, he's my favorite battering-ram general." Elwood shook

his head in mock disappointment, keeping an eye out for Chais's reactions. His small frown grew as a furrow formed between his silver brows.

"Battering ram? Leak? What are you talking about?" Chais finally cut in.

"'Battering ram' is what we call the forces attacking the center and largest area of the Unknown. If they win, we win the war. 'Leaks' are the forces that aid the battering ram. They win the small battles that give us an advantage, like an information or supply route," Finly explained, taking pity on the strange Feykin sitting on his cot. Chais nodded solemnly as he absorbed the information.

"Anyway. About that help?" Elwood asked, tucking the moment away to tease the colonel with later. "What are you willing to supply us?"

"I'll get you a map with the labeled must-avoid areas. I would love to send some men with you but I can't spare any at the moment," Finly sighed. He quite literally forced himself to his feet with the help from the chair and opened the tent flap to send the soldier stationed outside after the supplies. Within seconds, the man had brought a copy of a map. Finly nodded his thanks and took the paper. He laid it out on the floor. Each and every movement was agonizingly slow as he grumbled about sore muscles and how transforming put a strain on the body.

"Just avoid this area in general, and you should be fine," Finly said, gesturing at the entirety of the map.

"So basically, you think we're screwed," Lilith groaned, eyes glowing in the dim light. She and Chais had gotten up to get a better look at the map. Both of them hovered just across from Finly. "Why can't we just get home without a suicidal plan?"

"Because that won't be any fun, now would it?" Elwood grinned and stood up from his chair with seemingly far less effort. Ignoring every screaming and complaining muscle in his body, he bent down and snatched the map out from under the others. His body was going to hate him later—Relevard's silence only proved the point. Stupid dead Fey. He got to rest whenever he wanted while an unlucky Fey had to keep them both alive, Elwood thought, glaring into the dark tent fabric.

"Thanks, we'll be taking our leave then," he said out loud,

"All right. Get out of here, you idiots," Finly laughed. He pulled away the tent flap and allowed thin streams of silver to enter the space. "Good luck."

Elwood opened his mouth to reply when the shrill scream of alarms pierced through the air. Adrenaline burst through his body once more and he pushed past Finly, throwing open the tent door.

The front line of tents was ablaze, and the sickening scent of iron churned his stomach.

They were under attack.

ACKNOWLEDGMENTS

THIS BOOK WAS CREATED THANKS to the aid and support of more people than we can count, but we're going to try to anyways because what else is the acknowledgements page for?

First, a million thanks to our parents. If not for their unwavering moral and financial support, we never would have finished writing, much less publish it. They barely flinched at the incredibly large costs, allowing us to do what we loved without needing to worry about the prices that came with it. They've been our biggest fans since the beginning, and it was their motivation and kind words that drove us to who we are now. Thank you, mom and dad, for everything. Without you, we would not be here, recognizing our passion for writing and creativity. Heck, without you, we wouldn't even be here.

Our next round of thanks is directed towards our table. Our second family, a group of misfits that fit together far better than a handful of crazies ever should. Each one has encouraged our writing and shown unrivaled enthusiasm at the publishing of this book. And a special thanks to our first editor Judy. She didn't do much and we're not sure if we can say this, but she tried. And despite not doing much editing, she was our first reader. Her excitement regarding the story and where it was headed helped us keep writing when we felt like stopping.

A thanks and a ninety-degree bow of respect to Bobby, our real editor. His critique of our writing and plot helped us become better writers than we could have ever become on our own. Thanks for sticking with us through frustrating grammar mistakes, millions of unfinished sentences, and too much writing or lack thereof. We're not perfect writers; we will never be. But with Bobby, we can get pretty far.

And of course, a huge thanks to our publisher Polly, who helped us two novices navigate through the journey of publishing. If not for her guidance, we would have been hopelessly lost. We entered this world with a scrapped piece of writing from an eighth-grade project, and now look at us. We never would have imagined that we'd get this far. So thank you, Polly. Crossing paths with you and My Word Publishing was truly a fortunate stroke of serendipity.

Do we split voices here? I think we do.

I'd like to sincerely thank my coauthor and partner in crime, Elizabeth. What a coincidence that we first met in creative writing class of all places, huh? You inspire me, and you continue to inspire me; time and time again, through your sketches and writing, you have proven to be the best friend and coauthor out there. You deserve the world, Lizzy. Thank you, truly, for being in my life.

My final thanks are going to my coauthor Briana. You are absolutely amazing and I could not have asked for a better friend and writing partner. Your talent in both writing and art leaves me breathless. Bri, over the three years we have known each other, you have become more than just a friend to me. You're my sister, my partner in crime. And I cannot thank you enough for creating this wonderful book with me. You have potential to go so far in life, and I'm just glad that I get to be a part of it.

ABOUT THE AUTHORS

ELIZABETH IS A WRITER, wannabe artist, dungeons and dragon player and a space enthusiast. Most people would call her weird and impulsive, but she prefers unique and spontaneous. Having moved more than six times in eight years, she has mastered the ability of meeting new people despite being socially awkward on every degree. Her travels have also granted her insight on culture and story. She is a mess of sarcasm living in a state of a constant mid-life crisis and spends most of her time daydreaming for new writing projects that she will likely never act upon.

BRIANA IS AN AVID fantasy book reader and a constant victim to plunging into fandoms (she's okay though, the only casualty was her heart). If she zones out, she's probably thinking about food. She has a keen interest in all things imagination, from animation and drawing to writing and dungeons and dragons. She is also a self-taught digital artist, martial artist, and gamer who was a lead singer of a rock band. Briana currently spends her time trying to maintain some sense of direction in life and procrastinating on nearly everything.